DANGEROUS QUESTIONS!

"Have you got *Warhammer*'s papers?" he asked.

"Yes," Beka said. She reached into the right-side pocket of her jacket for the miniature blaster that always lived there, and put the business end of the little weapon against the back of his neck.

He froze. Then, with infinite caution, he lifted both hands and placed them flat against *Amsroto*'s hull.

Beka started breathing again. "Now," she said. "It's time you told me what your name really is, and how you wound up with a Mageworld scoutcraft parked in your docking bay . . ."

BOOK ONE OF MAGEWORLDS

THE PRICE OF THE STARS

DEBRA DOYLE
AND
JAMES D. MACDONALD

A TOM DOHERTY ASSOCIATES BOOK
NEW YORK

THE PRICE OF THE STARS

Copyright © 1992 by Debra Doyle & James D. Macdonald

Cover art by Romas

A Tor Book
Published by Tom Doherty Associates, Inc.
175 Fifth Avenue
New York, N.Y. 10010

Tor ® is a registered trademark of Tom Doherty Associates, Inc.

ISBN: 0-812-51704-0

First edition: October 1992

Printed in the United States of America

0 9 8 7 6 5

For Meggo and Duncan and John

Acknowledgments

We couldn't have done this without the help of a lot of people: Bruce Coville and the Tuesday Evening Literature and Carbohydrate Society; Mary Frances Zambreno; Andrew Sigel and Andrew Phillips and Nancy Hanger; and especially Sherwood Smith, first-reader extraordinaire, without whose enthusiasm we might not have finished the first draft, let alone gone the distance.

Prologue

NIGHT HAD come to Waycross on Innish-Kyl. Night, but not darkness or quiet. Bursts of loud talk and raucous music spilled out through open doorways, and the low thrumming of heavy machinery never stopped. Beka Rosselin-Metadi—tall and thin, with pale yellow hair tied back from a face too sharply planed for prettiness—strode through the crowded spaceport with a starpilot's fine disregard for the dirtside locals. The locals, in turn, took note of her purposeful air, and of her heavy war-surplus blaster in its worn leather holster, and let her pass.

In fact, Beka had no goal besides a cool drink and a few hours away from the ship. *Claw Hard* had been in hyperspace for two months on this latest run, plenty of time for Beka to grow tired of both the freighter and her crew. This stop at Waycross was Beka's first chance to get off-ship since Cashel; the layover at Raffa, the only other port on this run, had been too brief to allow the crew members any liberty.

Osa's probably afraid he'll lose the whole lot of us if he lets us out on the town, she decided as she stepped through the door of the Blue Sun Cantina. If her own duties as copilot/navigator hadn't ended when *Claw Hard* settled into the docking bay, she wouldn't be here either—she'd be off-loading and on-loading cargo with the rest of the freighter's crew. But except for Osa himself she had the only deep-space pilot's license on board, and *Claw Hard*'s captain was getting too fat and lazy to do his own ship handling.

Beka smiled thinly to herself. *If Osa wants to keep his copilot,* she thought, *he can damn well let me off the ship for a couple of hours.*

The door slid shut behind her, and she made her way through the crowd to the bar. The regulars at the Blue Sun weren't exactly the sort of people Beka had grown up with. Innish-Kyl was a frontier planet near the Mageworlds border zone, and Waycross had started out as a privateers' port during the worst years of the late war. Most of the cantina's patrons probably hadn't seen a respectable woman more than once or twice in their lives, and wouldn't know what to say to one if she showed up.

Luckily, Beka's much-mended coverall and worn leather boots—and the blaster—were enough to spare her the burden of respectability in this crowd. She found a place at the bar and pulled a ten-credit chit out of her pocket.

"Beer," she said in Galcenian. "Whatever you have on tap."

The bartender looked at her without speaking.

Beka sighed. *I wonder if it's my accent.* She didn't suppose the Blue Sun got many customers who spoke the universal tongue of the spacelanes as it sounded on the Mother of Worlds—but even seven years away from Galcen hadn't been enough to wipe all traces of home from Beka's voice.

It never fails, she thought with resignation. *A few hours without sleep, and I start talking like I'm just out of finishing school. Oh, well. Try again.*

"Beer," she said, enunciating clearly. "Tap."

The bartender blinked. "Yes, Domina."

Oh, damn. It wasn't the accent.

Beka exhaled slowly through clenched teeth. It wasn't the bartender's fault that random genetic factors had made her into a taller, thinner, plainer version of the civilized galaxy's most famous stateswoman. *But what anybody could think Mother was doing in a place like this—or maybe they haven't forgotten that she did come to Way-cross once, when she needed the kind of help that no other place could give.*

She drew a long breath. "Sorry to disappoint you, but I'm not the Domina. I'm not even a gentlelady. I'm a thirsty starpilot, and I'd like some brew."

The bartender gave her another strange look, then shrugged and turned away. He drew a mug of beer from the console behind the bar and slid the mug across the counter without speaking. Beka reached out to pick it up, but before her fingers reached the frosted glass she felt a touch on her shoulder.

She whirled, dropping her hand to the grip of the blaster. Then she saw who stood there—a slight, dark-haired man in dusty black, a plain wooden staff slung across his back on a leather thong. Her blue eyes widened with recognition, and she let her hand relax.

"Master Ransome," she said. "What are you doing here?"

"Looking for you," the man answered. "You're wanted down at the docking bays."

Beka raised an eyebrow. "Somehow I can't see the Master of the Adepts' Guild running errands for the likes of Captain Osa."

"I'm not," Ransome said. "Your father is here."

So you're running errands for Dadda instead . . . which means Mother has to be mixed up in this somehow. Beka felt the old, familiar anger stir to life at the thought. *Seven years. It's been seven years, and she still thinks I'm going to change my mind and come home. Or maybe Master*

Ransome is supposed to drag me back to Galcen whether I want to go or not.

She gave the Adept a wary look. "I thought the Space Force stayed away from Innish-Kyl."

"The Space Force has nothing to do with it. *Warhammer* is in docking bay sixty-two-D."

Beka took a long, deep drink from her mug. So her father had finally brought his old ship back to the port that had made her famous. *After all the times I asked him to take me to Waycross, back when I was a kid, and he said no, he didn't want to see the place again . . . and now he's here.*

She set down the beer and pushed herself away from the bar. "All right," she said. "I can take a hint. Let's go."

She followed the Adept through the crowded room and out onto the street. The rest of the Blue Sun's customers drew aside to let them pass—not out of any regard for her, she knew, but out of well-founded respect for anyone who carried an Adept's staff.

For centuries the galaxy's Adepts had kept to themselves, living apart from those who distrusted their power to sense and manipulate the patterns of the universe. Then strange, wing-shaped scoutships began appearing above the outplanets. A few years later the raiding parties followed, first on the frontier and then in the heart of the galaxy itself. And in the opening skirmishes of what became the Magewar, the once-distrusted Adepts became humanity's chief defenders against the power of the Mageworlds.

Now Beka Rosselin-Metadi glanced over at Master Ransome as they walked through Waycross's narrow streets. "Mother's up to something," she said, "and I don't like it. Are you going to tell me what's going on, or not?"

Ransome shook his head. "The docking bay isn't far."

She bit her lip and said nothing. A few minutes later they reached the low-walled, roofless enclosure where *Warhammer*'s flattened disk shape loomed against the white glow of the dock lights. Beka paused in the entrance to the bay.

"Damn, but she's still a pretty ship," she said, more to herself than to her companion. "Makes *Claw Hard* look like a flying rock. Did Dadda bring her in alone?"

"Not quite," said Ransome. "I was copilot."

"Just like old times," said Beka, as they crossed the open bay toward the ship. In her fighting days, the *'Hammer* had carried a full crew: pilot, copilot, engineer, and a pair of gunners. But Jos Metadi had flown *Warhammer* solo after the long conflict had ended, and had taught all three of his children to do the same.

Beka smiled a little in spite of herself. *Ari and Owen never loved it like I did, though—and I could fly rings around them both from the moment I was old enough to start learning.* The smile faded as quickly as it had come. *I wonder if Dadda would have taught me, if he'd known what I was going to do with all those lessons?*

She hesitated at the foot of the lowered ramp, and looked at her father's onetime copilot and oldest friend.

"Master Ransome, can you tell me what he wants?"

The Adept shook his head. In the shadow of *Warhammer*'s bulk, she couldn't make out his expression. She shrugged, and went on up the ramp.

The ship's door was open, and the faint glow of a force field stretched across the gap. Master Ransome reached out one hand toward it, and the light faded. He gestured at her to go ahead. She stepped through with Master Ransome following a staff-length behind. The air brightened again behind them.

Beka made her way forward to the *'Hammer*'s dimly lit common room. A lean, dark-clad figure half-lounged in a chair at the mess table: Jos Metadi, once captain of the privateer ship *Warhammer*, now Commanding General of the Republic's Space Force. Marriage to Perada Rosselin had given him the rank—in the old days before the Mage-war, "General of the Armies" had been one of the honorifics granted by custom to the consort of the Domina of

Entibor—but Metadi's own formidable talents had made the courtesy title into a powerful reality.

His chair spun round as the first footstep sounded on the common-room floor, and a small but deadly blaster appeared in the General's hand. After a moment the blaster disappeared again into its hidden grav-clip up Metadi's sleeve.

"Sorry," he said. "Old habits die hard."

Beka nodded, unsurprised. Innish-Kyl has that effect on people. She'd almost gone for her blaster herself back in the cantina, and she was nothing like the old hand that her father was. Behind her, she heard Errec Ransome half-laugh.

"You could get a bodyguard from the Guild any time you wanted," the Adept said. "Will you take one?"

"I'll take a bodyguard when I run into somebody who's even fonder of keeping my hide in one piece than I am," Metadi said. "And I don't think the creature exists." He turned back to Beka. "Sit down, girl. We have to talk."

Beka took a chair on the other side of the mess table and braced herself for a struggle. She hadn't written or spoken to anyone on Galcen—except, once in a great while, to her brother Owen—since that last, bitter quarrel the night she left home. She wondered what twist in galactic politics had convinced the Domina to send for the family's runaway daughter.

It must really be bad, she thought. The realization stiffened her resolve. *If Mother wants me to come back again, she's going to have to take me on my own terms, not hers.*

There was a long pause. Finally her father said, "You look like you've done well enough for yourself."

"I'm piloting for Frizzt Osa on *Claw Hard*," she said. "The ship's a pile of junk, and Osa's a bastard, but it's a job."

Metadi nodded. There was another pause. Finally Beka said, "I never expected to see you here."

"I never expected to come back," said the General. "The town's gone downhill since the old days—the Magelords turned Entibor into an orbiting slag heap, but that's nothing next to what peace and prosperity can do to a place.'' He gave Beka an appraising look. ''That blaster you've got—are you willing to use it?''

''I already have once,'' she said.

''Good,'' said Metadi.

Once again, conversation lapsed. *Warhammer*'s environmental systems kept up their low, almost subliminal hum. Beka looked from her father to Master Ransome, who had made himself inconspicuous after an Adept's fashion, leaning against the wall in a shadowed corner.

The Adept's face was hidden, and her father's was unreadable. Neither man seemed ready to break the silence. She drew a deep breath.

''How did you know I was going to be in Waycross tonight?''

The answer came quickly. It wasn't, she thought, the question they'd been expecting.

''Owen told us you were on *Claw Hard*,'' Master Ransome said. ''Learning your next port of call wasn't hard after that.''

''Owen,'' said Beka slowly. She'd kept in touch, over the years, with the younger of her two brothers, certain that the ally and co-conspirator of her childhood would never betray any secret she confided to him. If he'd come out with her ship's name of his own accord . . .

''Whatever Mother needs me for has got to be more than just family politics. Now, is somebody going to tell me about it, or are we going to sit here and make small talk until I have to get back to *Claw Hard* for lift-off?''

Her father looked at Master Ransome.

The Adept sighed, and came over to take a seat at the table. He glanced down for a moment at the tabletop, rubbing his finger lightly over decades-old scratch marks in the grey plastic, and then lifted his head again. ''The Domina of Entibor is dead.''

For a moment, the words meant nothing. Then Beka

heard a voice that had to be hers, although she didn't recognize it.

"So that's what the bartender meant. Mother is dead—and I'm the Domina now."

Errec Ransome's dark eyes were somber. "Yes, my lady."

"Don't call me that," she said automatically—the reflex of years. Inside her head, the old, old argument played on: *Mother is "my lady," not me . . . I'm going to be a star-pilot, one of the best, not just some kind of political figurehead . . . and someday I'm going to run so far away from Galcen that nobody will care who I am.*

Under the cover of the tabletop, her fists clenched so tightly that the nails, even trimmed short for handling a starship's controls, bit deep into her palm. She hadn't cried in public since she was twelve, and she was damned if she was going to start now. She pressed her lips together until they stopped trembling, and then turned to her father.

"When—how—did it happen?"

More silence. "Tell her, Errec," her father said.

After another long pause, the Master of the Adepts' Guild began to speak. "There was a debate in the Grand Council," he said. "Hearings, on the expulsion of Suivi Point. The Domina . . . your mother . . . was against expulsion."

Beka nodded. Suivi Point had been a blot on the Republic's honor for longer than she'd been alive; this wasn't the first time the wide-open asteroid spaceport had come near expulsion from the community of worlds. She remembered a family dinner, long ago on Galcen, and her mother saying to somebody—had it been Councillor Tarveet of Pleyver?—"Suivi's a disgrace, I'll grant you that. But if the Suivans leave the Republic, there'll be no way left to control them short of open warfare. And gentlesir, I've seen enough of war."

Tarveet. It was Tarveet, and that was the night I put a garden slug into his salad. Mother spanked me for it—but

I heard her laughing about it later. She didn't really like Tarveet any more than I did. . . .

Her eyes stung; she blinked once, hard, and kept her eyes on Master Ransome.

"The Visitors' Gallery was crowded that day. It always was, whenever your mother spoke." Master Ransome smiled briefly. "Even your father was there."

Which meant, Beka knew, that the debate would have been more than usually important—her father had no use for politics, as a rule. "It makes no difference to me what they decide," she'd heard him say once. "All it ever means is more work for the Space Force." Then he'd laughed, and smiled at her mother. "You shouldn't make so many speeches. It only encourages them."

She didn't dare look at her father now. Watching Master Ransome's face was bad enough. It made her wonder if the old portside story was true—that when Domina Perada Rosselin of Entibor came to Waycross in search of a new commander for the Republic's shattered spacefleet, she'd taken away the hearts of *Warhammer*'s captain and copilot both.

"Somehow," said Master Ransome, "the force field in the Visitor's Gallery went down. And there was an assassin. With a blaster. He got off one shot. Your father shot him before he could fire again."

Beka swallowed, and wet her lips. When she spoke, her voice sounded old and rusty. "That was how it happened?"

"Not quite," said the Adept. "Unlike your father, the assassin missed his target. All his shot hit was the floor of the Council Hall. But one of the flying shards of marble from the floor struck your mother. It was just a scratch, barely enough to justify visiting the Council's medics. But she went . . . and somebody had given them Clyndagyt instead of their usual variety of antiseptic spray."

"I don't understand," Beka said. "There's nothing wrong with Clyndagyt. It's what we've got on *Claw Hard*."

Her father spoke again, for the first time in what felt to Beka like hours. "Clyndagyt works just fine, as long as nothing's managed to sensitize you to it. And that's hard to do—about the only way to get sensitized was in one of the Mageworlders' biochemical attacks. But almost everybody who was at the Siege of Entibor lived through a couple of those—and your mother wouldn't leave until the Magelords had just about wiped the whole planet slick. She had some kind of damn-fool notion about staying there and making them kill her in person."

Beka bit her lip. "She never told me that."

"It makes a lousy bedtime story," said her father. "And anyway, I talked her out of it. Now let's get down to business."

So it comes around to family politics, after all, Beka thought. She clenched her fists again under the table.

"No," she said. "I'll say to you what I said to Mother seven years ago. I don't give a damn about duty and family and all that. I'm not going back to Galcen and letting myself get made over into the next Domina of Lost Entibor."

Her father shook his head. "As it happens, I didn't have anything of the sort in mind."

"Then what—?"

"You say that *Claw Hard*'s a pile of junk and Osa's a bastard. How would you like to be captain of *Warhammer* instead?"

She caught her breath. "Me? Pilot *Warhammer*?" For a moment, in spite of all that she'd just heard, the prospect dazzled her like walking out of a cave into the sunlight. Then she shook her head. "I don't have the kind of money a ship like the *'Hammer* would cost. And I'm not taking any family favors."

"Don't worry," said her father. "I'm not in the business of doing favors, family or otherwise. And I'm not asking anything you can't afford."

"There's more than one way of looking at that," said

Master Ransome quietly. "And I don't particularly approve of what you're doing."

"Then stay out of it," said her father. "I don't approve of everything the Guild does, either—but I don't interfere in things that aren't my business."

He turned back to Beka. "Are you interested?"

"In getting *Warhammer*? Of course I'm interested."

She looked about the common room—cramped, grey, and utilitarian—and thought about all the things that had made this ship a legend during the Magewar. The heavy dorsal and ventral energy guns. The cargo holds that had once held the captured treasures of the Mageworlds trade. The speed no ship of her class had ever equaled.

I could stick to small cargo, Beka thought, *pricey stuff, and run it fast. With those guns, even flying solo I wouldn't get in too much trouble. I could outshoot anything I couldn't outrun.*

She bit her lip—that was fantasy, and she knew it—and met her father's gaze directly. "Ships like the 'Hammer don't come cheap. And I haven't exactly struck it rich out here."

"I don't want money," General Metadi said. "I want to know who planned your mother's murder."

"Planned?"

"What do you think, girl?" he demanded harshly. "A lunatic with a blaster could happen any time, and a shorted-out force field could be bad luck, and the wrong antiseptic could be delivered to the Council medics by accident—but not all three at once. Somebody wanted your mother out of the way, and wanted it badly. Hired blasters cost money, but getting that Clyndagyt past Security must have cost even more."

"You're talking about somebody very, very rich," she said quietly. "And very, very powerful. And I'm very, very sorry, but I gave up running around with people like that seven years ago. Much as I'd like to help you stake out our unknown friend for a cliffdragon's breakfast, and much as I'd like to have the *'Hammer* to call my own—no.''

''We're talking about somebody who either comes from Suivi Point or has connections there,'' her father continued. ''And that, my girl, is exactly the sort of person you've been running around with for the past few years. Do you deny it?''

She shook her head, the brief flare of resentment gone. ''No. But if all you want from me is inquiries out on the fringes of the law, you don't have to buy them with *Warhammer*. I'll do it for free.''

''That's no good,'' he said. ''You'll never be able to follow up anything if you have to go where Osa and *Claw Hard* drag you. You take *Warhammer*; and I get the names, when you find them.''

She looked about the *'Hammer*'s shadowed common room. ''A ship like this—for nothing more than a couple of names? I can't take her, Dadda; it's not enough.''

''She's my ship,'' said General Metadi, ''and I say what she's worth. The names will do.''

For a long time, Beka sat without answering, listening to the whisper of forced air through *Warhammer*'s vents, and to the soft in-and-out of her own breath. The two sounds mingled in her ears, like the breathing of a single creature.

A ship of my own, she thought. *I used to say I'd give anything to have one. So now I get to prove it.*

''All right, Dadda. You have a deal.'' She squared her shoulders, and extended her hand across the mess table to seal the bargain free-spacer's fashion. ''Your names—my ship. Done?''

Her father met the grip with his own. ''Done.''

PART ONE

I. Mandeyn: Embrig Spaceport

AT WELL past local midnight in Embrig Spaceport—port of call for the wealthy provincial world of Mandeyn—the Freddisgatt Allee ran almost deserted from the Port Authority offices to the Strip. The warehouses lining the Allee blocked most of the skyglow from the lighted docking areas beyond, and Mandeyn's high-riding moon shed its pale illumination only in the center of the broad Allee.

Beka Rosselin-Metadi whistled an off-key tune through her front teeth as she took a leisurely return walk down the Allee to her ship. The black wool cloak she wore against the cold of Embrig's winter night swirled around her booted ankles, and if she'd put a bit of extra swagger into her stride as she left the Painted Lily Lounge—well, she figured she was entitled.

Damn right you're entitled, my girl, she told herself. *You made a tidy profit on carrying those parts for Interworld Data, and you've got another good cargo already on board for Artat—not bad work for a twelve-hour lay-over with time out for dinner with an old shipmate.*

The *Sidh* had been her first ship after leaving home, and she'd been junior to everyone on board, including Ignaceu LeSoit. The knowledge that LeSoit and his friend Eterynic were crewing now on the luckless *Reforger*—still in Embrig after three days, Standard, without finding a cargo—hadn't spoiled her evening in the least. Now that Beka was captain of her own ship, she lined up cargoes two ports ahead; if she could, so could anybody.

Maybe I should think about hiring a crew of my own, she thought. *Copilot, say, or an engineer who knows a bit of gunnery. A gunner, that's the ticket; then I could push my routes out further into the fringes, and get a bit closer to what I'm really after—*

Something hit her behind her right knee, hard. The leg collapsed beneath her, and she fell onto her back in the street.

"What the—" she began, and swallowed the rest of it when a blaster bolt ripped through the air where her head had been.

A second blaster answered, firing from a point above and beside her. She rolled toward the nearest wall, where her black cloak stood a chance at blending into the shadows, and grabbed for her own sidearm. Her hand came up empty.

She pressed herself flat against the metal siding of the warehouse. *I'm a shadow,* she thought. *Just a shadow that moved across the picture for a moment.* The trick had always worked for her brother Owen when they were both young; maybe it'd work for her if she tried hard enough.

Out in the street where she'd been walking a stranger stood, a blaster in each hand. He fired once toward the rooftop opposite; Beka heard the clatter of a dropped weapon and the heavy thud of a falling body. A left-handed shot down the intersecting alley brought a scream followed by silence.

As the outcry died, she heard a faint ratchety noise from farther along the road, a clear, distinct sound in the frigid air. The stranger heard it, too: he whirled and fired both blasters down the Allee. The man who had stepped from the shadows holding an energy lance flew backward and lay still.

The stranger turned to where Beka was lying and gestured at her to come out.

Beka unpeeled herself from the wall. Her knee hurt, and she'd dragged her cloak through the slush when she rolled clear. The wet wool slapped against her legs as she limped out into the light and said, "Who the hell are you?"

"A friend," said the stranger. He holstered one of the blasters, and held her own weapon out toward her.

She looked at the grey-haired gentleman, dressed for the weather in a long winter topcoat with silver buttons. Without the hardware—and if she hadn't seen him use it— she'd have figured him for a teacher of languages and deportment at a young ladies' finishing school.

She took back the blaster, checked the charge and the safety, and put it away. "Friend, huh?" she said when she'd finished. "I suppose those other guys weren't?"

"Not if your name's Rosselin-Metadi. Can you walk?"

"If it's back to my ship and out of here, yes. I've got a lift-off at zero-four-hundred local, and I'm not in the mood for long explanations."

"Then here's a short one," said the grey-haired gentleman. "The odds in town are running twelve to one against you making it that far."

"Short and sweet," said Beka. "Almost enough to make me bet against myself. What's your angle, Professor?"

The gentleman gave a dry chuckle. "I'm playing the long shot," he said. "I believe the Allee is clear of amateur talent for the moment—my suggestion is that you make what haste you can to your ship and wait for me there."

"And then what?"

"And then I'll tell you some things you ought to know."

The gentleman gave Beka a polite half-bow, stepped sideways into the shadows, and vanished. *The Adepts do it better,* Beka told herself. Then she looked back down the Allee, empty except for her and the dead. *But not by much.*

She made it home to *Warhammer* without any more trouble. As always, her spirits lifted at the sight of the familiar bulk of her ship, looming in silhouette against the white glare of the dock lights.

My ship. Damn, but that sounds good. In spite of the pain in her knee, Beka grinned as she gave the *'Hammer* a prelift walkaround.

"My lady?" came a cultured voice from the entrance of the docking bay. "Permission to come aboard?"

She jumped, thought about going for her blaster, and decided the hell with it. *If he'd wanted to kill me, I'd be dead by now anyway.*

"Permission granted, Professor," she said. "And let's make that 'Captain,' if you don't mind."

"My apologies, Captain."

The grey-haired gentleman came forward out of the shadowed entryway as she toggled off the force field at the *'Hammer's* ramp. The readouts on the security panel by the side of the main hatch showed clear, so she went on through and gestured for him to follow.

"Welcome aboard *Warhammer*," she said.

She brought the force field up again behind her visitor. After a second's thought, she closed and sealed the hatch as well. She'd finished all the paperwork with the port and with her cargo before leaving the docks at the start of the evening, and anybody wanting in now wasn't likely to be friendly.

Beka led the way to the *'Hammer's* common room. "Wait here while I check things out for lift-off," she said, dropping her wet cloak onto the deck beside the mess table. "Then I'll have a few minutes clear for talk."

She waited to see the stranger settled into one of the padded seats, then pulled a clipboard out of its bulkhead niche and started working her way down the prelift checklist. First stop, the main hold: crates of fresh Mandeynan *crallach* meat, destined for the gourmet trade on nearby Artat, all on board and secure for lift-off. Then—limping from one station to another—she did the operational checks on all the systems and backups, from the realspace engines to the cockpit controls.

Checkout complete, she flipped on the cockpit comm system. "Port Control, this is Free Trader *Warhammer*. Request permission to lift on time."

"Free Trader *Warhammer*, this is Port Control. Scheduled lift time your vessel zero-four-one-four, I say again zero-four-one-four."

She signed off, and switched the countdown timer to show minus minutes in real-time running. She had about half an hour, Standard, before lift—not really enough time to tend to her leg, if she wanted to give her visitor's tale the attention it deserved.

She took care of the leg anyway in the privacy of her cabin, stripping off her boots and trousers and examining the damage. The knee was swollen, with a nasty red welt on the upper part of the calf in back. By morning she'd have a spreading purple bruise.

Son of a bitch must have used the edge of his boot, she thought. *Well, tape it up, my girl, and get on in there. You can't put off hearing him out much longer.*

In a clean coverall and soft shoes, with a sprain-tape bandage around the injured knee, she returned to the common room, detouring by way of the galley nook to pour two mugs of cha'a from the hotpot.

"Now then," she said, setting the mugs down on the mess table. "I believe you promised me an explanation."

"Ah, yes." The gentleman took a mug of cha'a and leaned back against the padded seat. "If you decide to trust me," he said, sipping the hot drink, "I can get you out from under the death mark you've had on your head for three systems now."

Assassins, she thought, and felt a sudden chill. *Face it, they've got you outclassed—and you can't stay in space forever.* "Out from under for how long?"

"Permanently."

She thought about it a moment. "Manage that," she said, "and I'll owe you a big one. What would I have to do?"

"It's quite simple, really. Lift off from here on time, and hit your next port as scheduled, after making a layover of six hours Standard and taking in tow a second vessel of the *'Hammer'*s mass."

Simple. Right. And I'm a Magelord. She sipped at her cha'a, wishing it were cool enough to gulp down and have done with it. "Layover where?"

The grey-haired gentleman reached into an inner pocket of his coat and brought out a slip of paper. "You'll find the coordinates here."

She took the paper and gave it a quick glance, then bit her lip for a moment while she did rough calculations in her head. "I'll need to check the navicomps for this, Professor. You're asking me to take a hell of a risk on trust."

Her visitor sighed. "For what it's worth under the circumstances, you have my word that I mean you no harm."

She looked at him for a moment, wishing she had her brother Owen's ability to see what moved behind a stranger's eyes.

"I'll believe you," she said. "For now, anyway. Call it taking care of the one I owe you from back on the Freddisgatt."

She stood up, grimacing at the pain in her bruised leg. "Stow the mugs in the galley and strap yourself in for lift-off. By the time the navicomps spit out an answer on this one, I'll have to be sealed for launch and powered up."

The lift-off clock read three minutes and counting before she called back to the common room on the internal communicator. "All right, Professor, you've got your layover. But as soon as we're in hyperspace I want the whole story."

It had better be good, she thought, getting ready to raise Port Control on the external comm system, *to make it worth putting the* 'Hammer *through something as chancy as this is going to be.*

She scowled at the *'Hammer'*s main control board. That damned detour was going to mean blasting at 160 percent of rated max power the whole way out. Not to mention some pretty tight maneuvering to make it look good from out front. *Blow this one, my girl,* she told herself, *and you could wind up doing a real good meteor imitation.*

But with an expert at the controls, the *'Hammer* could handle it—thanks to the foresight of her previous owner. Long ago, at the start of his privateering days, Jos Metadi had put the profit from *Warhammer*'s first hunting foray into new, outsized engines for his ship—engines half again the standard size for a vessel of the *'Hammer*'s class. They cut into her scant cargo space; they made her cranky to handle, fuel-hungry, and a bitch to repair; but combined with the guns, they turned a harmless-looking merchant ship into a deep-space predator, and let her run flat out with a full hold at speeds even racing craft had trouble matching.

And—for the times when that still wasn't enough—the flip of an extra switch on the control panel would take all the safety circuits off line, and the autopilot right along with them. "Then everything depends on you," her father had told her years ago. "Either you guess right about how much she can take, or you go up like a supernova."

Beka swore under her breath as she reached for the external comm. *Just because you never could resist a dare . . .* She keyed the handset on the comm panel. "Port Control, this is *Warhammer*. Switching to Inspace frequency. Over."

"This is Port Control. Roger, switch, out."

"Launch Control, this is *Warhammer*. I have departure clearance. Over."

"*'Hammer*, this is Launch Control, roger, you have departure clearance. Lift on my signal, I say again, lift on my signal. Stand by, execute, out."

Beka pushed the forward nullgravs to max, tilting the *'Hammer*'s nose skyward, and fed power to the main plant. In a roar of engines, the freighter slid through the atmosphere and out of the planet's grip—slowly at first, and then steadily faster. At normal speed, Beka aimed for the jump point to Artat, took the run-in, and went into hyperspace. She counted off five seconds on the control-panel chronometer, then dropped back into realspace again, with

Mandeyn showing on the sensors as a bright star dead astern.

Following the navicomp leads, she swung the 'Hammer into a tight spiral and commenced a new run-to-jump—much faster this time. She fed power to the hyperspace engines, and the stars blurred and faded through blue to black as the 'Hammer broke through.

"Now we see if Dadda's little girl is half the pilot she thinks she is," Beka observed to nobody in particular, and switched on the override.

An alarm *whurrpp*ed. She silenced it with another switch, and then pushed the main control lever all the way forward. The readouts on half a dozen gauges flashed into the red, and danger lights started blinking all over the control panel.

She reached to her right and flipped a third switch. The danger lights began burning steadily.

"You still there, Professor?" she asked, over the ship's internal comm system.

"Still here, Captain." Her passenger sounded unruffled by the double jump.

"Then unstrap and get up here to the cockpit. I'm going to cut life support to the rest of the ship in about two minutes."

"Coming, Captain."

Beka passed the time waiting for her passenger to appear in taking nonessentials off line—the guns, the galley, the lights. When he arrived, calm as a professor of galactic history showing up for class, she closed the vacuum-tight door behind him and switched off life support to the 'Hammer's after sections.

"Take a seat," she said, with a nod sideways at the copilot's empty spot. "I'm going to cut ship's gravity."

She waited for him to strap in before taking that last system out. "And now," she said, "while I fly this thing, you can tell me a story."

"The first thing I ought to tell you is that you're going to come out of hyperspace inside an asteroid belt."

"Lovely," she said, keeping her eyes on the gauges and readouts in front of her. Her fingers played over levers and knobs as she held the power plant in balance and the ship on course. "Absolutely outstanding."

"My apologies. But we lack the time for a safer approach. We're going to a place where I've stockpiled a great deal of useful equipment over the last few years, and I wanted to make it hard to find."

"Congratulations." A needle wavered. She turned a control rod back half a degree. "Now, tell me more about this price you say I've got on my head. I suppose it accounts for the dustup back on the Allee?"

The Professor made a dismissive gesture with one hand. "Amateur talent, as I said. I rather suspect you owe your survival that long to your former shipmate LeSoit. He's a professional these days—in a minor way, of course."

"LeSoit," she said. *He never did say outright he was crewing on* Reforger, she reminded herself. *Only that his buddy Eterynic was.* "My old friend Ignac'."

"Don't be too harsh on him, Captain. The local bullies probably held back as long as they did out of unwillingness to interfere with a professional hit. But when he let you head back to your ship alive . . ." The Professor shrugged.

Beka frowned at the engine status readouts. "Well, that's one I'll have to owe LeSoit—though I must say the bastard might've warned me."

"That," said the Professor, "would have been thoroughly unprofessional on his part. He came close enough to stepping over the line as it was."

Beka stole a quick glance at her visitor. "You wouldn't," she asked with growing suspicion, "be one of those professionals yourself?"

"At one time or another," he admitted. "Among other things."

"Wonderful," said Beka. A readout that had stayed green so far flickered and went red. She swore under her breath, and backed the power off another hair. "I have better things to do right now than play guessing games. If you're going to kill me, why didn't you do it dirtside?''

"I'm not planning to kill you, my lady. Just the opposite.''

"That makes twice you've called me 'my lady.' Like I said before, the word's 'Captain.' ''

"As you wish. But I was a confidential agent of your House for many years. A certain sentimental regard for the niceties is hard to avoid.''

"Entibor's an orbiting slag heap,'' said Beka, "and Mother sold off all House Rosselin's assets to finance the war. I'm *Warhammer*'s captain, and that'll have to do.''

"For some things, perhaps,'' said her passenger. "But simple freighter captains don't merit assassins tailing them across half the civilized galaxy. You have a dangerous hobby, my lady: the word is that Captain Rosselin-Metadi asks too many questions in the wrong places.''

"Do I, now?'' She forced herself to keep her attention on the controls.

"Far too many questions,'' said the Professor, "for someone who carries your not exactly inconspicuous name. Such inquiries were bound to cause talk, coming so soon after what happened to your mother.''

Beka bit her lip, hard. She still didn't like to think about that. *All those years, I kept promising myself that someday I'd go back home and tell Mother the real reason why I couldn't stand it on Galcen anymore. It wasn't her, it was all the rest of them, the Council and the Space Force and the damned Entiborans-in-exile. Mother let them drain her dry, year after year after year, and I could tell they'd do the same thing to me if they could. . . .*

She shook her head to clear it, and concentrated on keeping her ship on course.

"I began asking questions myself,'' her passenger continued, "as soon as I learned of the Domina's death. And the first thing I heard was that the family's footloose daughter had a ship of her own at last.'' He paused. "I'm probably not the only person to wonder if the *'Hammer'*s new captain got her ship on the promise of future services.''

"Explains why people I've never met are shooting at me," she said. "Any idea who put them up to it, Professor?"

"At the moment," said her passenger, "no. Later, once we've shaken the hunters off your trail, we can look into that.''

She stole a second or so away from the control panel to turn her head and look at him directly. " 'We,' huh?''

"If you don't mind the idea of assistance.''

"I like the idea of improving my chances," she said, most of her attention already back on the *'Hammer'*s engine-status display. It still showed the same, but the steady thrumming—felt, more than heard—of the freighter's metal skeleton had smoothed out a bit.

She chanced easing the power back up, and added, "But what you're talking about doesn't come cheap.''

Back on Mandeyn, a pallid sun rose over the streets of Embrig Spaceport, and the Freddisgatt Allee stirred to reluctant life. Massive ground transports trundled up to the loading doors of the huge warehouses, the heat of their heavy-duty nullgravs melting the ice that had formed on the slushy street in the cold hours just before dawn.

If the Allee's business day was just beginning, the Strip—that narrow, rowdy buffer between the docks and the stolid, well-behaved city of Embrig beyond—was only now shutting down its operations. The Painted Lily Lounge, like all the other establishments, switched on the CLOSED sign and swept out the last of the drunks along with the dirt off the floor.

The door of the Lily's back room slid open with a faint whine. Inside, Gades Morven the gambler sat alone amid the litter of the night's business, practicing false cuts with a deck of playing cards. He looked up at the new arrival, a thin, dark-mustached man with a heavy blaster.

"I wondered when you were going to show up,"

Morven said. "There's people out there who aren't happy with you at all."

The newcomer shrugged. "You hired me. They didn't."

"They may not see it that way," said Morven, dealing out hands faceup onto the dark tablecloth. His pale grey eyes watched the cards as they fell.

"Damn it, LeSoit," he said as he dealt, "do you have any idea how many people saw their credits go out the airlock when *Warhammer* lifted off?"

"I just do my job and draw my pay," said LeSoit. "It's not my business if people place the wrong bets."

"Well, you may have to make it your business soon enough," the gambler said. "Somebody's bound to claim I rigged the deal on this one, the way you stuck with that bitch from the moment she made port."

LeSoit's dark eyes narrowed. "Your money buys you protection," he said, "and that's all it buys. Who I socialize with is my own business, and the *lady* used to be my shipmate."

Morven gave the spread of cards one quick, colorless glance, and gathered them up again with practiced fingers. He shuffled the deck and held it out for the cut.

"Still, LeSoit, people are going to talk."

The dark man cut the cards and handed back the deck. "Tell them to talk to me," he said. "I can handle them."

He watched as Morven, without answering, began dealing out a new table full of cards.

"Besides," LeSoit added, as the crown, coronet, scepter, and orb of trefoils fell one by one onto the tablecloth in front of the gambler himself, "it's not the people who lost money that I'd be worried about."

II. Nammerin: Space Force Medical Station; Downtown Namport

LIEUTENANT ARI Rosselin-Metadi crossed the open ground to the Med Station's Number Two aircar with easy, unhurried strides. A hard rain was falling on the landing field, but only newcomers to the station tried to escape bad weather. Here in Nammerin's equatorial region, rain fell every day for half the year, and violent storms roared through at least twice a week during the other half. This was the drier-but-stormy season, and the downpour plastered Ari's thick black hair against his skull.

In the shelter of the aircar, a lean, fair-haired man stood waiting. His uniform was less rain-soaked than Lieutenant Rosselin-Metadi's, but only because there was less of it to get wet. By most standards Nyls Jessan would be considered tall, but Ari was nearly seven feet in height and massively built, with powerful muscles overlying long, heavy bones—the legacy of a paternal grandfather whose name not even Jos Metadi had ever known.

"Our chariot awaits," said Jessan, with a theatrical flourish toward the aircar's open door. "We've got a civilian casualty requesting an assist at gridposit seven-two-eight-three-four-nine-two-five.''

His speech carried faint traces of a Khesatan drawl. Nobody at Nammerin's Medical Station could figure out what an aristocrat from the most elegant and civilized of the Central Worlds was doing in the Space Force, and Lieutenant Jessan, in spite of his ready flow of light chatter, had never volunteered the information.

Ari climbed into the waiting aircar. In a few minutes, with Jessan at the controls, they were flying in and out of drifting patches of grey cloud, with the lush vegetation of the equatorial zone spread out beneath them.

Nammerin was a young world, plagued by constantly shifting weather patterns, but the civilized galaxy was hungry and expanding in the aftermath of the war. So—to keep the agricultural machinery on Nammerin's vast water-grain farms from rusting untended while other worlds went hungry—the Space Force's medical and disaster relief teams worked overtime on behalf of the planet's scattered population.

''Well,'' said Ari, as soon as they'd leveled out. ''What do you think is waiting for us?''

''Could be anything,'' said Jessan. ''While you were up-country on leave we got three cases of Rogan's Disease at the walk-in clinic.''

''We shouldn't be seeing Rogan's here at all,'' protested Ari. ''It's a dry-world problem.''

Jessan shrugged. ''We've got it anyway, and tholovine's scarce in this sector. It's not even part of the standard kit.''

''You can thank the Magelords for that,'' Ari told him. ''Tholovine was a big part of their combat chemistry. Ever since the war ended and word got out, none of the major supply firms will handle the stuff. The dry worlds make just enough to handle their local problems, and that's it.''

The Khesatan lieutenant raised an elegant golden eyebrow. ''Sounds like you've been hitting the journals.''

''I had an interest,'' said Ari shortly.

Jessan opened his mouth and then shut it again. The

Domina's murder had rocked the civilized galaxy only a few Standard weeks after Ari first reported for duty on Nammerin. Around the Med Station, by unspoken agreement, the subject was never discussed.

The wind picked up as the aircar continued on. On the ground below, tall trees bent and tossed like stems of grass, and drainage ditches raged like turbulent rivers. Stiff gusts buffeted the craft as it flew.

Ari was the first one to break the silence. "It's going to be a wild ride coming back."

Jessan glanced over at him. "Are you trying to talk yourself into a piloting job?"

"Who, me?" Ari contrived to look innocent. "I wouldn't think of spoiling your fun."

But to himself, he had to admit that Jessan's comment had the ring of truth. The Khesatan was a good pilot, one of the Med Station's best, but Ari was better. Flying, after all, was in his blood. His crazy sister Beka—wherever she was right now—might be better at deep-space piloting, but she'd never cared much for working with the smaller atmospheric craft.

· *Her loss,* thought Ari. *Flying's not really flying if gravity doesn't have a chance to get you when you're careless.*

The aircar flew on. Soon a raised concrete strip came into view on the ground below, and Ari abandoned his private thoughts in favor of checking the chart screen.

"That's our posit, all right," he said to Jessan. "Looks like a farmer's landing pad."

"I bet somebody stuck his hand in a seed hopper again," replied Jessan absently. Already, the descent was taking most of the Khesatan's attention. The low-altitude winds appeared determined to push the craft off its approach and land it in the thick, soupy mud surrounding the pad. At last the aircar came to a halt on the concrete surface, and Jessan let out a satisfied sigh. "So far, so good. Now, where do we go from here?"

"Where" turned out to be a nearby line shack, a windowless prefab structure crowded with farm equipment and sacks of seed grain. A pocket glow-cube, set high up on a metal shelf, cast a pitiless white light down onto the floor where a human lay beneath a pile of blankets, sweating and shivering both at once. A hulking, grey-scaled being crouched beside the pallet. The creature rose to its feet as Air and Jessan walked in.

Just my luck, thought Ari. *We're dealing with a Selvaur.* The saurian—a male, from the crest of green scales rising off his domed skull—stood as tall as Ari himself, and bared a predator's fangs at the two medics. The voice that came from his chest was a deep rumble, speaking not in Galcenian but in a growling, inhuman tongue.

About time you guys showed up.

"Sorry," said Jessan, as he went down on one knee beside the man on the pallet. "We came as fast as we could."

Most humans on Nammerin had picked up the trick of "hearing" the Selvauran language, since there were almost as many of the big saurians on Nammerin as on the creatures' home world of Maraghai. Actually speaking the seemingly wordless, rumbling language was another matter—few humans had either the patience or the vocal range to manage the task.

Sorry's not the word, the Selvaur growled in reply to Jessan's apology. *This human is my sworn brother. If he dies, you die.*

"I'll keep that in mind," said Jessan, without looking up. He'd already opened the medikit from the aircar, and was working over the ailing man. "Talk some sense into him, will you, Ari?"

"My pleasure," Ari said. He stepped past the kneeling Jessan to stand in front of the Selvaur. This close, their eyes were on a level. Ari took a deep breath and pushed his voice down to the bottom of its range. *If this man dies, it's the will of the Forest, and not the work of anyone here.*

The Selvaur's vertical pupils dilated for a moment in surprise. Then the big saurian recovered his composure. *Who taught you to speak like a Forest Lord, thin-skin?*

Ferrdacorr son of Rrillikkik taught me the Forest

Speech,* Ari said. *He fostered me among his own young-lings in the High Ridges, and brought me into his family as a son.*

Again, startlement showed briefly in the Selvaur's yel-low eyes. It wasn't unknown for a Selvaur and a human to swear blood-brotherhood, but formal adoption was almost unheard of. *Have you gone on the Long Hunt, then, and made your Kill?*

Ari thought of the white scars along his back and ribs, and the double row of white puncture marks in the flesh of his left arm—only part of the price he'd paid to call himself part of Ferrdacorr's clan. *I have,* he said.

The Selvaur shook his head, a gesture he must have picked up from the humans he worked with on Nammerin. *Ahh.* He looked over at his partner, and then back at Ari. *Will he be all right, now that you're here?*

I don't know yet, Ari said.

He moved away from the Selvaur, and knelt down be-side Jessan. "What have we got?"

Jessan shook his head. "We'll need the lab work to confirm it, of course—but if this isn't third-stage Rogan's I'll toast my commission and eat it for breakfast."

"Rogan's," said Ari. "Damn."

The Selvaur made a nervous sound deep in his throat. *Is he going to die?*

Maybe, said Ari. It was unbecoming for one Forest Lord to lie to another, even in kindness. *Help us move him to the aircar. If we get him to the hospital, he may have a chance.*

The return trip was every bit as bad as Ari had feared, with the wind picking up, and the sick man shaking with chills and screaming in delirium the whole way. At last, though, they got the farmer checked in and under care, and made their way, wet and muddy, to the Junior Offi-cers' staff lounge for a cup of hot *ghil*. Off-worlders found the local drink sludgy and bitter, but like everybody else at the medical station, Ari had been on Nammerin so long the stuff was beginning to taste good.

The staff lounge was a converted storage dome, furnished with a half-dozen stackable chairs and a lumpy couch that someone had picked up secondhand at a flood sale. A holoset stood in the center of the dome atop its packing crate. Jessan clicked on the set, and the latest episode of "Spaceways Patrol" flickered into view, its colors dulled and its outlines fuzzied by atmospherics.

Ari sat back on the couch and gave his mug a gentle shake before taking the first sip—*ghil* was warming and filling and a natural stimulant, but it did tend to leave sediment in the bottom of your cup.

"Rogan's Disease," he said. "What next?"

"You never can tell on this planet," said Jessan. "The week after I got here—two years ago this LastDay morning, but who's counting?—the CO's pet sand snake got mildew. Had to freeze-dry the beast to kill the stuff."

"Wouldn't that kill the sand snake, too?" asked Ari. You never could tell about Jessan's wild stories. He told them all with the same straight face, and it was usually the unlikely ones that turned out to be true.

"Oh, no," said Jessan, shaking his head. "Just sent it into premature hibernation."

"And then, I'll bet," said a woman's unfamiliar voice from the doorway, "he had to put it under the ultraviolets to reset its clock. Come on, Jessan, tell us another one."

Ari rose, ducking out of habit even though the lounge's ceiling provided ample headroom, and turned toward the door. He saw a human female of about his own age, a small, plain-featured person whose thick black hair was twisted up into a knot at the back of her head. She wore a Medical Service uniform without insignia.

"Gentlelady," Ari began, and then saw the polished wooden staff slung across her back on a leather cord. "Mistress," he corrected himself.

Jessan chuckled. "Llannat, this is Ari Rosselin-Metadi. Ari, this is what else showed up while you were gone— Llannat Hyfid, our brand-new Adept. She's my relief."

Ari gave her the full Entiboran bow of respect, just as his mother had taught him years ago. "Mistress Hyfid."

She made a face. "Call me 'Llannat,' please. I'm from Maraghai, and the 'Mistress' bit makes me uncomfortable."

There weren't a lot of humans living on Maraghai, but the Selvauran distaste for human ranks and titles tended to rub off on the few who did. Ari looked at Llannat with a bit more interest. *Do you understand Forest Speech?* he asked.

The answering smile lit up the young woman's dark, bony features like a lantern on a cloudy night. "Oh, yes—but I can't manage two words of it without having a sore throat for a whole day afterward. How did you learn it so well?"

"There was a Selvaur who knew my father during the Magewar," said Ari. "I was fostered with him on Maraghai. It was part of some agreement he and my father made before I was born, back when my father talked the Selvaurs into joining the fight."

Ari watched Llannat Hyfid putting the pieces together as he spoke. "That's right," he told her, "Rosselin-Metadi as in the late Domina and the Commanding General. And you probably know my brother Owen—he's an apprentice in the Guild. Me, I'm about as sensitive as a brick."

"He has the manners of one sometimes, too," said Jessan. "It comes from talking with too many holovid reporters."

"You probably wondered," said Ari, "why I took my leave here on Nammerin instead of going home. I'll tell you why—Galcen probably has more holovid cameras than this planet has water-grain seeds."

"I still call it a waste of good leave time, roughing it in the backwoods on this quaking mudball," said Jessan. "But there's no accounting for taste. Speaking of roughing it—I finally got my orders this morning, and do you know where they're sending me next?"

"No," said Ari, smiling a little. "Where?"

"Pleyver," said Jessan. "Flatlands Portcity."

Ari whistled. Flatlands wasn't Waycross, but the Pleyveran port had been wide open enough in the bad old days to serve as one of his father's best ports of call. "I didn't know Space Force had a station there."

"We don't," said Llannat. "Don't listen to his griping, Ari—they're making him a lieutenant commander and putting him in charge of setting a place up."

"So I can spend my time in a one-man office treating stranded spacers for social diseases," said Jessan. "It'll be a picnic, I can tell you."

"Life around here isn't exactly going to be a tea party either," said Llannat. "Four cases of Rogan's Disease just came in from a logging camp upriver."

"Four?" said Ari. "Plus the three we've got and the one we brought in . . . that's more than just a fluke. It's an outbreak."

Llannat nodded. "One of the old cases died while you were collecting the latest one. And without any tholovine, we're going to lose some more."

"Didn't anybody put in a request for some?"

"I did," said Jessan. "As soon as the first case showed up. But you know how it works: *if* Supply can hurry things up, you might see some tholovine before next flood season. And by then it'll be too late."

"Too bad we don't have some right now," Ari said. "We could handle the problem while it's still small."

"And if I had hyperspace engines," said Llannat, "I'd be a starship. Where are we supposed to get the stuff—on the black market?"

There was a silence. Ari and Jessan looked at one another.

"Munngralla," said Ari.

"Right," Jessan said. "If anybody can get it, he can."

"Wait a minute," Llannat cut in. "Who's Munn-gralla?"

"He's a Selvaur who runs a curio shop down in Namport," said Ari. "At least, that's what he does officially. Unofficially . . . rumor says he's the local Quincunx rep."

"I see," said Llannat. If the Adept had any qualms about dealing with the most notorious organization of smugglers and black marketeers in the civilized galaxy, she didn't show it. "But is he likely to have tholovine on hand?"

"You name it," Ari said, "and Munngralla will sell it. But not for decimal-credit prices."

"Never mind the price," Jessan said. "We can always find cash someplace. The question is, how do we get in touch with him? If he thinks we're working for Security, he won't take the job no matter how much we offer."

Another long silence. Then Llannat looked over at Ari. "You did say he was a Selvaur. . . ."

Ari sighed. "This sounds like something the CO doesn't want to know about."

Jessan nodded. "He'd just worry."

The things I do for the Service, Ari thought, as the duck-boards laid across the intersection buckled under his feet and then pulled free of the mud in a series of sucking noises.

After yesterday's rains, the town of Namport lay steaming under the late-afternoon sun. A smell of decaying vegetation and other unwholesome substances rose from the muddy streets. Like most of the roads in this lowland agricultural district, the thoroughfares of Namport were unpaved. The shaggy tusker-oxen used as draft animals by the small farmers didn't care for hard surfaces, and nullgrav-assisted vehicles didn't need them; so when wet weather came to Namport, foot traffic was left with mud on its boots.

Ari stepped off the duckboards onto the raised wooden sidewalk. He'd worn civilian clothing for this expedition— a dark shirt over uniform trousers and boots—and a glance at his reflection in a shopwindow showed a looming, piratical figure. A heavy Ogre Mark VI blaster completed the effect.

The Mark VI had been Jos Metadi's, back in the days when the General still carried a sidearm openly instead of hiding one up his sleeve. When Ari left Galcen to join the Space Force, the blaster had gone with him—"for luck," his father had said, although Ari had never needed to wear it until today.

Halfway down the block, Ari spotted the sign he was looking for: FIVE POINTS IMPORTS, G. MUNNGRALLA, PROP.

G. Munngralla, Prop., hadn't wasted valuable credits on a holosign; the words were spelled out in fading gold paint on the shop awning over the sidewalk. When Ari reached the door of the shop, he saw that the same legend had been painted on the glass of door and window, along with a stylized depiction of a five-planet star system.

Ari knew as well as anybody else that Nammerin was the fourth planet out in a ten-planet system. He smiled at the sight of the design. So far, so good.

He pushed the door open—no fancy sliding doors with body-heat sensors for Munngralla, just ordinary cheap metal hinges, in need of a good oiling—and stepped inside. The air in the shop was cool and dry: Selvaur-cool, which made it two-shirts-and-a-jacket weather for a human. After the muggy heat of downtown Namport, Ari found it hard to keep his teeth from chattering.

He shouldered his way past a rack of pugil sticks and a pallet-load of boxes labeled "genuine Entiboran fused-rock paperweights—certificate of authenticity included," and came up against a Changwe temple gong bearing a hand-lettered sign in Maraghite script: PLEASE RING FOR SERVICE. There was no mallet in sight.

Carrying it a bit far, aren't you? Ari asked the absent Munngralla. *How many humans can read Maraghite in the first place? I'm lucky Ferrda took the time to be thorough with his responsibilities. And as for your missing mallet . . .*

He pulled his right arm back a little and struck the heavy cast metal ball with the side of one large and solid fist. The bell gave voice.

A single deep note tolled through the shop like a moan. A small grey lizard, frightened by the sound, ran out from behind a shelf of jars and into a crack in the wall. In the display cases, frangible items vibrated against one another on the glass shelves, setting up a high, brittle tinkling.

Ari struck the gong again.

All right, all right. Let an old wrinkleskin get his mid-day sleep, why don't you?

G. Munngralla—two meters and then some of not even slightly wrinkled Selvaur—pushed his way through the beaded curtain separating the back of the shop from the storefront.

Ari grinned at him, making sure to bare his canine teeth. *You're no wrinkleskin—and since when do the Masters of the Forest sleep in midday like animals?*

Who are you calling "animal," thin-skin? growled the shopkeeper. Selvaurs didn't like that name any better than other sentients did, and they took insults worse than some—Ferrdacorr would have knocked Ari across the room for showing such bad manners, and Munngralla might try yet.

But Ari stood tall enough in his spaceboots to meet Munngralla's bad-tempered glare straight on, and at a guess had a handspan more breadth in the shoulders. He hooked his thumbs into his belt, braced his feet, and held the predatory grin.

"I rang," he said. "I have some business to discuss."

It's all for sale, said Munngralla.

Ari's lip curled. "I don't need a pugil stick today, thank you. And as for the Entiboran paperweights—there's enough of them floating around the galaxy to build a whole new planet. Someday, though, you're going to get a real Entiboran in here, and he's going to wreck the place for you."

Ask me if I'm worried, said Munngralla. *Do I look worried?*

"Do I look like a Security Officer?" countered Ari. Then, switching languages again: *Do I sound like a Security officer?*

The Selvaur narrowed his eyes at him. *Talk is cheap, thin-skin. Can a Forest Lord or a Brother vouch for you?*

Ferrdacorr son of Rrillikkik, said Ari. *He hunts the South Continent High Ridges these days, but he went after other prey during the great war against the Mageworlds.*

Ahh, said the Selvaur. *That Ferrdacorr. If he answers for you, we shouldn't have any trouble doing business.*

"I'm glad to hear it," said Ari, in Galcenian again. "The Forest Speech isn't for thin-skinned throats."

That's true, agreed Munngralla. *Now, which will you have—a service, or merchandise?*

"Tholovine," said Ari. "In quantity, in a hurry."

If you're after chemical weapons, I carry some already made up, said the Selvaur. *No need to risk synthesizing your own.*

Ari bared his teeth—in real anger, this time. "If I ever need to hurt someone that badly, I'll beat him to death with my bare hands," he said. "It's just as quick and whole lot cleaner."

Suit yourself, said Munngralla. *How do you want your tholovine—powder, elixir, or pressurized spray?*

"Pure brick. Hospital grade."

Who's paying?

"Me," said Ari. "Come on, even an unblooded youngling knows better than to ask that. I'm good for the money."

Munngralla looked at him a moment. *Will Ferrdacorr pay if you default?*

Ari nodded, and dropped again into the Forest Speech. *I'm family. He'll pay.*

Munngralla extended a scaly hand—another human gesture. *Then we have a deal. I can have the first delivery for you by midnight tonight.*

"What's the price?"

Eight hundred credits the brick.

Ari pulled his own hand back. "No deal. The stuff's not illegal; just hard to get. Five hundred, or I go someplace else to do business."

Seven hundred.

"Six."

Six-fifty—take it or see where going someplace else gets you on this planet.

"Six-fifty," agreed Ari, and this time he didn't pull away from Mungralla's grip. "We have a deal."

Be here at midnight, the Selvaur reminded him. *And bring cash.*

"I'll be here," said Ari; and then—because Ferrdacorr had taught him courteous behavior—added in Selvauran, *Good hunting.*

Munngralla gave him a growled *Good hunting* in reply, but Ari was already halfway to the door. It swung open as he came near, and Ari had to retreat into the rack of pugil sticks to miss knocking over the Selvaur's next customer. The man glared up at him in passing.

"Sorry," said Ari, with a shrug. "I couldn't see the door through all those boxes of rock."

The man glared harder, and Ari braced himself for an unpleasant scene. But the stranger never made whatever retort he'd been planning to deliver. Instead, the pupils of his eyes dilated, his mouth snapped shut, and he ducked past Ari without a word.

Fear? wondered Ari. But he didn't think so—that hadn't been the look of someone who'd managed to lose his temper first and notice the other man's size afterward.

Not fear, then. Recognition?

He'd never seen the stranger before in his life; but he was not, he knew, a difficult figure to describe, and he'd been in and about Namport often enough on Med Station business.

Probably one of Munngralla's other customers, Ari decided. *I wonder what he was after, if spotting somebody from the Space Force was enough to set him on edge like that?*

On second thought, I probably don't want to know.

III. Asteroid Base
Artat Nearspace
Nammerin: Namport

T ALK IN *Warhammer*'s cockpit had lapsed as
the task of keeping the freighter on course
took up more and more of Beka's attention. Now, with the
flight-time clock marking off the few seconds remaining
in hyperspace, she looked over at the copilot's seat. Judging from his closed eyes and even breathing, her passenger
had fallen asleep.

"Wake up, Professor," she said. "We're about to drop
out of hyper and start dodging asteroids."

He didn't answer, but Beka had other things on her mind
than waiting to see if he'd heard. She took a deep breath to
calm herself. *We need to lose momentum real fast—there's
going to be a lot of rocks out there. This had better work.*

At one second before dropout, she switched in the realspace engines on maximum thrust. Then, as the ship came
out of hyperspace, she threw the *'Hammer* into a 180-degree
skew-flip, and felt herself pressed hard into the pilot's seat
as the freighter backed down at twelve gravities.

The cockpit darkened around her. In the center of her

field of vision, the readout on the relative motion sensor showed high velocity astern. The negative numbers unwound toward zero as *Warhammer*'s main engines fought momentum. Beka was close to blacking out—she couldn't see the lights and dials around the edge of the control panel—and she needed all her strength to reach for the master power switch.

-2, -1, 0 . . . Cut Power!

The release from deceleration threw her forward against the safety belts. Recovering, she slapped the Shield switch to divert energy to the ship's passive defenses. "Override, off," she said aloud, talking herself through the checklist while her head cleared. "Sensors, on. Life support, on. Gravity, on. Let's have a look and see where we are."

She switched to the Damage Control readout for an assessment of just how bad the trip had been, and decided that Dadda's little girl could pat herself on the back. Damage was light, and the cargo hadn't shifted at all.

"Any one you can walk away from, eh, Professor?"

Her passenger looked a bit groggy—as well he should after a high-G brake—but his imperturbability was still intact. "I've seen worse," he said.

He worked his hand past the safety webbing into an inner coat pocket, and brought out a second slip of paper.

"Broadcast this recognition signal on this frequency," he said, handing the paper to Beka, "then listen for the directional beacon you'll find answering it on this channel. The sooner we get to work, the better."

Beka made the trip through the asteroid field as quickly as she dared, homing in on the source of the beacon—a big, cave-pocked asteroid. "Dock in the third cave from the elevated pole there," said her passenger. "Just beside the sunset line."

She took the *'Hammer* into the cave at a gentle cruising speed, and watched the rock walls become first smooth stone and then polished metal. Soon the cave was looking more like the docking bay of a small space station.

"Set her down over there." Her passenger indicated the

area next to another small freighter, one that to an un-practiced eye might have been *Warhammer*'s twin.

Beka looked the freighter. "Now I understand what you have in mind."

"That's right. Ex-Free Trader *Amsroto*, old *Libra* class. By the time we get done, nobody'll ever be able to prove that she wasn't the *'Hammer*."

"That's going to be a lot of hardware down the drain," said Beka, as *Warhammer* settled onto the floor of the bay. "And you still haven't told me how I'm going to pay you for it."

Her passenger began unbuckling his safety webbing. "Would you believe me, my lady, if I told you I was doing all this out of a sense of obligation to a member of your House?"

"No," she said flatly. "That stuff died out years ago."

She thought she heard him sigh. "So it did, Captain. So it did. Do you have the papers listing your hull number and engine numbers?"

Beka undid her own restraining belts and stretched. "In my cabin," she said. "I'll bring them out."

"Right," said her passenger. "Then you start shifting your cargo to *Amsroto* while I stamp the numbers on her. How soon must we lift out of here, to tow *Amsroto* to Artat on time?"

She checked the cockpit chronometer and punched some figures into the navicomp. "We've got six hours forty-nine minutes thirty-five seconds Standard until the jump to hyperspace," she said. "Make it six hours even to do the job."

"Let's move, then."

By the time she'd fetched *Warhammer*'s papers from the cabin locker and returned to the cockpit, she could see her passenger already waiting by the open entryway of *Amsroto*.

"Works fast, doesn't he?" she said aloud, and tucked the bundle of papers inside the quilted jacket she'd picked up to take the place of her still-sodden cloak.

The sound of her footsteps on the *'Hammer*'s ramp echoed in the nearly empty bay, and her breath rose in a curl of mist. The Professor—if he was in fact the proprietor of this little hidey-hole—didn't believe in wasting energy on extra heat.

Out of long habit, she turned to her right at the foot of the ramp. "Let's have a look at you," she told the ship. Sensors and damage control comp caught a lot of things a pilot would miss, but . . . "computers go down, and numbers lie," her father had said many times. "Always check for yourself."

In the course of her walk around *Warhammer*, she saw that the hidden bay held a surprising variety of different spaceships. A single-seat fighter, framework tilted at an angle suggesting that its last landing hadn't been a gentle one, occupied deck space between a meteor-scarred cargo drone and a pleasure yacht decked out like a party cake in blue and silver trimming; and off in a corner beyond a dozen or so other antique craft, a battered-looking Mage-built scoutship hunched on the deckplates of the bay like a scavenger bird on a rock.

Beka stood very still for a moment, then nodded to herself, slowly, and continued her walk around the *'Hammer*.

By the time she'd finished and walked over to *Amsroto*, the Professor was busy smoothing the serial numbers off one of the hull plates with a hydro-burnisher.

"Have you got *Warhammer*'s papers?" he asked, bending to drop the burnisher into an open tool kit.

"Yes," she said. She reached into the right-side pocket of her jacket for the miniature blaster that always lived there, and put the business end of the little weapon against the back of his neck.

He froze. Then, with infinite caution, he lifted both hands and placed them flat against Amsroto's hull.

Beka started breathing again. "Now," she said. "It's time you told me what your name really is, and how you wound up with a Mageworld scoutcraft parked in your docking bay."

"*Defiant?*" asked her passenger, sounding imperturbable as ever. "I own her. As for names . . . names change, and the galaxy has forgotten mine. But I was Armsmaster to House Rosselin, when Entibor was still a living world.''

"I'll be damned," said Beka. "Everybody thinks you're dead.''

"An excusable mistake," said the Professor. "I . . . retired abruptly at the end of the war, and didn't keep up my old acquaintances. My lady, can we abandon this rather awkward conversation for one a bit more civilized?''

"I keep telling you, it's 'Captain,' '' said Beka, slipping the hand-blaster back into her jacket pocket.

The Professor lowered his arms and faced toward her. "You believe in playing for high stakes, Captain," he said, turning his right hand palm-up to disclose a tiny single-charger needler.

Beka closed her eyes and let out her breath in a long, shuddering sigh. "My father always said," she remarked, "that there was no feeling in the galaxy quite like noticing you were still alive after all. Now I know what he meant.''

The Professor slipped the needler into his coat. "Was all that really necessary, Captain Rosselin-Metadi?''

She took the 'Hammer's papers out from inside her jacket. "Yes," she said. "I couldn't think of any other way to learn if I could trust you, except to see whether you killed me or not.''

The Professor took the papers from her outstretched hand—she wasn't shaking, which surprised her a little—and said, "A bit drastic for most people, but effective. As long as you've decided to trust me, Captain, may I trouble you for one thing more?''

"I suppose," said Beka. "What do you need?''

He made a deprecating gesture with one hand. "Just a small amount of your blood.''

"What the hell for?''

"Additional verisimilitude," said the Professor. "It's the little touches that mark the work of an artist. At the same time that I—call it 'acquired'—Defiant, I came into possession of her medical kit as well. Since she was

Magebuilt, the kit included an emergency supply of undifferentiated general-purpose tissue.''

''You want to replicate me?'' Beka backed off a step, shaking her head. ''Oh, no, you don't!''

The Professor made an exasperated noise. ''A Mageworld biochemist with a full laboratory setup might have been able to coax a replicant out of that glop, but I can't. It's nothing but first-aid stuff—doesn't know whether it wants to be a liver or a leg, but slap it onto an open wound instead of tape or synthaflesh, and you'll heal overnight without a scar.''

''Handy,'' said Beka. ''But the blood—''

''It's one way to initialize the match,'' said the Professor. ''*Amsroto* still needs a pilot, after all—or at least, the convincing remains of one.''

Beka nodded, and began to smile. ''Professor, I like the way you think.''

A little over sixteen hours later the *'Hammer*—with the newly renamed and reloaded *Amsroto* attached to her belly by landing claw—approached the dropout point for the Artat system. Beka had kept *Warhammer*'s hyperspace velocity down to normal or a little below for this leg of the trip, and the control panel showed mostly green, with only occasional blinks of amber and red in protest at the ship's doubled mass.

The lights blurred as Beka fought down a massive yawn. She counted back—yes, it had been close to forty-eight hours since the last time she'd gotten any sleep, back when the *'Hammer* had been running on autopilot for Mandeyn.

Good thing there isn't much more of this. I'm nearly seeing double already.

''Are you sure this is going to work?'' she asked the Professor, more to keep her mind from wandering than for any other reason.

''Of course it'll work,'' said her passenger. ''No one puts a contract out on a corpse. And every holochannel in the galaxy will carry the news when the rich, famous, and beautiful Beka Rosselin-Metadi spatters herself and her father's historic spacecraft all over some backworld.''

When Dadda finds out I'm still alive, Beka thought, *he's going to kill me for doing this to him.* Aloud, she said, "I'm not rich. Or famous. Or beautiful, either."

"You will be by the time the news announcers get through with you," the Professor promised. "As soon as the obsequies are officially over we can go back to Mandeyn and pick up the trail. Whoever wanted you dead, Captain, is almost certainly connected to the one who ordered your mother's assassination."

She gave him an inquiring look. "What makes you think you can find either of them?"

"I've been a number of other things in my time besides Armsmaster to your House," the Professor said. "As a professional myself in that line of work—I can find them."

For a moment there was no sound besides the *'Hammer's* own ambient noise. "So," Beka said, when the pause had stretched out long enough, "how do we go about finding our assassin? It's a big galaxy out there."

"The easy part," said the Professor, "is going to be finding the person who actually engineered the job. Only about six people in the business could handle an assassination that subtle—and I didn't, which leaves five to check on."

"What's in all this for you? Last I heard, hired killers didn't take charity cases."

She heard her passenger sigh. "Archaic as it sounds, my lady, I swore an oath of loyalty to your House. And no matter what your occupation, you're still the Domina of Entibor."

Beka shook her head. "I don't believe this." A buzzer sounded. "Coming out of hyperspace!" she announced with relief.

The stars reappeared. As always, the sudden glory of the sight took Beka's breath away. *If I ever get tired of seeing that,* she thought, *it'll be time for me to give up piloting.*

The Artat system lay spread out beneath them. "Third planet in's our target," she said. "Let's tell the nice people that we're here."

In a few minutes, she had contact with Port Artat over

a voice circuit. "Inspace Control, Inspace Control," she said into the comm link, pitching her voice as low as possible to help out the transmission, "this is *Warhammer*, *Warhammer*, checking into the net, over."

"*Warhammer*, *Warhammer*, this is Inspace Control, Inspace Control. Roger, over," came the faint reply.

"This is *Warhammer*. Request permission to orbit Artat, over."

"This is Inspace Control, roger, permission granted, out."

"And that," said Beka, as the link clicked off, "was the easy part."

Warhammer drove on toward the cloud-covered world, and began her orbit. Beka activated the link again.

"Inspace Control, this is *Warhammer*. Request permission to land at Port Artat."

"*Warhammer*, this is Inspace Control. Commence your landing approach."

Turning to the Professor, Beka said, "Here it goes. I'm starting autopilot on *Amsroto* now." Then, over the comm link: "Inspace, '*Hammer*. I am declaring an in-flight emergency. Stand by, over."

"What is the nature of your emergency?" squawked the voice from the comm link.

Beka ignored it.

"What is the nature of your emergency? Acknowledge!" insisted the voice link a second time.

Again, Beka ignored it. She watched the split screen of the navicomp—data from the '*Hammer* above, from *Amsroto* below. When *Amsroto*'s half-screen showed the old freighter firmly on course for her appointment with the planet's surface, and when all the dirtside trackers had locked in on the incoming emergency, Beka released the landing claw.

The navicomp screen went blank as the link with *Amsroto* broke off. *Warhammer* shot away from *Amsroto* at max acceleration to jump speed.

"Now!" said Beka, and jumped the '*Hammer* blind.

Again, she gave it a five-second count before dropping out into realspace, and breathed a sigh of relief when the ship emerged in one piece. She'd worked out the calculations as best she could in advance—but a blind jump taken without a proper run-up still pushed the odds more than she liked.

The navicomp was up again. From the data it was giving her, she'd missed the estimated emergence point by more than just a bit. She thanked whatever deities happened to be listening for not bringing her out of hyper inside a star, and then got to work fixing the *'Hammer*'s location and charting a return course for the Professor's asteroid.

After the acrobatics with *Amsroto*, Beka was glad to make a normal hyperspace jump for a change. As soon as the stars had gone blue and vanished she engaged the *'Hammer*'s autopilot. Then, yawning, she unfastened her safety belts and stood up.

"That's it," she said, rotating her shoulders to relieve muscles gone stiff from tension. "I'm off to get some sleep."

"Six hundred and fifty credits," Ari said without preamble as he slid into the booth at the Greentrees Lounge, where Jessan and Llannat Hyfid sat waiting. "By midnight."

"I hope it's in small, unmarked bills," said Llannat with a straight face, "because that's all we have." Like the others, the Adept had come in civilian clothes—in her case, a plain coverall in dull black fabric. Her staff was propped ready to hand against the side of the booth.

"It couldn't hurt," said Ari. "You have the cash with you, Jessan?"

"The bag's right here," said the Khesatan. "But this is going to just about kill the wardroom slush fund. After payday, we'll probably be able to pick up a little bit more."

"If we don't," said Llannat, "it had better be a very small epidemic."

"Meanwhile," said Ari, "we've got a lot of time to kill, and this place has the best cheap food in Namport, so we might as well have dinner."

The sun set over the spaceport as the three junior officers applied themselves to a leisurely meal. "Here's to riotous living, Namport style,'' said Ari, after the waiter had trundled out the first serving dishes. ''Broiled groundgrubs and marsh eel soup. There's certainly nothing like it on Galcen.''

Llannat grinned, and pulled a broiled grub off its skewer with her teeth. ''That's the truth—I haven't had a meal this good since I left Maraghai.''

Ari dished out a helping of marsh eel soup from the just-arrived pot and presented it to Llannat with a flourish. ''They bring out the local beer to drink with this,'' he said. ''You're supposed to pour some of it into your soup to punch up the broth a little.''

The Adept looked dubious. ''I don't know—''

''We aren't on duty, we aren't in uniform, and we aren't on an official mission,'' Jessan said. ''So what's the worst they can do to us—make us medics and send us to Nammerin?''

''No,'' said Ari, after a moment's thought. ''The worst they can do is court-martial us and send us home. Considering that what we're doing is technically illegal, I for one wouldn't mind being able to list 'intoxication' as a 'mitigating or extenuating circumstance.' Here comes the beer now.''

As he spoke, another waiter brought out a tray of beer bottles and began setting up a pair by each place. ''One for the soup,'' explained Ari to Llannat, ''and one to drink.''

She picked up one of her bottles and inspected the label. '' 'Tree Frog Export Dark'?''

''Always demand the best,'' Jessan said, popping the seal on his first bottle and pouring some into the soup bowl.

The Adept shrugged and opened a bottle. ''If my friends could see me now,'' she said. ''Into the soup it goes.''

''That's the spirit,'' said Ari, pouring a good dollop of Export Dark into his own bowl and stirring vigorously. ''All the same, there's better stuff than Tree Frog, if we're going to do any serious drinking.''

''Not here in Namport, there isn't,'' said Jessan, ''unless you count that aqua vitae they distill from purple mushrooms—which I personally wouldn't.''

''I wouldn't either,'' said Ari. ''But take a look in that bag you're carrying.''

The Khesatan reached under the table, fumbled for a moment, and brought up a tall, narrow-necked bottle filled with dark amber fluid. Ari nodded toward the bottle.

''Does that look like purple mushrooms to you?'' he asked.

Jessan turned it to inspect the label. His eyebrows went up as he read. ''Galcenian brandy . . . prewar Uplands Reserve . . . I'd say it looks more like a minor miracle. How did you come by this stuff on a lieutenant's pay?''

''Family cellars,'' said Ari, with a shrug. ''Before that it was part of *Warhammer*'s liquor supply—and who knows how my father got it. I brought it with me to Nammerin as a consolation prize for getting assigned here, and wound up being too busy to drink it.''

''So what's an heirloom like that doing in a bar like this?'' asked Jessan. ''Meaning no disrespect to Greentrees, of course.''

''I dropped it into the carrybag before we left base,'' Ari said. ''Seeing that you're leaving for Pleyver, and Mistress Hyfid has just arrived, and you've got a promotion that we still haven't celebrated properly—''

Jessan cut him off. ''Are you proposing to share this jewel with us?''

''I am.''

''In that case . . .'' The Khesatan regarded the bottle for a moment before popping the seal. He poured a generous shot into a clean glass, and then repeated the ritual twice more for Llannat and Ari.

''A toast to our beloved Commanding General!'' Jessan said. ''After all,'' he added in an aside, ''it's his brandy.''

Ari laughed, and drained the glass. He held it out to Jessan for a refill. Llannat, meanwhile, had taken a small sip. Now she sat leaning back against the wall of the booth, with the glass cradled between her hands.

"This stuff isn't booze," she said, after a few moments. "It's a religious experience."

Ari looked at her. "The patterns of the universe as seen through the bottom of a bottle?"

She cocked an eyebrow at him and took another small sip. "Why not? It's a part of the universe like everything else."

"Including Tree Frog beer?"

"Sure," she said. "But this stuff's like all of autumn caught in a glass: the sun, the breeze from the high slopes, the wineberries after the first frost. . . ."

The Adept's dark eyes grew hazy and faraway, looking at something in the middle distance that only she could see. Ari watched her uneasily—she didn't appear to be the sort who was given to prophecies and visions, but you never could tell. She came out of the reverie without saying anything unnerving, however, and applied herself to the marsh eel soup as though nothing had happened.

Jessan, meanwhile, had bowed to local custom and was washing down the strong-flavored soup with more Tree Frog beer. After Llannat's brief excursion into mysticism, Ari found himself unwilling to spoil the memory of that first taste of brandy, and contented himself with refilling his water glass.

The soup was followed by tusker-ox steaks in red spore sauce, and then by a jellied fruit pie. At last, midnight drew near. Ari stood, and Jessan handed over the bundle of cash.

"There you are," the Khesatan said. "Remember—try to keep a low profile. As low as possible, that is."

"Very funny," said Ari. "Just make sure that you two have the scoutcar ready to pick me up at fifteen after. I'd hate to have to walk all the way home."

IV. Nammerin: Namport
Galcen: Prime Base

THE AIR outside the Greentrees Lounge hit Ari
like a wet towel. Clouds obscured the night
sky, and a warm mist hung in the air and made hazy circles around the streetlights. Despite his relative abstinence
at dinner, Ari found himself light-headed—probably, he
decided, some sort of interaction between the Tree Frog
Export Dark and the Uplands Reserve. He shrugged and
started walking.

Greentrees and Munngralla's curio shop were on opposite sides of town, with the port area sprawling between
them. Ari took the long way around, swinging in a half-
circle through streets that were for the most part lighted
but empty. Even in a galactic backwater like Nammerin,
portside on a LastDay night could get rough—and while
the Mark VI blaster could probably settle any trouble that
didn't answer to mass and strength alone, the combination
would be sure to get him noticed.

The CO's entitled to a little discretion, he thought. *And
anyhow the long way is faster.*

The district of seedy rooming houses and small shops where G. Munngralla's Five Points Imports did business was far enough away from the spaceport to close down at night. Most of the storefronts in the buildings along the muddy streets had grillwork up over their darkened windows—this wasn't a district that could afford security force fields and all-night displays. Streetlights here came one to a corner, making the intersections into puddles of bright light that never reached far enough to illuminate the middle of the block. The random glow from upstairs windows cast odd blocks of light and shadow onto the rutted streets; but not even that light reached the sidewalks under the shop awnings.

Ari kept one hand near the holstered blaster and moved as quietly from shadow to shadow as he knew how. He might not be able to disappear from plain view in broad daylight like his brother Owen the apprentice Adept, but he'd learned to hunt like a Selvaur in the forests of Maraghai, stalking the fanghorn and the rock hog on foot and bringing them down barehanded.

Now he moved in silence down the street leading to Munngralla's shop, and cast his mind back to the hunting lessons of his adolescence. *Watch everywhere, youngling,* Ferrdacorr had told him. *And listen, always. You humans have no noses, but better eyes than the Forest Lords—and you personally, at least, have something that passes for a sense of hearing.*

Nothing out of the ordinary seemed to be happening in the street itself. Something scaly and four-legged was digging through an overturned trash barrel; and upstairs in the building on the next corner a woman's voice berated somebody named Quishan for an unspecified, but apparently habitual, offense. But Five Points Imports was as quiet and dark as its neighbors to either side.

Ari reached out a hand to give the door a gentle push—mechanical hinges could make more noise than a feedback regulator about to go down hard—and got no result at all. Munngralla had locked up the shop.

Careless of him, thought Ari. He checked his chronometer. *I'm right on time.* And then, still standing with one hand reaching out to touch the doorknob, *He'd never be that careless. Not with a deal coming up that might lead to a long-term contract. Somebody else must have locked the door.*

He moved closer to the door, and put one ear to the crack between it and the jamb. Deliberately, he blocked out the scrabbling and rustling from the overturned trash barrel, the shrill voice with its accusations against the luckless Quishan, and the ever-present rumble from the port . . . and listened.

He heard nothing at first, then something: a distant, arrhythmic thumping and bumping from deep within the shop. If Munngralla had good soundproofing in his back rooms and upstairs apartments—which as the local agent of the Quincunx he more than likely did—those bare hints of noise implied that all hell was breaking loose somewhere.

Then Ari was sure of it, because faintly through the other sounds came a deep, ragged-edged roaring—the war cry of a Selvaur outnumbered but refusing to go down.

"Right," Ari said aloud, and took hold of the doorknob again. One quick, sharp jerk, and the door swung open without further trouble. Munngralla would have to repair the doorjamb and replace the lock.

Inside the shop, the noises were more distinct, though still muffled. Ari ran for the beaded curtain at the back of the shop, snatching up a pugil stick from the display rack as he passed. By night, the beaded curtain hid a solid metal door—thick enough for soundproofing, but still not strong enough to hold against a well-placed kick. It caved inward, leaning drunkenly from the only remaining hinge. Ari slid past it and into the back hall.

He ran up the steps three at a time, to where a slanting rectangle of light shone out into the upstairs hallway. The last door wasn't locked. Munngralla must have come upon the intruders before they could secure that final barrier against unexpected interruption. As Ari reached the last step, a body flew out the open door and slammed against the opposite wall.

From the looks of it, Munngralla was still fighting. Ari hefted the pugil stick, let loose his own version of Ferrda's fighting-roar, and charged in.

The Selvaur stood with his back to the far wall of a cabinet-lined workroom, swinging a length of metal shelving in murderous arcs that kept his attackers from closing. Munngralla's enemies—whoever they might be—hadn't stinted on the manpower. Not counting the casualty out in the hallway, Ari saw at least five humans still pressing the fight with clubs and knives.

He swiped the butt end of his pugil stick across the back of the nearest skull. The man collapsed onto the tile floor, fouling the footwork of two other attackers as he fell. Munngralla caught one of them along the side of the head with his length of shelving, and Ari heard the crack of shattering bone. That man also went down, his head bloody. The leading edge of Munngralla's piece of shelving showed a red stain.

One of the men turned and came at Ari with a knife angled low to slash across the gut. Ari blocked with the butt of the pugil stick, striking the knife man's forearm so hard that the wood shivered against his hands like an electronic shock.

The knife hit the floor with a metallic clatter. The man went grey-white but kept coming forward.

"Oh, no, you don't," said Ari, who had no desire to get the man's left-hand knife in the belly at close quarters. He smashed the haft of the pugil stick against the man's nose. The knife man screamed once before going down.

Blood from the man's broken face made the stick slippery under Ari's fingers. He shifted his grip a little and moved in toward the only attacker still standing. Munngralla swung his piece of shelving into the man's ribs as Ari cracked the same man over the head from behind.

Then the sound and heat and smell of a blaster bolt tore through the air, and Munngralla let out a roar of pain.

Ari swore. They'd both forgotten the second of the two men who had stumbled earlier. Smaller than the others, and possibly more prudent, he'd rolled sideways and come up under one of the worktables. Firing from that refuge, he managed to get off a second shot, but the bolt went wild as Ari tore the table loose from the floor and hit him with it.

Nobody fired any more blasters after that, and only Munngralla moved. The big Selvaur dragged himself to his feet, and Ari saw that most of the grey-green scales along his left arm and side had been burned away.

"It's going to be a day or so in accelerated healing for you, I'm afraid," Ari said, as soon as he had breath.

Never mind that, growled Munngralla. *We have to get out of here fast.*

"You think somebody called Security?"

I know what was on the shelf that idiot hit with his second bolt, said the Selvaur. *Heat starts the reaction— we've got about five minutes before it all explodes.*

"I wondered why they held off so long with the fireworks," said Ari. Habit already had him checking to see if any of their fallen adversaries were alive. Most of them looked past help, but both his first victim and the man he and Munngralla had taken out together were still breathing. "We can't leave these two here."

Why not?

Because I said not, snarled Ari, in Selvauran. *Are the Forest Lords hunters, or do they murder like the thin-skins?*

The Selvaur grumbled an obscenity, but nevertheless picked up one of the survivors with his good arm, as lightly as if the limp body were a rag doll. Ari knelt to lift the second surviving attacker. It took more of an effort than he'd expected, and his head spun as he rose again to his feet. He closed his eyes for a second or so, and the dizziness subsided.

That's what you get for mixing Galcenian brandy with Nammerin beer, he told himself. *File that away for future reference. . . .*

Come on! roared Munngralla from the hall outside. *The whole upstairs is going to blow in about two minutes.*

Ari took a firm hold on the unconscious man and started out after the Selvaur. At the top of the stairs, he paused. "What about the tholovine?"

Under the counter, snarled Munngralla from the foot of the stairs. *But we haven't got all night.*

"I know, I know," Ari said, starting down. The staircase looked steeper and more rickety than it had when he was charging up it a few minutes ago. A streak of drying blood ran down the plastered wall opposite the stairwell. It looked like that early casualty who'd come flying out through the door had made it away under his own power.

In the shop, Munngralla paused only long enough to shift his burden and pull a small, tidily wrapped brick from behind the Changwe temple gong before running on out through the ruined doorway. Ari followed at a breathless lope.

He jumped off the raised sidewalk to get a running start for the far side of the street—and then, in a roar of sound and a blinding light, came the explosion. Scraps of brick, plaster, and flaming wood rained down, setting the shop awning afire in several places. Five different burglar alarms in nearby shops went off in a jangling discord. Someone in the next building started having hysterics. And all up and down the block the doors flew open, discharging people in every imaginable state of dress and undress.

Ari picked himself up from his knees in the mud. The man he'd brought out still breathed, for a miracle; Ari half-carried, half-dragged him the rest of the way to the far sidewalk. Munngralla was already there, sitting on the edge of the raised walkway and watching the flames reaching skyward from the blown-out windows of his shop.

The force of the explosion, and the frantic overburdened

run, made Ari's head start spinning again. He laid his man down on the wooden sidewalk next to the man Munngralla had carried out, then sat down himself and waited for the vertigo to stop.

"What," he asked aloud as soon as he had breath, "was all that about, anyway?"

They didn't like the way I operate.

"Complaining to the Small Business Board wasn't good enough for them, I suppose."

The Selvaur gave a sardonic growl of laughter and pushed himself to his feet. *We'd better leave before Fire and Security show up.*

"What about—?" Ari flapped a hand at the two casualties stretched out behind them on the sidewalk.

Let Security handle them.

"I suppose that is easier that explaining," agreed Ari. Rising seemed to take almost more effort than he had energy for at the moment, and his head reeled. "Damned if I'm ever going to touch your local booze anymore."

Come on—we haven't got much time left.

The sound of an aircar's engines came to them on the night breeze, and Air shook his head. "Correction. We don't have any time left. Here they come."

But the scoutcar that settled on its nullgravs in the center of the street had Space Force markings. The side door slid open and a dim figure appeared, beckoning wildly.

"Come on—hurry!" shouted Llannat Hyfid from the open door.

"Here's our ride," said Ari to the Selvaur, and ran for the aircar with Munngralla at his heels.

On Galcen, the first blue shadows of evening gathered over Prime. From the old waterfront district beside the bay, the twilight spread up through the government buildings and commercial towers of the city proper, then out into the sprawling suburbs and over the city-beyond-the-city that was Prime Spaceport Complex.

The commerce of the civilized galaxy passed through

Prime Complex—water-grain from Nammerin, raw minerals from Lessek, wool from the Galcenian highlands, passengers from everywhere. The Republic's Space Force maintained its central administrative headquarters there as well. South Polar Base might do better for planetary defense, but when it came to keeping an eye on the rest of the galaxy, Prime was the only place to be.

In keeping with Prime's importance, the Officers' Club there boasted the best food of any Space Force base on Galcen, which wasn't saying that much—and the best wine cellar of any base in the galaxy, which was saying a great deal. Commander Pel Florens, whose ship left orbit in the morning for a long, dry patrol of the Mageworlds border zone, had already accounted for most of a bottle of prewar Infabede red while listening to his onetime Academy roommate Jervas Gil.

Commander Gil, an undistinguished-looking officer whose medium height, medium weight, and thinning hair of a medium shade of brown tended to fade from memory almost before he left the room, was not happy. He had confined himself to plain water from the table carafe, and to three cups of cha'a, strong and dark—not from preference, but because he had the duty—while he unburdened himself to his friend.

"I tell you," he said, "it isn't fair. I was set up."

"What's not fair?" Florens asked, a bit muzzily.

Commander Gil's head, if not happy, was clear. He signaled to the waiter for another cup of cha'a and enumerated his grievances.

"Here I am—career Space Force, first ground tour in five years, and what do I get? Flag Aide to the Commanding General! Career enhancing, right? Guaranteed my own command after this, right? Wrong! Dead people don't get command, and by the time this is over, I'll be dead."

Florens poured the last of the Infabede red into his wineglass. "Cheer up. It can't possibly be as bad as a Mageworlds patrol."

"Oh, yes, it can," said Gil. "All day, telling sweet

little old ladies that General Metadi absolutely does not speak at flower shows. When I'm not arranging surprise inspections. Or writing holiday greetings to the troops. Or talking to the holovids. I'd take two Mageworlds tours back to back and I'd smile if it meant I never had to talk to another reporter.''

He glanced at his chronometer, gulped the last of his cha'a, and stood up. ''Hate to leave you like this, Pel, but I want to get some sleep before I go on watch. If somebody starts a war between midnight and zero-eight-hundred Standard, I'm the lucky son of a bitch who gets to wake up the General.''

The flames of G. Munngralla's Five Points Imports lit up the Med Station scoutcar, hovering on its nullgravs above the muddy street of downtown Namport. Ari and Munngralla hit the door at a run and hurled themselves into the aircar's cargo bay. Llannat slammed the door back across the opening and dogged it shut. ''All right, Jessan,'' she shouted, ''go!''

The aircar sprang forward and up, leaving the confusion in the street below to dwindle out of sight. Ari pulled himself up to a sitting position on the floor of the cargo bay, and saw Llannat already working over Munngralla's blaster burns with antibiotic cream and bandages from the aircar's kit.

''You're a bit early,'' he said. ''Not that I'm objecting, you understand.''

''She had a feeling,'' came Jessan's voice from the pilot's seat. ''So we decided to hustle on along. And it does look like you've surpassed yourself. What was it—arson?''

''Nobody told me, either,'' Ari said, struggling to his feet and making his way up to the empty seat next to Jessan. He collapsed onto the upholstery with a groan, his head ringing. ''Damn, I'm tired.''

''Don't go to sleep yet,'' said Jessan. ''We have a contact on an intercept course—and he's not transmitting a Security identifier.''

Ari remembered the blood trail down the staircase. One of the attackers had managed to call for help, and get it.

He cursed under his breath—and then cursed again, more quietly, at the stab of headache that followed. "Try to shake them," he muttered. "They aren't very nice people. And I think they're mad at us."

Jessan answered with something Ari couldn't catch. The headache and vertigo were hitting him now with redoubled force, and a deafening roar filled his ears. He closed his eyes and leaned his head back against the seat, and was only dimly aware of the aircar's increasing speed.

There's more to this than mixing beer and brandy, he thought with an effort. The aircar heeled sharply, throwing him sideways against the safety webbing. He groaned.

A hand—cool and professional—touched the side of his face. "You're worse off than Munngralla," Llannat Hyfid's voice said from behind him. "Why didn't you tell us you'd been hit?"

"Wasn't." After his head stopped echoing the syllables, he added, "Thought it was the beer."

"If you're drunk," said Llannat, "I'm a Magelord."

He's not drunk. The grumble of Munngralla's Forest Speech was almost inaudible through the roaring in Ari's head. *But it was the beer.*

The hand dropped away from Ari's face. He sensed, rather than heard, the Adept turn back toward Munngralla.

"Poison? Which one?"

Mescalomide.

"How do you know—never mind. We'll handle it."

"Mescalomide's a blood agent." Jessan's voice, oddly faint and worried. "He needs a stimulant."

"He needs a complete blood change. What we've *got* is a stimulant."

"I know, I know . . . damn!"

The aircar heeled again.

He heard Llannat's voice. "Keep this damned thing steady for a few seconds, will you?"

The aircar leveled off, and Ari felt Llannat's fingers

pushing up his sleeve. Something cold and sharp pricked his skin, the arm ached for a second or two, and then the chilly sharpness withdrew. Almost at once, his head began to clear.

If I don't die in the next few minutes, he thought, *I'm going to spend the next few weeks feeling truly rotten.*

He opened his eyes and squinted at the control panel. He could see the readouts, all right, with an unpleasant, stimulant-induced clarity. "We're not doing too well."

"You're not doing so good yourself," said Llannat. "You're close to checking out on us."

"I'll try not to." He ignored the dull ache in his skull and focused on the control panel. "Right now, we're all in bad shape."

"I know," said Jessan quietly. "I'm not good enough to shake them, either." He paused, and then asked, "Are you up to handling the controls?"

Ari shrugged, and wished he hadn't—the motion made his headache worse. "I could give it a try, if you don't mind a rough ride."

Llannat grabbed his shoulder. "You're in no condition—"

But Jessan was already unbuckling his safety webbing. "Give him another shot of stimulant. I'm no Adept, but I have a bad feeling about those guys behind us."

Ari slid into Jessan's vacated seat. He glanced at the controls and readouts, barely noticing Llannat swearing under her breath as she pushed up his other sleeve and jabbed the needle into a vein. The Sarcan scoutcars used by the Medical Service had the same instrumentation and basic airframe as the Sadani armed scouts; right now he wished this particular Sarcan had a Sadani's gun as well. "One of you better get on the comm link and start yelling for help."

"I already tried," said Llannat. "No joy. Somebody's jamming our frequencies."

The row of lights on the lock-on indicator under the

long-range scan went out, then turned on again one by one.

"Somebody's also lighting us up with fire control," said Ari. He checked the location of the pursuit on the Position Plotting Indicator scope. "Stand by!"

He tilted the aircar's nose toward the zenith and fired the jets up to maximum. The little aircar stood on its tail and headed skyward.

The Thrust Level Indicator lights shone amber as Ari struggled to gain altitude. On the long-range scanner, the image of the pursuing craft overshot the point where the medical aircar had begun its climb, and skidded clumsily as it began its own climbing turn. The Sarcan's lock-on indicator went back to its random analysis pattern—the fix was broken.

Jessan cleared his throat. "Ari, the base is the other way."

"I know. The bad guys expect us to be going there. Why should we make things easy for them?"

"I'll tell you why," said Llannat from behind him. "I can't keep giving you stimulant shots forever. If you don't get to the Med Station for proper treatment inside of about ten minutes, you're a write-off."

"I hear you," said Ari. The second aircar was gaining again—it looked like a private job built purely for speed. The Sarcan's lock-on indicator blipped at him as the weapons systems astern tried again for a fix.

"Let's do something else this time," he said. "Hold on." He cut power and emissions, pushed the controls all the way forward, and began a ballistic dive.

Ari was flying blind now, trying not to give himself away with his own electronic signals. And again, the lock-on broke.

"Why hasn't he fired on us yet?" asked Jessan.

"Maybe because he wants prisoners," said Ari. "Or maybe because we've been dodging him every time he locked onto us."

But mostly because he has TurboBlaster 25s and they've got nothing for range, added Munngralla.

"How do you know that?" Llannat asked.

Because I sold them to him.

"You sold—who is he?"

Disgruntled customer.

"Oh."

Still accelerating under the pull of gravity, they flashed downward past the other aircar as it climbed. But the pursuit was more alert this time. The mysterious aircar pushed over into a dive as they dropped past, and began gaining on them again.

"Oh, hell," said Ari. "Time to do something desperate." He switched on the engines to put the aircar into a power-dive straight for the surface. "Follow me, you bastards, and let's see who falls apart first."

The thin red line that indicated the location of the ground reappeared at the bottom of the altimeter. The second craft was sticking close behind, and the lock-on indicator pipped again as the first of the Dangerous Altitude lights lit up. Ari maintained his vertical dive. A burst of light came from astern, and the aircar shook with the *whump* of a grazing hit.

"That was close," said Jessan. "You might consider dodging them again."

"Not yet," said Ari, his eyes on the altimeter. By now, six of the Dangerous Altitude lights had lit. "Not yet." The dark of the planet's surface filled the main window. A seventh light flashed on. "Now!"

He pulled back on the controls, wrenching the aircar out of its power-dive and into a vertical climb. Once again, the other pilot overshot the turnpoint. But this time he hit mud and rocks instead of air, and a column of flame rose up through the forest canopy.

"Should have watched his height instead of watching me," said Ari, and put the aircar back onto the approach to base.

A klaxon hooted. The energy level indicator showed in

the red zone, a hair above empty. "Damn! That hit ruptured the fuel tank. I've got to land this thing now."

Setting the aircar down on the closest flat piece of ground was harder work than he'd expected, but he managed. "End of trip," he said, leaning back against the seat. "The base perimeter should be right through those trees. Sorry about cutting things so close."

He shut his eyes. The stimulants and the adrenaline boost of the chase had already begun to fade, and the backlash was setting in. He fumbled with the buckles of the safety webbing, but Llannat's capable hands took over and released him.

"You have to get to Emergency right now," she said. "Can you walk?"

"Never mind that," said Jessan. "Get on the comm link, and tell them to send out some orderlies with a stretcher."

Llannat tried the comm link. "It's still down," she said.

Jessan took over the link, and tried again. "Damn. I don't like this. Llannat—take Munngralla and walk the perimeter until you find a gate or a guard or a comm booth, and tell them to send help. I'll stay here with the Terror of the Spaceways, and try to keep him from checking out for good."

"No," said Llannat. "You go with Munngralla while I stay here—please. I have a feeling about this."

The aircar's cargo door slid open with a metallic scrape and a heavy clunk. Ari heard Jessan and the Selvaur climb out and go crashing off through the underbrush. The door didn't slam closed behind them, and after a few moments he turned his head enough to see back into the cargo bay.

Llannat stood in the open door of the unlighted bay, looking out at the night. Her right hand went to the clips beside the door and recovered the staff she had stowed there. She held it loosely at her side, but something in her posture made the hairs rise on Ari's neck.

She spoke—not in a whisper, which would carry, but in

an almost subvocal murmur. "Whatever happens, stay in the aircar."

"What's wrong?" Ari asked.

Llannat replied without turning her head, and in the same low murmur as before. "A bad smell in the winds of the universe, my friend. Somebody earnestly desires your death."

V. Nammerin: Namport
Galcen: Prime Base
Artat: Port Artat

SOMEONE WANTS *to kill me*, Ari thought. *Well, I'd figured that out already. The question is . . . why?*

He saw Llannat stiffen. Something had moved out of the trees and into the open ground by the aircar—something that made no sound, and that he could track only by watching Llannat shift position fractionally as she followed its progress.

A voice spoke from the darkness. "Adept. Give me Ari Rosselin-Metadi."

Llannat didn't move from her position in the open door. "Lieutenant Rosselin-Metadi isn't mine to give anybody."

"Let us abandon playing with words," said the strange voice. "What matters is that nobody is here to guard a dying man but you—and who can say, afterward, whether help that comes too late might have arrived in time? Stand aside."

"No."

"Then on your own head be it, Adept."

A globe of scarlet light sprang out of the blackness beyond the cargo doors, illuminating a shadowy figure that seemed to have no face.

It's a mask, Ari told himself. *Or a hood. Nothing more.* He didn't want to think about how much power the stranger must be wielding, to have it show up so plainly against the night—or about what the poison in his blood must be doing, to make him of all people aware of the patterns and currents of power. *Owen said once that I was so dense I'd need to be halfway dead before I'd notice power at work. He was mad at me when he said it . . . but it looks like he was right after all.*

The stranger threw the scarlet globe toward the aircar. In the same instant, the darkness surrounding Llannat Hyfid flared into an aurora of vivid green. When the red fire struck that barrier, it faded and died, and the green aurora vanished as suddenly as it had come.

Ari heard Llannat release a long, shaky breath. Then the Adept seemed to draw herself together. She leapt down from the open door into the clearing with a scuffle of wet leaves, and brought up her staff two-handed before her as she landed. Streamers of green fire followed her movement across the darkness beyond.

Scarlet lightning blazed up as the black-robed stranger lashed out at the Adept with a staff of his own—this one short enough to grip one-handed, rather than in both hands after the fashion of Galcen-trained Adepts. Wood cracked against wood as Llannat blocked the blow. Then the combat moved out of Ari's range of vision, leaving him nothing to go by except the mingled sounds of scuffling footsteps and heavy breathing, punctuated by sudden flares of green and crimson light.

He heard the stranger laugh. "You're overmatched, Mistress."

There was silence, and then a blaze of green light washed over the clearing.

"I'm still alive," said Llannat's voice. "You have to

win this fight. I only need to keep from losing it too soon.''

Ari heard the stamping footsteps again, and the crack and swish of the staves. *I wish Owen was here,* he thought. For somebody who acted like he wasn't interested in reality most of the time, his younger brother was surprisingly dangerous in a fight. But Owen the apprentice Adept was safe up on a mountaintop away from it all, where he hadn't needed to fight anybody in earnest since he was about fifteen, and outside the aircar the sound of Llannat's footsteps had begun to falter and drag.

That leaves you, Rosselin-Metadi.

Ari pushed himself to a more upright position with an effort, and tried to focus his night vision on the aircar's medical kit, lying open on the deck just behind the pilot's seat. Yes . . . there was still one hypo-ampule of the stimulant. He reached down—almost fell over—caught himself on the edge of the control panel—and then he had it. He straightened, head spinning and vision fading to black, and propped his right shoulder against the seatback while he fumbled in search of a vein in his left arm. *There!*

He paused for a second—this might kill him, as surely as mescalomide or the stranger's crimson fire. *If Llannat goes down,* he reminded himself, *you'll be scavenger bait anyway.* He shoved the ampule home.

The needle stung in his flesh for a moment, and the false clarity of the stimulant returned. He pushed himself to his feet, standing bent-over under the aircar's low ceiling, and braced his left hand against the wall of the cargo bay for balance. With his right, he pulled the heavy blaster from its holster. Then he began to move in silent, careful steps toward the open door.

He didn't know how he was going to handle climbing down. His knees were obeying him, for the moment, but he wasn't inclined to depend on them very much. When he reached the door, he held on to the edge of the opening with his left hand and looked out.

The fight was still going on. Llannat and the stranger

moved like shadows within the brilliant auras of red and green that suffused the entire clearing with an uncanny, pulsating glow. Against that light, the dark lines of the staves crossed and recrossed in a pattern Ari didn't know well enough to follow, except to see that Llannat was being forced back, step by step, toward the aircar.

Ari saw her bring her staff up to block a swiftly falling blow, and heard her footsteps catch and slide. Then the Adept went down; but she kept her staff between herself and her opponent until the ground knocked it out of her hands.

The stranger struck again as Llannat went sprawling, but she had her feet under her and was rolling away. The blow bit into the earth instead, and Ari saw Llannat struggle upright—empty-handed, but still between her adversary and the open door.

The stranger took an easy step forward, holding his staff in a loose, almost careless grip. Ari saw Llannat brace herself, heard her draw a long, shaky breath—

The hell with this, he thought, and fired.

He saw the bolt reach its target. The scarlet light in the clearing faded as the stranger fell backward, hit the ground, and disappeared.

Nice trick, that, Ari thought. Then the backlash of the stimulant hit him, and he collapsed forward out of the open door onto the wet ground.

". . . I'm the lucky son of a bitch who gets to wake the General."

Halfway through the midwatch at Galcen Prime Base the message came in from Port Artat, and Commander Gil's words came back to haunt him.

At least the General was sleeping here at the base, Gil reflected as he reached for the comm link to the General's quarters, rather than out at the family's house in the country. Not that there was much family living there anymore, which was probably the reason the General had taken to spending more and more of his nights at the base. . . .

Gil told himself to stop stalling, and activated the link. He drew a deep breath, and started talking as soon as the buzzing on the other end stopped.

"General Metadi. General Metadi—wake up."

"I'm awake, Commander. What's the problem?"

Gil swallowed. "Sir, it's—there's been an accident with a merchantman, sir. It requires your personal attention."

"The hell you say! I'll be down in Control in five minutes."

In fact, only about three minutes had passed before the General stalked in—wide awake, fully dressed, and looking for answers.

"What've you got, Commander?"

Commander Gil picked up the message printout. "The CO's Situation Report from the Station on Artat, sir."

"Artat," the General said. "Brief me."

Gil compiled. "It's a small, cold world in the Infabede sector, population nine hundred million. Second Mechwing is based there—SERVRON Five's people. Nearest inhabited neighbor is Mandeyn, about thirty hours' distance in hyper."

The General looked unimpressed. "So what the hell has Artat come up with that's worth getting me out of bed?"

"This, sir," said Gil unhappily.

He handed over the printout, and let the brief message answer the General's question for him. A spaceship identifying herself as *Warhammer* had declared an emergency prior to landing at Port Artat. The ship had crashed and burned. A lifepod had been seen to eject, but the jets on the pod had failed to ignite and the chutes had failed to deploy. The pod had exploded on impact. There appeared to be human remains. The sketchy report ended with the words "amplifying info to follow."

Gil busied himself at the message terminal. Not for all the worlds in the galaxy would he have stood and watched the General read that printout. He waited until he heard the unmistakable sound of a message crumpling inside a clenched fist before he turned around again.

"Do you wish to convene a Board of Inquiry, sir?"

"Damn right I want an Inquiry," said the General. "I want to head it. We're going to Artat. Let's move."

The trip out, in the fastest vessel available at Prime, proved every bit as bad as Gil had feared. He had all he could do at the outset, just keeping the General from taking the controls himself. Even under happier circumstances Metadi liked to push engines closer to redline that Gil cared to think about; and as for the present, Gil wouldn't have ridden in a hovercar with a driver who looked like General Metadi did.

The rest of the trip the General spent pacing the passageways of the craft—in a bad temper and not afraid to let everyone know it—while officers and crew scrambled to stay out of his way.

The arrival at Port Artat's Space Force Station was, if anything, worse. The station itself held no more than a pair of local defense fighters and a scoutcraft; and judging from all the posters and holodisplays, the only building spent most of its time as a recruiting office. At the sight of his office doorway sliding shut behind General Metadi himself, the commanding officer gave a visible shudder, then pulled himself together with such force Gil fancied he heard bones clicking.

If the General saw the shudder, he ignored it. "All right, Commander—what do you have?"

Wisely, Gil thought, the CO decided to follow the General's lead and dispense with formalities. "All bad news, sir, I'm afraid. There . . . ah . . . wasn't much left."

"There usually isn't," snapped the General—Gil saw the CO wince. "Let me see the paperwork."

The station CO punched up a file on the desk comp. "We have the preliminary field investigation and the results of the lab reports. I'm afraid that's about it, sir . . . I'm sorry."

The reports showed that there hadn't been much left at all: a field of fragmented, burned *crallach* meat (with a note that the last known cargo of the *'Hammer* had been *crallach*, insurance claim appended); serial numbers taken from parts identified as having been at one time engines, and a serial number from the main hull structural member (numbers matched to the registration papers of Free Trader *Warhammer*, data from the Galcen Ministry of Ships and Spacecraft); pathologist's report from the wreckage of the lifepod, showing that tissue samples from the mess inside matched the gene type of one Beka Rosselin-Metadi as recorded in Central Birth Records on Galcen (copy of same appended); official notice taken that Beka Rosselin-Metadi was listed as captain of *Warhammer*, next of kin listed as General Jos Metadi (record of emergency data [page two] appended).

Commander Gil swallowed, feeling a little sick, and turned away from the comp screen to stare out the office window at Port Artat's flat grey landscape.

From behind him came silence, filled only by sporadic clicking from the comp keys. The General was taking his own sweet time with that report. Gil shook his head. Money could not have paid him to look closely at some of the stuff in that file. A crashed lifepod is not pretty.

"I want to examine the site of the wreck."

When the General's harsh voice broke the silence, Gil jumped. He turned around and saw Metadi, pale and tight-lipped, regarding the Station Commander with a look of grim impatience.

"The site of the wreck," said the Station Commander, sounding to Gil like a man trying very hard not to start babbling. "That would be the Ice Flats, sir."

"I read that," said the General, with a gentleness that made Gil shiver. "I said, I want to examine the site of the wreck."

"Yes, sir," said the Station CO, in the voice of one who has decided that nothing worse could possibly happen. "I'll see to it, sir."

The trip out was by aircar, and in very deep silence.

The Ice Flats—a vast expanse of open ground extending beyond Port Artat to the north and west—had all the scenic charm their name implied. Except for a large pit surrounded by a larger blackened area, nothing distinguished the crash site from the rest of a blank landscape. Pieces of twisted metal littered the Flats in every direction, and a freezing wind blew across the site, cutting through Gil's Galcenian spring uniform and his borrowed Artatian cold-weather jacket like a laser cutting through bone.

The General didn't seem to notice the weather at all. He stood by the Base's aircar with the cold wind whipping his hair around his face, and fixed the station CO with a look that was even colder than the wind. "Who's in charge of the investigation on-site?"

"Petty Officer Ilesh, sir," said the Base CO. Do you want to talk to him?"

The General nodded, once. "Bring him over."

The Station CO signaled to a serious-looking young man dressed in dirty fatigues. He approached the General and saluted smartly.

The General regarded Ilesh with the same cold eye he had given everything else on-planet so far, and asked, "What makes you think that this is my ship?"

"Mostly circumstantial evidence, sir."

"Show me what you have."

"There isn't much to show," Ilesh said. "Witnesses identified pictures of *Warhammer* as the ship that they saw coming in. We found part of the keel, with serial numbers, and the log recorder with the last three flights, and we have the engines: Gyfferan Hypermasters, standard for the class."

Gil saw a corner of the General's mouth quirk in what might have been a bleak smile. "Very good, Ilesh. Satisfy an old man's morbid curiosity—where'd you dig up the specs on a ship that was fifty years out of date when I got hold of her?"

"Back volume of *Jein's Merchant Spacecraft*, sir. Station library."

Again the bleak smile. "Good thinking. Have you towed the wreckage away yet?"

Ilesh shook his head. "No, sir. It's right over there."

He pointed at a tangle of metal pieces that looked to Gil like nothing so much as one of the more tasteless monuments to the Siege of Entibor. The General looked at the pile for a moment, and then began a slow walk around it. In silence, he made one complete circuit, then stooped and picked up something that Gil recognized as part of a starship's main control panel.

Metadi turned the bit of metal over and looked at the chips and wiring on the back. One or two chips he even pried loose and rubbed free of soot with his thumb for closer examination, before dropping the panel back onto the pile. Then he moved on to another fragment of metal, this one too large and heavy to lift. He knelt beside it on the icy ground, and ran his finger over the weld that had joined it to the main hull.

Then he rose to his feet and glanced over at Petty Officer Ilesh. "Where's the rest of the engines?"

"That's all there ever was, sir."

The General stood looking at the pile of blackened metal for a little while longer, and then turned away. "I've seen enough," he said. "Let's go back to town."

At the base, he was terse with the Commanding Officer. "I want the completed investigation in my hands by ten-hundred Local, tomorrow. It will show that the ship that crashed was the *'Hammer*, and that the cause of the wreck was nonspecific mechanical failure rather than pilot error. It will further show that *Warhammer*'s captain was Beka Rosselin-Metadi, and that she did not survive the crash. I will accept that investigation as complete and correct, and announce the results to the news channels fifteen minutes later. After that, the investigation will be closed. Do you follow?"

The station CO looked like a man who'd just taken a half-dozen stun-bolts in the midsection, but he nodded. "Yes, sir."

"Good. Commander Gil!"

Gil abandoned the attempt at invisibility he'd been earnestly cultivating for the past several hours. "Yes, sir?"

"The personal details—if you could take care of those . . ."

Gil felt a surge of sympathy. "Of course, sir. Do you have any specific instructions?"

After a moment, the General nodded. "As soon as the investigation's closed, do whatever you can to pry the . . . remains . . . away from the pathologists, and see that they're—that she's—shipped home to Galcen for a proper funeral."

"And the wreckage of the *'Hammer*, sir?"

"Put the pieces into low orbit and let them burn up on reentry," came the curt reply. "I don't want parts of my ship showing up in every souvenir shop from here to Spiral's End."

Two weeks after the fight in the clearing—or so the date stamp on his medical chart informed him—Ari Rosselin-Metadi came out of the accelerated healing pod in the Medical Station's hospital dome. Llannat Hyfid was waiting beside his bed in the convalescent ward, which surprised him a little. She appeared uneasy about something, which also surprised him. After the cool head she'd shown during the aircar chase and what followed, such nervousness seemed out of character.

"What's wrong?" he asked. "Are you all right?"

"Look who's talking—it's going to be two weeks of bed rest before you're fit for light duty. Jessan almost didn't make it back in time."

He nodded. Even the slight movement made his head swim, and he had to wait a moment before going on. "Close?"

"In more ways than one," she said. She looked away, seeming unwilling to meet his eyes. "For a moment back there I thought I was a write-off, too. Thanks."

"Call us even." He paused again, and then went on. "I thought that all the Magelords were dead."

Llannat appeared to be contemplating something in the far corner of the ward beyond him. "The great Magelords are as dead as the Adepts could make them," she said, after a long silence. "But they left their spies and their apprentices behind, especially in the outplanets. With the war lost and the Mageworlders stuck behind the border zone, there isn't much for the leftovers to do but cause petty trouble. The Guild usually takes care of them as soon as they show up."

"I'll bet your particular Mage had something to do with that outbreak of Rogan's," said Ari thoughtfully. "At a guess, the Quincunx furnished him or his boss with a mutated form of the dry-world virus—and the customer didn't like it when Munngralla turned right around and tried to sell us the cure."

He stopped. When Llannat didn't take up the conversation again, he went on, "How *is* Munngralla anyway?"

The Adept seemed relieved by the change of subject. "Gone," she said. "Just as soon as we got you into the pod and stabilized."

"Didn't want to stick around for explanations," guessed Ari. "Since he probably also furnished your friends with the mescalomide for my beer."

There was another long pause. Then Llannat shrugged. "Maybe. But you seem to have earned his gratitude somehow. He left the tholovine behind when he disappeared. Two more packets have shown up on the CO's desk since then, and the Rogan's cases are responding nicely."

She fell silent.

Ari waited a moment, and said, "It sounds like everything's worked out for the best. So what's the problem?"

The pause this time stretched out even longer than before—so long that Ari began to feel the first touches of a faint, indefinable dread.

And then, reluctantly, as if she'd delayed it as long as she could before speaking, she told him what had happened to *Warhammer* on the Ice Flats of Port Artat.

VI. Mandeyn: Embrig Spaceport
Galcen: Prime Base; Northern Uplands

WINTER HAD tightened its grip on Embrig in the week or so since *Warhammer* had blasted out of the spaceport. The snow tonight lay in drifts against the buildings along the Strip. Beka shivered in spite of her Mandeynan-style overcoat, and told herself it was the cold.

She didn't believe herself. *I feel like I have a target painted on my back.*

So far, though, her disguise seemed to be holding, somewhat to her own surprise. The long coat with silver buttons, the tall boots polished to a high gloss, and the loose white shirt with its elaborate neckcloth and ruffles at the cuffs might be the height of manly fashion in Mandeyn's northern hemisphere—just the same, Beka suspected that on her the overall effect was more androgynous than anything else.

She'd said as much to the Professor, back in his asteroid hideout, but he'd just shrugged and said, "You get all kinds in a big galaxy."

He'd even waved aside her offer to dispense with the

long yellow hair that hadn't been cut since the start of her schooldays back on Galcen. Instead, they'd wound up dying the hair an unremarkable brown and tying it off into a queue with a black velvet ribbon, making her the picture— or so the Professor claimed—of a young Embrigan dandy with a taste for violence and low company.

The heavy blaster riding low on her hip, she supposed, was where the violence came in. That, and the Professor's only concession to what she'd always thought a real disguise should look like, a red optical-plastic patch covering her entire left eye from cheekbone to brow ridge. And as for low company—ahead on the corner, the Painted Lily Lounge flashed its gaudy holosign against the night.

"Remember," said the Professor, "your name is Tarnekep Portree, and nobody crosses you more than once."

"I feel like an idiot," muttered Beka. "A *scared* idiot."

The Professor chuckled. "Trust me, the effect from out front is admirably sinister. Ah, here we are."

The street door of the Painted Lily slid apart before them. They entered, passing through a chilly antechamber whose inner door waited to open until the outer door had closed—a common setup anyplace in the galaxy where the weather outside got more than average hot or cold, and one that had never made Beka nervous before.

First time for everything, she thought, as she turned over her coat to the cloakroom attendant. That left her in shirt and trousers, and feeling even more like a target in spite of the blaster. *Oh, well . . . here we go.*

The front room of the Painted Lily had a dance floor, a bar, and too many little round tables, all competing for the available space. A small band—brass, woodwind, keyboard, and electronic drums—played a tune that had first been hot the year she'd left Galcen for good.

She hooked her left thumb into her belt, and let her right hand hang casually just below the grip of the holstered blaster. Maybe she had only used the damned thing once in her life, but nobody here knew that. She lifted her chin a little, and gave the room a slow, tight-lipped scan. One or two of the Lily's patrons had looked up, half-curious, as she and the Professor entered; when her glance hit them, they look hastily away.

It's got to be the eye patch, she thought. At her left hand, the Professor gave a faint chuckle; Beka wondered if that was what he'd meant by "admirably sinister."

The Professor, who carried no visible weapons, wasn't making anybody nervous—but his waistcoat of black moire spidersilk, and his neckcloth and ruffles of white lace, earned him the personal attention of the Painted Lily's manager.

"And what would the gentlesir's pleasure be tonight?"

The Professor smiled. "Just a quiet hand or two of cards—ronnen, tammani, whatever's going on."

"You'll want Morven, in that case," said the manager, with an answering smile. "Double tammani's the game tonight."

"Excellent," said the Professor. "Lead on, good sir. Come, Tarnekep."

Beka followed the manager and the Professor across the Lily's crowded floor, dodging waiters, dancers, and little tables. A narrow hallway lit by amber glow-globes in wrought-metal brackets led to the back room where Morven the gambler ran his games. The manager pressed his thumb on an ID plate set into the wall, and bowed the Professor in as the door slid open.

Beka entered unheralded at the Professor's right shoulder. As the door slid shut, she paused, taking in the harsh yellow light that replaced the outside's cozy dimness, the gaudy-colored tammani cards falling onto the green baize tablecloth, the gamblers too intent on their game to look up at the latest arrival—and Ignaceu LeSoit.

Oh, damn, we've had it, Beka thought in despair. Her old shipmate leaned against the far wall, looking like nothing so much as an out-of-work spacer too broke to play—except for the heavy government-surplus blaster, twin to her own. *Which it damn well ought to be, since we picked them up in the same curio shop at Suivi Point when I was the new kid on the* Sidh *and Ignac' was showing me the town.*

She dropped her hand to the blaster grip and braced

herself for defiance, reminding herself that it wasn't in her blood, either side, to go down without a fight. But to her amazement no recognition showed in LeSoit's eyes—only a quick, appraising glance that took in her appearance and categorized her all at the same time.

He nodded to her once, as one professional to another. She nodded once in return before moving to lean against the opposite wall with a casual air only just now borrowed from its original owner. *You always did say I learned fast, Ignac'. Let's hope it's true.*

The Professor slid into the seat to the right of the grey-eyed man shuffling the cards. "Deal me in, Morven."

The gambler looked up. "I've been expecting you," he said, and began dealing out a new round.

"As well you should have been," said the Professor, watching the cards falling facedown onto the green cloth. He gathered up his hand and continued. "I would have stopped by to collect earlier, but I had some business out of town. Now—would you be so good as to pass me four of the ten-thousand-credit chips, two of the one-thousands, and the rest in tens and hundreds mixed?"

Morven hesitated. "I don't have that kind of money right in front of me. When I cash in, I'll draw your winnings. I pay my bets."

"Of course," said the Professor. "Did anyone suggest the contrary? Until then, if you could stake me to a couple of hundred to help me pass the time . . ."

"No trouble," said Morven. He slid over a stack of chips—small ones, Beka supposed. Her own skills didn't go beyond solitaire kingnote and a fair game of ronnen for decimal-credit stakes. She'd never been much for gambling; she worked too hard for her money to enjoy seeing it go out the airlock because she'd guessed wrong about a run of cards. The players around the table didn't seem to share her prejudice, though. Most of the chips tended to wind up in front of Morven, but as the evening wore on a respectable stack began to grow in front of the Professor as well.

She quit counting the hands early on, having discovered

that a game of cards, if you don't care for it, is even more boring to watch than to play. The gilded antique chronometer above the door read well past local midnight when Morven dealt out the cards yet again and announced, "A thousand or better to stay in, gentle sirs and ladies."

The Professor slid a gold chip into the center of the table. "I'm in."

Two of the remaining gamblers—a spacer-captain in the colors of the Red Shift Line, and a plump woman in an Embrigan gown of bright green velvet—matched the gold chip with their own. The others looked at their cards, the table, and each other, then laid down their hands.

At ten thousand, the spacer-captain folded, and when the stakes reached twenty thousand the woman in green shook her head regretfully. "It's not my night tonight," she said, gathering up her fur-lined cloak. "Another time, perhaps."

With her departure, the big table was empty except for Morven and the Professor. Across the room from Beka, LeSoit moved a fraction away from the wall, shifting his weight back onto his feet and casting a quick glance in Beka's direction as he brought his hands clear. She met the glance and followed suit. Now, for certain, was a time to be ready for trouble.

"Twenty thousand," said Morven again. "Are you still in?"

The Professor lifted two black chips off the stack before him and put them out onto the table. "I'm in."

The sun had finished setting over Galcen Prime Base in a blaze of red, and the blue-white floodlights of the spaceport were coming on against the dark. Commander Gil watched from behind the safety line as the scheduled Space Force mail courier from the Latam sector settled gently onto the tarmac, and wished with all his heart that he could be elsewhere.

His duties over the past two weeks had not been congenial ones. First had come the unpleasant task of escorting Beka Rosselin-Metadi's remains, such as they were, from Artat to Galcen. Then had come all the panoply and protocol of a full state funeral for the young woman who had been, however briefly and against her will, the last Domina of Entibor. Organizing that had been bad enough, but at least the details had all been codified centuries before—from the order of precedence for the eulogists to the color of the memorial garlands.

Tonight's exercise, however, was something else again. "She was a starpilot," the General had said to Gil. "And her ship was known. They'll be expecting a wake, down in the commercial spaceport. See to it, Commander."

Gil went off to do the General's bidding. This time, he didn't have any formal guidelines to help him—but anyone who'd made commander in the Space Force had spent time waiting for ships in various ports, and anyone who'd spent time hanging around the ports had seen at least one freespacer's wake. Some people even remembered how they'd got home afterward.

After Gil had settled on a day for the wake, he went down to the largest tavern in the port quarter.

"Drinks on the house," he told the manager. "Send the bill to General Metadi on his personal account."

The manager was only too glad to make the rest of the arrangements, including spreading the word around the port. For a really high-class wake, with this much advance notice, every spacer in Galcen Prime would probably show up. No one wanted to risk the bad luck involved in shunning somebody else's final party. That only increased your own chances of ending up unmourned in a "starpilot's grave"—spacers' slang throughout the civilized galaxy for a piece of drifting wreckage.

Gil's visit to the port quarter took care of the main part of the occasion. But much as the General might like to be down in the spaceport with the rest of the crowd, Gil was determined that neither the General nor his family would be out in public any time soon.

"More beer," said Gil to himself, and set off to arrange a private memorial celebration at the General's home.

Now, a week later, thirsty spacers were already starting to line up for drinks at the Circle of Stars, just outside the spaceport gate. Elsewhere in Prime, Gil hoped, other men and women would be setting out for the Rosselin-Metadi estate north of the city—as was the man Gil was meeting, in this last errand of the night.

"He'll want to fly up here himself," the General had said, after the latest message from Nammerin. "See that he doesn't."

The courier's ramp lowered to the tarmac, and a man in Space Force dress uniform emerged. He paused to look about at the foot of the ramp, and then headed for the spot where Commander Gil stood waiting.

The new arrival was big and broad-shouldered, but not until he'd almost reached the safety line did Gil fully appreciate his size. Unlike most very tall men, Ari Rosselin-Metadi wasn't a gangling ectomorph—at a distance, his well-proportioned frame tended to disguise his height. Close at hand, though, he loomed over Commander Gil like a small mountain. At the regulation six-foot distance, he stopped and saluted.

Gil returned the salute. "Lieutenant Rosselin-Metadi?" he said formally. "Commander Gil. Flag Aide. Your father sent me to meet you."

The lieutenant nodded, more a weary inclination of the head than a response. In the stark glare of the port lights, his face was pale, with blue-purple smudges under the eyes.

"Yes, sir," he said. The voice was a deep rumble, with the catch of exhaustion in it. Gil had ridden mail couriers on a space-available basis himself a time or two, and suspected that the lieutenant had probably been sleeping on top of the mailbags for a day or more in order to make it to Galcen tonight.

Not exactly what the doctor ordered for someone just out of a healing pod, Gil thought. *He looks ready to drop.*

"Let's go," he said. "The aircar's over that way."

The lieutenant was silent during the walk to the aircar. When they got there, he lowered himself into the passenger seat without argument, fastened the safety webbing, and let his head fall back against the padded seat. He didn't slump or slouch—something about the set of his shoulders convinced Gil that the lieutenant would sooner collapse altogether than betray himself that way—but nevertheless his posture had the boneless quality of near-total exhaustion.

"We've got about an hour's flight time ahead of us," said Gil, "and Nammerin to Galcen's a bitch of a trip however you handle it. So you might as well grab a bit of sleep."

"Yes, sir," said the lieutenant again.

In the back room of the Painted Lily, the stacks of chips stood just about even.

Neither the Professor nor Morven had spoken more than a few words in the past hour. The game went on in a silence broken only by the riffle of cards, the click and slide of chips counted out and pushed across the tablecloth, and the quiet monosyllables of gamblers intent upon the flow of the game.

Beka had tried to follow the play for a while. She'd stopped after realizing, a bit queasily, that the chips on the table represented more money than she'd ever seen together in one place. Instead, she watched Ignaceu LeSoit, standing relaxed but ready on the opposite side of the room—and when she saw that LeSoit wasn't watching her, or even the Professor, as much as he was watching Morven, she let her own attention slide casually over to the gambler, and stay there.

It was nearly daybreak by the gilded chronometer over the door when the Professor's courteous voice broke the silence.

"I trust you will not take it amiss, Gentlesir, if I ask you to count your cards onto the table one by one— slowly."

"With pleasure, sir," said Morven, and flipped down the first of his cards. "One."

I wonder if he really is cheating? thought Beka. And

then, *Let the Professor worry about the damned cards. You worry about LeSoit. He's been watching for something ever since the stakes reached twenty thousand.*

She heard the sound of another card slapping against the tablecloth.

"Two," said Morven.

Even then, she almost missed it. Morven laid down a card and counted "Three," shifting position just a fraction at the count—and LeSoit went for his blaster.

She grabbed for her own weapon.

You don't have a chance, girl, the voice of sanity yammered in her head. *He's moving too fast. You're a hotshot pilot but a damned lousy gunfighter.* . . .

LeSoit had his blaster clear already, and she could see it coming up to point at her as he stepped away from the wall.

Her own piece was hung up on the holster or something. She dragged it free.

She watched LeSoit's blaster coming to bear on the danger he thought she was, and struggled—too slowly, like swimming in mud—to bring her weapon up in time.

I'm sorry, Ignac', she thought, with more regret than fear. *It looks like you're going to kill me after all.*

LeSoit's blaster pointed straight at Beka, but no bolt came. Instead the room echoed to the short, angry buzz of a needler, and LeSoit fell forward, his weapon dropping from his hand.

"The game, I fear, is ruined," said the Professor, turning up his left hand to reveal his tiny palm-gun.

Beka's own blaster had finished its upward arc from holster to target, and its blunt muzzle pointed unwaveringly at Morven. She couldn't tell from where she stood if LeSoit was breathing or not, and right now the gambler looked like a good person to kill if he wasn't.

"Restrain yourself, Tarnekep," said the Professor. "Your colleague will survive to find himself a more honest employer."

He made the needler disappear again, and regarded the gambler with a gentle—almost sorrowful—expression.

"What shall we talk about now?" he asked. "Perhaps we should talk about why you were offering heavy odds against a certain freighter captain lifting her ship?"

The gambler swallowed. His face had gone grey-white, like dirty snow. "I take bets on anything people are willing to bet on. Why did you bet that she would make it?"

The Professor smiled a little. "Let's just say the proposition intrigued me. Who was gunning for her?"

"I don't have anything to say about that."

"Scruples, Morven?" asked the Professor. "You amaze me."

Something small and glittering and knifelike appeared in his hand where the needler had been. Beka saw Morven flinch and close his eyes.

"I see you recognize this little item," said the Professor. "A relic of the war, like Tarnekep's blaster there—but a good deal harder to come by. Now, once again: who placed the death mark on Captain Rosselin-Metadi?"

Morven swallowed again, and wet his lips. "All I heard for sure was that Suivi Mercantile Trust was holding the funds."

"That's not enough, I'm afraid," said the Professor. "Tell me more."

He turned the small bright object so that it caught the light. The gambler flinched again.

"I can tell you who killed the Domina—"

"Old news," said the Professor. "The blaster man was a psychotic second-generation Entiboran-in-exile named Samos Lerekan, with a grudge against the Republic in general and Perada Rosselin in particular."

He leaned forward and laid the small object against the side of Morven's neck. "I was hoping you'd have something better for me."

The gambler seemed to stop breathing for a second. "I can tell you who switched Clyndagyt for the regular antiseptic at the Council Medical Center," he said carefully. "But that won't do you any good."

"I'm curious," said the Professor. "Tell me anyway."

"Beivan Vosebil."

"Beivan," said the Professor, withdrawing the small bright object a little. The gambler's eyes strained sidelong with his efforts to see the weapon—or whatever it was—in the other man's hand.

The Professor kept the object poised a hair away from the skin of Morven's neck. "Beivan," he said again. "One of the best. And why won't my friend Beivan be able to help me out?"

"He had an accident."

"I see," said the Professor. "Well, then . . ."

Beka listened with an odd empty feeling to the names that her father had given her his ship to find. It insulted the *'Hammer* somehow, she felt, to say that the ship was worth something as cheap and easy as this—threatening a pudgy gambler in the back room of a spacers' bar.

I can pay you back now, Dadda, she thought. *I wish this felt like enough.*

Maybe because the whole thing did feel too easy, she had to look away from the little object that wasn't a knife, and from the gambler's pallid, clammy face. Her gaze wandered to Morven's trained cardsharp's hands, and she blinked at an unexpected insight: that a good line of patter was the essence of any con.

"Gilveet Rhos handled the electronics," Morven said, but Beka wasn't listening anymore. She had already seen how the Professor rewarded answers by moving the small bright object a fraction farther away from the gambler's neck each time. By now, Morven's babbling had gained him a good two fingers' worth of breathing space.

Beka drew a deep breath of her own and let it out carefully. *If he makes a move at all,* she thought, keeping her eyes on his hands, *he's going to make it now.*

Morven ran a good game, she had to give him that. He kept the scared-witless routine going all the way down to the end, when he gave his right hand the twitch that would release a hand-blaster from its hidden grav-clip, and she shot him for it.

The acrid afterstink of a full-power blaster bolt filled the small closed room, overlaid with the odor of cooked meat. Morven the gambler lay facedown on top of his last hand of cards, with most of his head burnt away.

The Professor picked up the hand-blaster from the tabletop where it had fallen, and held it out to Beka. "Yours, I believe . . . my thanks, Tarnekep. I grow remiss in my old age."

Beka nodded, not trusting her voice much or her stomach either, and took the little weapon. She slipped it into the waistband of her Embrigan-style trousers, and was about to return the heavy blaster to its holster when a hand reached up from the floor to make a grab for the far side of the table.

The green tablecloth began sliding, and the hand scrabbled blindly for a better purchase. By the time Ignaceu LeSoit had secured his grip on the table's edge and pulled himself to his feet, Beka had both blasters leveled and ready.

She looked at LeSoit's own recovered and half-aimed weapon and shook her head.

Beside her, the Professor chuckled. From the sound of clicking plastic, he was already gathering up his winnings with a fine disregard for the mess on the table. "I'd take Tarnekep's advice, young man, if I were you—he's a gentleman of few words, but what he has to say is usually decisive."

LeSoit's eyes moved from the large blaster to the smaller one, and then down to the gambler's body. After a moment he shook his head. "He's not worth getting killed for."

Reversing his blaster, he held it out across the table butt-first toward Beka. "You could have burned me, Tarnekep, but you didn't . . . I owe you for that."

Beka shook her head again. "Keep it," she said, a sudden hoarseness making her voice sound strange even to her own ears. "Nobody owes anybody anything anymore. We're even." '

VII. Galcen: Northern Uplands
Mandeyn: Embrig Spaceport

COMMANDER GIL took the aircar up over the crowded buildings of Galcen Prime and turned northward. As the little craft sped toward the more sparsely inhabited uplands, Gil stole another glance at his sleeping passenger and reflected on what little he knew about General Metadi's oldest son.

Ari Rosselin-Metadi. Born in the last, violent years of the war, when the Magelords bent their entire might against his mother's world. Sent to live among his father's allies, the Selvaurs of Maraghai, as the Mageworlders' battering of Entibor escalated into a steadily tightening siege.

Three years that siege had lasted, under the pressure of the Magelords' ultimatum: either the Domina Perada surrendered the Resistance Fleet, now a formidable weapon in the hands of her husband the General, or she would see her planet turned into a wasteland. No effort of the Resistance could break the siege; and nothing the Magelords did could break the Domina's resolve. But when the war at last ended, with the Magelords destroyed and their ships grounded behind the border zone, Ari Rosselin-Metadi came home to Galcen, not to Entibor.

The boy must have been already half a Selvaur by then, Gil reflected; he'd certainly spent more time with the big, predatory saurians than he had with either of his parents. He'd gone back to Maraghai again as an adolescent, for an even longer stay, and this time his Selvauran foster-father had made the adoption official. Gil wondered, briefly, what language the lieutenant thought in, when he found himself alone—and whether that, or something else, was responsible for the faint remoteness behind his eyes.

The flight ended with the lieutenant still asleep. Gil brought the aircar down onto a level, grassy field near the General's house. More small craft were already lined up along the edges of the field, together with an assortment of ground vehicles and hoverbikes.

"Here we are," Gil said.

The lieutenant blinked, then opened his eyes fully and glanced out at the cluttered field. "I don't believe it," he murmured under his breath. "Father must have invited every free-spacer on the planet."

"It just looks that way," said Gil. "Most of them are still down portside."

"Good place for them," said Lieutenant Rosselin-Metadi. He sighed. "Well, no point in putting it off . . . let's go."

The house on the hilltop was big and sprawling, the residence of a family that had been comfortably well off, though not among Galcen's fabulous rich. The spoils of Jos Metadi's privateering days had gone into its construction, but the wealth of House Rosselin had not—the Domina Perada had thrown all of her family's immense fortune into the war against the Mageworlds. Perhaps, Gil thought, she hadn't believed that she'd survive to need it.

At the front door, Commander Gil paused and reached out a hand to palm the ID plate. As General Metadi's aide, he was in the building's temporary recognition files. But the door slid open before he could touch the black plastic square, and he knew the security system had recognized his companion.

The front hall of the General's house appeared to be empty. As Gil stepped forward, however, a tawny-haired young man in a beige coverall materialized out of nowhere. After a moment, Gil realized that the man had been waiting there all along. What had seemed like invisibility was just a self-effacement so complete as to be uncanny.

The young man and Lieutenant Rosselin-Metadi regarded one another for a moment without speaking. There was a distinct family resemblance between the two, mostly in the clean, arrogant Rosselin profile that had made the Domina Perada beloved of artists all over the galaxy. Once again Gil ran through his mental data base on the General's family. The young man in an apprentice Adept's plain garments would be Owen Rosselin-Metadi, the middle child, born at the end of the Magewar when Entibor was already burnt out and lifeless. Not quite twelve months had separated this one from Beka.

Born so near each other, Gil thought, *those two must have been close.*

Strangely enough, though, it was not Owen but Ari—who by Gil's reckoning had spent most of his childhood and adolescence on distant Maraghai—who seemed the most affected by his sister's death. Ari had the bruised, wary look of one who has experienced too many shocks in too brief a time; if his brother felt a similar pain, it was hidden far back behind the cool, measuring expression in the younger man's hazel eyes.

Finally the lieutenant broke the silence. "Owen. I didn't expect to find you playing door guard."

The other shrugged. "I do whatever Master Ransome asks me to. And somebody has to make the holovid reporters go away."

"Death and damnation," said Ari. "Have you been getting those up here?"

"They come and go," Owen replied. "We've only had

three so far this evening. I told them to leave, and they left.''

Gil said nothing, but he suspected there had been more to it than that. Ari's brother had that air about him, just as Errec Ransome had it—a stillness overlying something strange and possibly dangerous. About Ransome there was no question; these days he was Master of the Adepts' Guild, but during the Magewar he'd made quite a name for himself among the privateers of Innish-Kyl.

The General's younger son was a more puzzling case. Gil didn't know much about him. For the last ten years, since he'd turned fifteen, he'd been apprenticed to the Guild, spending most of his time in their Retreat far back in the Galcenian mountains. Just the same, that elusive quality of danger was there. The holovid reporters would have gone away without question, if Owen Rosselin-Metadi had told them to.

Ari, however, didn't seem impressed. The big lieutenant only shook his head and stepped past his younger brother into the main part of the house.

Time to find the General, Gil thought, *and report.*

He nodded politely at the lieutenant's brother, and moved out of the soundproofed entryway into a confusion of smells and noises. The big room downstairs was full of men and women—and a handful of assorted aliens whose sexes Gil didn't feel qualified to guess—all talking at once in at least three languages and a dozen or more different accents, from pure Galcenian to unadulterated Portside. In one corner a couple of junior officers from Prime Base played double tammani with an elderly woman in Entiboran court dress and a diamond tiara; in another, a young lady Gil recognized as Councillor Vannell Oldigaard's granddaughter flirted tearfully with a muscular free-spacer who'd somehow made it up from the port.

The air was dim and hazy, and heavy with the smells of perspiration and spilled beer. Gil looked about for the General, and finally spotted him: a tall figure in dark civilian clothes, leaning against the wall in a corner of the crowded room and regarding the procedings with a sardonic eye.

Gil made his way through the crowd to the General's side. "Mission accomplished, sir," he said. "I picked your son up at the Base, no problems. Is there anything else you need me to do?"

The General shook his head. "Not at the moment. Take it easy for the rest of the evening. Consider yourself off duty."

"Yes, sir," said Gil dubiously, and went off to the long table laden with kegs of beer and bottles of other potables.

Ari Rosselin-Metadi was already there, pouring himself a glass of the rough local vintage. *Bad idea*, Gil commented to himself. Uplands wine was harsh, flinty stuff—far better distilled into brandy than drunk—and the commander didn't think a man just out of accelerated healing had any business going near it. But Lieutenant Rosselin-Metadi didn't look like someone who would appreciate helpful suggestions.

Make that one more thing I have to watch out for, Gil thought, resigned. *If he manages to kill himself or start a fight or something, the General won't remember I was on liberty.*

Lieutenant Rosselin-Metadi wasn't the only person who'd decided to drink now and worry about a hangover tomorrow. By this time quite a few of the guests were more than a little drunk, and some of them were singing.

> *"Now stand to your glasses steady—*
> *The galaxy's nothing but lies.*
> *So here's to our friends dead already,*
> *And here's to the next one who dies."*

Gil regarded the vocalists with displeasure. He knew the song, of course—just about everybody in the Space Force did—but he'd been hoping to get through the night without having to listen to it.

I should have known better, he thought. The ballad was a staple of occasions like this, when the mortality of flesh and the fallibility of machines preyed heavily on the mind.

But Gil had read the accident report on Beka Rosselin-Metadi's crashed lifepod, and as the singers moved on to another verse, he found the morbid images too accurate for comfort.

> *"Take the carbon rods out of my kidneys,*
> *Take the navicomp out of my brain,*
> *Take the hyperdrive switch from my larynx,*
> *And assemble my starship again."*

Nothing had been left of Jos Metadi's daughter but a smear of pulped flesh mixed with metal fragments. Commander Gil had spent several sleepless nights trying to forget the pictures the singers had just called back to mind.

The hell with it, he decided suddenly. *If I crack under the strain of arranging a state funeral and two wakes, the General will have to break in a new aide a year early. Can't have that.*

He drew himself a foaming mug of beer from one of the kegs on the table, and began threading his way through the crowd to the door. Outside in the night air, his spirits began to improve almost at once. He settled himself on the front bumper of a conveniently parked hovercar, one of a dozen or so littering the grass in front of the house, and set about making the beer last awhile.

He had just finished draining the mug and was pondering, undecided, whether to go back in for another one or stay outside in the warm spring night, when the front door of the house slid open. A familiar figure paused for a moment, silhouetted by the light, and stepped out.

The door closed again. The General moved away a little from the lighted doorway and stood looking up at the stars.

Gil never saw the second shadowy form detach itself from the darkness and move to the General's side. He only knew that it was suddenly there. Gil tensed, and for the first time regretted that he'd never adopted the General's well-known habit of always going armed.

But the voice that broke the silence was a familiar one:

the Master of the Adepts' Guild was well known to the officers at Prime Base.

"Looking for the *'Hammer*?''

"Errec! Sneaking up on people like that is going to get you shot someday. By me, if you're not careful."

Gil heard the Adept's quiet laugh. "I'm not worried about it," Ransome said. "If you were planning to shoot me, you'd have done it a long time ago. We need to talk about Beka."

"I didn't think you'd stay fooled for long," said the General. "How'd you guess?"

Master Ransome sounded impatient. "My apprentice's sister, my best friend's child—did you think I wouldn't feel it if something like that had really happened?"

"I suppose not," said Metadi. "Who else knows about this?"

"Owen, I think—he and Beka were always close—but he isn't saying anything, and I'm not going to ask. Beka, of course, and whoever's with her. You and me. No one else."

"Beka's got someone with her?" asked Metadi sharply.

"Yes," said the Adept. "But I can't see anything clearer than that. I want to know what tipped *you* off—and don't try to convince me you've started seeing visions at your age."

Perched on the bumper of the hovercar, empty beer mug clutched in one sweating hand, Commander Gil shut his eyes and shivered. He'd thought Artat was cold, but that planet was nothing next to the temperature of his blood right now. His somber-hued clothing, and the moonless night, had kept him from being noticed so far—but the Adept Master, so rumors ran, could see in the dark. And this was not a conversation the General's aide was meant to overhear.

"I looked at that wreck, Errec," General Metadi said. "Not just the pictures and reports. And that ship wasn't *Warhammer*."

"You're sure?"

"You can bet on it. They'd found a piece of the main control panel—not much, but enough. I couldn't find any of the rewiring I did on the *'Hammer*—and believe me, I did plenty, between the secondary gun controls and the combat override. But the real kicker is the engines.''

''Special modifications?''

''You'd better believe it. That freighter on Artat had the old Gyfferan Hypermaster engines—standard for the class, so nobody was surprised. But the first thing I did after I got the *'Hammer*, as soon as I had the cash for a down payment, I had Sunrise Shipyards rip out her old engines and put in the big Hyper King Extras. And just to make certain that particular card stayed hidden up my sleeve, I bribed the yard's manager to keep all the work off-the-record.''

''So that's how she got her legs,'' murmured the Adept. ''I always wondered. You decided to let the ID stand?''

''Somebody went to a lot of trouble to make it look like the *'Hammer* and her captain had vanished from the spacelanes,'' said Metadi. ''I didn't want to disoblige them. If Beka had to set up something like that, she needs all the cover she can get. Only one thing worries me.''

''What's that?''

''Rigging a crash isn't impossible—I can figure out two or three ways she might have done it, and an old *Libra*-class freighter isn't hard to come by if you're not particular—but I can only think of one way to come up with matching tissue samples.''

''Replication?'' asked the Adept.

The General nodded. ''And I haven't heard of anybody working that sort of trick in years.''

''Mageworlds technology? You wouldn't.''

''It used to be around,'' said the General. ''More than some people want to let on. But even back then, it cost. And the people who used it . . .''

''I see,'' said the Adept. ''It appears your daughter has decided to keep some dangerous company.''

''She knows what she's doing—I hope,'' said the General. ''But I tell you one thing: if I live to see this mess cleared up, she's going to be glad she's gotten too big to spank.'' He stretched, and added, ''Right now, though, it's up to her. What do you say we go inside and and show those young pups what a proper wake looks like?''

Gil watched them go inside. When his chronometer showed that another thirty minutes had passed, he left his seat on the hovercar's bumper and followed.

He had no doubt that he'd just survived the most dangerous few minutes of his life. The Master of the Adepts' Guild was a peaceful and gently spoken man, these days, but he'd been something far different in his youth, when he'd fought the Magelords as Jos Metadi's copilot during the worst years of the war. And nobody—then or now—had ever accused General Metadi of being either peaceful or gently spoken.

Gil knew with a cold certainty that if either man ever learned that he'd overheard their conversation, the Space Force would be short one commander before the echo died.

For Ari Rosselin-Metadi, Beka's wake had been going on for what seemed like forever. He'd been meticulously polite to everyone he'd encountered, from his father's aide to Beka's old schoolmate Jilly Oldigaard, but the air of unreality about the proceedings refused to go away. It all felt like a party in a particularly bad dream—a continuation, somehow, of the nightmare he'd been trapped in since his mother's death. One of these days, he supposed, the nightmare would stop, and he could wake up and start hurting.

His head ached, right now, from the wine and from the presence of too many people and from the lingering aftereffects of his bout with mescalomide poisoning. A hyperspace journey in a Space Force courier ship didn't count as bed rest, and he knew it. He'd held himself together so far the best he could, but the sounds of the wake had started blurring into an indistinct rumble, and the edges of his vision were turning fuzzy.

I've got to get some fresh air, he thought. *Before I pass out and embarrass everybody.*

He left the room as inconspicuously as possible, and

found the back stairs up to the rooftop terrace. That part of the house had been shut off for tonight's wake, of course, but the domestic computers still recognized him as family and opened the doors for him to pass. He wondered, briefly, if anyone had erased his mother's and sister's ID scans from the household data bank—or did the house wait, unknowing, for Beka and the Domina to come home, quarreling as usual but still alive, from a day spent together in downtown Prime?

They were too much alike, he thought, as he walked out onto the upper terrace. *Mother wanted Beka to have the kind of life that the war took away from her—which Mother probably wouldn't have enjoyed all that much herself—and Beka wouldn't take it.*

The night above the terrace was starry, without a moon, and the scent of evening-blooming flowers drifted on the night breeze. From here, the sound of the wake was indistinguishable from the noises of any other party. He sat down on the ledge surrounding the terrace, and looked out over the Upland Hills.

"You shouldn't be here." His brother Owen seemed to materialize out of the shadows beside him. "You look like you're about to fold up and go under."

"I'll be all right."

"Most people who've just come out of a healing pod have the good sense to stay in bed for a while afterward." Owen paused. "And somebody who's being hunted by Magelords shouldn't wander around making himself an easy target."

Ari glanced at his brother. "Who told you about that?"

Owen looked back at him calmly—Owen was always calm, so calm that Ari wondered sometimes if his younger brother even noticed the real world at all. "Whatever the Magelords do interests the Guild."

"That wasn't what I asked," said Ari. "I want to know how you found out about something that's classified so secret I'm not even supposed to think about it in public."

"Stuff like that always finds its way to the Guild eventually," said Owen. "Master Ransome gets four or five messages every week from public-spirited souls who think they've seen a Magelord in their back garden."

"And he shows all those reports to you."

Owen nodded. "Somebody has to check out the rumors."

"I wouldn't call chasing Magelords a job for the Guild's oldest living apprentice," Ari said. His voice had an edge to it, both from the growing ache inside his skull and from the sting of realizing that the Guild's report had probably come straight from Llannat Hyfid.

His brother didn't rise to the insult. " 'An apprentice can stand where an Adept cannot.' "

"Is that all you've learned in the past ten years?" asked Ari. "How to quote proverbs?"

"No," said Owen. "Not quite." He paused again, his hazel eyes going distant as he contemplated something Ari couldn't see. "But I have learned how to let go of what I can't help anymore . . . and you need to do that, I think."

"Spare me your advice," growled Ari, nettled. "If you'd been a bit less generous with your advice to Beka, she might still be alive."

Not even that accusation could ruffle Owen's perpetual calm. The apprentice Adept only shook his head and said, "You know better than that."

"If you say so," Ari said. "But we both know you helped her get that first berth out of Galcen. Didn't you even try to talk her out of going?"

"Only long enough to see that she'd go whether I helped her or not," Owen said. "So I did my best to make certain she got a fair start, and then . . ." He shrugged. "Like I said, you let go of what you can't change. You need to do the same thing—go downstairs to bed, and don't think about Beka anymore. Nothing you do tonight is going to help her where she's gone."

The morning sun over Embrig gave the streets of the port a watery yellow light, but no warmth. Beka hunched her shoulders inside the long coat, and wished she were already back on the '*Hammer*—currently the *Pride of Mandeyn*, with a set of papers to prove it.

So far, at least, Embrig Security didn't seem to be chasing anybody. Either the Lily's manager figured that a cheating gambler was no loss to society, or Ignaceu LeSoit had waited a lot longer than the ten minutes he'd promised before officially recovering from the stun-bolt and discovering what had happened. The manager hadn't been inclined to argue with Tarnekep Portree when he cashed in the Professor's collection of chips on the way out, either; the former Armsmaster to House Rosselin would be leaving the planet richer by over a hundred thousand credits, as well as by a handful of names.

I ought to feel better about this, Beka thought. *I'm out from under the death mark, I've got a good lead on the bastards who killed Mother and wanted to kill me . . . I really should be happy right now.*

She wasn't, though—and the feeling that she ought to be only added to her increasing bad temper.

"You can't imagine how glad I'll be," she said moodily, as they turned the corner into the Freddisgatt Allee, "to get off of this lump of dirt and out into clean space again. I still have some debts to pay."

The Professor shook his head. "You told me you bought your ship for the promise of names, my lady, and now you have them. Beka Rosselin-Metadi may have died on Artat, but there's no need for Tarnekep Portree to keep on living. You can adopt a less uncomfortable persona, if you like, and go look elsewhere for a cargo."

Beka stopped dead in the middle of the Allee. "Shut up," she said, "and listen to me for a change."

The Professor didn't say anything, so she went on.

"All my life," she said, and a small corner of her mind was shocked by the bitterness in her voice, "I've been explaining to people what I want to do, and then listening to them explain back to me why I can't do it, until I've just about had it with explanations. So I'll tell you this once, and that's it: names aren't enough. I'm going to track down the bastard who arranged for Mother's death, and I'm going to bring him home to Galcen with a ribbon tied around his neck. And *that's* how I'm going to pay for my ship.''

''Then will you allow me to help you?'' the Professor asked after a moment had slipped by.

''Why should I?'' she demanded. ''What does any of this have to do with you?''

''Call it an old man's gesture of apology, Captain,'' he said, with a melancholy smile. ''I was . . . tired, after the Magewar ended, and sickened by the loss of Entibor. I told myself that my oath was no longer binding, and I left the remnants of House Rosselin to their own devices.''

''Which got my mother killed, is that what you're saying?''

He bowed his head in assent. ''If I hadn't abandoned my responsibilities for so long, her enemies might never have dared . . . but it's too late to remedy that. Not too late, though, for making them regret it—and at my age, Captain, it might be a good idea to begin such a project by finding a younger partner with an aptitude for the trade.''

''Meaning me?'' she asked.

''You have the reflexes for it,'' he said, ''and something of the temperament, not to mention a pilot's skills and a ship like no other. The rest''—he shrugged—''is training and practice.''

''I see,'' she said. ''Maybe we could work out a compromise. You need a partner. I need a copilot and a gunner if I'm going to push my trade routes out into the frontier worlds—and one or two of those names Morven spilled had an outplanets ring to them. How are you on starship gunnery, Professor?''

''I used to be quite good,'' he said. ''Of course, that was a war or two ago, and I'm sadly out of practice.''

''You're hired anyway,'' she said. ''Let's get the hell out of town.''

PART TWO

I. Pleyver: Flatlands Portcity

BEKA ROSSELIN-METADI rapped her knuckles against the clear plastic window in the Pleyveran branch office of General Delivery—"open thirty-three hours a day, organic sapient on duty guaranteed." The two chronometers on the far wall read 1824 Standard and 2520 Local, and the day clerk was drowsing in her chair, with her feet up on the bulk-mail bin and her back to the door.

If she's sapient, thought Beka, *I'll eat my pilot's license.*

After a twelve-hour stretch of tough realspace navigation through the Web, as starpilots called the Pleyver system's fluctuating magnetic fields, Beka didn't feel inclined toward sympathy for the bored and planetbound. Even with *Warhammer* securely docked in orbit up at High Station, her tension and exhaustion had yet to dissipate.

Once her business on-planet was taken care of, though, she had hopes. Commercial shuttles lifted regularly for High Station from the surface port, which meant that she and the Professor could relax in Flatlands for a few hours after they'd finished their dirtside business.

Not that the high life in this town is anything to write home about. If the Prof hadn't gotten word that Flatlands Investment, Ltd., has some stuff in their data banks that we ought to sneak a peek at, I'd have taken the 'Hammer straight on to Innish-Kyl. I hope whatever's in there is worth it. . . . With no cargo to pick up or deliver, we're going to have to eat the docking fees.

Beka rapped on the barrier again, louder. The day clerk unplugged her earphones—from the tinny music that drifted across the comm link to the outer office, she hadn't been using them to monitor General Delivery's data net—and turned her chair around.

"Name?" the clerk asked, looking up for the first time at her customer. The pupils of her eyes widened, and after a couple of seconds she wet her lips and added, "Sir."

"Tarnekep Portree," said Beka. She ignored the clerk's hesitation. Tarnekep's face, with its red plastic patch covering the entire left eye socket from brow to cheekbone, could unnerve people sometimes. The fact that Tarnekep's angular, thin-lipped features (eye patch and dyed brown hair excepted) were also her own was something that Beka tried not to think about too often.

"Tarnekep Portree," she repeated, "captain, *Pride of Mandeyn.* Any messages for me or my ship?"

The clerk blinked and came out of her momentary trance. "I can't check until you enter your password, sir."

Beka picked up the stylus on its plastic leash and scrawled a sequence of letters and numbers on the counter's datapad. The line of script glowed for a second as the office comps matched handwriting and pressure patterns against her samples on record. The datapad beeped.

"Will that do?"

The clerk dropped her eyes to the inside comp screens. "Searching now, sir."

After a moment she shook her head. "Nothing up on the bulletin board or in the private message files, sir."

"Try the bulk mail."

The clerk turned her chair around and burrowed through the bin full of cartons and envelopes. "Nothing that I can—wait a minute, how about this?" She held up a thin envelope. "Marked 'Hold for *Pride of Mandeyn*,' no return address."

"That'll be mine."

The clerk put the envelope into the security lock and cycled it through. Beka picked up the stiff envelope and pried at the seal with one close-trimmed fingernail. No luck; she shrugged, and drew out the knife she always carried these days, a double-edged blade in a forearm sheath. The ruffled cuff of her white spidersilk shirt fell back over her wrist as she slit open the envelope and pulled out the thin sheet of paper inside.

She eased the dagger back out of sight up her sleeve and scanned the paper, frowning:

Re your last message: Gilveet Rhos, freelance electronics expert, out of circulation past Standard year. Current status unknown. Break; new subject. If you need a bolthole sometime, the Space Force Medical Station and Recruitment Center in Flatlands has its own shuttle pad. The officer in charge is reliable and discreet.

"I need to send a reply," she said, folding the paper and jamming it into a trouser pocket. "Where's your keyboard?"

The clerk nodded toward a pull-out shelf set into one wall of the little office. Beka activated the keyboard, punched in a series of access codes and a single sentence of text—*Message received; info noted*—and signed off again.

"How much do I owe you?"

"Twenty . . . wait a minute. There's a message for you now. Must have been flagged when you signed on. Make that twenty-five, with a printout. Do you want it charged to your account?''

''No, I'll pay cash.'' Beka shoved across two twenty-credit chits, and took the sheet of flimsy and her change. For a second, she thought the brief message might be word of a cargo—even though none of the *Pride*'s usual contacts had known about her side trip to Pleyver—but the printout made no mention of freight charges or shipping dates.

Captain Portree, she read, *our firm desires to retain your services on a matter of grave import. Our representative will meet you in Florrie's Palace at 2100 Standard.*

''Damn,'' she muttered. ''There goes the R and R.''

She was still frowning as she left the General Delivery office and headed back toward the shuttle dock to link up with the Professor. The appointment at Florrie's came uncomfortably soon after the hours when she and the Professor intended to be rummaging through FIL's computer system. *But we can't afford to ignore the invitation. . . . We've put too much effort into giving Tarnekep the sort of reputation that gets him mysterious offers like this one.*

Outside at the shuttle dock, she paused to lean on a railing overlooking the landing zone half a mile away. Another of the regular shuttles had just come down and let off its passengers. After a few minutes, the Professor came out of the the dock office to join her. She turned away from the activity on the pad.

''All set?''

''Set.''

They headed for the arches leading into the tunnels of the Flatlands transport grid. The Professor, as usual, walked a discreet few steps behind and to her right. From that position he could guard her back; and while neither of them would interfere with the other's field of fire, they remained close enough together for conversation.

''Anything turn up in the way of a cargo?'' she asked as they came out of the tunnel onto the platform for the inbound transitway. ''Or do we have to lift empty?''

Another, unexpected voice cut across the Professor's reply. "Spacer—hey, spacer. Could you help me out with a couple of credits? Just a couple of credits, and I'll tell you something you want to know."

The voice had the wheedling tones of a dirtside panhandler, and the pitch was an old standby. Beka turned.

Her brother Owen stood half-in, half-out of the shadows at the end of the transit platform.

Beka looked at him for a moment, saying nothing. She hadn't seen Owen since the night after her coming-of-age party eight years ago, when they'd gone down to the port quarter in Galcen Prime and found her a junior pilot's berth on the *Sidh*. He'd been an apprentice in the Guild for three years then, almost ready to take an Adept's vows although seemingly in no hurry to do so. She wondered if he'd ever taken them; he'd never spoken of the matter in their occasional brief exchanges of correspondence. He certainly didn't look much like an Adept; even eight years ago he'd possessed the knack of making himself, at need, into an unnoticed fixture of the local landscape, and at the moment he looked like a spaceport bum.

And what do I look like to him? she wondered. *Does he see his little sister, or does he see Captain Tarnekep Portree?*

Or would he tell me there's no difference?

She didn't like that idea at all. Living inside Tarnekep's skin for so many months had already brought the Mandeynan gunfighter's personality too close to her own comfort. The last thing she wanted to hear was that she'd pulled Tarnekep out of herself in the first place.

She kept her eyes on her brother. "All right, spacer—start talking."

Owen nodded. "You're looking for the portside office of Flatlands Investment, Ltd. Is that right?"

Startled, Beka forced herself to maintain Tarnekep Portree's cool regard. There was no point, she knew, in trying to figure out how her brother had come by his information.

He'd say he had a dream, or a feeling, or something.

*And it might even be true. Or maybe Master Ransome
eavesdrops on the same messages the Professor does.*

"What if I am looking for them?" she asked.

"Then you shouldn't go there tonight."

She stiffened and looked down her nose at him. "I don't
even know you, spacer," she said, very much in Tarnekep's voice. "Who the hell are you to say what I should
and shouldn't do?"

"Gently, Tarnekep," murmured the Professor. "Gently.
The young man wishes you well. Our appointment can be
as easily kept by one as by two—wait for me at Florrie's,
Captain, and I'll handle our business at FIL alone."

"No," she said flatly. "I take my own risks."

"Not this time," said Owen. Her brother paused, as if
weighing how much he ought to say next. "There's more
going on here than you know, or than I can tell you. I have
a visit of my own to pay FIL."

"Ah," said Beka. *Guild business,* she thought, but knew
better than to say it out loud. "I need the information FIL
has in its computers," she told Owen. "I was counting
on getting it out of there tonight."

"I think I can guess what you're after," said her brother.
"I can get it for you if you let me."

She still didn't like the idea. "How will you know what's
important and what isn't?"

"We can rely on the young man's judgment, I think,"
the Professor cut in. "If I'm wrong, another chance can
always be found, or can be made."

Beka made up her mind. "You've got it," she told
Owen. "I'll be having dinner at Florrie's."

"At Florrie's," echoed her brother. He stepped back
into the shadows as a glidepod slid up to the platform, and
then he was gone.

Florrie's Palace was what the Professor in one of his
primmer moods would have referred to as a house of ill
repute: the biggest, busiest, most red-plush-and-gilt-trim-
bedecked whorehouse in Flatlands Portcity. Upstairs, the

Palace's employees plied their specialized arts. Downstairs, however, the Portcity's finest chef supervised a restaurant crew whose expertise made respectable hoteliers weep with envy.

So you might as well relax and enjoy your dinner, Beka told herself. *And remember to thank your brother for the favor someday. You wouldn't have had time for a meal like this if Owen hadn't shown up.*

At the dinner's end, Beka poured the last of the wine into the crystal goblets and leaned back in her chair.

"This is good. . . . I'm glad we got the chance to relax and take some of the edge off things." She gave a tired sigh. "That Web approach is a bad one. My father claims he made it in six hours once, but I wouldn't like to try. And I wish whoever's meeting us knew enough to let a pilot get some rest after a run like that."

"The message you received sounds like someone is hiring for a professional assignment," said the Professor. "We can't afford not to show interest."

"I'm a merchant-captain," complained Beka. "How did I get myself into somebody's files as a hired killer on the side?" She held up one hand to stop the Professor before he could speak. "Never mind, I already know who to thank. And our contact's about to show up."

The contact—a florid, beefy type—plopped himself down at their table without invitation. "You boys enjoying yourselves?"

Beka turned Tarnekep Portree's piebald gaze—one eye bright blue and the other a blank patch of red one-way optical plastic—onto the newcomer, and watched him wilt a little under that unspeaking regard.

"I'm Captain Portree," she said, after the silence had drawn out long enough. "You sent a message about a job?"

"Sure did," said the contact, recovering his enthusiasm. "We've heard all kinds of good things about you—a real pro, is the word—and I've got a sweet deal lined up for you."

The Prof's rumor-machines certainly have been busy, Beka thought. She smiled, and let their contact sweat for a few moments. "Indeed," she said finally, without inflection. "What exactly is your deal? And who are 'we'?"

"This isn't the best place to talk," said the contact. "Why don't you come along upstairs?"

Beka drained the last of the wine, and set down the empty glass. A stray drop slid down the stem to stain the white tablecloth. She pushed back her chair, stood, and was obscurely pleased to find that she was taller than the stranger by a head or more.

"Let's go," she said. "Come on, Professor."

"No," said the contact hurriedly. "My principal wishes to deal with Captain Portree alone."

Beka glanced over at her copilot. He looked concerned—he'd told her many times, during the past few months of training and practice, that splitting up a team was not a good idea. But the meeting upstairs sounded important, maybe even bigger than the data banks at FIL, and she couldn't afford to let the chance go by.

"Good enough," she said to the beefy type. "Professor, you wait here. Buy yourself some more wine—I'll be back to help you finish the next bottle."

She followed the contact up the Palace's broad curving staircase to a bank of lifts on the second level. The lift took them up to a penthouse office: plush-carpeted, wood-paneled, and soundproof. A closed door set into the paneling behind the desk led to somewhere deeper within the office complex.

A quick, automatic count showed her six men lounging about the room. One or two had the slab-jawed look of hirelings who only thought when the boss told them to think, but the others had the quick, dangerous air of freelance operatives. Few of them carried blasters openly, but she knew that appearances meant nothing.

The banker or lawyer or whatever who rose from behind the desk had a smile like a holovid hero. "Well, Captain Portree—it's a pleasure to see you in the flesh at last."

He held out his hand, and Beka met it with hers. The holovid hero's grip turned out to be firmer than she'd anticipated, but that was all right. Hours of work at *Warhammer*'s control's, or helping the dockworkers shift cargo, had put more strength into her own long fingers than most people expected, whether from Beka Rosselin-Metadi or Tarnekep Portree.

"The pleasure is all mine, Gentlesir," she said. "How can I be of assistance?"

The holovid hero sat down again and waved her to a chair opposite. "To be quite candid, a certain young officer in the Space Force has recently come to our attention."

Beka leaned back in her chair, and placed her fingertips together. The dandy's ruffles cascading over her wrists in a froth of pure white spidersilk hid the hilt of the dagger, but her right hand knew in sinew and bone the quick, smooth motion that would bring it into view like a snake striking.

"An entanglement of that kind is likely to draw more attention than the average," she said aloud. "I suppose you're prepared to set the price accordingly."

"We are, indeed," said the holovid hero, with a smile that dazzled. "My principals have authorized me to offer you five hundred thousand—half in advance, and the other half upon fulfillment of the contract."

Oily bastard, Beka thought, and smiled back at him over her steepled hands.

"Excellent," she said. "And the name, Gentlesir?"

"Ari Rosselin-Metadi," he said. "A Medical Service officer, and a man impossible to mistake once you have his description. Unfortunately, the lieutenant has proved difficult for my principals to deal with unaided."

Ari, you big idiot, thought Beka, still smiling across her hands at the man behind the desk. *What have you gotten into?*

"I take it you want him dealt with more or less permanently, then," she said.

"Permanently," agreed the other. "You'd have to use the utmost discretion, of course, because of the, ah, previous incident."

Beka forced herself to keep her voice level and disinterested. "Don't worry. Blaster-work in full view of the entire Grand Council and the lady's husband isn't my style."

"That whole affair should have been better-managed," said the holovid hero. "Vosebil was good enough to change the antiseptic at the Medical Center, and smart enough to subcontract out to the best. He could have poisoned the Domina any day of the week with less publicity."

"The way the holovids plastered that affair all over the civilized galaxy, I'd have said 'publicity' was the whole idea."

"Trust me, Captain Portree. Publicity is the last thing that Dahl&Dahl are looking for. We were not pleased with Gentlesir Vosebil's handling of his assignment." The holovid hero's sculpted lips narrowed in disdain. "We hope, Captain, that you can manage something less flamboyant for the Rosselin-Metadi contract."

Beka's fingers ached where she pressed them together. *Only a few more minutes of this,* she promised herself. *Then you can be sick to your stomach in decent privacy.*

"My methods are my own choice," she said. "Or hire a different man to do your killing for you."

"No, no," said the banker-or-whatever, smiling yet again, all flashing white teeth and practiced sincerity. "We make it a rule not to dictate to our professional contractors. The choice of techniques is entirely at your own pleasure."

"That's better."

"Then you'll take the contract, Captain Portree?"

She nodded. "I'll take it."

The man from Dahl&Dahl rose and held out his hand for the ritual handclasp that would seal the bargain.

Beka stood up and reached across the desk to return the

grip. *Don't flinch, girl. You're Tarnekep Portree, and you've done a lot worse than shaking hands with a smooth-faced, smiling son of a bitch who just hired you to kill your own brother.*

The man from Dahl&Dahl was saying something, and she forced herself to keep on listening.

"We'll send you the background material and the initial payment through the General Delivery drop by thirty-three hundred, Captain Portree, and it's been a pleasure doing business with you."

Beka let go his hand. "That's it, then."

"One more thing . . ."

She paused, tensing. "Yes?"

"There will be an additional payment, of course, equal to that we have already agreed on—but first, there is someone else for you to kill."

Oh, damn, she thought. *How am I going to get out of this one without blowing Tarnekep's entire reputation sky-high? They're going to drag in some poor idiot they've already decided needs to be dead, and solve three problems for the price of one—check me out, and get rid of the idiot, and give themselves a crime they can put into the data net with my name on it any time they get tired of working with me. Damn, damn, damn.*

The Professor, she felt certain, could handle such an execution without a qualm. Whoever these people had on hand for sacrifice was marked for death already, and a full-power blaster bolt was quick and merciful compared to some of the things an ingenious mind could devise.

But the Prof's been doing this for more years than I've been alive, and I'm still new. I don't know. . . .

Then the door behind the desk opened, and her uncertainty became a purely academic matter. Two more men emerged from the inner chamber, dragging her brother Owen between them.

"Kill this man for us," said the lawyer, or whatever he really was. "Now."

She couldn't tell if Owen was unconscious, or just

deeply drugged; he hung limp in the grasp of his captors, and his head drooped too low for her to see his face. He still wore the dirty coverall he'd worn at the port. She looked away from her brother, and gave the lawyer her best Tarnekep sneer.

"Where the hell's the challenge in something like this?" she demanded. "Any schoolkid could do the job."

"You're being paid," said the man from Dahl&Dahl. He leaned back in his chair. "Call it a sign of good faith."

The two men propped Owen up against the wall. Bereft of support, he slid down and collapsed in a sitting position on the floor, his chin resting on his chest. The two men backed away. They were well trained; neither one crossed between Beka and her designated victim.

Slowly, she pulled her blaster, and pointed it at the slumped form of her brother. She could feel the other occupants of the room watching her, waiting to see if the notorious Captain Tarnekep Portree could perform as advertised.

"Take care," said the holovid hero. "We don't want any accidents."

Beka glanced in his direction. The handsome lawyer or whatever he really was wore an expression of anticipation—bright-eyed and wet-lipped. No matter what happened next, this one was going to enjoy watching it.

"Accidents, *hell*," snarled Beka. Her right foot lashed out in a move the Professor had taught her, catching the nearest of Owen's two guards in the kneecap. He gave a grunt of pain and collapsed. Beka twisted around and shot his companion in the gut. "I'm doing this *on purpose*."

The sound of the blaster echoed in the closed room. She saw Owen push himself to his feet, stumbling a little but definitely not unconscious, and she tossed him her blaster as he came up.

Without waiting to see if he caught it, she yanked out her double-edge blade from its forearm sheath and launched herself across the lawyer's desk in a low, flat dive. A blaster bolt heated up the air behind her. The man from Dahl&Dahl was standing up and reaching for something as she came at him; she slashed the knife across his throat.

Blood from the cut artery sprayed everywhere. She dropped behind the desk as another blaster bolt seared the polished wood. More blasters fired, the bolts passing close overhead. Then, suddenly, the room was quiet again. Only two men remained standing, one by the wall—her brother—and, by the door through which she had entered, the Professor.

"I took the liberty of following you upstairs," the Professor said calmly, reholstering his blaster. "When I heard firing, I made what haste I could to lend assistance."

Beka pulled herself up to her feet. There was blood on her knife, and more blood covering the ruffled front of her shirt; she stood for a moment, uncertain, then wiped the blade clean against her sleeve.

She put the knife back in its sheath and turned to her brother. Owen stood leaning against the wood paneling, with the blaster she'd thrown him hanging loosely from one hand.

"Are you all right?" she said.

He shook his head as if to clear it. "Well enough." He pushed himself away from the wall and held out the blaster. "Here. You'll need this before long."

"You don't sound all that well." She took the blaster, checked the charge, and slid the weapon into its holster. "What happened?"

"I'll be fine," he said. "It was a trap. I knew that from the beginning, of course, but I thought it was for you." He gave a faint, shaky laugh. "I was wrong. But they waited a bit too long to spring it—I found what you were looking for."

Owen fumbled in a pocket of his coverall. "They missed it when they searched me. I was almost all the way under by then, but I held together long enough to make sure of that."

He held out a plastic disk no bigger than a gaming chip. "Take it," he said. "It's got everything you wanted."

"Thanks," said Beka. She pocketed the datachip. "You coming with us to High Station?"

Her brother shook his head. "No. I have some unfinished business to take care of first. But if you can draw away the people with blasters—"

" 'The people with blasters?' Who the hell are they?"

"Better if you don't know," he said. "I can get away from them, though, if I don't have to worry about getting my head blown off at the same time."

She bit her lip. "If I didn't owe you a big one for getting me that berth on the *Sidh* . . . all right. Give me and the Prof five minutes. I'll make certain they spot us leaving by the front door."

II. Pleyver: Space Force Medical Station

LIEUTENANT COMMANDER Nyls Jessan ran a hand through his straight blond hair and turned off the desk comp with a satisfied sigh. "Another day, another eight-point-six-five credits. Everything taken care of in back, Namron?"

"All secure, Commander."

"How about that spacer off the *Stellar Cloud*?"

"Sent him home at eighteen-thirty with capsules and a prescription, sir," said Namron. "Unless somebody rings our doorbell during the night, we're empty."

Jessan pushed his chair away from the desk and leaned back to look at Namron. Seen from that angle, with the light of the setting sun glinting off a row of service medals that went back to the Magewar, the petty officer made an impressive sight. Jessan wondered yet again whether Space Force had assigned the older man to Pleyver with an eye toward offsetting his own distinctly unheroic appearance.

But looking like a recruiting poster come to life didn't stop Namron from being an efficient corpsman as well as good company with his limits. Jessan leaned his chair even further back, and propped his boots up on the edge of the desk.

"If I had the choice," he said, "I'd put the clinic on an outpatient-only basis indefinitely. Right now, if we have a medical disaster bad enough to fill all the beds, I don't know where we'll find the staff to handle it."

Namron nodded. "Any word on when Space Force is going to send us a few more people?"

"They're still trying to work out the allowance list," said Jessan. "But even a reservist would help." He sighed, and contemplated the toes of his boots with dissatisfaction. "I'll put through the request for more personnel again in the morning. Maybe somebody will read it this time."

"Like they did the one for the healing pods?"

Jessan gave a theatrical shudder. "Don't remind me about that," he said.

The clinic's accelerated healing setup had been scheduled to arrive via the Space Force shuttle from High Station six months ago. So far, the supply shipments had included any number of improbable items, but the pods remained undelivered.

He stretched and yawned. "Oh, well. Time to pack it in and get some sleep, just in case the dawn flight comes in at midnight again."

Namron shook his head indulgently. "The pilot hasn't been hatched who likes to show up in town after the bars are closed."

"Let's hear it for Flatlands and its exciting nightlife," said Jessan, with a marked lack of enthusiasm. Pleyverans liked to think of their planet's only spaceport as a wide-open den of iniquity, but the Portcity's tawdry fleshpots held few attractions for a native of Khesat. As Jessan had written to Ari Rosselin-Metadi shortly after arriving on-planet and taking stock of the situation, "Flatlands is the sort of place that gives decadence a bad name."

Footsteps from the back of the clinic heralded the arrival of Clerk/Comptech Second Class Peyte with a folder of printout flimsies. "Comps and comm links all secure, Commander. Got anything else for me?"

Jessan reached up an arm and snagged the folder. "Nothing before the supply shuttle gets here. Check with Petty Officer Namron before you turn in."

"Roger out, Doc." Peyte disappeared again into the back of the clinic.

Jessan riffled through the printouts, trying to decide whether taking them to his quarters would really put him ahead of tomorrow's workload, or only keep him from getting to sleep.

Without warning, the buzzer at the clinic's front door broke the late-hours quiet.

"So much for a restful evening," Jessan said with a sigh. He swung his feet back down to the floor and brought his chair upright. Across the room, Namron was already toggling the clinic door open.

Two men—one slight and grey-haired, the other tall and much younger, his narrow face disfigured by an ugly red eye patch—waited on the threshold with blasters in their hands. The panels had barely reached full dilation before the pair shoved past Namron and flattened themselves against the walls to either side of the entry. The younger man slapped the toggle switch with his free hand.

Mandeynan, thought Jessan, taking in the man's ruffled shirt and queued-back brown hair. His heavy blaster, and the dried blood stiffening the front of his expensive shirt, said something more: this particular Mandeynan was dangerous, and already in bad trouble.

The door shut with a click. Jessan came to his feet. "Do you need medical assistance?"

The older man's left arm hung motionless in the way that spelled "broken" to a trained eye, but he shook his head. "No time. Do you have a comm link here?"

"Of course," said Jessan.

"Get on it, then," said the Mandeynan. "Call Space Force, and tell them to come in heavy."

Jessan looked from the grey-haired gentleman to the

beardless dandy in the bloodstained shirt. "Mind telling me what's going on first?"

"Later," snapped the Mandeynan. He edged over to one of the front room's tall, narrow windows and peered out at the darkening street, blaster at the ready. "Make that call while you still have the chance—they'll be here any minute now."

" 'They'?"

The Mandeynan gave Jessan an angry glance. "Damn it, will you stop asking questions and make that call?" As he spoke, a blaster bolt flashed into the interior of the office, melting a curly-edged hole through the window-pane next to the Mandeynan's head and scorching the material of the far wall.

The older man shook his head. "Too late, I'm afraid."

The Mandeynan fired twice out the broken window. "We're not dead yet, Professor. For the last time, Commander—where do you keep the comm room in this place?"

That accent's pure Galcenian, thought Jessan. *He's more than just Mandeynan, no matter how he dresses.*

"Through the door to the back and make a right," he said. "Who are you people?"

"I'm Tarnekep," the young man said, and snapped another shot out the window. "And that's the Professor."

The Mandeynan fired one more time, and sprinted for the interior of the clinic. Then Jessan heard a muffled *whump* from somewhere outside, and all the lights went out.

"What the hell?" came a shout from deeper inside the building. Peyte, that would be, seeing one of his beloved comps go down.

Tarnekep's voice came from near the back door. "Just how many people are in here?"

"Three," said Jessan. "Me and Namron, and that was Peyte you heard in the back."

"Where's your weapons locker?"

"This," said Jessan, feeling his urbanity starting to wear thin, "is a walk-in clinic and recruiting center. We don't have a weapons locker."

His eyes were adjusting to the twilight filtering in from the street. A bar of light from a hand-torch swept across the room as Peyte walked into the office.

"Hey, Doc! We lost power!"

"Turn that off!" snapped Jessan and Namron together.

Peyte turned the light off, so that only the grey light from outside remained, and asked in plaintive tones, "What's going on around here, Doc?"

"Visitors," said Jessan. "That's Tarnekep there by you. He wants to use the comm setup. Go show him how."

"Whatever you say, Doc. C'mon, you."

The two men vanished into the back. After a moment, Peyte's voice said, "Damn. The relays are out."

Tarnekep's voice said something brief and nasty. *So he dresses like a Mandeynan,* thought Jessan, *and talks like a Galcen-born aristocrat . . . and swears like a spacer in back-alley Gyfferan. Not your usual mix, at all.*

Peyte and Tarnekep reappeared. "Somebody's taken out our communications," said the comptech.

"I heard," said Jessan. He looked over to where the Mandeynan's pale face made a lighter blur against the twilight. "What's going on here, anyhow?"

"Our ship's docked up at High Station," said the Mandeynan. "And the locals have closed the commercial shuttle port."

Jessan shook his head. "If Security's after you, I can't do anything to help."

Tarnekep snorted. "Do Security Enforcers fire into Space Force installations without talking first—even on Pleyver?"

Jessan knew that the Mandeynan was right, which meant the men shooting at them were somebody's private troops. *And in that case,* he thought, *I can't solve my problems by handing these two over to the folks outside.*

The Professor's quiet voice cut into the conversation. "If need be, Commander, Captain Portree and I will surrender ourselves into Space Force custody."

"No," Jessan told him. "Consider yourselves under

Space Force protection instead. You wouldn't be the first spacers to bite off more trouble dirtside than they could handle. And let's wait until Security gets into the act before we start talking about surrender. Peyte!''

''Sir?''

''Is the comm set in the hovercar back in working order?''

''Fixed it yesterday, Doc. You want me to make a dash for it and get a call patched through to High Station?''

''I'd better do that part,'' said Namron. ''Those guys out there don't seem too particular who they're shooting at, and your coverall's going to look like civvies in a dim light. That goes for you, too, Commander.''

Jessan had to agree. His working uniform, like Peyte's, lacked flash—but Namron's glittering splendor, meant to impress potential recruits, would mark the petty officer as Space Force from the moment he came into view.

''Get the patch through to High Station,'' he said. ''Tell them we've got a bit of trouble down here with somebody's private army, and ask them to send the shuttle down stat. Then get in touch with local Security.''·

''Yes, sir!''

Namron saluted and headed for the door. The Professor toggled the panels open and Namron stepped through, the last of the fading light reflecting from the heavy gold braid of his dress uniform. Seconds later, a blaster bolt came zinging out of a window across the street. The scarlet beam caught Namron in the chest, just above his impressive row of service ribbons.

The petty officer staggered backward and fell against the building's outer wall to the left of the door. A second later he twitched and tried to rise.

Jessan ran for the doorway. ''He's alive,'' the Khesatan called over his shoulder to Peyte. ''Go get a shock set.''

''Sure, Doc,'' said Peyte. ''I'll be right with you.'' The clerk/comptech vanished into the back.

As soon as Jessan reached the door, he dropped to his belly and crawled the last few feet toward the injured man. He grabbed Namron's right arm, but neither his first nor.

his second try got him enough leverage to move the man inside. A blaster bolt scorched a line into the pavement ahead of him as he inched himself farther out.

Suddenly, a long-legged figure sprinted past him. It was the Mandeynan. Without saying a word, the youth ran forward, took hold of Namron's left shoulder, and heaved the bigger man sideways. Jessan caught Namron under the armpits and started dragging the petty officer inside. He heard the high whine of a blaster going off nearby. Then he was inside with his patient, and the door was cycling closed.

The petty officer groaned—under the circumstances, a beautiful noise. Peyte reentered the room, a medical kit in his hand.

"Let's get Namron bedded down," said Jessan. "I don't know how long it's going to be before we can get him out of here and into a healing pod."

As he finished speaking, a white flash lit up the entire front row of windows, and the building rocked with an explosion.

Peyte stared out at the street. "Those bastards blew up the hovercar!"

Moments later, the room's remaining unbroken windows bulged and deformed inward, then shattered onto the floor. Dark shapes filled the window frames, clambering in and firing blasters as they came. Tarnekep and the Professor fired back until the room was filled with crossing streamers of colored fire. As suddenly as it had begun, the assault ended, leaving behind a only a deafening silence and a couple of bodies on the floor.

Funny, thought Jessan, straightening up from where he'd flung himself across Namron when the glass started flying. *You'd have thought there'd been more of them, from the racket they made coming in.*

Now all he could hear was a scrabbling sound. He looked, and saw one of the bodies moving, trying to crawl toward a blaster lying on the tiles. Tarnekep must have caught the same faint noise; before Jessan could shout a warning, the Mandeynan turned away from the windows and swung one boot in a short, fast arc that connected with the crawling man's head. Jessan heard a snapping noise, and the body lay still. Tarnekep stooped for the weapon and stuck it into the waistband of his trousers.

"Anyone hurt?" the Professor asked.

"I'm fine," said Tarnekep. "But we can't hold this room. Not with all these damned windows."

"True. Are there any other ways into the building, Commander?"

"No more windows," Jessan said, working over Namron as he spoke. "Two doors, and the cargo bay in the rear."

"Then I suggest we fall back."

A blaster bolt flashed into the room as the Professor spoke, searing the plast-block of the opposite wall. Jessan took that as a hint and began crawling backward, dragging Namron along with him. The other two followed.

Peyte, shaken but unflappable, brought the pillows and blankets into the comm section. The self-powered emergency glows on the control panel had cut in when the power died. By their dim luminescence, Jessan and the comptech bedded Namron down among the equipment—warming him, raising his legs, and putting a pressure bandage over the blaster wound in his side.

"Move that desk in front of the door for a barrier," said the Professor. "We're going to see more fighting before the night's over."

Jessan nodded at Peyte. The clerk/comptech took up one end of the desk and said, "Seems quiet enough right now."

"It'll get noisy again," said Tarnekep shortly from the desk's other end. When the table had been moved into place, the Mandeynan wiped the sweat off his face with one bloodstained sleeve and asked, "Where can we cover the other doors?"

"The corridor makes a T branch a little way back from here," said Jessan. "You can watch both doors from there. And the stairs and elevator from lower stores come up just around the corner."

Tarnekep nodded. He took the spare blaster from the

waistband of his trousers and handed it to Jessan. "Do you know how to work one of these?"

"This may only be the Medical branch," he said, "but it's still the Space Force. Yes, I'm qualified."

"Then you and Peyte go back and hold the rear doors while the Professor and I keep them out of the front."

Jessan took the blaster and stood up. "Just who are those people out there?" he asked, checking the charge on the weapon. Half-full—it could be worse. "Assuming I make it through the night, having their names is going to make writing the report a whole lot easier."

"If I told you," said Tarnekep with a thin smile, "they'd probably want to kill you, too."

"Namron didn't know their names, and it didn't help him a bit."

The two strangers were silent; Tarnekep bit his lip. After a moment, Peyte said, "They can't just sit out there and shoot at us all night."

"No, Peyte," said Jessan wearily, "they're probably going to come inside so they can shoot at us even better. Everybody else in the district is closed up, remember, and it's a long time until morning."

"Sorry, Doc." Peyte sounded crestfallen, the way he usually did whenever his knowledge of people didn't match his handiness with robots and computers.

"Don't worry about it," said Jessan. "Come on—looks like we get to guard the back doors."

He and Peyte walked toward the rear. With the power down and the air circulation off, the corridor smelled of dust and anesthetics. The medical odor gave Jessan an idea.

"Wait a minute," he said, as they passed one of the treatment rooms, and ducked inside. Working mostly by feel, he picked up three small cylinders of oxygen and a large bottle of antiseptic. Arms full, he hurried back out.

Peyte looked at him curiously. "What're you going to do with those, Doc?"

"Give somebody a surprise."

Jessan piled up his loot near the far door and retired

with Peyte to the crossing. He settled down on the tile floor, leaning back against the plast-block wall and stretching his long legs out in front of him. A few feet away, he could hear Peyte doing the same.

"Rest while you can," he said to the clerk/comptech. "I'll take first watch."

"Are you kidding, Doc? I joined the Space Force for excitement, and all I've done so far is look up the right forms for signing underage semisentients. Do you think a repair crew's going to be along soon to fix the lights?"

Jessan shrugged. "I don't know. A crew will probably come out as soon as the Power Service notices a break in the net—but how many crews have to turn up missing before Power gives in and yells for Security?"

"In this neighborhood?" asked Peyte. "At least a dozen."

Silence for a few moments, then Peyte spoke up again. "Who are those two guys, anyway? That one with the eye patch—there's something funny about him."

"A number of funny things, if I don't miss my guess."

"Yeah. I was right next to him, trying to work the comms—and Doc, that's not his blood he's got all over him."

"I didn't think it was," said Jessan. He frowned a little. There was a noise—or had he imagined it?—down at the end of the hall.

Firing broke out again in the front room. The bolts of energy flowing into the front office lit the whole clinic as far back as the rear corridors in an aurora of multicolored light. The sound of the blasters almost drowned out a hollow booming at the far door. *Never mind the sound-and-light show*, Jessan said to himself, as the door fell inward and half a dozen attackers surged forward into the hall. *You've got trouble of your own back here.*

He took careful aim—*Just like a target range, nothing to worry about*—and fired into the stuff he'd left piled up at that end of the corridor. The bolt ruptured at least one of the oxygen cylinders, and the sideshock broke the bottle of antiseptic wide open. Flammable liquid mingled with pure oxygen escaping from the ruptured cylinder, and the resulting fireball rolled up and down the hall in both directions before it faded.

"My, my," said Jessan, with some satisfaction, as the ceiling gave way and buried the back door under a heap of rubble. "That *was* impressive."

From the front, Tarnekep's rather breathless voice called, "You two all right back there?"

"We're fine. They won't be trying that door again, either. How are you two doing?"

"Making it. Do you have a moment to come play medic?"

"It's what they pay me for."

Jessan handed his blaster to Peyte. "If anything tries to get in from the outside, shoot it."

"Got you, Doc."

Jessan ran toward the front. The table still stood across the inner door, and a quick check reassured him that Namron's condition hadn't changed, but the throat-clawing aftersmell of a blaster fight hung undissipated in the stagnant air. Tarnekep sagged exhausted against one wall, and the Professor sat at the comm station, checking his blaster one-handed with intense concentration. Jessan looked over at Tarnekep, and the younger man made a tired gesture in the Professor's direction.

"Right," said Jessan. "Let's see about you, then— 'Professor,' did you say to call you?"

"I didn't," said the grey-haired man. "But it suffices."

"Then 'Professor' it is," agreed Jessan. "Tarnekep . . . if you could be so kind as to bring over one of the extra blankets, I can rig a sling for this arm. There's no accelerated-healing setup here, I'm afraid, and until the power comes back on there's no way to mend the bone for you, either. If you like, though, I can give you something for the discomfort."

Under the cover of the cheerful babble, he examined the injured arm. More than once, the skin and muscles under his fingers tensed in reaction to what must have been considerable pain, but the grey-haired man didn't make a sound. So he wasn't surprised, when he'd finished, to see the Professor shake his head.

"Not now, Commander. Perhaps when this is over."

Jessan took the blanket that Tarnekep held out to him, and began fashioning a sling. "How did you do this to yourself, if the answer isn't too embarrassing to repeat?"

"I dived into a gutter a bit too hard," said the Professor. "I'm afraid that city fighting is a game for the young."

"Everybody to their own amusements," said Jessan. "Now, this is going to hurt a bit . . . there. Mind telling me what the fuss is all about, while we're at it?"

But it was Tarnekep, not the Professor, who answered. "A friend gave us your name."

"Nice of him."

"The small army out there wasn't our idea," said Tarnekep. "The original plan was to spend a quiet night in the clinic playing double tammani, and sneak out in the morning with your usual shuttle traffic."

"There's a supply run coming in at dawn," said Jessan. "We can leave town with the empty boxes."

" 'We'?"

"We," Jessan said firmly. "I don't fancy staying behind and explaining to all these people just where the two of you went. As far as they're concerned, high orbit strikes me as an ideal negotiating distance."

He gave a final twitch and pat to the improvised sling, and stood back. "Now, if you gentlesirs will excuse me, I think I'd better rejoin Peyte in the rear corridor."

III. Pleyver: Space Force Medical Station

BEKA'S LEGS trembled with exhaustion and the adrenaline surge of the firefight. She propped herself against the support of the comm-room wall, and watched as the blond lieutenant commander made his exit.

He stooped over the wounded man again on the way out, and said something light and cheerful-sounding in reply to a thready question, but the set of his shoulders as he headed out into the corridor gave his voice the lie. She bit her lip hard.

Damn you, Owen. Do you realize just how much your getaway is costing?

The Professor still sat in the comm chair where he'd collapsed at the end of the last bit of fighting. His back was as stubborn-straight as ever—but his eyes were shut and his face looked grey and haggard in the half-light of the emergency glows. *You can put that one on the tab, too, Owen,* she thought bitterly. *'City-fighting is a game for the young'—and knocking somebody out of the way of a blaster bolt is a game for romantic idiots, not for old men with brittle bones.*

She cursed, and slammed her fist against the wall. Then she put the scraped knuckles into her mouth to suck away the fresh blood on them.

At the sound of flesh hitting plast-block, the Professor opened his eyes and brought his blaster to the ready. "Trouble, Captain?"

She took her hand down again, flexing fingers that ached from gripping a blaster. "That was just me, Professor. They're still quiet out front."

"So I thought. And from the sound of things, our medical acquaintance has taken care of the back way for a while. A resourceful young man . . . a friend?"

She gave a weary chuckle. "He doesn't even know me. And I didn't know about the clinic until this afternoon."

The Professor looked thoughtful. "I take it you heard from your father."

"A letter at the mail drop. Some interesting stuff, and the word about this place—in case I needed a bolthole sometime, he said." She shook her head. "He certainly called that one right."

Jessan returned to the intersection, where Peyte made a shadowy, vigilant shape in the blue-green twilight. The Khesatan settled down in his old position against the wall and asked, "All quiet back here?"

"Like a tomb, sir," said Peyte. "How's Namron?"

"Holding on." Jessan looked down the hallway toward the pile of rubble. "With that way blocked, they'll try the other door next."

"Not the cargo bay?"

"No. The outside door down there is blast-armored against launch. It'd take a laser cannon to get through there."

Peyte was silent for a moment. Then he said, "You know, Doc, we might be better off down in the bay."

Jessan thought about it. "There'd only be the one door

to worry about . . . give me the blaster, and go back up front. Tell Tarnekep I want to talk with him.''

''Right, Doc.''

Peyte headed up the corridor. Jessan leaned back against the wall, blaster in hand, to wait on developments. After a few minutes he heard footsteps coming from up front— not Peyte's familiar tread, but a quick, light stride that had to belong to the longer-legged, more slightly built Tarnekep.

The footsteps halted a few feet away. Jessan looked back and saw the tall Mandeynan standing for a second in dim silhouette against the light of the glows, before he moved closer to the wall and became only a vertical shadow.

''Peyte said you wanted to talk with me.'' The voice wasn't promising.

''That's right. I think we ought to go down below into the cargo bay.''

''That's what Peyte said.''

''You have some trouble with that?'' Jessan kept his own voice as neutral as possible. Already during his tour of duty in Flatlands he'd had to talk a blaster away from a blind-drunk and homicidal spacer, and he was beginning to think of that night as a garden party compared to this one.

''The Professor doesn't like the idea of leaving the front office unguarded.''

Jessan caught the phrasing. ''And you?''

''I can live with it. How close is the cargo bay to the shuttle pad?''

''Just the other side of the blast doors.''

Silence for a moment, then, ''Your man Namron. Can he take being shifted that far?''

''If it comes down to a choice between moving him or letting him collect another blaster bolt—'' began Jessan. He stopped. ''Damn,'' he said quietly, as the remaining undamaged door into the upper building tore free of its hinges and slammed onto the floor of the hall.

Massed blaster fire lit up the passage. Jessan dropped

to a prone position and started squeezing off shots from the shelter of the corner. *If we didn't have to discuss everything in committee we'd be down in the cargo bay right now.*

"Firing blind's not going to do any good against so many," said Tarnekep from behind him. "Cover me!"

The lean figure sprang past him into the intersection and ran for the far wall.

Jessan squirmed far enough forward to see the broken door and began firing as fast as he could press the stud. At the same time, out of the corner of his eye, he saw the Mandeynan send three quick bolts down the hall in the course of his dash across the gap. Only one of the shots ended with the harsh sound of a miss against plast-block.

He's good, conceded Jessan, still firing. *But what in the name of all that's sane and normal is he doing now?*

Tarnekep had paused for only a few seconds on the far side. Now the Mandeynan stepped away from the sheltering wall into the center of the junction, turned half right, and brought his blaster up at arm's length like an old-style duelist. Then he began to fire aimed shots into the broken doorway at a slow, deliberate rate.

He is insane, thought Jessan, as the blaster fire from down the hall limned the Mandeynan's unmoving, upright figure in a lurid halo of light. *Nobody in their right mind takes chances like that.*

Jessan's own fire was continuous by now. He had the stud pressed down hard in its socket, and was depending on the blaster's feedback regulator to keep the weapon from going on overload. Beams of energy played around the far end of the hall like hallucinatory party streamers. Jessan couldn't tell if he was hitting anything or not, but he hoped that the constant fire might keep the other side from taking time to aim.

Still Tarnekep stood in the center of the hallway, aiming bolt after steady bolt. With each shot, the fire from outside slackened, until there was silence.

Tarnekep lowered his blaster. Jessan waited a moment.

When no renewed firing lit up the air, he stood up and faced the shadowy gunfighter.

"Right now, Portree, I could make out a good case for locking you up in a padded room." The brief, intense firefight had left his professional manner in shreds and he knew it, but he was past caring. "If you get yourself killed, where does that leave the rest of us?"

"I didn't get killed," said Tarnekep, then turned and stalked back toward the comm room without another word.

Jessan shook his head slowly, and slid aside the readout cover plate to check the charge on his blaster. The little glowing numbers showed the weapon's energy level a lot closer to flat than he liked. "The Academy target-shooting team was never like this," he muttered, and resumed his watch down the hall.

Beka got as far as the comm-room door before her legs buckled under her. A grab for the doorjamb stopped her from crumpling to the tiles in the middle of the corridor.

She made it to the wall, sliding quietly down that instead, and sat there, head between her knees, until the black fog cleared out of her skull. She'd almost fainted once already, back where the hallways crossed, when fatigue had slammed into her like a high-G lift-off as soon as the firing stopped. Pride alone had kept her back straight and her voice steady long enough to get past the lieutenant commander without collapsing; she was surprised that she'd made it this much farther.

Be honest. You're surprised that you're still alive.

She pushed herself back onto her feet, hanging on to the doorjamb again for support, and took a couple of deep breaths. Tired . . . she'd never been so tired . . . threading the Web for twelve hours straight, and then all this. She knew that if she collapsed a second time she wouldn't be able to get up again until she'd slept herself out.

Keep moving, my girl. Onward and upward.

Shoving away from the wall, she straightened her shoulders and strode into the comm room with a fair imitation of Tarnekep's usual arrogance. The Professor was still sitting in the control chair, but the clammy grey look that had frightened her into yelling for the medic was gone. Petty Officer Namron didn't look any better, but he didn't look much worse either. She supposed that would have to do.

The desk still lay across the outer door, and the young comptech—Peyte, that was his name—kept watch at the improvised barricade. He looked round as she came in; so did the Professor, who would normally have risen to his feet like the stickler for proper behavior that he was.

"Time to pull back," she said. "I've looked, and there's a chance we can get down into the cargo bay."

The Professor nodded toward Namron. "What about him?"

"We're taking him with us." She looked at Peyte. "You take his right side, I'll take the left. We'll have to leave the bedding here."

"Right," said the clerk/comptech, standing up. Beka switched her blaster to her left hand and followed Peyte over to the corner where Namron lay in the shelter of the heavy hyperspace comm setup. He was pale, but conscious.

"This isn't going to be pleasant," she told him. "But it beats staying behind to get shot at."

Namron blinked, and shook his head from side to side on the pillow. "Just leave me one of the blasters and I'll do fine," he said faintly. "You don't have to—"

"Don't argue," she said. "You can't spend Hostile Fire Pay if you don't stay alive to collect it. Ready, Peyte?"

"Ready."

Together they picked up Namron, Peyte supporting him on one side and Beka on the other. "Let's go," she said, and they started off down the hall like some awkward, six-legged beast, with the Professor hanging behind to cover the rear.

Jessan heard the thump and shuffle of footsteps approaching from up front—Peyte and Tarnekep, supporting

Namron between them. "Any trouble back here?" asked Tarnekep, when the little procession had drawn even with the junction.

"Not a peep."

"Well," said the Mandeynan, "either they're waiting for us down below, or they're not. Is your cargo lift tied in to the main power lines?"

Jessan nodded. "We'll have to use the auxiliary stairs."

"Lifts, stairs, doors all over . . . if I didn't know better, I'd say you people *wanted* to make this place easy to get into."

"Well, as a matter of fact—" Jessan caught the irony just a second too late and stopped, shaking his head in disgust. The Mandeynan gave a brief snort of laughter. Peyte snickered.

"Gentlesirs." The Professor sounded patient but tired. "Commander—are these back stairs normally kept locked?"

"Of course. There's a lot in here worth stealing."

"Then you'll have to lead the way. Tarnekep and I aren't keyed to your locks."

"Come on, then," said Jessan. "Easy with Namron, now."

Blaster at the ready, Jessan stepped around the corner. He more than half expected to get his hair parted by an energy beam as soon as he appeared in the hall, but nothing happened.

The stairs were halfway down the hall. Beyond them, at the far end, the outside door yawned blackly into the night. Jessan covered the distance in a dozen quick strides, the others hurrying behind him with no attempt at quiet. Once at the stairway door, he switched his blaster to his left hand long enough to palm the ID plate. The lock clicked open, and Jessan gave silent thanks to the designer who'd thought to make the auxiliary door panels self-powered.

Self-power didn't run to working a slide mechanism, though. Like most auxiliaries, this door was mounted on hinges instead. He shoved the door hard, and had his blaster pointed down the unlit stairwell before the swinging panel slammed against the inside wall.

Nothing happened. "Just like a holovid hero," he muttered, feeling a bit silly.

"Shut up, damn you," said Tarnekep's voice in his ear. "And get on in there."

Pinched a nerve, did I? thought Jessan, stepping through the door and standing aside to let the two men carrying Namron come past, with the Professor on their heels. *I wonder how.*

He shut the door behind the older man, and locked it. "Peyte," he said into the solid darkness, "do you still have that hand torch?"

"Just a moment, Doc."

There were scuffling sounds, a grunt of pain from Namron and a muffled "Sorry!" from Peyte, and the torch came on. Its actinic glow made the faces of the little crowd standing together on the upstairs landing look drained and colorless—not, Jessan suspected, that even north light on a good day could have made much difference at the moment.

But Peyte was grinning like an idiot, and Jessan found himself grinning back. "What the hell," he said out loud. "If I wanted a quiet life I'd have studied flower arranging and ornamental tree-sculpture. Let's go on down."

The cargo bay, when they finally reached it, proved to be as empty of life as the stairwell. The light from Peyte's hand torch played over stacks of crates and boxes to the massive blast doors at the far end.

"Nobody home," said Jessan. The words echoed in the high-ceilinged chamber.

The Professor looked somber. "They'll realize soon enough that we've abandoned the upper floors."

Jessan locked the lower stairway door. "We have a while yet. Peyte, you and Tarnekep get Namron settled by the back door. That'll be our way out when the shuttle comes in, and I'm damned if I want to see him dragged any farther than I have to."

"What about blankets, Doc?" the clerk/comptech asked. "This floor's going to be colder than a Magelord's heart."

"Wait a minute and I'll find you something," said Jessan, craning his neck to scan the roomful of shipping containers. *Where . . . ah, there.*

He headed over to the crate he'd spotted and started working the lid off. "Here we are," he said over his shoulder. "Good-quality reclaimed synthetic, thermal weave, preserves body heat down to some incredible temperature below zero, allows for the free evaporation of sweat, does everything but function like a healing pod—which is what those misbegotten paper-pushers in Supply swore on their mother's graves these blankets were going to be."

He came back to the group with a stack of blankets in Space Force basic beige, and with Peyte's assistance soon had Namron bedded down as snugly as circumstances allowed. The Professor watched the proceedings with an expression of polite interest, but Tarnekep prowled back and forth among the stacks of boxes like a thin, patch-eyed ghost. Jessan recognized from experience the compulsive activity of someone who must either keep moving or collapse.

"Commander." The Professor spoke quietly, his eyes on the tall, restless figure in the bloodstained shirt. "I am concerned about the stairwell."

Stairwell, my foot, thought Jessan. Aloud, he said, "They'll have to cut through the doors top and bottom to get to us—we'll have warning. And with luck they won't come around the back. Too much chance of getting burned if the dawn shuttle comes in early."

"With luck," said the Professor, still watching Tarnekep prowl among the boxes. "Without it . . ."

He shrugged his uninjured shoulder. "One does what one can. Your improvisation in the upper hallway comes to mind—do you have supplies for something similar down here?''

"I'm afraid not,'' said Jessan. "Except for what's in the treatment rooms, the chemicals are all in the flammables locker. Safety regs.''

"Very proper,'' said the Professor, but his expression was grim.

Jessan hesitated for a moment. What he was contemplating now would probably get Supply so angry with him that he'd never see the healing pods at all. *The hell with that*, he told himself. *Right now you're not likely to see morning if you don't do something about it.*

"Look in those boxes nearest the blast doors—that's the emergency supplies for an aircar we don't even have yet. If there's anything in there that looks useful, haul it out. Take Peyte with you to do the heavy stuff; that arm has got to be giving you hell.''

The Professor moved off without protest in the direction of the blast doors, summoning Peyte to follow with a nod. Jessan sat down on the cold concrete next to Namron to check the pressure bandage; as he worked, he could hear the sound of boxes being ripped open, mingled with a stream of chatter from the irrepressible Peyte.

"Monofilament—scalpel blades—yo! Look what I found here!''

"What's that?'' The voice asking the question was Tarnekep's; it sounded like the gunfighter's prowlings about the cargo bay had brought him back to the doors again.

"Survival Kit, Aircar, One Each.''

"So?''

"So there's an emergency transmitter in here someplace.''

"Dig it out,'' said Tarnekep. "Maybe we can raise somebody after all. Commander!''

Jessan gave Namron a final quick once-over and rose to his feet. "What's the problem?''

"Help me shove some boxes around. We need to clear out fields of fire around the stairs and lift entrance.''

The slightly built Mandeynan was stronger than he looked; he and Jessan moved boxes until they'd emptied out nearly the first third of the bay and had thrown up some quick-and-dirty barricades, one set facing the stair and lift doors across the open space, and the second about halfway back to the far wall.

Jessan heaved a shipping carton marked "Boxes 120 Lint-Free Wipes, Disposable—100 Count" onto a crate stenciled "Table, Folding, Metal—Property Republic Space Force Medical Corps," and asked, a trifle breathlessly, "What's the plan behind all this, anyway?"

"We need covered lines of retreat," said Tarnekep, panting.

The Professor looked around from holding the hand torch for Peyte. The clerk/comptech was elbows-deep in an open crate.

"If we can't hold them up front," the older man explained, "we'll need to fall back to the secondary position. If we can't hold them there, we fall back to the door. Then it's each for himself out the back, or fight to the last man in here."

"Damnation and hellfire!" Peyte came up from the packing crate empty-handed except for a plastic-laminated printed sheet.

"What's wrong?" asked Jessan.

"The transmitters' power sources are shipped separately. But we do have complete instructions for installing them."

Tarnekep muttered something that Jessan didn't quite catch, and then asked, "Commander—any chance that the power sources are here?"

"We're dealing with the Supply Department," he said. "There's a chance of finding almost anything. But with all the comps down, I wouldn't make bets on locating those power sources tonight. Anything else useful in the box?"

"So far—" began the Professor.

A yelp from Peyte interrupted him. "Hey! Here's something, Doc—take a look."

Jessan came over and read the label on the carton. "Emergency rations, including stimulant tabs. 'Use of this medication by persons in a duty status strictly forbidden except under emergency conditions.' " He looked from one grey, dust-and-sweat streaked face to the next. "Fine. By the power vested in me by the Grand Council of the Republic, I hereby declare this an emergency. Share out the food and fluids, and everybody take one of those pills."

The solid rations tasted even worse than space rations usually did, and the liquids tasted like the body fluids they were supposed to replace, but they did their job. Jessan found himself feeling, if not optimistic, at least somewhat more steady. *Once the stimulant tabs kick in, we'll really be on top of the world . . . probably just in time for the party.*

Tarnekep finished his share of the rations; Jessan was relieved to see some color reappearing in the narrow features. The Mandeynan swallowed off the stimutab with the last of the liquid and looked over at Peyte and the Professor. "Anything else in there?"

"Flare launcher and flares," said Peyte. "I'm taking those."

Tarnekep held up a hand for silence. "Noises in the stairwell."

"Places, everyone," said the Professor. "I'll cover the lift door. Commander, you take the flank—shoot down the length of the front wall toward the stairwell door. Peyte, stay here with Tarnekep. When they break through, put a multistar cluster behind them. I want them backlit and us in shadow."

Jessan moved off to his left for the position the Professor had indicated, behind a pile of boxes at the stairwell end of the bay. The grey-haired man had vanished somewhere off to the right, and Jessan caught a glimpse of the top of Tarnekep's head over the boxes in the center before he heard the Mandeynan snap, "Put out your light!"

The hinges of the stairway door glowed a bright orange-red for a moment against the darkness, and then the door fell forward into the cargo bay.

"Here they come!" the Mandeynan's voice shouted over the crash of the falling door. "Fire, damn you!"

Jessan heard a dull *whump!* as Peyte fired the flare launcher. A glowing red streak shot in a flat arc across the cleared-out space and into the open door. Brilliant white light poured out of the doorway from the burning flare, and reflected on clouds of thick white smoke. The attackers—black shapes against the light—ran forward through the smoke and glare.

Jessan fired into the packed figures before they could spread out. More streaks of blaster fire zinged in from behind the barricades where the Professor and Tarnekep lay hidden.

The attackers were no slouches either—they fired as they came. *So many of them,* thought Jessan. *Who the hell can throw this many into a private war?*

Then the blaster bolts were coming in his direction as well, and he didn't dare look any longer. He could only take quick snap shots in what he knew was the direction of the opening—a group of three, duck, a burst of five, duck, while the attackers kept on coming.

IV. Pleyver: Space Force Medical Station

B EKA SAW the hinges of the door glow red.
"Here they come!" she shouted as the door
fell inward. The clerk/comptech beside her hadn't moved.
"Fire, damn you!"

The flare launcher went off with a *whump*, and the attackers charged in through smoke and blazing light.

You've only got a little time before their eyes adjust,
Beka thought. *Make the most of it.*

She heard the clerk/comptech shout a warning as she
stood up for a clear line of sight on the attackers' point
man. A blaster bolt burned into the stack of boxes with a
sound like water hitting hot metal. She ignored it and fired,
smiling with satisfaction as she saw the bolt connect.

Got you, you bastard! She aimed and fired again.

A harsh grating noise broke her concentration. She
looked to the right and saw the lift doors opening. *They
must have climbed down the shaft,* she thought. Peyte fired
off another flare toward the new sound, and the blaster

beams that had been coming from the Professor's position switched from the stair door to the lift entrance.

Peyte's flare exploded into deep crimson flame. Over by the stairway door, meanwhile, his first star was guttering out. The white light faded and died. Seconds later five attackers burst out of the smoke in front of the barricade, looming enormous against the bloodred light of the second flare.

They're right on top of us! Beka shot the first one, and then another, but the other three kept coming. She took aim at the closest, and fired again.

Nothing happened.

No charge. You've had it, my girl.

She threw the useless weapon full force at the nearest of her assailants. The heavy blaster hit him squarely in the forehead, and he went down. She heard the sound of the flare launcher going off again beside her. The star hit one of the two remaining men in the belly. He screamed—a high, rising note that got inside her skull and wouldn't stop—and began to roll on the floor.

Beka drew her knife and braced herself as the last man leaped over the barricade and tackled her. He was almost as big as her brother Ari, and had momentum on his side. She went down backward with him on top, and barely remembered to fall the way the Professor had taught her.

She felt a muscle in her leg twist anyway as she hit the concrete, with the big man landing on top of her at full length.

"What the hell?" she heard him grunt, on a note of surprise. "This one's a bitch!"

She shoved the dagger home between his ribs.

His heavy body went limp, pressing her down on the floor. She cursed in every language she knew, and half-pushed, half-squirmed her way out.

The clerk/comptech was staring at her. Beka thought for a moment that he'd heard the dead man's last words, and felt a surge of blind panic. Then she followed his eyes down to the bloody knife she'd pulled from the man's side as she wiggled free, and understood.

She gave Peyte what she hoped was a reassuring smile. The young man flinched. She shrugged. *The hell with it, then.*

She stood the rest of the way up and took a deep breath. The lieutenant commander would have to hear her from up in the front, and the Professor from wherever he had moved to since he'd fired last.

"Fall back!" she shouted. "Fall back!"

Tarnekep's voice came to Jessan over the sound of blaster fire. "Fall back! Fall back!"

About time, Jessan thought, and headed for the second pile of boxes. He was the first one there; a moment later, by the faint light still glowing off the interior wall, he could see Peyte coming, with Tarnekep limping alongside half-supported by the clerk/comptech's shoulder.

"Are you hurt?" he asked, as soon as they got close enough.

"No," said Peyte. "Just a twisted leg—not too bad. One of the bastards got over the barricade and jumped him."

"Let me have a look," said Jessan. He went down on one knee and reached out to make an examination by touch in the near-dark.

Tarnekep pulled away in a move that had his bad leg almost buckling, and the dying light glinted off a knife blade in the Mandeynan's hand.

"You keep your damned hands off of me!"

Jessan drew his hand back and stood up slowly. "That's fresh blood," he said, in as calm and even a voice as he could manage. "Yours?"

"Of course not."

But the knife didn't go away, and Jessan watched the Mandeynan's tense face for a stretched-out moment before another voice said, "Gently, Tarnekep. The young man meant no harm."

Tarnekep gave a long sigh, and Jessan saw the lean frame relax. The four of them leaned against the packing crates while the last light from the star-flares faded and died.

Muffled sounds came from the darkness toward the front of the bay. "How's the charge in your blaster, Commander?" the Professor asked.

"Damn near flat, I'm afraid."

"Then you'll need to make every shot count. But still—better to shoot as though you have all the charge in the world, than to let them know you're running out. Tarnekep?"

"I ran dry up front," said the gunfighter.

"Stay out of it unless they overrun us. Peyte—how many more flares do you have?"

"We're down to the last one."

"Save it, then."

More noises drifted toward them from the forward part of the cargo bay.

"Commander," murmured the Professor, "if you would be so good as to throw out a piece of your spare change . . ."

Jessan fumbled in his pocket for a tenth-credit bit, and tossed it out over the crates in the direction of the rustling noises. The coin hit the concrete with a high, metallic *chink*, and a blaster beam lanced out at the sound.

The Professor fired at the source of the bolt. By the brief light of the shot, Jessan saw a man fall to the floor—dead or cowering, he couldn't say.

Another beam flashed up through the stacks of boxes. Jessan fired back, with no result that he could see. The firing speeded up and began to work its way closer, shot by shot. He and the Professor were soon returning to fire alternately between them, and there was no time left to wonder about results.

"My compliments," said the Professor, when the interchange slackened for a moment. "For a medic, you shoot well."

"You've guessed my guilty secret," said Jessan. "I was

on the Academy target team, the year we went to the Galactic finals. But believe me—'' Two beams passed close above his head, and he threw himself against the boxes. ''—I made a habit of standing at the other end of the range back then.''

''It's only a matter of time before they rush us,'' said Tarnekep's voice out of the darkness near his ear.

''You're just saying that to cheer me up,'' replied Jessan under his breath. ''I'd hate to think—what's that noise?''

A pause followed. The Professor traded blaster bolts with someone unseen out in the darkened bay, and the faint sound grew steadily louder.

''Light orbit-to-atmosphere cargo craft, putting down on jets,'' said Tarnekep, with more emotion in his cool voice than Jessan had heard all evening. ''Your shuttle's coming.''

''Right,'' said Jessan. ''I don't know about the two of you—but when the Midnight Special pulls out, the Space Force is going to be on it.''

''You won't get any argument from us, Commander,'' said the Professor. ''Time to fall back to the doors. Peyte, if you would be so good as to lend Tarnekep your shoulder again and move on out ahead—''

''No trouble.''

''Excellent.''

Jessan heard the clerk/comptech and the Mandeynan moving off at a limp-and-shuffle.

''Commander, you and I will have to cover the rear. I anticipate a rush as soon as our friends hear the shuttle and realize we're leaving.''

''We can always hope they're deaf and stupid,'' said Jessan. And then, as at least five blaster beams lit up the air in front of him from positions uncomfortably close—''No, I guess they're not. Let's get going.''

''Wait for a count of five, then move back,'' said the Professor, fading off into the darkness.

''Right,'' said Jessan, to the air where the older man had been a second earlier. He directed a beam of his own into the darkness and began a subvocal count.

One . . . two . . . fire again . . . three . . . damn, that came close! . . . four . . . standing here lighting myself up like a holosign at midnight, I must be crazy . . . five, and move!

A blaster fired from behind him—the Professor, that would be, taking up the job of providing cover. Jessan loped past him toward the doors, counting as he went. On *five*, he stopped running and began firing to another count, until once again the Professor's blaster lit up the darkness.

A long-legged man in no particular hurry could cross the clinic's cargo bay from lift doors to blast doors in a little over a Standard minute, and run it in less. In objective time, Jessan realized, their leapfrogging journey back to the auxiliary door couldn't be taking much longer—*which fails to explain,* he thought, caroming off a metal crate he'd forgotten was in the way and swearing in High Khesatan, Galcenian, and Nammerinish backwater-talk all at once, *why enough time's gone by since we started for hell to freeze over and all my hair to go grey.*

He found the back wall by running into it, and was so grateful for its presence that he didn't bother to swear this time. He only sagged against the reinforced plast-block, breathing hard, until he could ask, "Are we all here?"

"All present or accounted for, Doc," said Peyte, "And Namron's still with us."

"Had it easy," came the petty officer's faint voice from the floor. "Only had to lie here and watch the fireworks. Must have been . . . fun up front."

"A laugh a minute," Jessan assured him.

"Tarnekep," said the Professor, "you have good ears. Has our taxi landed?"

"She's down," said the Mandeynan. "But let's give them a while longer to open up and lower the ramp."

"Can you walk on that leg?" Jessan asked.

He heard the gunfighter laugh, a bit shakily. "The question is, can I run on it?"

"Adrenaline's a marvelous thing," said Jessan. "Run now, pay later—but I think you'd better take my blaster and let Peyte and me carry Namron."

Whatever Tarnekep might have said was cut short by a whoop from Peyte. "Here they come, Doc!"

Jessan slapped his blaster into the Mandeynan's lean, sinewy hand, then bent with Peyte to scoop up Namron, one of them under each of the petty officer's arms.

They backed up to the auxiliary door, and Jessan reached around to slap the ID plate. He heard the locks click over, and threw his shoulder against the opening lever. The door swung open. He and Peyte half-backed, half-fell with Namron out onto the apron around the shuttle pad. Tarnekep and the Professor followed, firing back into the darkened bay.

"Son of a bitch!" Peyte yelled, as a blaster beam flashed past them out of the bay. The bolt came so close that Jessan could see Peyte's indignant expression by its light. The clerk/comptech lifted his flare launcher and fired their last flare back into the doorway.

"Come *on*," said Jessan to the comptech. With Namron hanging limp between them, they turned and ran awkwardly toward the shuttle. The supply craft sat door open and ramp down in the center of the landing pad. Its pilot and flight engineer stood together at the top of the ramp, paralyzed by the scene.

Jessan had to admit the sight was spectacular. Sizzling rays of red, green, and blue-white came from the auxiliary door and from both sides of the pad, filling the air around the shuttle with a brilliant, deadly interlace of colored fire. By the intermittent, strobe-effect light, he could see the Professor and Tarnekep running on either side of him and Peyte, and firing as they ran.

"Space Force!" Jessan shouted at the shuttle crew over the whine of the blasters. "We're Space Force! Let us in!"

One of the two figures on the ramp moved to do something—raise the ramp, toggle on the force field, duck out of the way, Jessan never knew. From out of the darkness came the ugly snarl of a crew-served energy gun, and one of the colored beams threading the darkness with light went into the doorway and brought down pilot and engineer together. One of the figures fell forward off the ramp onto the pad, and the next flash of light showed his head a blackened lump. The other staggered as the bolt hit, grabbed the frame of the door, and sank backward into the darkness as Tarnekep and the Professor reached the top of the ramp.

The one on the ground's dead for sure, Jessan told himself, as he and Peyte dragged Namron the last few steps over the threshold. *The one inside . . . get the door shut first, and then take a look.*

He hit the Raise Ramp button as soon as his boots touched the deckplates. Out of the corner of his eye he saw Tarnekep slam down the Close Door lever with a doubled fist and vanish in the direction of the cockpit controls.

"This one's still breathing," said Peyte, from the floor.

"Great. Let's get her and Namron strapped down in the passenger compartment."

They carried first Namron and then the shuttle crew member back into the passenger/cargo area. Namron looked like hell, but he was still alive—barring accidents, he'd probably make it to draw his pension after all. The shuttle crew member had caught the sideshock from the heavy beam that had killed her partner; her burns were nasty but not fatal.

"Watch those straps!"

"Sorry, Doc."

No time now to pick out cloth from skin . . . give her a general-purpose antibiotic and a painkiller, and sort things out when we get to High Station.

"Pass me the first-aid kit."

"I don't see one, Doc."

"You're standing on it, that's why—pass it over."

He'd finished taking care of the two casualties and was about to strap in for lift-off himself when the Professor reappeared. "Commander—could you come forward, please?"

"These two need me here."

"Do you know the passwords and procedure to get us into the Space Force docks on High Station?"

"Yes," said Jessan. "But—"

"Then these two need you more where you can get at the comm panel."

He's got a point, Jessan admitted to himself. "All right, I'm coming. Peyte, the casualties are all yours. Squawk if anything changes."

"Right, Doc. Be seein' you."

Jessan followed the Professor forward. The older man took the fold-down seat at the right rear of the cabin, which left only the copilot's seat to the right of Tarnekep. Jessan slid in and strapped down.

"How's it going?"

"Shut up," said Tarnekep, without looking away from the control panel. "I've never flown one of these before."

It might have been the first time he'd seen the controls, but the Mandeynan was doing a preflight run-up without benefit of checklist just the same. Space Force would have lifted the certification of any pilot who got caught cutting so many corners—if any Space Force pilot had dared to try it in the first place—but Tarnekep carried it out with an impression of competence that Jessan found oddly familiar.

Now where have I . . . never mind. He knows what he's doing, so let him be.

The medic looked away from Tarnekep's intent profile—with no eye patch visible, the sharply cut features didn't look so much vicious as plain dead-tired—and watched the external scan screens instead.

He wasn't encouraged by what he saw. Peyte's last flare had torched off the cartons inside the bay. The flickering red light illuminated teams of men at work out on the pad. One group was trying to burn through the shuttle's hull by means of concentrated blaster fire on a single point. Another group was busy at the airlock door with a torch. A third group was doing something just out of sight of the scan, down around the landing legs. Somehow, the fact that exactly what they were up to wasn't visible made Jessan more nervous than the activities of all the others put together.

Tarnekep finished his check-and-flip of the major systems and looked up at the scans. "Fry, you sons of bitches," he said, and hit the jets.

Sudden acceleration pressed Jessan back into his seat—far

too much boost for a craft with casualties on board. Just as he was about to protest, Tarnekep cut the power, flipped the craft onto its back, and began a rapid sideslip. Then, just as suddenly, the Mandeynan hit the boosters and headed for orbit.

I haven't had a ride like this since I left Nammerin, thought Jessan. *And a good thing, too.* He cleared his throat and asked quietly, "What was that trick in honor of?"

"In case they fired off a heat seeker," Tarnekep muttered, still intent on the controls.

"Oh," said Jessan, and abandoned the subject.

The shuttle exited the atmosphere in a pop-up, and then went into a flat dive to orbit, gaining speed all the while. Tarnekep was muttering under his breath. "No sign of High Station—must be farside right now. Commander—what's the frequency for Space Force Control?"

"One fifty-six point two," he answered. "Why?"

"Get on it, and tell them that we're coming in." The Mandeynan didn't wait for a reply, but went back to muttering over the console readouts. "Where the hell is High Station . . . ah, there's the bastard. Here we go."

The long fingers played over the shuttle's controls. With a touch of the lateral jets, the craft was falling around the planet along a new and fractionally different orbit.

Jessan pulled his attention away from Tarnekep's disturbingly familiar piloting to pick up the shuttle's external comm link. He keyed in the Space Force restricted channel.

"High Station Pad, High Station Pad, this is Medical Station Pleyver actual, over."

"Roger Medical Station, go," replied the tinny voice of the comm link.

How do I put this? he wondered. *Oh, well—details now, explain later.*

"Pad, I'm in trouble. I have casualties on board. Request you call dirtside Security and ask them to investigate the site of the former Space Force Medical Station. Over."

Silence from the comm link.

"Do we have a problem?" asked Tarnekep.

"Shouldn't have," said Jessan. "Right now, they'll be matching my call against my voicefile to see if I'm really me."

The comm link spoke up again. "Med Station, this is High Station Pad. Request you authenticate. Over."

"Pad," Jessan said again, "this is Med Station Pleyver. I authenticate one-five-seven. Request you authenticate. Over."

"I authenticate three-five-two," said the comm link. "Commander, are you all right? Over."

"I'm fine," said Jessan, "but I've got four casualties—"

The Professor's quiet voice came from behind him. "Two casualties—we won't be staying."

"Correction, two casualties, and there's been an attack on the clinic. Recommend you go to General Quarters. Over."

"We are going to General Quarters at this time," said the comm link. "Awaiting your report, out." The link clicked off.

Jessan gave a deep sigh. "And that should get us home safe . . . but I hate to think of the paperwork."

Tarnekep laughed briefly. "If you don't like paperwork, you're working for the wrong firm." A pause, and then, as the massive artificial moon came up over the rim of the planet, "There she is: Pleyver's better half."

High Station Pleyver had been one of the first of the orbiting communities built in the economic boom that followed the end of the Magewar. By now the enormous, gaudy globe housed everything from spacedocks to luxury hotels, and had only historical ties to the world below. Most of the time, in fact, the planet and its late-born satellite competed for the lucrative spacing trade.

Tarnekep looked at the station, and then at the console readouts. He did calculations in his head—if he did any at all—and fired the aft and lateral jets. The shuttle skidded obediently into a matching orbit for the approach.

It was a maneuver held at a higher speed than Jessan had ever seen, and done with casual, almost unconscious ease. He'd only known one other pilot who worked with such effortless assurance—and his friend Ari had gotten both his technique and his reflexes from the Magewar's most famous starpilot.

"If I didn't know better," Jessan said aloud, "from the way you fly this ship I'd say your last name ought to be Metadi."

The quiet in the shuttle cockpit congealed into a profound stillness. Jessan felt a cold sensation growing in the pit of his stomach. *I think I've just said something very stupid.* Next to him, without looking away from the forward screens, Tarnekep drew the blaster he'd taken from Jessan earlier and pointed it at the medic's head.

"I meant that as a compliment, you know," Jessan said, holding himself perfectly still. "The suggestion was only figurative."

The muzzle of the blaster didn't waver. On the other hand, he was still alive, which counted for something. Jessan looked more closely at the pale, intense profile of the man on his left.

Ari Rosselin-Metadi, who was bigger than just about anybody, would stand at least a foot taller than the Mandeynan, with a massiveness of bone and muscle lacking in the slim and wiry Tarnekep. In both men, though, the arrogant line of nose and chin could have come off any Entiboran coin ever struck—which let out any chance that the gunfighter might have been one of the General's youthful indiscretions come home to roost.

Ari's only brother is an apprentice Adept back on Galcen, I remember him saying so—and whatever this one may be, he's certainly no Adept. That leaves . . . no, that's impossible.

Jessan looked again. The Mandeynan's accent—pure aristocratic Galcenian, mixed with Gyfferan whenever he swore or talked piloting—could have been Ari's; but Tarnekep's voice was a light, clear tenor, instead of Ari Rosselin-Metadi's rumbling bass. And the gunfighter's loose Mandeynan shirt, with its elaborate cravat and ruffled cuffs, masked the lines of the torso and hid the betraying structures of neck and wrist.

Wrong. It's not impossible. If it were impossible, she wouldn't be pointing a blaster at your head right now.

"Beka Rosselin-Metadi," he said. "I sent your brother a Card of Grief when I learned of your death."

She didn't say anything. The shuttle held on its course for the High Station Pad, and what he could see of the pilot's face was as closed and unreadable as before.

He felt no surprise, only a kind of inevitability, when he heard the Professor speak up behind him. "Commander," said the soft, polite voice, in an accent he recognized too late as prewar Court Entiboran, "I'm afraid you'll be coming with us."

V. Pleyver: High Station
Nammerin: Space Force Medical Station

THE PASSENGER liner *Gravity's Rainbow*, four days out of Galcen and the sleekest commercial ship in the Red Shift Line, slid into the spacedock at High Station and began discharging passengers. For most of the elderly trippers and too-wealthy young people coming down the ramp, Pleyver was only the first stopover on *Rainbow*'s Outplanets Adventure Tour. Commander Jervas Gil, however, had come to High Station on business.

He turned his back on the *Rainbow* and her tour group and headed for High Station's Customs and Immigration checkpoint. The carrybag in his left hand held enough changes of uniform to last him for two weeks, and the dispatch folder tucked under his right arm contained a letter.

Gil knew the letter by heart. It began: "FROM: COMMANDING OFFICER, REPUBLIC SPACE FORCE. TO: COMMANDER JERVAS GIL, RSF, 7872–0016. SUBJECT: INVESTIGATION. 1. YOU ARE HEREBY DIRECTED TO TRAVEL BY THE FIRST AVAILABLE

MEANS TO PLEYVER, THERE TO INVESTIGATE THE CIRCUMSTANCES SURROUNDING THE LOSS OF SPACE FORCE MEDICAL CLINIC AND RECRUITING COMMAND ON THAT WORLD. . . .''

The rest of the letter directed him to present his findings of fact, his opinions, and his recommendations to his commanding officer within twelve days. Since the commanding officer in this case was General Jos Metadi, whatever Gil decided to recommend was guaranteed attention at the very highest levels.

Highest levels . . . right, he thought, as the Customs and Immigration man looked at his passport and his orders. *If I'd known two years ago what it was going to be like up here on the 'highest levels,' I'd have gone down on my knees to my detailer and asked for orders to a Reserve Force Retrofit Stores Ship instead. . . .*

He'd been in his office back at Prime Base, drafting the General's testimony for the upcoming session with the Council's Appropriations Committee, when Metadi had come in and tossed a folder of message flimsies onto his desk.

"How'd you like a few days away from politics, Commander?"

"If you can spare me, sir."

"I can write my own speeches for a week or two," said the General, "and you look like a man who could use a break."

"Frankly, sir," Gil told him, closing down the testimony file on the desk comp, "I could."

The General nodded at the folder full of messages. "Well, this will give it to you if anything can. How do you feel about Pleyver this time of year?"

"I've already started packing," said Gil. He began keying in a search of the port complex's data base for vessels outbound toward the Pleyveran system. The news from Flatlands Portcity had been the talk of Prime Base all morning, ever since the first message had come in from the Supply Detachment on High Station. "What's the latest on that mess?"

"Nothing good," said the General. "One dead, one missing, two still in healing pods—and all they can see from upstairs is a pile of smoking rocks where the clinic used to be."

"That's bad."

"Damned straight it's bad. I want to know who did it, and I want to know why. Go out there, Commander, and find out just what the hell did happen."

"I'll get right on it, sir," said Gil. "Any other instructions?"

"It's all in the folder," Metadi told him. "If anybody bothers to ask, you can tell them you're acting for me personally—that might get you a word or two extra out of some of the old-timers, even these days. Don't try it on the local law, though. For all I know, they've still got a warrant out for me in Flatlands Portcity."

"A warrant," said Gil, without much surprise. Most histories of the Magewar claimed that before the start of his privateering days, Jos Metadi had been an independent merchant captain. A few of the less laudatory texts, however, went so far as to point out that such a designation often covered a great deal of questionable activity. "If it's not a breach of etiquette, sir—what for?"

"Not much," said the General. "The last time I put in there—a couple of years before the Resistance recruited me, it would have been—one of the locals decided he didn't like my number two gunner. The gunner got mad and punched him out, and that would have been the end of it, except that the big guy with a blaster at the other end of the bar turned out to be the local's bodyguard. One thing led to another, and then we ran like hell for the spacedocks and left town in a hurry. Wound up threading the Web in something like six hours instead of twelve, because somebody dirtside whistled up a squad of Security fighters to chase us all the way to hyper. And I haven't been back to Pleyver since."

"Probably wise, sir," murmured Gil. "Six hours through the Web?"

"Well," said the General, "I used to round it down to six in those days for bragging purposes, but from high orbit to hyperspace jump it was probably closer to seven. I've turned respectable since then," Metadi finished, "so I'll say it was six-and-a-half."

Six or seven, Gil thought, remembering the conversation as High Station's lift system took him from the commercial docks to Space Force's section of the orbiting structure, *if he really did it, I'm impressed.*

Gil had taken advantage of professional courtesy, and observed the *Rainbow*'s realspace progress through the Web from the liner's bridge: twelve hours of what he recognized as tricky piloting even in the hands of an expert. *Give me a courier ship running empty, and I might try doing it in eight-point-five . . . but seven's right out. And as for six . . .*

Gil shook his head.

The lift opened, and he stepped out in front of a pair of armor-glass doors marked with the Space Force crest.

Time to get to work.

Halfway through second lunch shift at the Space Force Medical Station on Nammerin, Llannat Hyfid checked her chronometer and frowned.

Bors Keotkyra caught the motion and looked up from his bowl of nut-butter soup. "What's wrong?"

"If Ari's working through lunch again—"

She paused, looking across the tables toward the door of the mess dome. She'd thought for a moment . . . yes. A familiar pattern was making itself felt among the varied presences in and around the crowded building. She relaxed and smiled a little in relief. "It's all right. Here he comes."

Bors gave her a nervous look that didn't change when the doors of the mess hall opened and Ari walked in.

Llannat suppressed a sigh. She knew that expression. It was the reason Adepts took great care not to make the rest of the civilized galaxy nervous—whether over outworn tales of dark sorcery or the real fear of abuse of power. For that same reason, the Guild forbade its fully-trained Adepts to hold rank in the Space Force, although still allowing them to serve.

Llannat herself had never planned to wind up in such an awkward position, doing an officer's work without an officer's place in the chain of command, but when Ensign Hyfid's latent sensitivity to the currents of power had unexpectedly ceased to be latent and became impossible to ignore, her superiors had sent her to the Adepts for basic instruction. They hadn't thought that Master Ransome would go further, offering her an apprenticeship in the Guild—but he had, and she had accepted.

So what do I get for all my hard work? she thought. *Stared at like I had two heads because I knew who was on the other side of that door.*

"Good morning, Ari," she said aloud, tilting her head back to look the big lieutenant in the eye. "I thought for a while we weren't going to have the pleasure of your company."

Ari put down his tray on the table across from her and pulled out the chair. "I was packing crash-trauma kits for Emergency," he said, sitting down. "They've got the sterilizers back on line again, so we spent the morning playing catch-up."

He started to work on a plate of steamed gubbstucker. Once you got used to the texture—which admittedly took some doing—the fibrous root had a flavor not unlike good Maraghite mud eel. After a few mouthfuls, he stopped chewing long enough to ask, "Any hot gossip?"

Llannat shook her head. "Not today—sorry."

It didn't take a Adept to guess what Ari had really been asking about. Nyls Jessan had been stationed on Nammerin before getting the nod to start up the new Space Force clinic on Pleyver, and the whole staff had been hit hard by the news from High Station. Ari, though, was taking it harder than most.

Bors Keotkyra made another try at conversation. "Hey,

Ari. Did you catch last night's episode of 'Spaceways Patrol'?''

Ari shook his head. "I was working late over in the Isolation dome."

"You should have seen it. I thought Serina's dress was going to fall right off her this time."

Llannat tried not to wince. Bors had a good heart and he was trying his best, even if his methods did lack subtlety. "You guys think Serina's dress is going to fall off her every time," she said. "Haven't you ever heard of glue?"

Bors grinned. "Not for that."

"I missed the show last night myself," she said, "but I'm planning to catch the late rerun when I come off watch this evening. Black Brok's about to take over the galaxy again, and I want to watch." She turned to Ari. "How about you?"

"No, thanks," said the Galcenian. "I was thinking of spending time studying up for the re-quals. I haven't cracked a micro text since I got out of school."

"Yeah—you were too busy doing micro." Bors took up the familiar complaint. "That's the thing about those exams. They're slanted against all us people out here working at medicine instead of sitting home memorizing it."

The comm link on the wall gave its usual blink-and-beep to get the room's attention, followed by a three-tone sequence. Ari shoved back his chair and stood up.

"Death and damnation. I can't even get a quiet lunch around here."

Llannat watched, frowning, as he went over to the link and punched the Respond button. The sound of Ari's signal sequence had sent a wave of foreboding washing over her, but the feeling refused to verbalize itself or resolve into anything specific. "Visitor for you, sir, over in Outpatient," said the crackling metallic voice over the link.

"Roger, I'll be there, out."

Ari was already halfway to the door by the time the link clicked off.

"Don't let them throw my food away," he said over his shoulder as he went out. "I'll be back as soon as I take care of this."

The door shut behind him. After a couple of seconds Bors said, "Do you think the big guy's all right?"

"What do you mean?" Llannat asked. Her sense of disquiet deepened.

"He's pushing himself awful hard. And it's like pulling teeth to get him to talk these days."

"Look, Keotkyra," she said patiently, "the man's seen his mother assassinated and his sister killed in a messy spaceship wreck, he's doing a tour of duty on a planet where somebody's already tried once to kill him, and now he's found out that his best friend is missing in action. Just because a man's built like a brick wall doesn't mean he is one."

"Hey, Jessan was my friend, too," protested Bors. "What I meant is, I'm worried about Ari. He'd probably punch me out for saying so, but he ought to have somebody looking after him."

Llannat glanced over at her tablemate. "Don't sweat it, Keotkyra," she told him. "Somebody probably is."

Ari walked past the central lab and pharmacy domes toward the field hospital's outpatient wing. The day was shaping up to be a nice one by local standards, with just enough light rainfall to make the compound's force field glow a faint pink overhead. The storms of high summer were still months in the future, and the winter floods had subsided to nothing but a soggy memory. There hadn't even been an earthquake lately.

Inside the Outpatient dome, Esuatec had the desk watch. "I just got a strange one," she told him. "Said he had to talk to you personally, and then he couldn't wait. Left a present for you, though."

"A present?"

Esuatec nodded. "A pair of dice." She dropped the white cubes into Ari's hand. "I didn't know you gambled."

"I don't," he said. "Was that all?"

"No, there was a message, too: 'The same as before.' Mean anything to you?"

"Absolutely nothing," said Ari. "And for this I'm missing lunch. What did the guy look like?"

"Little bitty spacer type. Not a local."

"One of ours?" asked Ari. RSF *Corisydron* had been on maneuvers in the Nammerin system for a week now, and they'd seen one or two crew members in Outpatient already.

But Esuatec shook her head. "Not Space Force, no."

"Could you recognize him if you saw him again?"

"Only if he was wearing the same clothes," said Esuatec. "He looked just like everybody else, if you know what I mean."

"I know," said Ari. "If he comes back, sit on him if you have to, but don't let him leave till I get here. See you later, 'Tec—I want to get back and finish my lunch before mold starts to grow on it."

"Got you covered, Ari. Later."

As he'd expected, his plate of steamed gubbstucker was cold by the time he got back. The mess hall was empty except for Llannat Hyfid, still nursing a cup of cha'a. The Adept had been a good friend when he needed one, over the past few months, and she'd plainly been waiting for him today.

"What happened in Outpatient?" she asked as he sat down.

"Nothing."

"You sure aren't acting like it."

"I'm puzzled," said Ari. "That's all."

He turned his hand over and spilled the dice onto the table. They came to rest against the napkin dispenser, showing a three and a two. Moodily, he scooped them up and threw them again. "So tell me—does 'The same as before' mean anything to you?"

"By itself? No." Her dark eyes followed the dice as he picked them up and tossed them again. "Why?"

He shook his head. "No reason."

"What's the trouble? Maybe I can help."

The kindness undid him. His eyes blurred and his throat tightened. "Nothing is ever the same as before. Nothing."

"Ari," said Llannat's soft voice from across the table, "there's no such thing as luck or chance."

He shook his head. "I don't want to talk about philosophy right now, thank you."

"I'm not talking about philosophy, I'm talking about those dice. They've been turning up fives ever since you started throwing them."

Ari blinked and threw the dice again—watching them, this time. "Three and two. Four and one. Three and two." He scooped up the little cubes and clenched his fist around them. "It's the Quincunx. It has to be."

"Just what we needed," said Llannat. "I still have nightmares about the last time."

"So do I, believe me. I thought we were dead for sure."

"If it hadn't been for you, we would be."

"I could say the same thing about you," he said. "We were both lucky, I guess."

"Now *you're* talking philosophy," she told him. "Believe me, there's no such thing as luck. Everything has a purpose."

"All right, then. You tell me what the message meant."

"Let me hold the dice."

Ari hadn't expected her to take up the challenge; he kept forgetting that Llannat Hyfid was an Adept as well as a medic. He handed the dice over anyway. She put the little ivory cubes between her palms and closed her eyes. After a minute or so, she spoke.

"The same place, the same people, the same time, the same trouble."

"Clear as ditch water," he said.

"They wanted it to make sense to you, and nobody else," she told him, opening her eyes. "What were the first things that came into your head?"

"Munngralla's curio shop," he said without hesitation. "The Quincunx. Midnight. And my . . ." The silence stretched out too long.

"Your what?"

"I was about to say 'my sister,' but they couldn't mean that. There's no way they could have known. So it's probably intended to mean a killing."

"There you have it," she said. "A warning—or a summons."

"A summons, I think," said Ari. He tapped the pips on the dice with one blunt fingertip. "Five dots . . . Five Points Imports. The rest of it doesn't matter, since they couldn't count on me finding an Adept to read the patterns."

"Then take the warning as a gift," she said. "Now that you know there's danger, are you still going in?"

"I don't see that I have a choice."

"There's always a choice," she said. "But I promised I wasn't going to talk philosophy. Do you want a backup?"

"No thanks," he said. He scooped the pair of dice off the tabletop and put them into his shirt pocket. "Helping me out before almost got you and Jessan killed. If trouble's looking for me again, this time I'm the only one it's going to get."

VI. Pleyver: High Station
Nammerin: Namport; Central Wetlands

HREE DAYS after his arrival at High Station, Commander Gil shoved his chair back against the office wall and looked at the blank screen of his desk comp in disgust. Only a polite regard for the tender sensibilities of the clerk/comptech the station had assigned to him as a runner, secretary, and clerk kept him from tearing his hair out in handfuls.

But I'm seriously tempted, he thought. *Everything I check comes up zeroes—and the General isn't likely to take 'Sir, I haven't the faintest idea' as an acceptable report.*

Gil sighed. "All right. Let's take it again from the top."

"Bringing up the timetable now, sir," said the clerk-comptech, and Gil watched the familiar data moving in a slow scroll up the screen of the desk comp.

Item: two strangers enter clinic. Time approximately 2200.

Item: Flatlands power grid goes down in the Ilx-3 sector. Time 2209.27.

Item: Certainly a dozen, possibly as many as a hundred, unknowns attack the clinic from at least two directions at once. Time approximately 2215.

"Stop," said Gil.

The scrolling halted, and Gil exhaled wearily. "Before we go any farther, let's take another look at that pair of mysterious strangers."

"Datadisk two," said the clerk, feeding the slice of plastic into the comp. "Classified files from Space Force Intelligence; unsworn statements of Clerk/Comptech Second Class Peyte, Portmaster Sharveelt, and Dock Complex Loading Boss Bevan Cemliah; supporting data from Far Station Pleyver and Embrig Security on Mandeyn."

"And a whole lot of good it does us," finished Gil, as the first file came up: text on one side of the screen, and on the other a blurred image lifted from one of the port complex's security cameras. The grainy flatpic showed a young man caught in the act of looking back over one shoulder at something behind him, giving a good angle on the eye patch, the long queued-back hair, and the immaculate ruffled shirt that—if CC2 Peyte's observations could be trusted—was shortly to be soaked with blood.

"Tarnekep Portree," said Gil. "Captain, *Pride of Mandeyn*. By all accounts at least as vicious as he looks. Rumored to work as a hired killer more or less for the fun of it. But no hard facts or even solid gossip; only thing the Central Criminal Data Net could turn up was a 'Wanted for Questioning' from Mandeyn, about eight Standard months back. Somebody shot a gambler's face off, and Embrig Security's mildly curious about it. And that, my friend, is it for Captain Portree: possibly one of the galaxy's major hard cases, possibly not. Next file."

Another flatpic from port security filled the screen. This time the picture showed a slight, grey-haired man whose face reminded Gil of his old mathematics instructor.

"Gunner/copilot on *Pride of Mandeyn*. Called 'Professor,' which isn't surprising. No record on him anywhere at all, which is."

"Maybe the 'Professor' identity is a new one, sir," suggested the clerk.

"I'll buy that," said Gil. "Not that it gets us any further at the moment . . . next file."

The statement of Portmaster Sharveelt began its progress up the comp screen: arrival time and crew list for the *Libra*-class freighter *Pride of Mandeyn*, Tarnekep Portree commanding; information—backed up by the Port Accounting Office—that the *Pride* had paid, in cash, High Station's docking fee for a three-day stay . . . "didn't bitch about it either, the way most of those independents do"; further information that six hours and forty-nine minutes later the *Pride* had left High Station without filing a movement report or asking for a refund . . . "and I've seen independents forget to file before, but this is the first time I've ever seen one leave early without screaming for his money back."

Gil leaned forward. "Put the next bit on audio—there's some stuff I want to hear again."

"Switching to audio playback, sir," said the clerk, and Gil heard his own voice coming out of the desk comp's on-board speaker:

"Do you recall anything else unusual about that evening, Portmaster Sharveelt?"

"No, not really, Commander. Things were pretty tame down at our end. Didn't even have any of the dirtside commercial shuttles coming up. We usually get four a night from Flatlands, but that night we didn't get anything at all between the twenty-one-thirty and the zero-eight-hundred."

"Does that sort of thing happen often?"

"Not at all. Maybe the bosses dirtside are crooked, but the shuttle operators are real spacers. I've been here since High Station was nothing but an orbital platform, and they've had maybe one or two flights canceled in an av-

erage month—a few more during the spring storms. But three shuttles in one night—no, never.''

Gil signaled to stop the audio. "This job is turning my brains to sludge. I should have caught that part the first time. Make a new entry in the timetable file: 'Twenty-one-thirty to zero-eight-hundred, commercial shuttles removed from service.' ''

He leaned back, smiling for the first time in several hours. "I think we're finally starting to get a handle on this thing. Is there any cha'a around the office?''

"No, sir, but Requisition Processing, down the hall, has a galley urn set up. If you like, I could—''

"Fetch some? Please do. I can handle the comp while you're gone, no trouble.''

The clerk headed out the door. Gil dragged his chair back up to the keyboard and punched up the next file: the unsworn statement of Dock Complex Loading Boss Cemliah, who'd been overseeing a post-off-load inspection at dock #237 when the *Pride* lifted from #238. Gil toggled on the audio playback and let the loading boss's hoarse tones fill the little office.

"I saw three men come onto the dock, walking fast, just before she lifted. . . . They all looked kind of rocky, if you ask me. The one with the eye patch had blood all over him and was limping pretty bad, and the old guy had his arm in a sling. . . . Yeah, one of 'em was a tall man in a Space Force uniform—nah, I couldn't tell you his rank. . . . How the hell am I supposed to know if he was going along willingly? He wasn't screaming and kicking, if that's what you want to know. I got a job to do, Commander—I can't check out everything funny-looking that goes down between here and the storage bays.''

Cemliah had been an unpleasant sort, Gil reflected, but at least the loading boss's statement had cleared up the mystery of Lieutenant Commander Jessan's disappearance. Wherever the Khesatan medic was at the moment, he'd left High Station on board *Pride of Mandeyn*.

The *Pride* herself could be any place in the galaxy by now. She'd gone into hyperspace just beyond Far Station,

the manned beacon platform that marked the outer edge
of the Web and Pleyver's closest jump point. Far's time-
tick, correlated with departure information from the High
Station docks, gave the *Libra*-class freighter's time for the
Web run as six hours and twenty-one minutes.

Commander Gil wondered briefly what the General would
have to say when he read that bit. Depending on which of
Metadi's stories you chose to believe, Tarnekep Portree had
managed to trim the former privateer's unofficial record by
anywhere from nine minutes to half an hour.

That was hot piloting, any way you looked at it, hot and
more than a little desperate. Gil remembered the General,
in the office on Galcen: "Somebody dirtside whistled up a
squad of Security fighters to chase us all the way to hyper."

"Somebody dirtside," said Gil aloud, as the door slid
open and closed again behind the clerk and a hotpot of cha'a.
"Sir?"

"We've been taking this from the wrong end all along. Pack
a spare set of skivvies—we're going down to Flatlands."

Ari left the hospital aircar in a lot on the outskirts of
Namport and went on foot to the seedy district where
G. Munngralla had kept his shop. With RSF *Corisydron*
back in Nammerin orbit for the weekend, and the Strip
full of liberty parties bent on fun and mayhem, he had no
desire to emphasize his connection with the Space Force
presence on-planet.

To the same end, before leaving base, he'd traded his
uniform for a free-spacer's outfit of shirt, trousers, and
boots. And if anybody who saw him was going to remember a Selvaur-sized human packing a heavy blaster, and
never mind what clothes he was wearing—well, they'd have
to spot him first. Llannat Hyfid might have been able to
pick him out as he moved from shadow to shadow, but
nobody else in Namport tonight was likely to have her
combination of an Adept's talent and an upbringing on the
sparsely settled world of Maraghai.

Ari had been fostered on Maraghai himself, and when

Ferrdacorr son of Rrillikkik swore to raise a friend's son like his own, the Selvaur did exactly that. By the time Ari left for the Academy, he'd made his Long Hunt in the high-country ridges with the rest of his agemates, and could move through underbrush with no more noise than a passing thought. When he reached the vacant lot where Five Points Imports had stood, he knew that he hadn't been followed.

In the months since explosion and fire had gutted Munngralla's shop, plume-grass and creeper vines had moved in and taken over the rubble-filled lot. Ari leaned against the brick wall of the building next door, letting its shadow hide him while he watched the grass stalks nodding in the warm, humid breeze. One patch of grass dipped its feathery blossoms against the wind; he marked the position and kept on waiting.

When a quarter-hour's vigil brought nobody else to the lot, Ari decided that the rendezvous might not be a trap after all. Just the same, he pulled his father's blaster from its holster before he spoke.

"Over here."

"Doc?"

"Over here," he said again, and watched the grass bend and rise as the other made his way across the lot by way of the weed-covered perimeter.

The little man emerged from the overgrowth at Ari's elbow. "You the big medic?"

"Look at me," said Ari. "Take a good guess. Is there a message?"

"You got a pair of dice?"

"Yes."

"Give them to me."

Ari dropped the dice into the other man's palm. "Here you are. What's the word?"

The little spacer pocketed the dice. "Two parts. First thing—from now on out, you're a member of the Brotherhood. Munngralla stood sponsor for you, because you helped him when he needed it."

"Thanks," said Ari.

I think, he added to himself. He wasn't sure what his superiors in the Medical Service would say if they found out one of their junior officers was a member of the galaxy's biggest criminal guild—but he didn't for a moment suppose he'd like to read their comments in his fitness report.

His father the General, on the other hand, was certain to find the whole idea hilarious.

"You mentioned two things," said Ari. "What's the second?"

"A warning," said the little man. "Our friends in the profession say that someone's put out a contract on you."

First poison, then a Magelord, and now a hired assassin, thought Ari. *What did I do to deserve all this?* "Do you know who they're getting for the job?"

The little man shrugged. "Someone named Portree—a Mandeynan with an eye patch. We didn't hear anything more. If you need to, though, you can call on the Brotherhood for help."

"How?"

"You know how to find the five-spot already," said the spacer. "Tell them you've traveled a long way for the sake of a proper word. That should get you whatever you need."

"Thanks," said Ari again.

"Live well," said the other, and vanished back into the shadows.

Ari was in the CO's office first thing the next morning, so early that the commanding officer's pet sand snake still dozed on its bed of heat-bricks in front of the office safe. At Ari's footstep on the threshold, it uncoiled a foot or so of its mottled length and raised its head to give him an unblinking amber stare.

"Just me," said Ari, smiling as the heavy wedge-shaped head subsided onto the bricks. He and the sand snake were old acquaintances by now. In another moment the CO emerged from the inner office, a steaming mug in one hand and the first of the day's message printouts in the other.

"Ah, Rosselin-Metadi. What brings you in here so early?"

"Something I found out last night, sir. I think you ought to know about it."

The CO added the printouts to the snowdrift of flimsies already covering his desk. "Something you found out," he said. "And what's that?"

"Well," said Ari, choosing his words carefully. "You remember the people who helped us with the Rogan's epidemic?"

The CO nodded. "I remember them—with gratitude, I might add. The latest word from Supply is that we might see the first shipment of tholovine sometime next month."

"Next month," Ari said. "Does Supply live in the same galaxy as the rest of us, sir?"

"They claim to," said the CO. "But I've heard otherwise. Anyhow, Rosselin-Metadi—what do you hear from your friends?"

"They say I've got a contract out on me."

"I see," said the CO, after a second or so of silence. "Did they happen to say why?"

"Because I make such a damned good target, I guess. . . . No sir, no reason."

The CO looked sympathetic. "Is there anything you want me to do about it?"

"No, sir. I didn't get anything solid. Only the warning."

"Well, write up what you heard, and leave it on my desk when you're finished. That way, if anything does happen to you, we'll have a place to start."

"No problem."

"Good," said the CO, nudging the sand snake with the toe of his boot. The snake uncoiled and flowed off in the direction of the inner office. "Another thing, Rosselin-Metadi."

"Yes, sir?"

"That blaster of yours—I don't care if it does make you look like Black Brok the Terror of the Spaceways. As of right now, you wear it wherever you go."

After getting his warning from the Quincunx, Ari spent the next two weeks looking over his shoulder and jumping at shadows. Nothing out of the ordinary happened, though, and eventually things like staying away from windows and not turning his back on the door became everyday behavior for him, the way the heavy blaster and its holster became just another part of his uniform.

He was in the Pharmacy dome one afternoon, finishing up the monthly controlled-substances inventory, when the wall comm link sounded his tone sequence.

"Rosselin-Metadi here."

"Hey, Ari—this is Dispatching. We just got one from a farmer out in the boonies. Looks like a house call."

"Why me? I'm not on for another two days."

Dispatching sounded amused. "He says he's got a delirious Selvaur on his hands. And since we haven't got a squad of commandos and a professional interpreter—"

"You decided to send me instead."

"Hey, 'only the best for those we serve,' right?"

"Right," said Ari, sighing. " 'Spaceways and away,' then."

He closed up the controlled-substances locker and headed for the station's hangar bay, stopping in at Weather for the current report ("light rain, chance of fog") and at Control for the coordinates of the farm.

"It's off at zero-two-zero-five-five-one-zero-zero on the other side of the Divide," said the comptech on duty. "That's going to be right on the sunset line by the time you get there, and pure hell to come back from if it's a bad case."

"I'm betting it's fungoid fever," said Ari. "We've seen a couple of cases the past week or so, and it drives the Selvaurs right out of their skulls."

He went on out to the aircar and gave it a quick walk-around. When he came back to his starting point, he saw that he wasn't alone any longer. Llannat Hyfid leaned against the cockpit door, dressed in her usual off-duty clothes—a plain black coverall, with the Adept's staff slung across her shoulders by its leather thong.

"I didn't know you were on call," he said.

"I'm not for a couple of days. But you're in for a long trip, and I thought I'd see if you wanted company."

"I could use the relief pilot," he admitted. "Especially if I end up bringing a delirious Selvaur back to base after dark. Did you let anyone know you were coming?"

"You can call it in once we're on our way," she said. "But let's get going—you don't want to lose any time."

"Another one of your feelings?" he asked, opening the door and climbing into the pilot's seat.

Llannat followed. She laid the staff down on the aircar floor and began strapped in for takeoff. "Something like that," she said.

The trip out wasn't bad at all. The mountains east of Namport loomed a dark green under the mist, and the grey clouds had thinned enough to allow some watery sunshine to light up the peaks. Once the aircar crossed over the Divider Range, the big water-grain farms of the central wetlands spread out from horizon to horizon in regular squares of pale yellow-green, latticed with silvery drainage canals and blotched with stands of massive, soil-holding *grrch* trees.

In the copilot's seat next to Ari, Llannat sat without talking. She had a knack of making her silence seem restful, and he wondered if it came from her Adept's training. Or maybe it was part of the basic model, like dark eyes and a kind heart, or long black hair that always had a few shorter strands curling loose from its regulation up-off-the-collar style.

Right now, she sat with her eyes closed and her hands lightly clasped in her lap—meditating, or perhaps just catching up on some sleep. Ari smiled in her general direction, and let the physical pleasure he always got from flying mix with the calm of her presence, putting him more at peace with himself than he'd felt in weeks.

The aircar droned on toward 02055100. The sun was falling down the sky behind them as they approached the landing zone. The control panel beeped, and a readout started blinking.

"There's the beacon," said Llannat, opening her eyes

and coming back to the here-and-now so smoothly Ari decided she hadn't been sleeping after all.

"Right," he said. "Let's go in."

The farm's landing pad was one of the raised concrete strips common out here in the wetlands. Once the aircar had settled to rest inside the markers, Ari powered down the engines and squinted out of the cockpit window at the empty landscape.

"Talk about the back of beyond," he said. "I thought the upcountry settlements were bad, but at least they usually send out a welcoming committee whenever Medical shows up in town."

Llannat bent to retrieve the emergency carry pack from its place behind the copilot's seat, and began giving the contents a quick checkover. "This looks like one of those big machine-worked operations. The farmer's probably with his partner."

"How are we supposed to find them?" grumbled Ari. "A dowsing rod?"

"Go that way," said Llannat, without lifting her eyes from the kit. She pointed toward the eastern horizon.

Ari followed the line of her gesture to where the ridge of a steep-pitched tile roof showed over the green of the sprouting grain paddies. He looked back at the Adept. Her head was still bent over the open kit, and he could hear her counting ampules of medication under her breath.

"All right," he said. "That way it is. The kit okay?"

"Just fine."

They left the aircar—Ari with the carry pack, and Llannat with her staff—and climbed down a rusting metal ladder to the surface. Ari promptly sank three inches into the mud. He pulled one boot free of the black ooze with a heavy sucking noise, and Llannat giggled.

Ari made a face. "Visit scenic Nammerin, where it rains twelve days out of every eleven. Come on, let's get slogging."

They started out along the raised earthen track between the water-grain paddies. The *slup-slupp* of their boots in the thick mud sounded loud against the late-afternoon stillness.

Ari heard the far-off rumble of farm machinery, and nearby in one of the grain paddies a drum-lizard throated out its deep, resonant *chunkachunk, chunkachunk*. Nothing else besides their footsteps disturbed the quiet at all.

Their shadows stretched out ahead of them as they approached the house, a deep-eaved stone building in a paved yard. "The place looks deserted," said Ari.

"The farmer's inside," said Llannat. "I can sense it." Her voice sounded strained. Ari wondered if the uncanny lack of noise and activity made her as uneasy as it was making him.

"I hope I was right about this being fungoid fever," he said. "If I was wrong and it's a psycho case, who knows what we'll find."

Llannat nodded without speaking, and unslung her staff.

Ari shifted the emergency kit to his left hand and drew the blaster from its holster. The door of the stone house was a hinged job of cured *grrch* wood—hard as iron, and almost as heavy. Ari pounded on the dull black wood with the butt of his blaster until the whole yard echoed, but no one answered.

"Try the knob," said Llannat.

Ari glanced over at the Adept. Her dark face had a tight, unhappy look to it, and her knuckles were bloodless on the hand that gripped her staff.

"You have a hand free," he said. "You try it."

He watched, blaster at the ready, as she worked the knob with her left hand, and gave the door a shove. It swung open.

They waited in tense silence for a few seconds. Nothing came out through the door—and as far as Ari could see or hear, nothing moved inside.

VII. Nammerin: Central Wetlands
Galcen: Prime Base

T HEY ENTERED the farmhouse together. Llannat kept behind him and to the right, Ari noticed, well out of the way of his blaster and with plenty of
maneuvering room for two-handed work with a staff.

Ari blinked in the dimness, and the vague interior shapes
resolved into typical farmhouse furnishings: a table and
benches made out of rough-hewn wood, a red brick floor
covered by a rug braided from dried water-grain stalks.
Cheap flatpix and a Nammerin Grain Cooperative Stan-
dard/Local Integrated Calendar made spots of color on the
drab stone walls.

But still no noise. None at all.

Llannat's left hand closed on his right wrist. "Ari," she
said, her voice hardly more than a whisper, "there's somebody behind us."

He tried to turn and bring the blaster to bear, but the
hand on his wrist suddenly had more than physical strength
behind it. His brother Owen had thrown him against a wall
the first and only time they'd ever fought, when Ari had

reached almost his full adult strength and his brother had
been all of fifteen. Ari didn't doubt that Llannat Hyfid
could do something similar if she chose.

"Ari, no," she said. "He's had a blaster on us since
we came in the door."

"Quite true, Mistress," said a voice behind them. "And
very wise."

The language was Galcenian, but the accept was not.
Court Entiboran? Ari thought incredulously as the speaker
continued.

"Please put up the blaster, Lieutenant—and the staff,
too, Mistress—and walk into the next room. There's
somebody there who wishes to talk with you."

Ari and Llannat walked ahead of the unseen speaker,
going through the large common room to the door of a
small tacked-on annex that housed the farm's comm set
and power generator. A red-faced, heavyset farmer sat at
the far end of the room, near the comm. To Ari, he didn't
look much like a man worried to distraction over a sick
partner.

*Come on, Rosselin-Metadi. You quit believing in that
delirious Selvaur all the way back out in the courtyard.*

"So they got you," said the farmer, sounding more disgusted than anything else.

They? thought Ari, and realized for the first time that
the farmer wasn't the only person in the room. A slim,
fair-haired man in spacer's work clothes leaned against the
right-hand wall, his blaster trained on the farmer. The man
had his face turned away—the better, Ari supposed, to
keep an eye on his prisoner—but something about that lean
build and careless posture nagged for recognition.

Ari made a low growling noise deep in his throat, a
noise that Ferrdacorr would have recognized as a thoroughly obscene comment on the whole situation. At the
sound, the fair-haired man half-turned toward the door.

"I don't believe," he said, smiling, "that I really want
to know what that means."

"You're supposed to be missing in action," Ari said

before he thought, and then realized how stupid it sounded. *Death and damnation, Rosselin-Metadi—couldn't you come up with anything better than that?*

"I don't quite know how to tell you this," said Jessan, "but as of now, so are you."

Ari doubled his right hand into a fist. "Jessan, if this is some kind of joke—"

The Khesatan medic shook his head. "We don't have time for jokes. Captain Portree is waiting."

Ari looked at Jessan's bland and guileless face, and felt a chill run down his spine. *"Someone's put out a contract on you,"* the Quincunx man had said.

No. I'm not going to believe that the friend who helped me get out of that fight at Munngralla's is working with someone who's been hired to kill me. There has to be another answer.

His fist unclenched, slowly. "All right," he said. "Let's go."

Next to him, he heard Llannat let out her breath in what sounded like a sigh of relief. Jessan looked past them both, directing a silent question toward the stranger they still hadn't seen. After a second the Khesatan nodded, and turned back toward the farmer.

"I really do apologize for all this," he said, and fired.

Ari watched, wordless, as the farmer crumpled over and slid out of his chair onto the floor. Jessan stepped carefully around the man's unconscious body to the comm set.

Behind Ari, the soft Entiboran voice spoke again. "You would have done better to use heavy stun. Once he recovers, he will undoubtedly report our presence on-planet."

Jessan had the access plate open now, and was groping inside the unit. "I don't exactly worship every dot and comma in the healer's oath," he said without looking around, "but I did swear to it, after all. And that farmer's a textbook example of a candidate for stun-shock syndrome: overworked, overweight, and not as young as he used to be."

The Khesatan medic came back out of the comm unit

with the resonator in one hand. "I'm sorry, Professor, but I'm not risking it. I don't want to get into an argument I'm probably going to lose, but there it is."

"I won't ask you to break an oath," said the stranger's voice. "But haste is now imperative. Lieutenant Rosselin-Metadi—Mistress—if you would precede us . . . ?"

Ari turned around, and got his first glimpse of the stranger as the slight, grey-haired gentleman stood aside to let them pass. The blaster the man still held trained on them looked, in the dim interior light, like a custom-modified Ogre Mark VI—a heavy weapon, and one Ari felt inclined to take seriously.

"Which way do we go once we're outside?" he asked.

"East," said the Entiboran. "Toward the trees."

"I'm afraid," added Jessan, coming forward from the rear of the room, "that it's going to be a bit of a hike."

Whatever else might have happened, Ari reflected, his friend's penchant for understatement hadn't changed. The setting sun made a blaze of scarlet at their backs by the time the four of them had slogged their way across a couple of grain paddies to the stand of towering *grrch* trees east of the farm. "Into the woods?" he asked.

"That's right," said Jessan. "It's not much farther."

Under the trees, a darkness like night already prevailed. Ari heard once again the farm machinery that he'd noticed from far off during the walk to the farmhouse. Now, though, he recognized the deep trembling in the air and in the earth underfoot as the noise of heavy-duty nullgravs, running on high.

Those things sound big enough to hold up a spaceship, he thought, and then remembered Jessan's words: *"Captain Portree is waiting."*

He wasn't surprised to break out of the woods into a clearing where the grey underbelly of a hovering space-craft hid all but a scrap of twilit sky. Below, everything was in black shadow where the ship's bulk blocked off the light. All he could see was an open passenger door and an extended ramp, its end several feet above the muddy ground.

Good move, he conceded, with a nod of respect to the unseen Captain Portree. *Anybody who tried to land here would sink.*

Jessan grabbed the ramp and scrambled aboard. Ari turned to Llannat. " 'A long trip,' " he quoted. "I ought to have known right then. . . . Do you need a hand up?"

The Adept shook her head. "I'm all right." She leaped, and stood looking down at him from end of the ramp. Ari shook his head. Catching the edge of the ramp in both hands, he swung himself up onto the strip of metal, then turned and, with a fatalistic shrug, extended a hand to the Professor. The grey-haired gentleman accepted his help with calm dignity, like an aristocrat being handed aboard his private yacht for a pleasure cruise.

"Please follow Lieutenant Commander Jessan forward while I close up for lift," said the older man. "We haven't a great deal of time to spare."

With Llannat once again keeping station slightly behind him and to his right, Ari followed Jessan along a narrow, curving corridor. The metal deckplates rang with the sound of their booted feet, and the note they struck had an oddly familiar resonance.

He looked again at the bulkhead panels. They only confirmed his growing suspicion. This was no brand-new craft, but one that carried the scars and stains of hard use. And he could name every scratch.

"Llannat," he said, low-voiced, "I know this ship."

She nodded. "I could tell. How much trouble are we in?"

"I wish I knew," he said, as they reached the common room. "Right now, I don't know what's going on."

As he spoke, the grey-haired gentleman hurried through the common room in the direction of the cockpit. "Strap in, all," said Jessan. "We're going to lift in a couple of minutes."

Ari found a seat on the acceleration couch and began

working the safety webbing with easy familiarity. Jessan and Llannat took longer; the Adept was still closing the last of the fasteners when she looked over at the Khesatan and said, "Isn't it about time you told us what's happening?"

"The captain will explain everything, I promise, just as soon as we get out of here. But let me tell you," Jessan finished with a quick grin, "you two got off easy compared to the way I was recruited."

"We heard about that," said Ari. "The rumors, that is."

"It was . . . interesting," said Jessan.

"I'll bet it was. What's the name of this ship?"

Jessan's grey eyes met his, wide-open and innocent. "She's the Free Trader *Pride of Mandeyn*, Suivi registry."

"Her real name, Jessan!"

The blond medic shook his head. "I think I ought to let the captain tell you that."

"I'm looking forward to meeting this captain of yours," Ari growled.

The ship's internal comm system gave a premonitory crackle, and a tinny, distorted voice announced, "Stand by for lift-off."

The background thrum of the engines rose in a deafening crescendo, and Ari felt himself pressed back against the cushions by the steady pressure of the lift.

Beka Rosselin-Metadi looked over at her copilot as *Warhammer* left Nammerin's atmosphere behind. "How did it go, Professor?"

"As Lieutenant Commander Jessan predicted," said the Entiboran. "With one unfortunate exception. Your brother did not answer the call alone."

Beka shrugged. "Those are the breaks. What did you do with the extra?"

"She came with us, my lady."

She bit her lip. "Damn it, Professor—I wanted to keep this a family affair. I'd counted on Ari being able to square things on his end once he knew the score, but we're probably already in the data net for kidnapping Jessan. If we start making a habit of snatching Space Force medics, not even my father is going to be able to get us out of it."

"Understood, my lady."

Her copilot sounded almost apologetic. Beka sighed. "All right, Professor. What is it you aren't telling me?"

"Our passenger is an Adept, my lady."

"An Adept," said Beka. Her mouth felt sour. "Lovely. As if my brother Owen hadn't gotten us into enough trouble already. How the hell did an Adept get mixed up in all this?"

"What her relationship is to Lieutenant Rosselin-Metadi," said the Professor, "I do not know. But she appears to feel a commitment toward his personal safety, and I am not such a fool as to test the strength and mutuality of that commitment under pressure."

"So we've got Ari's girlfriend along for the ride," Beka said. "That should make for an interesting trip . . . oh, damn." The electronic detector panel had started blinking red. "Someone's scanning us."

She watched, chewing her lower lip, as ship's memory worked on a matchup for the scanner pattern. What came up wasn't good. "A Space Force cruiser—probably the same one we spotted on our way in. What's the odds he'll let us pass without asking awkward questions?"

"Not good, I'm afraid," said the Professor. "He's dropping off fighters."

"I see them," said Beka, as the external comm began to scratch and crackle with the sound of a local broad-frequency signal. "Sounds like they want to talk a bit first, though."

"Freighter lifting from Nammerin," crackled the comm link, "this is RSF *Corisydron*. Come to neutral power and zero your guns, over."

Beka looked over at her copilot and raised one eyebrow. The Professor shook his head. She nodded, and turned her attention back to the control panel. Sensors showed that the cruiser had dropped off a total of six fighter craft, and was now accelerating on a matching course with *Warhammer*.

"Unknown freighter, unknown freighter, heave to. Stand by to be boarded, over."

She had *Corisydron* on visual now, a bright blob of light getting bigger every second. At any moment, the blob would resolve into the long, deadly triangle of a ship-of-war. She couldn't see the much smaller fighter craft yet, but the sensors could pick them up just fine, coming in three up top and three below. *Somebody's taking us real seriously.*

"Professor, time to man the guns."

"On my way," said *Warhammer*'s gunner/copilot, and left the cockpit at a run.

"Unknown freighter, unknown freighter. This is your final warning. Cut power. Over."

Blue fire lanced through space across *Warhammer*'s bow.

"Shields, full," Beka whispered to herself, and suited the action to the word. Then, over the internal link to the guns, "Professor, are you there?"

"In place, my lady."

"Under the circumstances, let's make it 'Captain,' " she said. "Listen, now. I have all the guns ganged to your panel. I don't want you to hit anyone—just scare the pants off them. Got that?"

"Understood, Captain."

"On my signal, then."

The external comm crackled again. "Unknown freighter, unknown freighter, have your personnel move forward. I am about to destroy your engines."

"Like bloody hell you're going to destroy my engines," muttered Beka. She grabbed the external comm. "RSF *Corisydron*, be advised that on my ship *I* tell my people where to stand!"

She shoved *Warhammer*'s throttle to full forward and cut hard right.

"Professor—now!"

* * *

Commander Gil had seen worse days than this one, his first back at Prime Base on Galcen, but not lately. He'd gotten in from Pleyver at the end of the base's regular working day, and Metadi had been waiting for him.

"Well, Commander?" the General had asked.

"I've got everything from Pleyver, sir," said Gil. "But I'm still waiting for a couple of reports from Intelligence."

Which was true, as far as it went. What rankled was that after two weeks he didn't have any firm conclusions to report.

Except that the clinic's a pile of rubble, which we knew; and Lieutenant Commander Jessan is missing, which we also knew; and the dirtside establishment on Pleyver is in this up to their fat necks, which might surprise some people but I don't think a moderately reformed ex-privateer is going to be one of them.

"Don't look for miracles from Intelligence," said the General. "You're not likely to see any. I'll read your report tomorrow—maybe something will have turned up by then."

With that, the General had departed for his aircar and the roomy, sprawling house in the northern uplands where he lived alone these days; and Commander Gil had headed—by way of a shower, a shave, and a change of uniform in lieu of a meal—for his own smaller office and an all-night job of writing.

He poured himself a cup of cold cha'a from the office urn and carried it over to his desk. The stack of datadisks and printout flimsies hadn't vanished while he was away. Draining the cup and setting it aside, he laid out his notes on his desk and began shuffling them. He was still shuffling when the office comm link buzzed.

"Commanding General's Office, Commander Gil speaking; this is not a secure line; may I help you?" he recited, his mind still on the slips of paper with their scribbled jottings.

''Is the General there? He's needed in Command Control at once.''

''Sorry. He's on his way home. I'll patch you through to his aircar.''

Gil punched the button to complete the connection, then stood and stretched. *He'll expect me at CC when he gets there, so I might as well go now and find out what's up.*

Command Control, when Gil arrived, looked the same as always—dim red lights, winking comp displays, and hushed activity—but he hadn't felt so much tension in the air since the time a spaceliner had suffered explosive decompression on its jump-run off Peygatai. Rescue efforts on that one had been a bitch; if the trouble now was even half as bad, this was going to be one of the nights when the Space Force earned its pay.

That's interesting, he thought, as the big holodisplay monitor in the center of Command Control winked into life. *They're lighting up the main battle tank.* That particular display meant only one thing: somebody out there in the civilized galaxy was doing some shooting, and the Space Force was planning to shoot back.

A comptech worked at one of the tank terminals, keying in a yellow sun and a ten-planet system. In the tank, the fourth planet out began to blink. That would be where the action was. Gil looked at the nearest comp for information.

The readout identified the blinking planet as Nammerin. *Where have I heard of that place recently?* Gil wondered, before remembering that Nammerin had been the missing Lieutenant Commander Jessan's last duty station before Pleyver. Close by the planet, a tiny blue triangle and a swarm of blue dots marked RSF *Corisydron* and six of her fighter craft. The lone red dot in the swarm would be the unknown/hostile vessel.

At the watch officer's command, the display in the battle tank enlarged to show only Nammerin and its moons, instead of the entire star system. Gil saw that the *Cory* was using the classic setup for blocking a jump to hyper. Right now, the *Cory*'s fighters were swarming the unknown, trying to prevent the hostile ship from maneuvering. Meanwhile the *Cory* herself would sit on the unknown's projected jump point, and let the fighters keep the hostile craft from finding another point for as long as it took to disable her.

The tactic worked most of the time, but not always. As Gil watched the battle tank, now being updated in real time by datalink from the cruiser, he saw the unknown moving ahead faster than the *Cory*'s fighters.

He pursed his lips in a soundless whistle. *Whoever that guy is, he must have hell's own power plant.*

"*Corisydron* reports her fighters under fire," announced the duty comm tech.

"Roger. Pass to *Corisydron*, Condition Red, Weapons Free," called the watch officer.

Gil strode over to the log comp to catch up on what had led to this point. Scanning the entries, he saw that the *Cory*, responding to a planetside distress call relayed through the Space Force Medical Station, had reported an unknown contact.

What's this? Probable kidnapping of two Space Force officers by the unknown . . . Mistress Llannat Hyfid and Lieutenant Ari Rosselin-Metadi. Damn. Not again.

So far, Commander Gil had been enjoying the situation more than not. As the General himself had said during the spaceliner mess, somebody who couldn't appreciate a good disaster had no business being in their line of work. Now, though, the nervous, adrenaline-rush excitement went out of him like air out of a punctured balloon.

He advanced the log screen. First contact—*Libra*-class freighter, not responding to signals. A shot across the freighter's bow. Then, at the point where Gil had walked in, the fighters' return fire and her increase in speed.

Gil stared at the comp screen. Out of the corner of his eye, he could see the blue lights blocking and surrounding the red one in the main battle tank, as the red dot side-slipped out of yet another of the fighters' trapping patterns.

A Libra-*class freighter. Same as* Warhammer. *Same as* Pride of Mandeyn. *Those ships haven't been made for almost a hundred years; and now I've run into three of them. And each one faster than the stats allow.*

A cold sensation started in the pit of Gil's stomach, and began spreading outward. The commander was hearing a voice in his mind—General Metadi's voice, speaking to Master Errec Ransome on a spring night eight months or more ago: *"I had Sunrise Shipyards rip out the old engines and put in the big Hyper King Extras."*

A second later, the comptech working the battle-tank terminal let out a yell. "We hit him!"

BEKA LOOKED ahead out of *Warhammer*'s cockpit window. The big cruiser was still hanging there, just this side of the *'Hammer*'s jump point on her current course. At least the shields were holding. So far, the fighters hadn't been able to close the range.

Time to figure a new jump, Beka told herself. *Try for a point barely astern of him. That's hardest for him to move to cover, and my course change'll be so small he might not detect it right away.*

She heard a hammering sound on the *Warhammer*'s starboard quarter. On the control panel, a warning light flashed to life.

"Damn," she said, under her breath. One of the fighters had scored a hit, in spite of the really spectacular light show the Professor was putting on. "Another good idea shot to hell."

She reversed thrust to put the *Warhammer* into a sudden slowdown. All six of the fighters sped past, jets glowing. Beka brought the *Warhammer* back to full forward, throwing in some up vector to keep the fighters bunched on the *'Hammer*'s ventral side. That way, they'd foul their own ranges, and have to waste time and power in avoiding collisions.

Besides, this wasn't the way the drill was supposed to go—maybe the pilots would outrun their own training. Her father always said that most fighter pilots were crazy kids still young enough to think they were immortal. The Republic hadn't seen any serious fighting since the Magewar; none of these pilots were likely to be combat veterans.

Not that I'm a combat veteran either, Beka reminded herself, *but I've heard all of Dadda's stories. Twice.*

Ahead of her, *Corisydron* moved to block the new jump point.

Son of a bitch figures the jump faster than I do. I'm going to have to get a computer upgrade next chance I get.

She caught herself estimating just how far back a comp system fast enough to outthink a cruiser would set *Warhammer*'s numbered account on Suivi Point, and began to laugh. *Later, girl, later.*

Now the fighters were coming in again, grouped in two wedges. One fighter began to falter and slow, and a trail of reflected sunlight started forming behind the limping craft—the sloughed-off lining of its jets, condensing in space's endless cold.

He's down hard with engine problems, she thought. *Only five to go—and I can't shoot them. Or I'll never be able to go home again.*

She put *Warhammer* onto a new course for yet another jump point beyond and astern of the cruiser. Closer and closer she ran, until finally the huge vessel began to turn—but away from *Warhammer*, not toward her.

Beka frowned. *What's this?*

Still frowning, she began the final tick-down for the run to jump. The cruiser finished its long, looping turn, and began accelerating again on a convergent course. The fighters continued to swarm on *Warhammer*'s ventral side, firing but doing no real damage at the longer range with their light weapons.

She checked the sensor readouts. Not only had *Corisydron* paralleled *Warhammer*'s course; the Space Force vessel had also matched speeds with the freighter. *Good thing we're inside the minimum range of his guns—and the fighters don't dare shoot us for fear of hitting him.*

But he's so close, his field is interfering with my jump. I can't jump with him so near, I can't turn without colliding with the little guys—time to see who's the fastest.

She pushed the throttle lever forward again.

Suddenly, warning lights blazed on all over the panel. Alarms began hooting and beeping. *Warhammer*'s controls vibrated under her hands, and she could feel the whole frame of the spacecraft starting to buck and tremble around her.

"Damn," she said aloud, over the rising howl of the freighter's oversized engines. "The bastard's got a tractor beam on me."

"He's maneuvering again," said the comptech at the tank terminal. "And he's fast."

Gil walked over to the watch officer. "Has he hit us?"

"Not yet."

Gil took a deep breath. "All right," he said to the watch officer. "I am ready to relieve you."

The watch officer stared. "What do you mean? This is *my* watch!"

Gil met the other man's incredulous gaze. The maneuvers in the main tank were shaping up as the nicest little space battle Command Control had seen in years—in the watch officer's shoes, Gil wouldn't have wanted to let go of it, either. *So here I am, about to cycle a perfectly good career out the airlock. Life's a bitch.*

He pushed down the urge to leave the whole thing in the watch officer's eager hands and asked, instead, "Commander, what's your lineal number?"

"Seven eight seven two, zero zero two three," replied the watch officer, in something close to a snarl.

"My number is seven eight seven two, zero zero one six. I'm senior to you, and I'm taking the watch."

"I protest!"

"Fine. Send a letter to the Board." Gil raised his voice to carry into the farthest reaches of the space. "In Control, this is Commander Gil. I have the watch."

The man he'd relieved snapped "Log that!" at the duty comptech. Gil ignored them both and walked over to the battle comm—Space Force's highest-priority, highest-security communications system.

"Give me the comm."

The petty officer gave him the handset. Gil keyed it and waited for the double beep of the crypto synchronizing.

"*Corisydron*, this is Space Force Control. Condition White, Weapons Tight. Break off at once, return to base. Acknowledge. Over."

"Dropped synch, over," a distorted, faraway voice replied.

Gil's lips tightened. The CO of the *Cory* wasn't any more eager to let go of this one than the watch officer here on Galcen had been. That "dropped synch" was a polite way of asking if the speaker on the other end still had all his synapses firing in order.

"This *is* Space Force Control," he repeated. "Break off at once. Return to base. Acknowledge. Over."

A long pause from the *Cory*, and then, "Will comply. Out."

Up in the main battle tank, the blue triangle and the smaller blue pips peeled away from the unknown. The red dot sped on, holding a straight-line accelerating course, then flickered out.

He's jumped.

Gil let out his breath in a long, shaky sigh. Behind him, he heard the *swoosh-snick* of the door sliding open and closing again, and then the General's unmistakable voice.

"Is somebody going to tell me just what's going on here?"

Gil turned to the officer he had summarily relieved. "You have the watch."

By now, the junior commander had choked himself nearly purple with suppressed rage. "Why, you—! Sir, he—!"

The General cut him off with a gesture, and kept his eyes fixed on Gil. "I suppose you have an explanation for all this."

"Yes, sir," said Gil.

Metadi's voice was quiet, almost gentle. "Would you like to share it with us, Commander?"

Gil finally found his own voice. "Perhaps we'd better go into your office, first. . . ."

With the dazzle of the jump still hanging before her eyes, Beka punched in a hyperspace course for the safe haven of the Professor's asteroid base, then leaned back in the pilot's seat with a sigh.

Time to go aft and straighten things out with Ari, she thought.

But her knees didn't want to hold her up, and what had started as a trembling in her fingers grew into a case of the shakes that went through her entire body.

You're amazing, she told herself. *A real classic. You can pilot anything with engines, you can hold your own in a knife fight against a man three times your size—and the very thought of walking up to your brother and saying "Hi there, I'm alive" takes all the strength out of your knees.*

She put her hands over her face—Tarnekep Portree's face, with the queued-back hair and the red plastic eye patch—and kept them there until the shaking stopped. Then she took a deep breath, wrapped Tarnekep's arrogance around her like a protective cloak, and got to her feet.

"All right, big brother," she said softly, settling Tarnekep's knife in its sheath and Tarnekep's blaster in its holster, "here I come."

* *-*

In *Warhammer*'s common room, Nyls Jessan felt the fleeting wave of disorientation as the freighter jumped into hyperspace, and let himself relax.

"Maybe I should have used heavy stun, after all," he said as he undid the safety webbing. "Oh, well—I suppose even being an interplanetary desperado takes practice."

Ari gave him a dark look. "Next time you drag me away from work to watch a space battle, Jessan, I expect better seats."

"I'll try to oblige," he said. "Ari, there's something you ought to know before—"

"No," said Ari. "I want to hear this Captain Portree of yours explain it to me himself."

Jessan flinched. *This is a fine time to remember that you've never seen the big guy get really angry . . . and Ari is not the sort of person who's likely to find Tarnekep Portree amusing. Not at all.*

He glanced over at Llannat. The Adept shook her head and gave a helpless shrug. The common-room door slid open.

Warhammer's captain stood on the threshold, surveying the three passengers with a disdainful, bicolored gaze.

Ari rose to his feet. In the cramped space of the '*Hammer*'s common room, he looked gigantic, and Jessan realized with a sinking feeling that for once the big medic was making absolutely no attempt to play down his size and strength.

He doesn't recognize her, thought Jessan unhappily. *Now there really will be hell to pay.*

"Captain Portree," Ari said, cold and carefully polite. "Or so I assume."

Beka favored her brother with a tight-lipped, crooked smile. "That's what they call me," she agreed.

She crossed her arms and leaned one shoulder against the bulkhead with an air of casual arrogance. "And I'd say you're that Lieutenant Rosselin-Metadi I keep hearing about.'' She shook her head. ''You really ought to be more careful about answering emergency comm calls.''

''In future,'' said Ari, ''I will be.'' The deep, even voice never altered—but Jessan could hear the anger in it just the same. ''How did you come into possession of this ship, Captain?''

Beka shrugged one shoulder. ''Let's say I bought her.''

Bloody-minded little bitch, thought Jessan, with a sense of despair. *Can't you see this isn't the time . . . ?*

''Let's say you didn't.'' Ari had taken a step forward. That much closer to Beka and the doorway, he looked even bigger. ''This isn't *Pride of Mandeyn*—we both know that, so there's no point in pretending. It's *Warhammer*, that was supposed to have crashed onto the Ice Flats outside Port Artat eight Standard months ago.''

He took another step closer to the doorway. ''What did you do to my sister, Captain Portree?''

This has gone far enough, Jessan thought. ''Ari,'' he said. ''Don't be too—''

Beka glanced in his direction for the first time. ''Stay out of this. It's between Lieutenant Rosselin-Metadi and me.''

Jessan swallowed, feeling a bit sick. *This is all my fault. She really did expect him to know her—after I figured out her secret, she must have been certain her own brother could do the same. But Ari just isn't flexible enough when it comes to looking at some things. . . .*

Beka had already turned back to her brother without waiting for a reply. ''Concerned about your sister, are you—Lieutenant Rosselin-Metadi?''

Ari clenched one hand into a massive fist. ''Portree, if you've hurt her—''

One corner of Beka's mouth quirked upward. ''Suppose I killed her? Than what, Lieutenant?''

''Then you're a dead man, Captain.''

The smile Beka gave her brother could have been either wistful or vicious. On Tarnekep Portree's face, Jessan had

to admit, the two would look the same anyway. She shook
her head, still smiling.

"For somebody so devoted to his sister, Ari, you're
damned unobservant. What happened—too much time in
the Space Force wipe out everything Ferrda taught you?"

Ari just stood looking at her.

Beka's half-smile twisted and turned nasty. "You're
supposed to be glad to see me, remember?—not acting
like I'm about as welcome as a plague of boils."

After a long moment Ari found his voice. "You've really outdone yourself this time, I have to admit that. Kidnapping, flying under false registration, firing on a Space
Force vessel in the lawful performance of its duties—
there's absolutely no way I'm going to be able to get you
out of this one."

Beka's lip curled. "I don't recall asking you to, big
brother."

"No," said Ari. His face was bone-white, and Jessan
realized unhappily that his friend was even angrier now
than he had been before. "Asking for help would mean
showing a bit of sense for a change. Tell me something,
would you—when you pull these crazy stunts of yours,
don't you ever, even once, think about what you might be
doing to the rest of us?"

Beka drew a sharp breath. If someone had shoved a
knife into her, Jessan thought, she might have made a
sound like that.

" 'The rest of us,' " she said, her lips pulling back
from her teeth in a snarl. "All *I* ever wanted from the rest
of you was to be left the hell alone—do you really want to
hear just how much luck I've had with that?"

Jessan stood up abruptly. "I've had about all of this that
I can stand. Ari—Beka—"

"Shut up, Jessan," said Ari, without bothering to look
around.

"Oh, yes," said Beka. "Mustn't have interruptions
while little sister is getting scolded."

Jessan looked from one pale and angry face to the other,

and wondered if brother and sister knew how much alike they looked right now. *Well, I wish them joy of it.*

"I'm going," he said. "Llannat?"

The Adept's dark face had gone the color of a dirty bedsheet, but she shook her head. *No,* said her voice, somewhere near the back of his skull. He jumped, and the voice continued. *Somebody has to stay and make sure nobody gets killed.*

"Better you than me," he murmured, and headed for the door. It opened to let him through, and shut after him on the sound of rising voices.

Jessan walked forward to the cockpit. He wasn't surprised to find the Professor there, slumped in the copilot's chair, looking out at the swirling pseudosubstance of hyperspace.

"How are they doing back there?" the Professor asked without looking around.

"They're having a fight. What are you doing up here?"

"Staying out of it."

"You knew they'd have one?"

"Let's say I expected something in that line." The older man turned to face him. "Do you have any siblings, Commander?"

Jessan shook his head. "No, I'm afraid I don't."

"And they let you off Khesat?" asked the Professor, with an expression of mild surprise. "The galaxy has certainly changed since I was young."

Jessan gave a weary laugh. "Not that much, Professor. My crowd's a cadet branch, and there's plenty of cousins left over to take up the slack. Not to change the subject or anything—but how long have we got before we come out of hyper?"

"About four days. We'll be on autopilot the whole way."

Over on the control panels, the status light representing the door to the captain's quarters lit briefly as the door opened and shut.

"Well," said Jessan, "it looks like round one is over. Shall we go back and aid the wounded?"

Only Llannat was still in *Warhammer*'s common room when they got there. Jessan raised an eyebrow at her. "What, no bodies?"

"I cycled them all out the airlock."

"That bad?"

"Not quite—but it was touch and go for a moment or two."

Jessan could hear the Professor busy in the tiny galley nook. *Good idea. We could all use something hot and nourishing right now, and that's a fact.*

"What happened?" he asked.

"Well . . . once you left, the argument turned mean."

"*Turned* mean?"

"You heard it here first," she said. "Finished when Beka slammed into the captain's cabin and Ari stomped off aft somewhere."

"Oh, dear," said Jessan, subsiding into one of the seats by the mess table. "Not an auspicious beginning."

"They'll come around," Llannat said. "You have to be reasonably fond of somebody in the first place, to light into them like that."

"Adept's wisdom?"

She shook her head. "Five brothers and sisters back home on Maraghai."

The Professor emerged from the galley with a steaming tray in each hand and a third tray balanced across his forearms. "Then you'll understand, Mistress, how it came about that when the captain saw a need to expand the crew of *Warhammer*, she turned first to her brother."

Llannat reached up and took the third tray from its precarious balance point. "Mmm, fresh cha'a . . . thank you, Professor. She ought to have given him some warning, first—he'd just gotten used to the idea that she was dead. The whole thing with the crash on Artat happened while he was in accelerated healing, you know. He went straight from the pod onto a courier ship bound for Galcen, but by the time he got there everything was over but the wake."

"He never mentioned that in his letters," said Jessan. The Professor had set the two remaining trays down on the battered surface of the mess table. Jessan reached out and pulled one of them over in front of his own place. "But then, Ari wouldn't."

"We'd have liked to be more tactful," said the Professor to Llannat. "But time was working against us."

"Count your blessings," Jessan added. "I got brought along at blaster-point . . . not that I blame you, Professor. Under the circumstances, I'd probably have shot me out of hand."

Llannat gave him an appraising look over the rim of her mug of cha'a. "Said the wrong thing at the wrong time, did you?"

"I'd had a long night."

"Don't we all, sometimes." Llannat took a long swallow of the cha'a, then cradled the cup in her hands. "But what if Ari doesn't agree to go along with his sister? What then?"

"Don't worry," said Jessan. "When he finds out what she's got in mind, you won't be able to stop him."

The tractor beam had rattled a few pieces loose in the 'Hammer's engine room—nothing dangerous, but stuff that ought to be taken care of while somebody remembered, before it got worse. Blinding rage had brought Ari to that part of the ship in the first place; once the worst of the anger had drained out of him, he went looking for a synch-meter.

He found one in the first spot he checked, in the cramped, out-of-the-way compartment where tools for the 'Hammer's internal repair work had always been kept. Then he went back to the engine room to work off the rest of his temper in bringing the hyperspatial reference block back into line.

He'd been at it for a good while when he heard quick,

light footsteps on the deckplates behind him. He swiveled around on his heels and looked up. "What are you doing down here?"

His sister dropped down to sit on the deck beside him. "You stole my line," she said. "I came to see about taking care of the damage, but it looks like you beat me to it."

"I was down here anyway," he said. He tightened down the last bolt on the access plate with particular care. "That eye patch," he said, without looking back around. "Do you really need to wear it?"

She chuckled. "Don't you like the effect?"

"No." One-way lenses like that usually covered prosthetic repair work too extensive to disguise any other way. "If you don't need the blasted thing, could you please take it off?"

"It really does bother you?" She sounded surprised. "Even though you're a medic and all that?"

"Even though I'm a medic and all that."

"Funny—it doesn't bother Jessan."

"Jessan's not your brother, damn it!"

Beka made a noise that was almost a giggle. Ari turned back around, and found her looking at him out of a pair of plainly functional blue eyes. She grinned.

"See?" she said. "Two. But I have to wear the patch whenever there's a chance I might be going dirtside."

"I understand," he said. "But—why, Bee? Not just the eye patch, but all of it."

She drew her knees up and linked her arms around them. "Well, you know how Dadda turned the *'Hammer* over to me in exchange for any information I could pick up about the people who killed Mother."

Ari nodded. "He gave me the general outline. I thought he was looking for an excuse to give you *Warhammer* without getting the registry papers thrown back in his face."

"He doesn't work that way," said Beka. "Neither do I. Anyhow—there I was with the *'Hammer*, and doing just fine, thank you. Low-bulk, high-speed stuff mostly; there's good money in that these days. And then somebody put out a contract on me.''

"That can really ruin your day," Ari agreed.

"You're not kidding. If the Professor hadn't stepped in and lent a hand, I'd be dead right now for real. But we rigged a nice piece of theater instead, and I wound up as Tarnekep Portree, merchant captain and part-time paid assassin.''

"You haven't really—"

She shook her head. "Not for money."

That leaves a lot of ground uncovered, Ari thought. He looked over at Beka. She was hugging her updrawn knees tightly and gazing into the middle distance, somewhere on the other side of the far bulkhead.

"What really happened back on Pleyver?" he asked.

"I made some people mad enough to chase us all the way across Flatlands. And after we'd gone to ground portside at the Space Force Clinic, the sons of bitches sent in a private army." She smiled briefly. "Your friend Jessan's got a cool head in a crisis. Too sharp-eyed for his own good, though; he spotted me for your sister just as I was bringing the shuttle into High Station.''

"So you invited him along for the ride."

"More or less. He's a cool one, like I said; told us we could either trust him with everything or cycle him out the airlock, but nothing else was going to work for more than a few hours. So we decided to trust him.''

"I'm more interested in why Jessan decided to trust you," said Ari. "Mind telling me just what it was you said to him?"

"Same thing I'm going to tell you," she replied. "I know who had Mother assassinated, and I'm going to track the bastard down and kill him. Want to come along?''

PART THREE

I. Asteroid Base

FOUR DAYS after lifting from Nammerin, *War-hammer* emerged from hyperspace. By tacit consent, the subject of Beka's intentions hadn't been brought up again during the otherwise uneventful trip. There'd be time enough for councils of war, Ari supposed, once the *'Hammer* arrived wherever his sister and her mysterious copilot had in mind.

For his own part, he supposed that he could work with Bee and not wind up throttling her. *Just remember that she's the captain,* he told himself, *and it's her ship. If you cared about that sort of thing, you'd have become a line officer, not gone into the Medical Service.*

The sigh of the ship's hydraulic systems taking the strain of planetfall brought him back to the present. The *'Hammer* settled down onto the landing surface. A minute or so later, Ari heard the noise of the ramp being lowered. Across the common room, Jessan unstrapped and stood up.

"We might as well go on inside," the Khesatan said to

Llannat and Ari. "Your sister and the Professor are going to be a while shutting down the ship. You know how starpilots are."

Ari stood and stretched. "I know that their brains don't function under natural gravity, which describes my sister pretty well most of the time. You've been here before?"

"Only once, for a few hours," said Jessan. "But I know how to get in."

Together, the three of them went out the *'Hammer*'s main passenger door and down the ramp. The freighter stood on her landing legs in the middle of an enclosed docking bay. Ari looked around at the assortment of spacecraft parked under the bay's echoing dome like so many hovercars, and whistled.

"Impressive, isn't it?" said Jessan.

Ari nodded. "I know collectors on Galcen who'd pawn their grandmother's jewelry for some of this stuff."

"Small-time," said Llannat beside him. "I know historians who'd hock the old lady herself for nothing more than a chance to prowl around in here for an hour or two. That's a Magebuilt scoutcraft over here, just for starters."

So it was—meteor-pocked and ugly and, as far as Ari had ever heard, unique in the civilized galaxy. *Not even the Adepts ever captured one of those*, he thought uneasily.

"Let's get on in," said Jessan. "It's chilly out here—we're inside an asteroid, or something that does a damned good imitation of one. You two must be freezing."

"Don't hurry on my account," said Llannat. "It's been almost a year since the last time I shivered, and I'm enjoying the sensation."

"Same here," Ari said, but he knew that a tropic-weight uniform wouldn't keep out the cold forever. When Jessan started off toward one side of the docking bay, he followed. He wasn't surprised when a section of rough-cut rock wall turned out to be a concealed door opening onto a small antechamber and a larger room beyond. "What about the main door over that way?"

"Don't try it. That one only looks like a door."

"What is it, then?" asked Ari, as the sliding panel snicked shut again behind them.

"A burglar alarm," said Jessan. "Or so your sister tells me. You wake up when the burglar starts screaming."

Llannat looked curious. "You believe that?"

"Implicitly," Jessan assured her.

"Probably wise," said the Adept, her dark face unreadable. Before Ari could speak, her expression changed, and she hurried past him and Jessan into the main room.

"Hey, Ari!" she called back over her shoulder. "You should see the setup in here!"

"Sickbay," Jessan explained as they followed Llannat into the immaculate tile-and-metal room. "About as far as I got last time. We had to stop here for some quick repair work on the other two."

"Anything bad?"

"Nothing they couldn't have handled without me," said Jessan. "Beka had a torn ligament in her leg, and the Professor had a broken arm—child's play for a setup like this. I wish I'd had some of this gear back on Pleyver."

"I wish we had it on Nammerin," said Ari. "That bonemender's the latest model from InterMedical Industries. We've got a flatpic of it stuck onto the old one in Emergency, so we can pretend a little sometimes."

"I'll tell you something interesting, though," said Llannat. "Everything new in here is really new, nothing older than a couple of Standard years, and the highest quality that money can buy. But all the other stuff, the little things that don't lose their potency or become obsolete—they go back to the Magewar, at least. What does that suggest to you?"

"That our friend the Professor has been in business for a long, long time," said Jessan, with a shrug. "But five minutes in his company will tell you the same thing."

"You can read more into it than that," Ari told him. "We all can. There's no need to go around it on tiptoe—two years ago something caused the owner of this very professional sickbay to refurbish it and restock it with enough gear to handle a small war. And two years ago somebody killed my mother.''

"Who was the last Domina of living Entibor," said Llannat, soft-voiced. "And the Professor is Entiboran.''

Ari thought about that for a moment. "It would explain a few things," he said. "Jessan, I'm suddenly very curious about the rest of this place. What else is there?''

"The door's right over that way," Jessan said. "Let's go.''

After the scrubbed-clean familiarity of the medical bay, entering the next room was like stepping through a doorway into another world. *And that's not just a phrase*, thought Ari, halting frozen in the doorway. *It's the truth.*

He couldn't move. He felt afraid to step onto the exquisite parquetry of the wooden floor. The delicate openwork carving on the long central table and the surrounding chairs made him feel large and clumsy, the way fragile or beautiful objects always did—an intruder in a world that was much smaller than it should be, and far too easily broken.

"There's more," Jessan said. "Look outside the windows.''

"I am looking," said Ari quietly. "I see it.''

The windows, tall and casemented, made the room's far wall into a curtain of glass. Beyond them, the sun was rising over a wide vista of forested hills, flooding the whole room with a ruddy light. Morning mist filled the valleys between the evergreens, and from somewhere outside the chamber came the sound of birds. One darted past the windows as Ari watched, a scarlet streak appearing and vanishing against the dark green of the woods.

"Where are we?" Llannat asked. Her voice, always gentle, now hardly rose above a whisper.

"Entibor," murmured Ari. "Years ago, while it was alive.''

"One of the private rooms in the Summer Palace," said Jessan. "But this—did you ever see such a high-quality holovid?'' He reached over to the wall, and flipped a switch.

Ari blinked. The table and chairs wavered, and became stark, heavy-duty pieces in plain metal, the sort of thing you couldn't break if you tried. Where the rows of windows had been, he saw open archways leading off down shadowy passages.

"The furniture," said Llannat after a moment, "has got to be real this time. Nobody would ever make themselves an illusion that ugly."

Ari had to agree. Without the holovid, the room and its furniture reminded him of the Namport Detention Center. "Can we have the Palace back?"

"Sure," said Jessan. He toggled the switch on again, and the dawnlit chamber reappeared. "I'd rather wait here for the others, anyway. I know there's sleeping quarters down one of the halls, but that's it—and I wouldn't want to wander around alone in here. No telling what you might find."

Ari sat down on one of the chairs. Even knowing what it really was, he half-expected the frail, pretty thing to crumple under his weight. Outside the windows, the sun rose higher over the Entiboran hills.

"Real-time holographic simulation," said Jessan, taking a seat at the far end of the table. "Whoever did the programming was an artist. You could probably watch it for days and not get an exact repeat."

"The Professor programmed it himself," said Llannat. "From memory, after Entibor was lost."

Ari turned his head, and saw the Adept standing just behind his right shoulder. She was watching the changing holographic landscape, and her eyes looked sad. He didn't ask her how she'd known about the room's programming. Being an Adept, she'd probably pulled the knowledge out of the air somehow. Instead, he ran a hand along the cool metal tabletop that looked like carved blond wood, and said, "Mother was just the opposite. She never let anything Entiboran into the house at all if she could help it."

The room's outer door slid open again before Llannat could answer him. Beka entered, followed closely by the Professor.

"Now do we find out what you've got planned?" Ari asked.

"We'll talk about it tomorrow over breakfast," Beka replied. "Nobody's committing themselves to anything until we've all gotten some sleep."

Ari spent the period of rest surrounded by more luxury than he'd thought existed outside the Central Worlds. The bathroom attached to his sleeping quarters was, by itself, a thing of wonder—black marble and tile, with a sunken tub that looked long enough to swim laps in. *After two years on Nammerin,* he admitted as he lowered himself into the steaming water, *and four days on the 'Hammer, it would take far less than this to impress me.*

He stretched out at full length in the tub and soaked until his fingertips began to wrinkle. Sonics might get you antiseptic enough to meet hospital standard, but they still couldn't make you feel clean. And the public bathhouses in downtown Namport, besides being strictly off limits to Space Force personnel, were in general good places to lose your wallet while picking up an eclectic assortment of the local diseases.

Enjoy it while it lasts, he told himself. *Whatever Beka's got in mind is almost certainly not going to be this much fun.*

He ducked under the surface to rinse the soap out of his hair, then stood and let the water run off his body. Stepping out of the tub, he wrapped himself in a nubbly bath towel roughly the size of a landing pad and returned to the bedroom.

Four of the bath towels might have stretched to make a coverlet for the bed itself, an enormous expanse of mattress between swagged-back velvet curtains. *It looks like a holoset for "Spaceways Patrol,"* he thought. *All that's missing is Sinister Serina in a glued-on gown.*

He shook his head regretfully over the omission and slid between the cool spidersilk sheets. The room lights slowly dimmed. Ari burrowed his head into the large feather pillow and fell asleep.

Light awakened him, streaming into the room from a source outside something that looked like a window but probably wasn't. Semitransparent glassweave curtains gave a hazy impression of manicured lawns and formal gardens stretching out beyond the leaded panes. He sat up in bed and looked around the room.

A dark, silent figure stood motionless in an alcove near the door. Ari tensed, then let out his breath in explosive relief. What he'd taken at first for an intruder was only some sort of robot, vaguely human in its general outlines, its black-enameled body surmounted by an ovoid of dark plastic. A red light flashed briefly within the sable depths of the mechanism's featureless mask.

"Good morning, sir." Despite the machine's outward appearance, the synthesized voice was pleasant and well modulated. "I trust you slept well. I shall fetch your clothing while you bathe, sir."

"Right," said Ari, rolling out of the wide bed. The carpet felt springy and cool under his bare feet, like freshly mown grass. When he emerged from the bathroom some time later, the bed had been made, and the robot had laid out a handsome suit of burgundy cloth.

He frowned at the garments. "Where's my uniform?"

"Being cleaned and repaired, sir. Do you require it?"

"No," Ari replied. "I don't suppose I'll be needing it for a while. But can't you find something that won't make me look like the bouncer in a high-class bar?"

"Something more subdued, then," said the robot. "If you would be so kind as to wait a moment . . ."

The robot picked up the pile of cloth and left the room with it, returning a minute later with another armload of fabric that turned out to be an otherwise identical suit in a quiet shade of forest green.

Ari wasn't at all surprised when the garments turned

out to fit him perfectly. He sealed the last fastener and turned back to the robot. "Tell me—can a man find a cup of cha'a somewhere hereabouts?"

"The others are waiting in the breakfast nook, sir."

"Lead on," said Ari. He followed the robot down a passageway to a sweeping staircase, and from there to a balcony overlooking something that looked for all the galaxy like a waterfall in a woodland glade. A milk white durnebeast drank, head bent, from the pool some thirty feet below. The slim, long-legged creature looked up as he appeared, then fled into the undergrowth.

Out on the balcony, three more members of the *'Hammer*'s crew sat together around a glass-topped breakfast table. Beka still wore Tarnekep Portree's clothing, but she'd left off the red plastic eye patch and had done something to her long hair to turn the single braid back to its familiar yellow. The others had clearly taken at least partial advantage of the valet robots' services. The Professor had switched from his free-spacer's outfit to a plain white shirt and black trousers cut in the old Entiboran style, and Nyls Jessan carried off a pale blue Khesatan lounging robe with an air of having just arrived from an early-morning session of birdsong and flute music.

Ari slid into one of the empty chairs and began filling his plate with shirred eggs and slices of grilled meat. "Where's Llannat?" he asked.

Beka shrugged. "Still asleep, I suppose. What does the robot assigned to Mistress Hyfid have to say?"

The valet robot that had escorted Ari to breakfast paused for a moment before responding. "My series-mate reports that Mistress Hyfid dressed and left her chamber some time ago."

"Then she ought to have gotten here by now," said Ari.

"Maybe not," said Jessan. He turned to the robot. "Did Mistress Hyfid have an escort when she left?"

Another pause. "She refused one, sir."

"There you have it," said Jessan. "She's lost."

The Professor shook his head. "An Adept? Unlikely.

Mistress Hyfid is undoubtedly going about her own business—but what it is, I wouldn't venture to guess.''

After a night full of confused and disturbing dreams about the gentle-voiced Professor, with his illusory windows onto an Entibor long dead, Llannat Hyfid had awakened to a room flooded with light—and to the knowledge that she needed to make up her mind before she went any further.

All right, she demanded of the universe, as the shower room's multiple jets and sprays of water sluiced the night sweat off her body. *Here I am. Now what do I do?*

She didn't get an answer. She never did, when she tried to push things that way. The prompting she'd gotten unasked on Nammerin had been so strong that she'd pulled away from a conversation in midsentence to make a dash for the hospital airfield, but that inner sureness had left her as soon as the 'Hammer lifted out of atmosphere and headed for hyperspace.

She turned off the shower room, twisted her long hair up into its customary out-of-the-way knot, and padded back into the sleeping chamber to get dressed. The robot had brought her a set of formal Adept's blacks while she showered: trousers and tunic and a clean white shirt, laid out in proper order on the new-made bed.

"I wish," she said, as she fastened the high collar of the black broadcloth tunic, "that whatever's pushing me around would tell me where I'm heading."

"I don't understand, Mistress," said the robot.

"Never mind," she said. "I was talking to myself."

It was close enough for truth, she supposed. The robot seemed to think so, anyhow. It hesitated a second before asking, "Would you care for breakfast, Mistress?"

She shrugged. "Why not?"

"If you would follow me, then . . .''

"No," she said. "I'll find my own way. Thank you."

The robot made demurring noises. She said no a second

time, more forcefully; the robot gave up and rolled away, still clicking with disapproval.

She sighed, and went out into the passage.

It looks like the decision is all yours, she told herself. *If you say you want out of whatever they're planning, they'll honor the request. The Professor's old-fashioned enough to understand an Adept wanting to keep her hands clean, and Captain Rosselin-Metadi wishes you hadn't come along in the first place. And those two are the ones who count.*

She didn't need the machine to tell her that breakfast was down the hallway and to the left. The rich, eye-opening aroma of fresh-brewed cha'a reached her nose even more distinctly than the mingled aura of the *'Hammer*'s crew came to her other senses. She swallowed once, and headed in the opposite direction.

"Mistress Hyfid's absence need not delay us any longer," said the Professor. "The robot can record and replay as needed. So—my lady?"

"Right," said Beka. "The latest bit started with a letter from Dadda. I'd set up a mail drop through General Delivery on Pleyver not too long after the Prof and I rigged that crash outside Port Artat, so I thought it was time to make a side trip to Flatlands and check it out. There was a message confirming something I'd asked about, and he told me about the new Space Force clinic in Flatlands. The officer in charge, he said, was discreet and reliable."

"Considering the source," Jessan said, pouring more cha'a into the translucent porcelain cups, "I'm flattered."

"As well you should be," said the Professor. "Pray continue, my lady."

"Right," said Beka. "Besides the word about the clinic, Dadda passed along what he'd learned: Gilveet Rhos, the man who did the electronics work when they killed Mother, hasn't been in circulation since then. It sounded like somebody wasn't happy with the way that job went down, which tallies with what out late friend on Pleyver had to say."

"Which friend was that?" asked Ari. The only Pleyveran he could name offhand was Tarveet, and the councillor had still been alive and making long-winded speeches the day before the 'Hammer hit Nammerin.

"The one who was hiring me to kill you, big brother," said Beka, with a crooked smile. "He never did give me his name . . . but he certainly was generous with everybody else's."

Something about her expression sent a cold finger tracing down the back of Ari's neck. "What did you do to him, Bee?"

"Nothing more than he deserved," she said. "Owen was in Flatlands—Guild business, I think; he was doing a passable imitation of a spaceport bum—and the bad guys caught him. I don't know how, and I didn't ask. But I'd just finished shaking hands on the original deal when a couple of goons dragged Owen into the room, and the head man wanted me to do him, too."

She paused. "So I shot a goon and cut the head man's throat, and after that things got violent."

There was a moment of silence. Ari didn't doubt that his sister had done everything she described—lying had never been one of Bee's particular vices—but he was damned if he'd give her the satisfaction of knowing that she'd shocked him. When he was fairly certain he could match Beka's offhand manner, he asked, "What happened to Owen?"

Beka looked worried. "I don't know. He stayed in Flatlands—unfinished business, he said. But he needed somebody to draw away the hired guns, which is how the Prof and I wound up ruining your friend Jessan's evening."

"Believe me," murmured Jessan, "the night had its moments."

Beka cast a quick glance sidelong at the Khesatan, but Jessan's bland face was an noncommittal as ever. With only a faint—and uncharacteristic—pinkness in her pale

cheeks to show that the exchange had taken place, Ari's
sister went on.

"After everything fell apart," she said, "we were, well,
busy for a while. But later on, I had some time to think.
And the longer I thought, the more the affair on Pleyver
started to smell like a setup. Like a whole damned series
of setups, in fact, all the way back to the start."

Ari set his knife and fork aside; the conversation had
killing his appetite a long time ago. "A setup? How?"

Beka leaned back and steepled her hands, tapping the
fingertips together. "Try this on for size, big brother.
Somebody wants to smash Dahl&Dahl and the Suivi lobby
so hard there isn't even a damp spot left on the pavement
afterward."

"It's conceivable," the Professor commented. "The
Dahls of Galcen are a powerful clan—as are their Suivi
cousins."

"Powerful," said Jessan, "but not well-loved." The
Khesatan surveyed the breakfast table's array of jams and
preserves, took a spoonful of something clear and green,
and began spreading it on a torn-off bit of fresh bread.
"Power and popularity," he continued, "don't usually go
hand-in-hand. Your mother the Domina was a notable exception to the rule."

"And that's why someone killed her," said Beka.

She picked up the silver butter knife from the side of
her plate and frowned at it for a moment. Then she
changed her grip in a single quick, blurred motion, and
started turning the blade first one way and then another.

"It's how I'd do it," she went on, her blue eyes following the glint of the breakfast nook's artificial daylight on
the polished metal, "if I wanted to make somebody squirm
and bleed."

"What do you mean?" Ari growled.

His sister smiled—not at him, but at the edge of the
knife. "Work it out for yourself. First, you get debates
going hot and heavy in the Grand Council over Suivi
Point."

"Tarveet of Pleyver," said Ari, remembering. "He introduced the original Expulsion Bill. Mother cut it to ribbons on the Council floor."

"The slug-eating idiot deserved it," said Beka, and went on. "Step two—assassinate the beloved public figure who happens to be the most passionate voice against expulsion. And step three—make certain your killers get caught, to lay the blame on Dahl&Dahl."

She tossed the knife from hand to hand for a few seconds, then flicked it out to take up a pat of butter from the crystal dish. "But they didn't count on Dadda," she finished. "And their assassin wound up too dead to interrogate."

Ari scowled into the depths of his cha'a. "Why would anybody believe that Suivi Point *wanted* to get kicked out of the Republic?"

"In order to gain freedom of action," said the Professor, who'd been listening to Beka with grave approval, like an instructor in keyboard and the voice at a favorite student's graduation recital. "And a release from the constraint of law."

"That would make sense to most people, you have to admit," said Jessan. "Your mother was hitting the 'how can we control them if we expel them' note pretty hard in her speeches."

Ari growled an obscenity under his breath in the Forest Speech—a language he'd always found more satisfying than Galcenian for such purposes.

"You won't get any argument on that from me," said Beka. "But think about it, Ari. If I'm right, and the original plan was a putup job, then so was everything else."

II. Asteroid Base: The Inner Depths

T HE INNER tunnels of the asteroid base ran deep. The Professor had taken over the upper layers for his holovid-enhanced· complex of luxurious chambers, but over half of the base's volume lay empty and unused.

Llannat Hyfid had sensed the structure's tremendous size as soon as she'd stepped out of *Warhammer* onto the floor of the docking bay. Something about the asteroid smelled familiar, too—an acrid-sweet odor somewhere between engine coolant and rotting meat, one that wasn't there at all if she made herself close down her sensitivity to the currents of power and rely on her nose alone. The smell had crept into her dreams, making her restless and uneasy in the huge bed, when back at the Nammerin Medical Station she'd slept untroubled on a standard-issue cot and mattress less than a quarter the size.

Now, as she moved downward out of the inhabited sections of the asteroid, the unpleasant nonsmell grew even stronger. However the Professor had come into possession of this place, she reflected, he'd scoured it most thoroughly afterward . . . but a full squad of cleaning robots couldn't get rid of a stink that was only there for an Adept to notice.

Back on Maraghai, the Selvaurs always claimed that trouble had a bad smell to it, and perhaps because of her upbringing she had a nose for such things. The practice yard of the Adepts' Retreat on Galcen, for instance: its hard-packed earth had always smelled faintly of blood to her, a relic of the slaughter done there in the opening days of the war, when the Magelords had attacked the Guild's inmost citadel and nearly brought it down. She'd gotten used to the smell in time, but most of the other apprentices never even noticed it.

There'd been a class of new students busy in the yard at staff practice on the day she took her Adept's vows, all oblivious of any lingering impressions from the past. One of the senior apprentices was coaching them. As she drew nearer, she recognized Owen Rosselin-Metadi—Master Ransome's personal student and, some said, his most trusted aide. Owen looked around from correcting one apprentice's faulty stance, took in her new suit of formal blacks and the staff, and began to smile.

Congratulations!

His "voice" came through strong and clear, even at that distance, and she knew that her own *Thank you* was a mumble by comparison.

He gestured in the direction of a shady spot over to one side of the yard. *Have time to chat before you go?*

Sure.

Just wait a minute, then, while I get them started on the next bit.

She leaned against the practice-yard wall and watched as he matched up the new students for two-person drill. Llannat wondered about Owen sometimes. He'd been a senior apprentice and a teacher when she first came to the Retreat, he was a senior apprentice and a teacher now that she was leaving—and if her training had taught her anything at all, it was how to recognize somebody already working on a level she wasn't ever going to reach.

He left the apprentices sparring with their staves and came over to join her in the shade.

"Congratulations," he said again. "You look good."

She wiggled her shoulders inside the stiff new garments. "I feel like somebody's about to come along and write me up for impersonating an Adept."

"Don't worry," he told her. "You'll get used to it. Where are you going now that you're finished here?"

She grinned at him, and whistled a scrap of an old melody.

" 'Back into space again'?"

She nodded. "I could have gotten waivered out, I suppose, but I like being a medic."

"And you don't like being an Adept?"

"I like it," she said. "I just don't think I'm ever going to feel easy with it."

"I don't know anyone who does," he said. "It's better that way, I think—always to be a little uneasy with power."

She looked at him curiously. "Is that why you're still an apprentice after all this time? Because you're . . . uneasy?"

"Uneasy?" he asked, startled. "No. Not that."

He paused, and then seemed to make up his mind about something. "Taking Adept's vows with your whole heart isn't just a matter of speaking the words," he said finally. "When you say the words and mean them, the experience changes you—or you change yourself, if you'd sooner look at it that way. And sometimes Master Ransome finds it useful to have an agent on hand whose aura won't show those changes to anyone who knows how to look."

"I see," she said. "I don't *feel* particularly changed."

"It's there, all right," he told her. "Master Ransome wouldn't have let you go if you weren't ready. Where's the Space Force sending you, anyway?"

"Nammerin," she said. "Almost like going home. Lots of Selvaurs, lots of big trees—"

"Lots of rain," said Owen. "My brother Ari's on Nammerin these days."

"That, too."

He gave her a measuring look. "Is that how it is, then?"

"That's how it is. Master Ransome sees trouble brewing on Nammerin, with your brother at the heart of it. So he did whatever it is he does to arrange these things, and I'm off to keep an eye on the situation."

She got a different look this time, almost a humorous one. Owen didn't explain the joke, though, but said only, "You'll have your work cut out for you—Ari's not the type to appreciate having a bodyguard."

"With any luck, he'll never need one."

Owen laughed under his breath. "Don't tell me you still believe in luck."

Llannat sighed. That was something else she'd be leaving behind her for good, and she was going to miss it. "No," she admitted. "Not any longer."

Owen never had explained why he found the idea of an Adept bodyguard for his brother amusing, either. Enlightenment on that score needed to wait until Nammerin, when she'd walked into the staff lounge one afternoon and heard Nyls Jessan telling some tall tale about the CO's pet sand snake . . . a nice enough beast, and one that didn't deserve the problems it had in adapting to the humid climate.

"Come on, Jessan," she'd said as she came through the door, "tell us another one."

And then the lounge's other occupant stood up from the battered, lumpy couch—and kept on standing, until he loomed up like one of the Great Trees of Maraghai under the ceiling struts of the converted storage dome.

"Gentlelady . . . Mistress."

The big man's deep, Galcenian-accented voice didn't stumble on either title, and the bow of respect he made, while a bit unnerving coming from someone his size, had none of the clumsiness she'd expected.

Someone's taught him how to move, she thought, obliv-

ious of Jessan nattering introductions in her ear. *Adept?*
No, he's got lieutenant's bars.

Besides, his aura showed none of an Adept's almost
unstable brilliance. *Strong,* she thought. *Strong and rock-
steady-solid . . . why does he make me think of home?*

"I'm from Maraghai," she said, while her mind worked
on sorting out the confused impressions. "And the 'Mistress' bit makes me uncomfortable."

The big man surprised her again. His rather guarded
expression changed to a genuine smile, and then she was
listening to the rumbling bass notes of a language she
hadn't heard in years, least of all from a human throat.

Do you understand the Forest Speech?

Humans from Maraghai were a rare breed, especially
in the Space Force. Caught in the glow of meeting somebody else who'd grown up under the Big Trees, it took her
several minutes to make the connection between the lieutenant and Owen's brother on Nammerin. Then she had to
struggle to keep her face from showing her disbelief and
her mouth from saying anything stupid.

*Master Ransome thinks a man like this needs a body-
guard? Lords of life—what sort of trouble can he be in?*

But she'd had to wait for the answer until the next night,
when a pleasant meal at the Greentrees Lounge in Namport had ended with a wild aircar ride and a fight to the
death in a jungle clearing. The heavy, rotting nonsmell
had filled the air again that evening—as it did now, even
when the passage that she'd been following dead-ended
abruptly in a blank wall.

Under her feet, though, she could still sense the lower
reaches of the base beneath. *This can't be the end of the
line,* she thought. *There has to be something more.* She
closed her eyes, and let the darkness intensify her awareness of buried passages extending coreward.

Over this way a step, she thought, suiting the action to
the words. *And another, and one more . . . here.*

She stamped on the floor with the heel of one sturdy,

standard-issue boot. The sound rang hollow. She opened
her eyes, and looked. No seams, just solid concrete.

Llannat propped her staff against the wall and knelt on
the floor. Then she put both hands flat against the concrete
and opened herself to whatever insight the material had to
offer. After a second, she lifted her hands again.

*There's some strong pattern-working in place here. No-
body gets any further who can't find the key.*

She took a deep breath, and let it out slowly. Finding a
way through the barrier was going to take a probe deeper
than she'd ever tried before, one reaching down into the
elementary particles of matter, and she didn't know if she
had the resources to carry it off. If she failed, she might
die down here, merged so completely with the material
she was probing that she couldn't pull free.

Even if she didn't fail, she'd be working so close to her
limits that she might come unbound from the physical
world altogether and become lost in the Void. Existing
outside of place or time, the Void touched all places and
all times equally, and the power that filled the rest of the
universe had no meaning there. An Adept who over-
stretched her abilities might fall into that bleak dimension
and be drained of energy before she could find the way
home.

Llannat squared her shoulders. *Time to find out if you're
more than just a medic in an Adept suit.* One by one she
lowered the barriers between her essential self and the
outside world, until nothing remained to stop her from
sinking into the slab of concrete beneath her hands.

Vertigo threatened to overwhelm her as her mind opened
up. She felt a flash of panic—*Trapped inside the stone
forever!*—and then steadied, reaching for the pattern of the
substance around her. When the universe settled down
again, she could feel subtle differences within the surrounding material. Long ago, she realized, someone had
hidden points of instability within the flooring to mark the
door to the other side: a door closed against the weak and

the timid, but open to anyone bold enough to search for the key.

Llannat pulled back into herself, breathing hard from the effort, but smiling. Now that she'd felt the markers the way she had, finding them a second time would be easy, like looking at pebbles on the bottom of a pool.

And then—she picked up her staff and rested it across her knees—*and then, you just slip right on through . . .*

She knelt on a landing at the top of a metal staircase spiraling down some kind of access tube. The rotting smell filled her nostrils, mixed now with the scents of wet earth and moldering vegetation. When she stood, the floor of the upper passage made a ceiling close above her head. The dim, sourceless lighting of the base's upper reaches was gone, leaving her in a kind of visible darkness.

She stared down the twisting metal staircase, making her way by feel, one hand grasping her staff and the other the stair rail. As she descended, the darkness grew less profound, until she could look down on thick rain forest far below her.

Where am I? What am I seeing?

She kept on climbing down the staircase, gripping the handrail even tighter than before. The wet jungle-feel was in the air all around her now, and the narrow metal treads felt slick and treacherous underneath the soles of her boots.

Once you've started, she reminded herself, *you can't go back. You have to go on through, or else be lost.*

She heard a high whine from the sky beyond. An aircar came in on a low approach, streaking over the forest canopy to land with a sudden braking blast in a small open area. Space Force Medical Service insignia caught the hazy starlight for a second as the cargo door of the aircar slid back.

Two figures—one tall and fair, the other taller and scaly-skinned—left the aircar and headed off into the jungle. After that, the clearing lay silent; nothing in it moved at all.

Llannat felt her breath catch in her throat. *I remember*

this. I was there. She kept on climbing down. She reached the end of the staircase, and stepped off the bottom tread onto the damp, leaf-covered earth.

She started across the open ground toward the open door of the downed craft. The stink of evil welled up around her, almost choking her, but she couldn't stop. There was something important that she had to do here, something that she'd been sent to accomplish. She saw a movement against the blackness of the aircar's cargo bay, and spoke to the moving shape.

"Adept," she said. "Give me Ari Rosselin-Metadi."

"Lieutenant Rosselin-Metadi isn't mine to give anybody," came the reply. The words were brave, but Llannat read another message in the currents of power she sensed interweaving in the darkened forest. *This little one is afraid. She stands between me and what I have to do—and she expects to die.*

Llannat shook her head at such foolishness. But she was ready to be merciful, within the limits of her business here.

"Let us abandon playing with words," she said. "What matters is that nobody is here to guard a dying man but you—and who can say, afterward, whether help that comes too late might have arrived in time? Stand aside."

"No."

"Then on your own head be it, Adept."

Llannat called forth power, drawing on the strength of the night, and the air about her shone a deep crimson. The small figure facing her called up power in turn. Against the aura's vivid green the other showed up clearly, and a sudden realization made anger rise up in Llannat like a burning tide.

She's taken my staff! thought Llannat. How the little stranger had done it, and left her with a shortened rod fit only for one-handed use, Llannat didn't know—*but I'm going to make the bitch sorry she ever dared to call herself an Adept.*

Llannat tried a few elementary moves with her shorter

staff to test the other's quality. Even working with an unfamiliar weapon, she found the little Adept sadly lacking, clumsy in her attacks and slow with her blocks.

What are they turning loose from the Retreat these days? she raged inwardly as they fought. *This one shouldn't be allowed out without a keeper.*

She turned an ill-timed combination of blows with ease, and pressed forward with a simple attack of her own—beginner's moves, fit for playing with such a novice. The strange Adept's training sufficed to let her stop most of the blows and evade the rest, but not even Master Ransome's expert teaching had brought her far enough to last much longer.

Llannat laughed aloud. "You're overmatched, Mistress." On the last word, she launched a series of feints at the stranger.

"I'm still alive," came the breathless reply. "You have to win this fight. I only need to keep from losing it too soon."

In spite of the bold words, the Adept was gasping for air. Llannat herself felt strong and fresh, and still able to draw on the power that surrounded them both.

I've given this little one chance after chance, she thought. *Now it's time to end the game.*

She stepped forward, whipping her staff into a series of blows. Power shone around her, making a haze of blurry red against the night. The other Adept blocked, and blocked again. But now Llannat fought in earnest, forcing her weaker opponent back step by step—and then a quick move sent the other stumbling backward. The young stranger, already overbalanced, lost her footing on the slippery ground and went down on her back. The impact knocked her staff from her hand.

Llannat took a step forward. On the ground in front of the aircar's open cargo door, the stranger was already clambering, weaponless, to her feet.

Poor fool. She still hopes to delay me, even if it's only for the moment it takes to smash her down.

Llannat put aside the temptation to give the little stranger a few seconds more of life, and lifted her staff for the killing blow.

There was a smell like lightning, and a hot flower of light blossomed from the dark interior of the aircar. The bolt of energy caught her in the chest, hard and burning, and she was flying backward, with the world tilting up behind her.

She fell back to the ground, through it, and came to rest in a bright chamber, surrounded by figures wearing black robes and masks like her own.

"Did you succeed?"

The voice was deep and slow, with an unfamiliar accent.

"I don't . . . know. . . ." The pain of the blaster wound in her chest was blurring her vision. The black-robed figures towered over her. "He was poisoned . . . as you ordered . . . but he had an Adept with him. . . ."

"An Adept!" came a voice from the circle. "How much does Ransome know?"

"Enough to make him wary, it seems," said the first man. "Very well; we can wait. Someone else can do our work for us—you know the ones I mean."

Llannat heard a harsh laugh of agreement from somewhere in the circle, and a third voice said, "That's right—let them take some risks for a change."

The room was going black before her eyes, and the pain of the blaster burn in her chest was taking over the universe. She could feel her blood running out of her, and her life with it, as she struggled to draw in enough air to speak.

"But . . . what about me? Can't you do something . . . ?"

"You have a point." It was the voice of the first speaker, the stranger in the circle. "Failure must always draw its reward."

He lifted a silver knife in the blackness above her. She saw the glittering blade growing larger, slashing down—the pain when it hit swallowed up the little hurt of the blaster burn like a sinkhole swallowing a pebble, and she couldn't hold on to life any longer, but sighed out her breath and let it go.

Llannat woke.

Or was I ever asleep? she wondered.

The air smelled clean around her—still and dusty, yes, but free of the rotting stench of evil. She was sitting cross-legged on a stone floor, with her staff lying across her lap.

One thing that hadn't changed was the darkness. She called forth power, and was satisfied when the air lit up with its familiar green glow.

I'm still myself. What happened wasn't real. True, I think, but not real.

She looked about her. She wasn't alone. Owen Rosselin-Metadi sat cross-legged on the floor across from her. He still wore his plain apprentice's coverall, a drab garment that could belong equally to a farmhand or to a spaceport mechanic. A staff lay across his lap, and his eyes were closed.

Llannat blinked. She recognized the room—its rough stone walls could only belong to one of the oldest chambers in the Galcenian Retreat. But she'd never been alone with Owen Rosselin-Metadi in any of those rooms.

Another dream? she wondered, and stood, as quietly as only an Adept can.

Silent as she had been, Owen must have heard her rising to go—without opening his eyes, he lifted his hand and gestured at her to stop. Then his hand fell back to his lap and he sat motionless once more.

"You're not dreaming," he said, his eyes still closed. "Or remembering. When the time comes, look for me here."

She stared at him, confused. "What do you mean, 'when the time comes?'" she asked. "And where *is* here? The asteroid? The Retreat? Somewhere else?"

Owen's face didn't change. With his hands motionless on the staff in his lap, and his eyes shut, he might have been a holovid frozen in midframe, except that he spoke.

"When you know why your second question has no answer," he said, "then you'll know that the time has come."

Llannat was still puzzling over his meaning when he opened his eyes. His pupils widened when he saw her waiting, almost as if he'd been unaware of speaking to her a moment before.

He stood up. "Let's find a way out of here," he said, and gestured toward the door of the chamber. "The path I need to take is in this direction, I think."

She followed him out into the hallway, and closed the door behind her. The power she had summoned earlier cast a flickering green light on the stone walls, and she saw more doors opening off the corridor to her left and right. She couldn't tell where they might lead to—all of them looked alike in the leaping, twisted shadows.

"What did you mean," she asked again, "to look for you here when the time comes?"

He shook his head. "Did I say that? I don't know yet what I meant, either . . . but I *will* know when the time comes, and so will you." He paused, and put his hand on one of the doors. "I have somewhere to go now. Don't follow me until you're certain that you should."

He pushed the door open as he spoke, and was through into an unlighted space before Llannat could say anything more.

The door swung closed and vanished, and the stone corridor vanished along with it. The faint green light remained, but it illuminated only a cramped space, no wider than she was tall and perhaps twice as long, enclosed on all sides by smooth walls, with no hint of a door or other opening.

She let her instinct turn her toward one end of the room. Then she walked forward, not breaking stride as she came to the wall. Her physical being blended with the apparent obstacle—she passed through—and Llannat found herself once again in the corridor above the hidden stairway.

She reached out with her feelings. The marks hidden in the concrete beneath her were still there.

Doors, she thought. *Hidden from anyone who lacks the strength and insight to use them. This is a strange place, and no mistake.*

She walked forward and out, toward the upper reaches of the Professor's asteroid.

"A put-up job," Ari repeated. He glanced across the breakfast table at his sister. *Bee must have thought more about this than she lets on. She's actually starting to make sense.*

"Care to get specific?" he asked.

"Well," said Beka, "whoever the bad guys are, Dadda shot their main plan right out of the air. Not long after that, I got the *'Hammer* and started asking questions. So then our mysterious somebodies got nasty—maybe they wanted to send a warning to Dadda, so that he'd keep out of things."

Ari grimaced. "They don't know him very well, do they?"

"Not everybody has had the privilege," said the Professor quietly. "Pray continue, my lady."

"I was knocking around the outplanets by then," Beka went on, "so they decided to kill me and lay a false trail pointing back to Dahl&Dahl. They fed fake information to a gambler on Mandeyn who was making book on my odds of getting off-planet in one piece, and he would have spilled his guts to anybody who leaned on him a little. But somebody killed him over a crooked card game before he could talk to anyone who mattered."

"Somebody," said Ari. "Any idea who?"

"Me," said his sister.

She paused a moment, as if waiting for him to challenge her, and then continued. "So our friends decided to try again with you as the target, and some humorous soul in their organization had a really bright idea: give the Rosselin-Metadi contract to Captain Tarnekep Portree.

That way you'd get yours for stopping whatever they were up to on Nammerin with that Rogan's epidemic—oh, yes, Jessan told me about that—and getting wrung out and hung up to dry by Space Force Intelligence would be just about what Portree deserved for wrecking things back on Mandeyn.''

Ari thought about it for a while. "If you're right," he said slowly, "then somebody's been playing all of us—even Mother—like so many game pieces. Nobody does that to my family if I can help it. Whatever it takes, Bee, I'm with you.''

"Thanks," said Beka. "We won't be working blind, either; Owen slipped me a hot datachip before we split up on Pleyver, and the comps here have been making it dance and sing. We've got a line on two or three different groups who might want Dahl&Dahl out of the picture—so now we go out hunting.''

She looked over at Jessan. "This isn't your quarrel, Commander. You don't have to consider yourself held here at blaster-point any longer.''

Jessan ran a forefinger around the rim of his empty cup. "Am I being invited to leave, Captain?''

Beka shook her head, but didn't meet his eyes. "No.''

"Then by all means count me in," said Jessan. The Khesatan's words were light as usual, but his expression, for once, was not. "If the Space Force isn't happy with me afterward—well, I can always resign my commission and go back home to Khesat.''

"I don't think you'll need to do anything quite that drastic," said a familiar voice from the stairway.

Llannat Hyfid came down the last few steps to the balcony. With an emotion that he couldn't put a name to, Ari saw that she was wearing an Adept's formal blacks, something she'd never done on Nammerin.

"Where have you been?" he asked as she slipped into the empty seat. "You damn near missed breakfast.''

"That's all right, as long as there's cha'a," she said,

and added, "I've been exploring. Professor, you have an unusual setup here. Did you know it was Magebuilt?"

The grey-haired Entiboran inclined his head. "I did, Mistress. But that was long ago . . . five centuries and more."

Ari poured a cup of the now-cool cha'a and passed it to Llannat. She drained it in one swallow and held it out again.

"More, please . . . ahh, thank you, Ari. Time doesn't mean much to the Magelords. This year, next year, a hundred years from now . . . they make long plans."

She set the cup down in its saucer and turned to face Beka. "You'll need an Adept where you're going, Captain Rosselin-Metadi. Will I do?"

III. Ovredis: House of Marchen Bres

I KNOW how I'm going to die, thought Commander Gil. *They're going to find me bored stiff at a garden party, with a polite smile frozen on my face and a too-small glass of wine in my hand.*

Though it was high summer in the southern hemisphere of Ovredis, the day was pleasant and cool. Gil steered his rented Silver Streak hovercar up the long, curving drive toward the country house of Marchen Bres, head of the Ovredisi Bankers' Guild, and tried to convince himself that he'd been lucky.

Back at the Prime Base, after he'd taken control of the space battle over Nammerin away from the watch officer and let the unknown *Libra*-class freighter slip away into hyper, Gil had thought for a few unpleasant seconds that he really was done for. The door of Metadi's office had clicked shut behind his heels, and the General himself stood there looking at him with a cold light in his eyes that Gil didn't like at all.

"Talk fast, Commander," the General invited.

Gil complied.

To his relief, the chilly, measuring look eased off as soon as he mentioned *Pride of Mandeyn*. By the time he got around to identifying the *Pride* as the mystery freighter over Nammerin, the General's expression had shifted to one of wintry approval.

The hard part had been explaining his conviction that both the *Pride* and the unknown were in fact the old *Warhammer*, without admitting to having overheard the General's private conversation with Errec Ransome. Gil scraped through that one by dint of fast talking and blurred logic, and concluded with a detailed comparison between a holocube likeness of the General's daughter at her coming-of-age party and the Security flatpic of Tarnekep Portree, for which he made up most of the key points as he went along.

Finally he ran out of ideas for improvisation, and finished by saying, "Sir, my report can't include any of that, and I can't prove a word of it. But I'm morally certain that's the way it happened."

"I think I have to agree with you, Commander," said Metadi gravely. "Have you discussed your conclusions with anyone other than me?"

"No, sir."

"Don't. My compliments, by the way, on an excellent piece of work."

"Thank you, sir," said Gil. He wasn't going to ask for clarification on that comment, he decided, not now or ever.

The General sat down at his desk with a faint sigh. "It's at times like this," he said, "that I really wish I could have some unbiased advice. What do you think I should do with you?"

"Accept my resignation?"

"Wouldn't work," said Metadi. "There'd be too much talk. No, Commander, I think the best thing to do is classify all the log entries for tonight, and let everybody in Control think it was one of Intelligence's little ploys."

"And what do we let Intelligence think, sir?"

"If they come around asking," said the General, "I'll

just point out that the third victim 'kidnapped' by our mystery freighter was an Adept. Then I'll tell them they're welcome to ask the Master of the Guild for more information any time they feel like it.''

Gil blinked. ''But the Guild doesn't run intelligence operations, sir—do they?''

For a second Gil wondered if he had finally managed to go too far—but the General only gave him a quizzical look and said, ''Commander, that's one of the questions I'm careful not to ask. Now, about that report of yours—''

''Yes, sir,'' said Gil with relief. ''I'll have the hard copy ready by morning, but to sum it up: as far as the Pleyveran affair goes, and leaving Lieutenant Commander Jessan's whereabouts out of the discussion, the *Pride*'s crew don't seem to have been the villains of the piece at all.''

''You're sure of that?''

''We have an eyewitness for most of the night's events,'' Gil said. ''He insists that the conflict involved the clinic staff plus the two strangers on one side, and an undetermined but large number of unknown attackers on the other.''

The General looked thoughtful. ''No idea who the attackers might have been?''

''Somebody's private army, sir,'' Gil said. ''You know how Pleyver is.''

''I know how it used to be,'' said the General, ''and I hadn't heard of it changing much. Anything else?''

Gil shook his head. ''Not much, sir. All I got when I went dirtside was the runaround. To hear the local authorities talk, there wasn't even a traffic jam in that sector on the night in question.''

''Don't sound so offended, Commander,'' said Metadi. ''A good con job's a work of art. How'd they explain away the rubble?''

'' 'Explosion in the flammables locker due to improper storage of volatile substances,' '' quoted Gil. ''But they forgot to sand away the blaster pocks.''

''What about casualties? How'd they explain those?''

''There weren't any,'' Gil said. ''Not officially. Unofficially, our eyewitness puts the killed and injured in the dozens. And even allowing for his youth and inexperience, I'm still inclined to put the actual number around twenty."

"It must have been quite a night," said the General. "Any idea what started it?"

"No, sir," Gil said. "The trouble seems to have begun in a dining establishment in the Portcity. But beyond the fact that the incident was both brief and violent . . ." Gil shrugged. "Nothing, sir."

"And no idea who sent in the private troops?"

Gil hesitated. "No, sir"

Metadi raised a skeptical eyebrow. "All right, Commander," said the General. "What else are you morally certain of, even if you can't prove a word?"

Gil took the plunge. "We can eliminate most of the local bosses right away. They wouldn't take on the Space Force in the first place. If they did, they'd lose what little goodwill they've got with the rest of the Republic. That leaves us looking at the off-world combines. They could risk losing one world without betting their entire bankroll."

The General looked thoughtful. "You're talking big fish there, Commander—Dahl&Dahl, Suivi Mercantile, the Five Families Group—folks like that."

"Exactly, sir," Gil said. "With its power base safe off Pleyver, a combine might undertake a local operation if the stakes were high enough."

"Makes sense," the General said. "Do you have enough to haul somebody in for questioning?"

"No, sir," said Gil, with regret. "Just having power isn't an actionable offense."

"Sometimes I think it ought to be." The General sat for a moment looking at the flatpic of Tarnekep Portree displayed on the desk comp. Finally he turned around again. "As of now, Commander, you're on special assignment. Find out who was behind that attack, and get what you need on them—I don't care how, so long as what you get holds up in court."

Armed with that sweeping authorization, Gil had spent the

remainder of the night making an electronic tour of the Republic's data bases. Some time near dawn, he found what he was looking for: the Pleyveran tax records for the "entertainment complex" known as Florrie's Palace, which listed the owner of record as Flatlands Investment, Ltd. Working back through a chain of several intermediaries, Gil came at last to a name that made his eyebrows go up.

"Well, well," he said to himself. He closed down the file and punched up a code on the desktop comm link.

"Space Force Intelligence, External Operations, Lieutenant Miya speaking."

"Miya, this is Gil. How soon can you people get onto Rolny and plant some surveillance on the head of the D'Caer Combine?"

"How heavy?" Miya asked.

"Heavy," said Gil. "If he talks in his sleep, I want a transcript in the morning."

"Hold on." A minute or so passed; then Miya's voice came on again. "Rolny's a tough nut to crack. Analysis shows we've got a fifty percent chance of losing any operative we send there to put in the equipment, fifty percent for losing whoever monitors it once it's in place. That's a seventy-five-percent probability of coming up dry before we even start, with no second chances."

"Any way to bring that down some?"

"Just a minute." Another pause, and then, "We might be able to pull it off under a couple of conditions. According to projections, the chance of failure goes down to twenty percent if the head man isn't home while we're wiring the place for sound."

"Is that acceptable to your people?"

"It's no summer picnic," said Miya. "But we've handled worse."

"Fine. Is he planning to be off-planet any time soon?"

"Hard to tell," Miya said. "He goes back and forth a lot between Rolny and his branch operations on Ovredis, but his schedule's unpredictable."

"I'm from Ovredis," Commander Gil said. "But you probably knew that already."

"Opened up your file at the same time I did his," agreed Miya. "And if you could be in place on Ovredis to tell us when D'Caer gets there and when he leaves, and maybe delay him a little . . ."

Two weeks later, Gil brought the Silver Streak hovercar to a stop under the portico of the Bres estate. Keeping an eye on the comings and goings of the head of the D'Caer Combine had so far been a matter of watching a series of reception halls and office buildings in the daytime and a string of casinos and pleasure complexes at night. Today, however, promised to be something different. Ebenra D'Caer had promised the head of the Bankers' Guild that he would, faithfully, attend the garden party this afternoon.

A footman opened the driver's-side door of the hovercar with a flourish. Gil left the vehicle floating on its nullgravs and stepped out onto the driveway, gravel crunching under his mirror-polished boots. He nodded at the footman, who slid into the seat Gil had just vacated. The craft purred off to the parking bays.

Gil headed for the broad marble stairs leading up to the double doors of the entrance hall. Pausing on the top step, he straightened his uniform jacket and brushed a speck of imaginary lint from the gold braid at the shoulder. Under cover of the motion, he took the opportunity for a quick scan of the grounds.

Now, what do we have here? Duty footmen out front; young couples flirting in the topiary orchard; a bunch of chauffeurs and menservants lounging around back by the parking bays—swapping gossip about their employers, if I know the type. Damn, but that one's big; he probably doubles as a bodyguard when the boss is on the road.

Gil climbed the steps and went in. As he stepped over the threshold of Marchen Bres's country estate, the doorman bellowed above the chatter that filled the atrium.

"The Right Honorable Jervas Gil, Baronet D'Rugier!"

Heads turned here and there among the fashionably overdressed people crowding the atrium's ornamental garden. Gil reminded himself that he wasn't on Galcen any longer. Back here on Ovredis, the local nobility still counted for something, especially with the wealthy but untitled mercantile families who actually ruled the planet.

After one quick glance at his dress uniform, however, the fashionable people turned back to their conversations. Gil knew what they were thinking, and smiled to himself.

That's right—good family but no money to speak of. Having the right ancestors got me into the gentry, and having no money got me into government service.

At least, though, the nineteenth baronet hadn't fallen so low as to depend on the buffet tables of the Bankers' Guild for his meals. Gil's Space Force dress uniform, with the shoulder loop of gold braid that marked him as a high-ranking officer's personal aide, served to make that much abundantly clear. Besides, if Gil had chosen to attend the party in mufti, the occasion would have demanded that the nineteenth baronet dress in a manner befitting his station— and Gil's old court-formal clothes, unworn since his last home leave, had grown distressingly snug in the waist.

Too much high life on Galcen, Gil thought. *And too much time behind a desk. I need to get out into space again, soon.*

He nodded amiably at a friend of his sister's, secure in the knowledge that for years he hadn't been connected with a party like this in anything besides an official capacity. He got a perverse pleasure, in fact, out of knowing that he wasn't in charge of this one. *Some other poor slob has to worry about running out of canapés and insulting the guest of honor.*

A brightly costumed waiter—the height of vulgar ostentation, but Marchen Bres didn't have breeding, only money—passed by with a tray of glasses filled with something pink and sparkling. Gil snagged a glass with the ease of long practice and continued his stroll through the atrium, sipping as he went.

Wide arches opened off the atrium on three sides. Gil made his way through the central arch into a long passage. At the far end, beyond a narrow cross-corridor, glass doors opened onto the formal gardens behind the house. To his right, beyond a scarlet ribbon stretched between carved marble newel posts, a sweeping staircase led to the private rooms above. Off to his left, in the Grand Ballroom, music and the drone of voices poured out together on the air, like honey with flies in it.

Gil hesitated a moment between a stroll through the gardens for pleasure's sake, and one through the ballroom for duty. *No shirking,* he told himself, and turned left into the ballroom.

All right, Commander, time to circulate. Listen to the gossip. See who's here. Find one of those little cakes with the nut toppings. . . .

Gil insinuated himself into the crush. At once, the babble of a dozen conversations assaulted his ears.

". . . dear Marchen hired one of the very *top* stage designers to plan the west view . . . Interworld Data up twenty points by closing LastDay . . . that stand of trees around the ruined castle . . . in three volumes, with an index, too boring for words, I assure you . . . hired a hermit to live on the grounds, just to add an air of mystery . . ."

The commander drifted away in the direction of the buffet tables. *The things I do for the galaxy. Today could turn out to be even longer than I thought.*

He kept an ear turned toward the chattering voices just the same, while he loaded up a plate from the buffet—nut toppings didn't seem to be in vogue this season, worse luck, but this made the fifth afternoon in a row he's been confronted by pink sugar icing and candied flower petals—and he was rewarded for his perseverance.

". . . Sapne."

He couldn't place the voice. The size of the crowd made such judgments difficult. But the planet's name caught his ear; it wasn't the sort of place he'd have supposed this crowd thought about very often.

The speaker's unseen companion seemed to agree. "But

Sapne doesn't even have enough population left to qualify as an independent world anymore.''

"One doesn't need people in order to be noble, my dear," said the first voice. "The ancestor of the House of Sapne-in-Exile was on his own Grand Tour when the Plagues hit—the duke told me so just yesterday—and he married off-world to found the present line."

Who've probably never been within half a sector of Sapne, thought Gil. After more than a year on Galcen, he knew the type. The civilized galaxy was cluttered with them—ousted royalty, deposed presidents-for-life, former chairmen of planetary boards—and sooner or later they all showed up on the Republic's capital planet. *Funny, though . . . I haven't spotted anybody so far who looked quite that spectacularly useless. I must be losing my touch.*

He wandered back out into the atrium with his plate of finger foods and took station against one wall, the better to keep a watch for visiting royalty and other objects of interest.

I'm going to starve, thought Beka, smiling in her best regal manner as she held out a hand for the head of the Ovredisi Bankers' Guild to kiss. *I've been living on pink cakes and little pale sandwiches for a solid month. I wonder what they're feeding the lowlife out back?*

She hated these parties. The tight sleeves and fitted bodices of this year's fashionable gowns left her with no convenient place to hide a knife. The sheath strapped to her upper thigh, just below where the skirt flared outward into a filmy cloud of pale green, gave her some comfort, but not much.

And nowhere to carry a blaster at all . . . I feel like I'm walking around naked.

She swallowed a laugh. *I'm getting as bad as Dadda.*

"Is something wrong, Your Highness?"

She shook her head at Marchen Bres. "No, gentlesir. A momentary spasm, only . . . a hereditary affliction, I'm afraid." She smiled at him again. "Fortunately it's not a serious one, though it's kind of you to ask."

The banker positively glowed.

Right about now, she thought, *if I asked him for a million in cash he'd hand it over and not ask for collateral.*

She'd never thought they could carry it off, back when the Professor had laid out his plans on board *Crystal World*, the tiny but extravagantly appointed pleasure yacht he'd brought out of mothballs for the occasion.

"Sapne?" she'd asked. "*Sapne?* Professor, nobody is from Sapne. That whole damned planet's nothing but a bunch of ruins and a few mud huts. The locals wear fur loincloths and trade colored rocks to each other for flat beer. I've been there," she finished. "I know."

"We will be the Royal House of Sapne-in-Exile," the Professor repeated. "An off-world branch of the family."

"It'll work," said Jessan. "There's already two Kings of Sapne and a Sapnish Pretender running around. The way planetary royalty intermarried in the old days back before the Magewar, a Rosselin of Entibor's probably got as good a claim as anybody else anyhow."

"You'll notice the Rosselins never bothered to assert one," Ari grumbled. They were gathered on *Crystal World*'s observation deck; like everything else about the little yacht, it was an exquisite miniature, and Beka's brother had been moving for three days now with exaggerated care, as though he expected to break something the moment he let down his guard. The caution had not improved his temper.

The Professor ignored him. "You, my lady, will be the Princess Berran, and Lieutenant Commander Jessan will be her brother, the Crown Prince Jamil. And Mistress Hyfid, if she agrees, will be Her Highness's companion-chaperone, the better to further the illusion."

Llannat looked abstracted—Beka was reminded of somebody trying to remember the date of the last solstice by counting the weeks backward—and then nodded. "I can handle it."

"Handle what?" Beka asked.

"Keeping us from being recognized," said the Adept. "The easiest way is with a single wide-range illusion—language, for instance. None of us know Sapnish, but give me some tapes to listen to for a few days and I can manage to convince everybody else that we're speaking it. It's not infallible, but it'll work better than fancy disguises.''

"You don't have to worry about me," Jessan said. "I can fake the accent when you're not around.''

"Excellent," said the Professor.

Ari looked suspicious. "And what am I supposed to be doing while the rest of you are enjoying the high life on Ovredis? Parking the hovercar?''

"As a matter of fact . . . ," said the Professor.

Ari regarded the Entiboran in silence for a moment, and then started to chuckle. "Why not?" he said. "Bee, I'll bet you twenty credits the food's better down in the servants' quarters.''

And so far, he's been winning, Beka thought, doing the gracious-smile bit again as Marchen Bres bowed himself away. *Where the hell is Jessan, though? He was supposed to meet the rest of us here, and I haven't seen him yet.*

The doorman's stentorian tones broke into her worries. "His Royal Highness Jamil, Crown Prince of Sapne!''

About time, thought Beka, half-turning to glance toward the door.

Lieutenant Commander Nyls Jessan strode into the atrium, flinging off his light summer cloak and tossing the swirl of purple satin over his shoulder to the doorman without turning his head or breaking step. Beka's eyes narrowed. The Khesatan medic had thrown the cloak aside with even more bravura than usual, and his whole bearing projected self-satisfaction.

He's got something hot.

Gil located the Princess of Sapne without much trouble, once he knew what he was looking for. The tall girl in frosty green wore a plain metal circlet around hair already twisted high up on her head in a shimmering, pale-yellow crown, but what first caught his eye was her stillness. The rest of the throng in the atrium milled about, collecting in groups and splitting up again, but the girl in green stayed in one spot, with a grey-haired avuncular gentleman keeping watch on her left hand and a sable-gowned duenna hovering on her right. Marchen's party guests came to her, it was clear, and not the other way around.

She wasn't bad-looking, either, in a thaw-me-out ice-maidenish sort of way. Marchen Bres got two smiles out of her while Gil watched, and went off looking like a man ready to sell company secrets just to get another one. *Time to circulate a bit more,* Gil told himself. *Maybe I can find somebody who'll introduce an overworked baronet living on his Space Force pay to a planetary princess.*

He stood away from the wall, and was making ready to ditch his now-empty plate when he heard the doorman's voice echoing across the indoor garden.

"His Royal Highness Jamil, Crown Prince of Sapne!"

The Princess turned her head sharply, looking back over one shoulder toward the door—and Gil froze. He set his plate down on a passing waiter's tray with a nerveless hand, while his mind played back first one picture and then another: Beka Rosselin-Metadi, age seventeen, looking out at the camera from the holocube on General Metadi's desk, her hair the same moonlit blond and her dress the same light green . . . and Captain Tarnekep Portree, age unknown and habits unsavory, caught by a Security camera in the act of glancing back over his shoulder with just that air of damn-your-eyes arrogance.

IV. Ovredis: House of Marchen Bres

"**G**OOD AFTERNOON, sister dear. How's the party?"

"Boring," said Beka.

Jessan smiled and gave her a brotherly kiss on the cheek. "D'Caer's on his way here now," he murmured.

Beka felt a warm glow that had nothing to do with the kiss. *Finally,* she thought.

That night of all-out war back on Pleyver had been a bad mistake on the part of the other side—or failing to win it had been, which amounted to the same thing. And while Tarnekep Portree and his copilot didn't have access to the social circles traveled in by the rich and regal, the Royal House of Sapne-in-Exile turned out to be another story.

"Is our driver ready?" she asked.

Jessan smiled, and tapped the comm link built into one mother-of-pearl cuff button. "He awaits our departure, dear sister—but we can't leave just yet, I'm afraid. I promised a good friend an introduction to my lovely sibling."

Beka looked down her nose at him. "That was a trifle

presumptuous of you, wasn't it, Jamil?'' She turned to the Professor. "Uncle—must I?''

"I'm afraid so, my dear, if Jamil has promised.'' The Entiboran gave Jessan a look of faint disapproval. "You shouldn't be so free with your sister's company, Your Highness. Dare we hope that this time, at least, your friend is a gentleman of good family, and not another of the local merchants?''

"A very rich merchant, Uncle,'' Jessan said. "And very lucky at cards.''

"Oh, Jamil,'' wailed Beka softly, "you can't have gambled away all your pocket money again!''

Jessan gave her and the Professor a scapegrace grin. '' 'Fraid so, Berran. And the news got round after Uncle stopped my allowance the last time—he wouldn't take my note-of hand.''

The Professor's faint disapproval changed to a stern frown. "Do you mean to tell me, Your Highness, that you made your sister the object of a public wager?''

"Caught, by the gods!'' said Jessan, with a reckless laugh. He looked over at Llannat, standing by in her modest black gown. "Tell me, Cousin Lana—will you have me if they cast me out?''

Llannat only sniffed. *Too wrapped up in her illusion weaving to do anything else*, Beka supposed. *Well, thanks to her, everybody else in the room is getting the impression of a royal family spat—in Sapnish.*

The Professor was doing a good job of it on his end, too. "Your Highness, you have overstepped the bounds of what is permissible, even for one in your privileged position. We leave for home as soon as this affair is concluded.''

"Oh, Uncle,'' Beka pleaded, "must we? Home is so *dreary*.''

"I'm afraid we must, my dear,'' the Professor said. "If your brother will not learn responsibility on his own, he must be taught. We will keep the promise which he so rashly made in your name, and then make our farewells.''

Jessan laughed a second time and chucked her under the chin. "Cheer up, sister mine . . . my friend Ebenra's charming as well as rich. You might even enjoy his company, if you can get away from Uncle and Cousin Lana long enough to appreciate it." He bowed and kissed his hand at them all. "I'm off to the punch bowl, dear hearts— collect me when it's time to leave in disgrace."

The man's wasted as a medic, Beka thought, smiling after him. *He should have gone on the stage.*

Commander Gil leaned his shoulders against the atrium wall. Right now, frankly, he could use the support, and never mind the cultivated air of negligent idleness he'd been trying to convey earlier. *So Beka Rosselin-Metadi is Tarnekep Portree is—the Princess of Sapne. Let's have another look at the rest of them, why don't we, Jervas?*

He let his gaze move from one member of the Sapnish party to the next. After that first revelation, the rest was easy. The grey-haired gentleman, for instance, could only be the copilot of *Pride of Mandeyn*, the one known around the spaceports as the Professor. And as for Crown Prince Jamil—if that wasn't Nyls Jessan playing royalty as if to the manner born, then Gil was never going to trust a Space Force ID file flatpic again. He gave a slight smile and an inward chuckle. *I could solve the mystery of the vanishing medical station right now if I wanted to, just by asking.*

The chaperone, though—that rather plain, unremarkable face didn't belong to anybody involved in the Pleyver affair. But the *Pride* had snatched an Adept off Nammerin along with Lieutenant Rosselin-Metadi, and Mistress Llannat Hyfid was a small, dark woman not unlike the princess's duenna. Very like, in fact. Gil thought about General Metadi and the questions he was careful not to ask, and hurried on to the next topic.

If the Adept is with Captain Portree . . . ah, Beka Rosselin-Metadi, then Ari Rosselin-Metadi must be somewhere hereabouts as well, and I haven't seen him. He'd certainly stand out in this crowd—right. That big chauf-

feur out by the parking bay. No wonder he looked so familiar.

Gil accepted another glass of the sparkling pink stuff from a passing waiter, and stood sipping it while he watched the Sapnish contingent over the wafer-thin crystal rim. The family seemed to be having a bit of a tiff right now—*Funny*, thought Gil, *I know who they are, but they're speaking a language I don't understand. For all I know, it might even be Sapnish.*

He took another swallow of the pink-and-sparkly, wishing that his conscience would let him switch to something stronger. What he'd seen went a long way toward explaining some of the mysteries he'd encountered lately, but left him staring at an even bigger one—just what were the General's daughter and her grab-bag crew up to on Ovredis?

As he slipped his drink and mulled the question over, the doorman's voice boomed out yet again.

"Gentlesir Ebenra D'Caer!"

A stir and a hum went through the crowd in the atrium, and all eyes, even those of the Sapnish contingent, turned toward the door. Gil wasn't surprised. The head of the D'Caer Combine might be only a common Gentlesir, and not even a Guildhead like Marchen Bres, but he still counted for more than all the local nobility and imported royalty put together.

D'Caer hadn't changed much since the last time Gil had chanced into his orbit, during a home leave nine or ten Standard years before. He was still tall and hatchet-faced, he still dressed with the same insulting plainness for office work and social occasions alike, and he still traveled with a bodyguard even taller and broader in the shoulders than he was himself.

I wonder if he stills feels up young ladies at parties? wondered Gil—who'd been amazed, on that long-ago leave, by the things a girl would tell an older brother who could be reliably sworn to secrecy.

Right now, Beka Rosselin-Metadi was looking across the atrium at D'Caer with a smile that for some reason made Gil remember CC2 Peyte's report on the fight in the cargo bay—and the comptech's description of Tarnekep Portree, white shirtfront soaked from neck to waist in somebody else's blood, standing in the line of fire and smiling as he took aim.

Whatever she's holding against D'Caer, thought Gil, *it's got to be something worse than roving hands on the dance floor. Bad enough to get help from her brother, and from the CO of a Space Force Station, and from an Adept. Not to mention General Metadi's tacit approval . . . and maybe Master Ransome's as well.*

Commander Gil could only think of one offense that warranted all that. "Damn," he muttered aloud to the dregs of his punch. "What am I supposed to do now?"

He's here, thought Beka. A chill of anticipation ran down her back as she looked over toward the door, and she smiled in spite of herself.

She smiled again at the sight of Jessan ambling back through the atrium, brushing cake crumbs off his fingertips with a napkin as he came. Jessan paused, gazed languidly around the room, and then started toward D'Caer with a cheerful cry.

D'Caer bowed, and Jessan did the "stand up, friend" routine with the hand that held the napkin. The older man straightened, and his dark eyes flicked about the room. The head of the D'Caer family had a hungry-predator look to him that made Beka wish for a moment that she'd come to the party as Captain Portree instead of the Princess of Sapne. Tarnekep knew how to deal with types like that, but the Princess Berran . . . *I wish that knife was easier to get to.*

His gaze hit on her, and took in her circlet and her little entourage. She forced herself to give him a courteous "have I met you?" smile in response. He turned to Jessan, and said something or other. Calling in his debts, probably.

Yes, that was it; here they both came. *Gracious, my*

girl, Beka reminded herself. *Act gracious. And don't mess things up this time!*

"Sister dear," said Jessan, with a mischievous smile, "allow me to make known to you my good friend Gentlesir Ebenra D'Caer, of the Rolny D'Caers. Ebenra, this is my sister, Her Royal Highness Princess Berran of Sapne."

"Your Highness," murmured D'Caer, making a bow even lower than Marchen Bres's as he kissed the hand she held out to him.

"Gentlesir D'Caer," she said, as demurely as she could manage, and looked up at him from under her eyelashes while blessing the years-ago schoolmate who'd showed her how.

I can't remember the last time I thought about Jilly. She'll never know her eyelash trick finally did me some good.

It appeared to work as advertised, too. D'Caer showed no intention of moving on to the buffet tables or joining any of the other groups scattered all about. Instead, he made innocuous small talk with Jessan and the Professor and glanced from time to time in her direction—nothing she would call offensive, but probably heady stuff for a sheltered princess. She made a point of catching his eye the next time he looked over at her that way, and then she did the eyelash bit again. The effect was even better the second time around.

Thank you, Jilly Oldigaard—I've got him hooked. Now to maneuver him off alone—but how is a sweet little innocent thing like Berran going to manage that? And right under the noses of her uncle and her chaperone, too!

As if on an unspoken signal, Llannat Hyfid sagged against Beka's right side with a gentle moan. "Oh, dear, Your Highness . . ."

Beka slipped an arm around the shorter woman to support her. The Adept had gone pale under her dark skin, and tiny drops of sweat beaded her forehead.

"Cousin Lana!" Beka exclaimed. "What's wrong? Are you ill?"

Llannat's drooping eyelids lifted. "I feel . . . unwell, Your Highness. The room is so hot. . . ." The eye on the side of the Adept's face away from Ebenra D'Caer closed, and then opened again, even as her faint voice went on, "Does Your Highness think it could have been the shell-fish salad?"

D'Caer gave a harsh laugh. "It's possible, by heaven, as long as Bres keeps on trying to serve it out of season."

"Damned inconsiderate of him, I call it," said Jessan. "Cousin Lana, light of my life, let me take you away from these crowds to recover yourself."

The Khesatan held out his arm, and Llannat took it with another little sigh. "Your Highness shouldn't go on so . . . but if you sister is able to spare me . . . I do feel most peculiar."

The two faded off into the greenery of the atrium garden, leaving Beka alone between the Professor and Ebenra D'Caer.

"Your Grace," D'Caer was saying, "I've long hoped for the chance to pay my respects to your niece. If I could presume to ask the favor of a stroll about the atrium in her company?"

The man certainly knows how to take advantage of an opening, Beka thought.

At her left, the Professor was going grave and protective again. "I'm afraid that with her companion taken ill—"

There's my cue. "Please, dear Uncle?"

Her "uncle" managed to appear indulgent and concerned at the same time. "I don't know what your mother would say, Your Highness."

"I'm sure," said D'Caer, "that a noble and kind-hearted lady such as she must be would say that no harm could possibly come of it."

The Professor smiled at Beka. "Very well, dear child— but only in the downstairs rooms, mind you, and don't stray out onto the grounds. It wouldn't be seemly without your cousin."

"Yes, Uncle," Beka said as she took the arm D'Caer held out to her. "We won't be long, I promise."

Not long at all, she thought happily, *now that we've got him.*

At his post against the atrium wall, Gil nursed along yet another glass of the sparkling pink punch—something put together, he suspected, from a recipe labeled "suitable for maiden aunts and Space Force commanders"—and watched the Sapnish royalty weaving their net around Ebenra D'Caer.

Right now the Princess of Sapne, a shy blush coloring her cheeks, was flirting with D'Caer like a schoolgirl. Knowing what he knew about Beka Rosselin-Metadi, Gil wasn't sure whether the sight made him want to laugh or gave him the cold shivers.

I wish I knew what they plan to do with him, Gil thought. *Then I'd know whether I ought to stop it, or just stand back and watch the fun.*

Without warning, the Princess's companion put a hand to her forehead, swayed, and collapsed against her royal mistress. *Good move*, thought Gil, after the colloquy that followed resulted in the Crown Prince Jamil leading the drooping chaperone out of the atrium. *Let's see what happens next.*

He watched as D'Caer spoke with the grey-haired gentleman. The Princess said something on a note of entreaty; the grey-haired gentleman seemed to waver; D'Caer spoke again, and it was settled. The older man withdrew, and the Princess took D'Caer's arm with a smile.

He works fast, thought Gil, frowning. *And so do they.* Neither Lieutenant Jessan nor the Adept had reappeared, and the man called the Professor had effaced himself as soon as D'Caer strolled off with the Princess. *Whatever they're planning, it's going to happen soon.*

D'Caer and the Princess made a couple of turns about the atrium. D'Caer, Gil noticed, was doing most of the talking. After the two had made their second circuit, Gil saw D'Caer say something to the Princess that made her drop her eyes to hide some emotion or other—modest confusion, one might say, but somehow Gil doubted it. She made a little gesture of one slim hand toward the hallway, and murmured something that made D'Caer look like a hungry man who'd just smelled supper cooking. The two of them headed, not rapidly but with purposeful steps, down the long hall.

Time to circulate again, Commander, Gil said to himself. *This could get interesting.* He moved away from the wall and wandered down the hallway after them, glass of punch in hand.

By the time Gil rounded the corner into the cross-corridor, the Princess and D'Caer had almost reached the door of the last room along. With a curt gesture, D'Caer waved off his ever-present bodyguard.

He's still the same charmer he's always been, thought Gil, as the Princess disappeared through the door—a delicate antique hung on carefully restored hinges—that her escort opened for her. *Doesn't want witnesses.*

The door started swinging closed behind the pair of them, apparently of its own volition.

Now they've got him, thought Gil.

He wasn't the only one thinking. D'Caer's bodyguard hadn't gone farther than the intersection of the two corridors when the door swung shut, and he was evidently brighter than most of the breed. The man's eyes widened as the significance of that quiet closure came home to him. He started down the hallway toward the suspicious door.

"Right you are," muttered Gil, and moved out on an intercept course. In a few long strides, he drew even with D'Caer's man, and then took one more step into a crashing collision that involved both the bodyguard and a passing waiter.

The three men went sprawling onto the marble floor—an effect that had required some last-minute contortions on Gil's part, but with which he found himself inordinately pleased. The wave of pink punch that drenched them all was a happy accident, but one that Gil intended to give due thanks for someday when this was over.

"Oh, my dear sir!" he exclaimed, helping the bodyguard to rise. "Oh, my *very* dear sir . . . !"

Jessan had his arms around D'Caer and was lowering him to the floor as the man's legs crumpled under him. The Khesatan looked at the lump beginning to form under D'Caer's right ear.

"Amazing," he said under his breath, "exactly how useful a first-rate medical education can be."

Beka looked up from straightening her gown. "Let's get him out of here before his bodyguard shows up."

"As you will, dear sister."

The two picked up D'Caer's limp body between them and walked him, toes dragging, to the window that looked out onto the garden. Ari, impressive in his chauffeur's uniform, stood waiting outside the open casement.

"Marchen's head gardener is going to fall on his pruning shears when he sees what your big feet have done to his floral borders," Jessan said.

Ari looked at Jessan and shook his head. "You'd make small talk at your own funeral." He took D'Caer's limp form and lifted it at shoulders and knees. "Got him. See you out front in five minutes."

Jessan closed and locked the window, then crossed the room, opening a hand holoprojector as he did so. He flicked on the expensive toy. The far side of the room wavered like concrete on a hot day and changed into a facsimile of itself—quite hiding, he was pleased to note, the reality behind it, including Beka Rosselin-Metadi in a pale green gown.

"A very high quality holovid," he murmured in satisfaction, and joined Beka behind the projection. With the illusion in place the room appeared empty, and the ribboned-off doorway to the back stairs stood open invitingly on the far side.

From where Jessan stood, he could watch through the

projection as the door opened and D'Caer's bodyguard stepped in. The big man was red-faced and his livery was in disarray. He looked as if he'd slept in his clothes and then given them for washing and pressing to an enthusiastic but untrained laundry maid. Jessan stifled a smile—the laundry maid had apparently used sparkling pink punch for cleaning fluid as well.

I wonder who we can thank for that? he thought. *It doesn't seem quite the Professor's style, somehow, or Llannat's either.*

The bodyguard crossed the room to the window and checked that it was fastened from inside. From there he went to the stairway, stepped delicately over the scarlet restraining ribbon, and disappeared in the direction of the upper floors.

As soon as he was out of sight, Jessan clicked off the holoprojector.

"Come, Berran," he said. "Our uncle is waiting."

She took his arm. He opened the door, and the two of them walked out, side by side. The Professor was standing with Llannat in the atrium.

"Uncle, I am weary," Jessan announced. "Shall we away?"

From Marchen Bres's reception-room window, a Space Force commander in a rumpled and punch-stained dress uniform watched the Sapnish party emerge onto the gravel driveway.

The big chauffeur—plainly Ari Rosselin-Metadi in livery—stood waiting beside the gleaming hovercar, braced at a stiffer attention than he'd probably assumed since he left the Academy. He handed up first the Princess Berran and her companion, next the Crown Prince Jamil, and finally His Grace the Duke. Then he rounded the vehicle and slid into the driver's seat. With a rising whine, the hovercar dashed away down the drive.

At the window, Commander Gil raised his too-small glass of wine in a silent toast.

V. Hyperspace Transit
Asteroid Base

VEN IN hyperspace, the observation deck on *Crystal World* offered a view of stars—not the real ones, of course, but more of the Professor's holographic simulations.

You have to admit it, Ari thought. *The man's an artist.*

As soon as *Crystal World* had left Ovredisi orbit and made her jump, Ari had brought the cha'a pot and a stack of cups from the galley up to the forward dorsal section of the little yacht. Here, a quarter-sphere of spaceworthy armor-glass replaced everything but the rear bulkhead and the deck, and a simulated starscape twinkled outside.

He could have taken his cha'a to the dining salon, a tiny masterpiece of etched glass and silvered-steel filigree work, but the smallness of the room made him feel cramped at the same time as its fussiness made him restless. On the observation deck, at least, he didn't feel as though his head was always about to crash into the crystal chandeliers.

Ignoring the assortment of wrought-metal chairs, he

seated himself on the carpeted deck where he could use one of the sturdier-looking hassocks as a backrest. A moment later, the door in the rear bulkhead slid aside. He looked around.

"Hello, Llannat," he said as the Adept stepped clear of the doors and let them slide shut again behind her. She'd lost no time in returning to her usual clothing, and "Cousin Lana" had apparently gone into the closet right along with her collection of demure black dresses.

Ari waved a hand at the collection of furniture scattered about the green-carpeted observation deck as if on a manicured lawn. "Have a seat someplace. Want some cha'a?"

She smiled. "So that's what I heard calling my name out here. Did you bring an extra cup?"

"I brought a whole stack of them," Ari said. He poured her some of the steaming drink. "The rest of the gang's probably going to show up fairly soon."

Llannat took the cup and saucer and sat down in a chair next to Ari. "How's our passenger?"

Ari shrugged. "You'll have to ask Jessan. He took over that end of things once we got D'Caer tucked away."

"Crew berthing?" she asked.

"That's right."

"Where are you going to bunk, then?"

The doorway opened as she spoke, and Jessan walked in. "Ari's in stateroom three, with me," said the Khesatan. "But if he talks in his sleep I swear I'm going to throw him out here with some pillows and a blanket."

Ari laughed. "You and who else?"

Jessan picked out a chair within easy reach of the cha'a-pot, straightened the cushion a little, and sat down. "There is that," he admitted; pouring himself a cup. "Maybe I'll just move out here myself. I have to check on D'Caer's condition every few hours anyway, if we're going to keep him under all the way to base."

"You don't have to handle the whole job yourself, just because you're feeling guilty about living it up while Ari and I waited on you hand and foot," Llannat said. "We'll take our shifts, too."

"Now, that's an idea I can approve of, Mistress Hyfid," said Beka. She came up the steep metal stairway from the *Crystal World*'s bridge, located below the observation deck in the yacht's forward ventral section. The Professor followed close at her heels. "With three medics tending him round the clock, D'Caer can't claim he didn't get quality attention."

She poured herself a cup of cha'a and carried it over to a chair-and-hassock set that offered a good view of the rest of the deck. Like Llannat, she'd taken the time to change her clothes, and once again wore Tarnekep Portree's Mandeynan-style clothing. Her yellow hair was tied back from her face with one of Portree's black velvet ribbons, and of Princess Berran, only a few smudges of makeup remained.

The Professor, not surprisingly, looked much the same as he had before: an elderly gentleman with a great deal of money and quiet, if a bit old-fashioned, good taste. Ari and the rest of the group on the observation deck watched in a sudden stillness as he filled a cup at the cha'a pot and sat down.

The Entiboran looked around the little group. "Captain," he said, "Mistress Hyfid, Lieutenant Commander Jessan, Lieutenant Rosselin-Metadi—the time has come for us to decide what to do with Gentlesir Ebenra D'Caer."

"You know what I want to do with him, Professor," said Beka. She stretched her long legs out on the hassock in front of her and regarded the polished toes of her boots with an expression that Ari found more than a little unsettling. "And I hadn't heard that it was a voting proposition."

"No, my lady," the Professor said. "But our advice, if you wish it, is at your disposal."

"Quite the diplomat, aren't you, 'Uncle'?" Beka said. "But you're right, I suppose . . . so who'll go first? How about you, Ari? You look like you're just bursting with things you'd like to say to me."

Ari counted to ten, slowly. *You knew she might get like this,* he reminded himself. *You thought you could handle it, remember?*

Aloud, he said only, "Go easy, Bee. You don't know for certain yet if he's guilty."

"Do you seriously think he isn't?" she demanded.

Before he could think of anything else to say, Llannat's gentle voice spoke up from the chair beside him. "We haven't got proof."

Jessan looked across at the Adept with a curious expression. "The comps back at the asteroid put his guilt at ninety per cent probable," he said. "Isn't that enough?"

Llannat shook her head. "Not for a private trial and execution."

An uncomfortable silence followed. She had, Adeptlike, put her finger on the problem. Jessan had never taken his eyes away from Llannat during the interchange, and when he spoke again his voice was low and unwontedly sober.

"What if D'Caer confesses?"

Beka gave a short laugh. "Him? You've got to be kidding."

Jessan glanced over at her as she spoke, and shook his head. "We've already got him doped to the gills—just vary the dose a little, and he'll answer anything."

"It's not quite that simple," said the Professor, "but the suggestion has merit."

Ari shook his head. "No. No chemicals."

Beka fixed him with a cold blue stare. "I don't care what sort of philosophical objections you picked up from your scaly buddies on Maraghai. This is no time to get particular."

He shook his head again. "If you want a confession that badly, I can always try reasoning with him."

She cocked her head. "Reasoning, big brother?"

"Strenuously, if necessary."

They gazed at one another across the observation deck, and Beka began to smile. "Sounds good to me."

"But inelegant," the Professor said. "Confessions gained in that manner always have a taint to them."

The grey-haired Entiboran looked directly at Llannat, and there was a long pause before he spoke again. "You could help us get the proof, Mistress Hyfid, if you would."

Ari expected to hear an angry denial from the Adept. Instead, she looked down at her hands and answered without raising her eyes, "No Adept has been trained as an interrogator since the end of the war."

"I have some small skill in the art," the Professor said. "With your assistance, I think we can get the confirmation we need without doing violence to D'Caer's person."

There was another drawn-out silence before Llannat said, "Or to his mind?"

Beka slammed her empty cup down on the glass-topped side table at her elbow with a violence that threatened to break cup and tabletop both. "Damnation take it, Mistress Hyfid! What the hell else do you want?"

"Gently, my lady," said the Professor. "Mistress Hyfid and I understand one another, I believe." He looked back again at Llannat. "I give you my word, Mistress. Neither invasion nor compulsion."

"And what if D'Caer does admit his guilt?" Beka asked hotly. "Then what am I supposed to do? Give him shuttle fare and send him home?"

Nobody else spoke, and Llannat was looking back down at her hands again. Finally, the Adept lifted her head and met Beka's challenging gaze.

"Captain Rosselin-Metadi," she said, "if Ebenra D'Caer condemns himself out of his own mouth and of his own volition, then you can do whatever you want with him and I won't lift a hand to stop you."

Someone was knocking at the door . . .

Ebenra D'Caer let fall the arm that he'd slid around the

Princess of Sapne's shoulders. His bodyguard stuck his head into the room.

"Your pardon, sir, but there's a call for you."

D'Caer scowled. "Can't you see that I'm busy?"

"It's important."

"Oh, very well."

He turned back to Princess Berran. "Excuse me, Your Highness, but I'll have to leave you alone here for a moment."

She smiled at him. Her blue eyes were bright and eager in spite of the modest blush that pinkened her pale cheeks. "I understand, Gentlesir D'Caer—but hurry back. Uncle will scold me dreadfully if I'm gone too long."

He kissed her hand. "I live for your smile, Your Highness," he said, and followed the bodyguard out.

The hallway and atrium of Marchen Bres's country estate buzzed with the sound of sociable chatter. The bodyguard walked ahead, making a path through the crush of party-goers as the two men made their way to a quiet alcove off the main atrium.

D'Caer followed his bodyguard into the alcove. The guard pressed a stud set into the wainscoting, and the back wall slid aside to reveal a secure comm-link console, its red "call waiting" light flashing on and off. D'Caer picked up the handset and the light went out.

"Get away at once," a rough voice whispered over the link. "They know everything."

"What do you mean?" he demanded. "Who are you?"

The rough voice didn't answer, but hurried on, sounding breathless and afraid. "Space Force Intelligence knows about the Council assassination. They've sent a man to Ovredis to arrest you."

D'Caer looked out into the main room. A Space Force commander lounged against the far wall, resplendent in his dress blues. *He hasn't moved since I came in. Is he the one?*

The commander glanced to left and right. D'Caer followed the glances. Now that he knew what to look for, he could count half a dozen muscular young men with military haircuts dispersed in key positions around the room.

A chill ran down D'Caer's spine. He set the handset back down without looking at it, and forced himself to gaze about the atrium with a casual air. *After all*, he reminded himself, *this isn't the worst scrape you've ever been in.*

Wait . . . there was the Princess again, standing just outside the alcove. He'd all but forgotten about that interrupted bit of diversion.

He frowned. "You shouldn't have come here, Your Highness."

"I was bored, sitting all alone," she said. "So I came looking for you."

He had no time now for royal fluffbrains, no matter how entertainingly innocent; he was about to send her back to her uncle when an idea struck him, and he smiled.

He stepped up to her and took her arm. "Then we can go together, Your Highness."

Her blue eyes widened. "Oh, but I couldn't do that— Uncle would be so *very* angry!"

D'Caer pressed his other hand against her waist, then tilted it up to show her a tiny hand-blaster. "We're going."

The fine blue vein in her throat leaped with the sudden race of her pulse, but she made no resistance as he guided her firmly through the press of bodies to the front door.

"Summon your vehicle," he whispered.

The Princess of Sapne tilted her head. The doorman said a few words over the in-house comm circuit to the parking bays, where the ranks of hovercars waited with their chauffeurs.

The royal family's hovercar was waiting when they reached the bottom of the steps. The driver, a huge man in Sapnish livery, leaped out to open the rear door and stand beside it.

"No tricks, Your Highness," D'Caer whispered in the girl's ear. "Or I will hurt you. Badly."

The girl gasped and bit her lip. D'Caer could feel her whole body trembling against him as they climbed into the hovercar's private rear compartment.

"The spaceport, and hurry," he commanded the driver.

The chauffeur inclined his head and shut the door behind them, then took his place behind the controls. The hovercar purred forward. D'Caer watched the countryside flowing smoothly past the windows for a moment, and then turned to the Princess.

"Ah, well," he said, and shifted the miniature blaster over to his other hand. "No reason why the moment should be wasted. Shall we resume where we left off, my dear?"

The Princess shook her head wordlessly, and shrank against the seat back in a useless attempt at evasion. D'Caer contemplated the fearful young woman for a moment. Then, still smiling, he reached out with his free hand to cup one of her breasts, firm and warm under the fabric of her gown.

"It's a good thing," Jessan said, "that you made Beka leave off her knife for this little charade. Otherwise we'd have to wash Gentlesir Ebenra D'Caer out of that hovercar with a hose."

"She's well in control of herself," the Professor replied, without looking up from the control panel of the asteroid base's main holoprojector.

"You hope," said Jessan.

He stood watching at the Professor's shoulder, one hand tapping out a restless rhythm on the panel's edge while the older man created an unrolling landscape around the mockup hovercar shell. Llannat Hyfid sat cross-legged on the cement floor of the projection room at some distance from them both, a small figure in Adept's black, eyes closed and features immobile as she held D'Caer in the beglamoured state that made him more susceptible to the Professor's holographic illusions.

"Still," the Entiboran conceded, as the overhead monitor showed D'Caer's hand sliding down below Beka's waist, "it might be wise to abridge the 'trip to the port' sequence. I doubt that he'll notice."

The hovercar whirred through the spaceport gates, flashed arrogantly past the commercial craft on its way to the private docking bays, and pulled up with a whine of nullgravs at the entrance ramp of a yacht painted in the blue and silver of the Royal House of Sapne. The driver pulled the side door open.

"Here so soon?" asked D'Caer. Briefly, he considered compelling the Princess to board the yacht with him, as a combination of insurance and entertainment for the journey, but something about the look of the huge chauffeur stopped him.

Loyal family retainer to the core, that one, he thought. *If I tried to abduct Her Royal Silliness, he'd pound me into the pavement before he noticed I'd shot him dead. As it is, I'll be in hyperspace by the time he's done calming her hysterics.*

"Thank you for the loan of the yacht, my dear," he said instead. "This will only take a little while."

He gave the Princess a farewell kiss that she bore with only a faint whimpering nose in her throat, and then slid out of the hovercar. "Good-bye, Your Highness."

He strolled up the boarding ramp and shut the hatch behind him.

"High time," Jessan muttered, as Beka and Ari climbed out of the mock-up hovercar and headed over toward the lift doors. Behind them, the appearance of the "spaceport" shifted and changed. The only parts that remained were those visible from the windows of *Crystal World*, docked back in the asteroid base's chilly, echoing bay.

Readouts flickered on the console screens. "There's his lift-off now," said the Professor.

The Entiboran touched a sequence of keys on the console control panel. The ship pulled down under heavy tractor beams, imitating the acceleration of launch, and the holoprojections outside the windows showed Ovredis dwindling away.

"I hope he enjoys the trip," Jessan said absently, most of his attention on the monitors that showed Beka and Ari's progress across the floor of the bay. Beka seemed mostly disgusted—she wore the expression of someone who's just found a dead insect at the bottom of the cha'a pot—but the look on Ari's face made the Khesatan shake his head.

Somehow I don't think Beka was the one on the edge of breaking back there.

The big medic had himself under control, though, by the time he and his sister stepped out of the lift into the projection room and came up to the control panel. "How did it go?" he asked.

Jessan shrugged. "You'll have to ask the Professor. But it looked good from out front."

"It damned well better have," Beka said. "As far as I'm concerned, the only question left is whether I give him to Dadda for a solstice present or cycle him out of an airlock with a space suit and half an hour of air."

"Perhaps we shouldn't be so hasty, my lady," the Professor said. A new light on the console had begun to flash. "Our friend wants to make a long-distance comm call through the planet's orbiting link stations."

"Interesting," said Jessan. "Are we able to oblige him?"

The Professor smiled. "Fortunately, we are prepared for the eventuality. At the moment, the comm links on *Crystal World* connect only to this panel."

The flashing red light changed to yellow as the Professor picked up a handset, and the speaker crackled. "This is Ebenra D'Caer on Ovredis," said a scratchy voice. "I want to talk to Nivome."

Nivome, thought Jessan. *I knew this felt too easy.*

"I'm sorry, sir," the Professor said. A readout panel beside the handset showed two wave patterns superimposed, indicating a distorter in operation at the Professor's end of the link. "Nivome isn't talking to anyone."

"He'll talk to me," said the scratchy voice. "Get him."

"If you insist, sir."

The imitation of an offended family servant had Jessan suppressing a laugh in spite of himself. Then the Professor switched off the comm link and turned to the others.

"Gentlesir D'Caer can stay in suspense for a few minutes," he said. "Meanwhile, we have trouble."

Beka bit her lower lip and regarded the monitor views of *Crystal World* with an expression that made her look more like Tarnekep Portree than the Princess of Sapne. Next to her, Ari shook his head in frustration and scowled at the comm set.

"Who's this Nivome?" he asked.

"Like the Professor said—trouble," Jessan answered. "If he's who I think he is—and the name's not all that common—he heads the Five Families of Rolny and makes D'Caer look like a pauper. Owns a couple of planets outright, that sort of thing. I met him a few times, back home on Khesat."

"Excellent," said the Professor, his face brightening. "Can you imitate his voice?"

"Not very well."

"Do the best you can, Commander. It's a long way from Ovredis to Rolny, and our friend won't be surprised to find himself contending with interference on the hyperspace relays."

"Indeed." Jessan reached for the handset. "I'll provide Nivome for you, then—but you'd better make that 'heavy interference.' "

"Ion storms, I think, in the Arcari sector," the Professor murmured, bending over the control panel once more. "Over to you, Commander."

Jessan closed his eyes for a second, calling up everything he could remember about Nivome's speech patterns from a handful of long-ago casual meetings. *Just a touch of the accent should do the trick for something this short. And don't worry about timbre and pitch. The Professor's ion storms can handle that. All right, then—here we go.*

"Rolny here," he said over the comm link. "D'Caer, this had better be important."

"It is. Space Force is onto us."

"Calm yourself, D'Caer," said Jessan. "What is there for them to find out?"

"You know damn well what!" snarled D'Caer's voice over the link. "And if they know I arranged the Domina's assassination, how much do you want to bet they don't know who put me up to it—and why?"

Out of his own mouth, Jessan thought with satisfaction. *And willingly, too.*

The Khesatan glanced over at Llannat, still deep in her trance. He wondered if the Adept knew what Beka had endured to fulfill her part of that bargain the two women had struck back aboard *Crystal World*.

"Are you sure about all this?" he said to D'Caer over the comm link by way of encouragement.

"It's true," the scratchy voice replied. "There was a Space Force man here to arrest me, but I got clear. You'd better do the same."

Time for a touch of panic, Jessan decided. "You can't show up here, D'Caer!"

"What kind of fool do you think I am? I won't go near Darvell. Just watch yourself."

Damn, thought Jessan. *If Nivome's holed up on Darvell then nothing can touch him. That place is worse than Rolny.*

"I can handle things on my end," he said over the link. "Is there anything else you want to tell me?"

"Nothing. Out."

The link clicked off.

"Now that," said the Professor, "was certainly informative. My congratulations, Commander, on an inspired performance."

"One manages," Jessan said. "What next?"

"The *'Hammer* and I are going to Darvell," Beka said. "Anybody who wants to come along, can—but I'm going regardless."

"And I, my lady," said the Professor. "Lieutenant Rosselin-Metadi?"

Ari ignored him. "You know I'm with you, Bee."

"Ari," she said, "you don't know what Darvell is like. It's not even part of the Republic."

The big medic shook his head and growled one of his Selvauran oaths deep in his throat. "I told you once already—I'm coming along. How about you, Jessan?"

"Of course," he said. *Darvell. Now I know I've gone crazy.* "I wouldn't miss it for all the worlds."

"Thanks," Beka said. "All three of you. I suppose we can ask Mistress Hyfid when she comes out of her trance."

"Are you taking volunteers for something?" came a voice, faint but clear, from across the projection room.

Jessan turned his head, and saw Llannat getting stiffly to her feet. The Adept looked like a good candidate for a hot bath, a solid meal, and twelve hours of sleep, but her step was firm enough as she came up to join the others at the console.

"We're planning to go visit Darvell and get ourselves killed," Ari explained. The prospect didn't seem to be bothering him much. "Want to come along?"

"You're all crazy," Llannat said. "Am I invited?"

The Professor made the Adept a formal bow. "Your presence, Mistress, would do our campaign great honor."

She smiled at the Entiboran. "Then how could I refuse?"

The console beeped.

"Hyperspace jump calculations coming in from *Crystal World*," Beka said. "Professor?"

"Let's see where he wants to go," said the Entiboran. In silence, they watched the numbers scroll up the console screen. Beka was the first to speak.

"I'll be damned," she said, as the Professor keyed in more commands, and the star-rush of hyperspace entry appeared in holoprojected glory before the cockpit windows of *Crystal World*. "The son of a bitch thinks he's jumping for the Mageworlds!"

VI. Asteroid Base

A RI'S DEEP voice broke the resulting silence. "The Mageworlds. Bee, are you sure?"

Jessan turned from the comp screen to see the big medic looking at the captain with a frown. In response, Beka pointed to the screen.

"The coordinates are right there, big brother," she said. "Work out the course for yourself if you don't believe me."

"I believe you, I believe you," said Ari. "But the Mageworlds . . . damn. Why can't things be simple for a change?"

Jessan shrugged. "The galaxy hates you?" He turned to Beka. "What do we do now, Captain?"

"Do?" She regarded the rest of them with a bright, challenging gaze. "As far as I'm concerned, *Warhammer* has an appointment on Darvell. All D'Caer's done is raise the question of timing. Professor—your opinion?"

"That first things come first, my lady," said the Entiboran, gentle-voiced as always. "Gentlesir D'Caer can keep indefinitely—my robots are equally proficient as valets and as jailors—but Nivome the Rolny owes your House a debt that is long overdue.''

Ari nodded. ''I agree.''

''Don't worry,'' said Beka. ''We'll see that Nivome pays up. But I've got a bad feeling about that Mageworlds jump.'' She glanced over toward Llannat. ''Mistress Hyfid, if anybody in the civilized galaxy knows about the Magelords, it's an Adept. What do you say?''

Llannat glanced around from the monitor she'd been frowning at while the others talked. ''What? Oh, D'Caer.'' She shook her head. ''D'Caer's not a Magelord. The smell's not on him.''

Beka stared at her. ''Damn it, we just *saw*—''

''Let me finish, Captain!''

Beka's eyebrows went up for a moment, and then, to Jessan's surprise, Ari's sister chuckled. ''Since you put it that way, Mistress . . . go on.''

Llannat nodded, but her eyes had already gone back to the image of *Crystal World* on the monitor screen. She kept on watching it as she spoke.

''What we just saw, Captain, means that we've got native-born citizens of the Republic in direct contact with the Mageworlds.'' She lifted her eyes from the screen, and her expression was sober. ''Anybody care for a try at reading the future? It shouldn't take an Adept for this one.''

Jessan felt cold. ''Speaking as a Adept,'' he said, ''how much breathing space do you think the Republic's got?''

Llannat gave him a bleak smile. ''Let me tell you something about seeing the future, Jessan—most of the time it's about as useful as getting anonymous notes in your mailbox. You want prophecies whistled up to order, go to a fortune-teller or pull slips of paper out of a hat.''

''In other words,'' Beka said, ''you don't know.''

The Adept sighed. ''Even Master Ransome's predictions are obscure, Captain, and I'm nowhere near in his league. But I know what the Selvaurs would say.''

''What's that, Mistress?''

" 'Hunt while you can. The weather may change tomorrow.' "

"Got you," said Beka. "That's it, then. But let's get D'Caer tucked away first."

Jessan heard the click of comp keys on the panel next to him as the Professor entered yet another set of commands into the projection room's control console.

"The gas in *Crystal World*'s intruder-immobilization systems will take effect soon," said the Entiboran. "After that, the robots can fetch D'Caer out of the yacht and convey him to the maximum-security cells."

Ari looked curious. "This place has some of those?"

"Of course," the Professor said. "One never knows when such things may come in handy."

"Fine," said Beka. "You know what's here, Professor, and what we're likely to need. How soon can we lift?"

The Professor thought in silence for a moment. "Allowing for dinner and a full night of rest before lift-off—if we start working immediately, Captain, we can lift within a Standard day."

"Then let's move, gentles," said Beka. "We're hitting Darvell, and our prisoner can sit here until we come home to collect him."

If we come home, thought Jessan, but he knew better than to say that aloud.

Ari stood in the center of the asteroid base's well-stocked and up-to-date sickbay, surrounded by the *'Hammer*'s first-aid chest, the emergency kit from the Nammerin Medical Station's aircar, and a collection of sturdy boxes and cartons. Behind him, the door to the docking bay snicked open, and he turned.

His sister entered, dressed in a coverall and spaceboots, and carrying a pocket comp. She hadn't yet taken the time to get back into her Tarnekep rig, for which Ari felt thankful. Beka was enough of a handful under ordinary circumstances, but wearing the face and affecting the style of her highly unpleasant Mandeynan alter ego made all her natural tendencies even worse.

She stopped just inside the door, and looked at the array of boxes. "Are you planning to pack out the whole sickbay?"

"As much of it as I can," he said. "I'd take the bonemender and the healing pod, if I thought the *'Hammer* had hookups for them."

"She's an armed freighter, not a hospital ship," said Beka. She glanced about the room again, and shook her head. "Well, you're the medic."

"I'll number the boxes in order of priority," he promised. "How are things going on your end?"

"The Prof is tuning up the electronic cloaking gear on *Defiant* now."

"Mmph," Ari said, pulling boxes of sprain tape and plain bandages down off the shelf in front of him and making a layer of them in the bottom of the nearest carton. He looked from the loaded shelves to the empty boxes. "I wish I knew just how much cubic was going to be free in the *'Hammer*'s hold. . . . How did an Entiboran gentleman like the Professor wind up owning a Magebuilt ship?"

His sister punched a code into the comp. "I never asked," she said. "I figure it's his own business what he did back in the old days."

"Even if it included trading with the Mageworlds? That's treason, you know."

Beka looked exasperated. "My word, Ari, but you can be stuffy sometimes! He was a confidential agent of House Rosselin for years before the war even started; if he picked up a Magebuilt scoutship it's probably because he needed one."

She paused, and her expression changed to something Ari would have pegged as fond tolerance, if he'd thought for a moment that Bee had it in her to be tolerant of anything.

"Besides," she went on, "the Prof may or may not have been a friend of the Republic's—if he had to choose between House Rosselin and the rest of the galaxy, I don't think he'd give the galaxy a second thought—but he's certainly been a good friend to me."

Ari frowned. "If he's such a good friend, why is he letting you go charging off into trouble on Darvell?"

The sickbay doors opened again, and Jessan entered—just in time, it seemed, to catch Ari's last remark. The Khesatan laughed. "Royalty, my good man, can do whatever it pleases," he said in his best Sapnish accent, "and it's not the place of a loyal family retainer to argue. Or so our friend the Professor seems to think."

"Let it lie, Nyls," said Beka.

But the look she gave the fair-haired medic wasn't nearly as chilly as Ari would have expected, knowing just how much his sister hated any reminder of her royal antecedents. House Rosselin had reckoned inheritance in the female line, and all the galaxy knew it. Calling the six-year-old Beka "sweet little Domina" was what had bought Tarveet of Pleyver that garden slug in his dinner salad, and Bee didn't seem to have mellowed any on the subject since then.

Right now, though, she and Jessan were looking at each other in silence, and Ari was at a loss to interpret either expression. Neither his friend nor his sister appeared inclined to speak first; Ari sighed, coughed to gain Jessan's attention, and asked, "What brings you in here?"

"The hoversled you sent for," said Jessan. "It's outside waiting to get loaded."

"That's right, Ari," said Beka. "Fill as many boxes as you want to. They won't take up more than a corner of the hold."

"Thanks," muttered Ari. He turned to Jessan. "How's the tune-up going?"

"Like a charm," said the Khesatan. "We can slip into Darvelline space by the back door and never be noticed."

"Why all the extra bother?" Ari asked his sister. "Why not just go in as *Pride of Mandeyn* on a normal run?"

Beka shook her head. "No way we can be the *Pride* for

this trip. What we'll be doing is nothing at all like the way a merchant does business—especially on Darvell.''

"You've been there before?'' Ari asked.

"No,'' she said. "I never needed to go out of the Republic to find a cargo. But I've heard some real horror stories.''

"What kind of horror stories?'' Jessan inquired, looking interested. "Blood sacrifices at the dark of the moon? Cannibals dancing in the streets? Carnivorous flora?''

"You've seen too many episodes of 'Spaceways Patrol,' '' Ari told him. "All right, Bee, enlighten us. What's Darvell supposed to be like?''

"It's so calm and law-abiding it's unnatural,'' said Beka. "Everybody's numbered off as they land, and outside the port compound it's strictly 'no spacers allowed.' You either stay on your ship, or you bunk in one of the government dormitories inside the fence.''

"What about the rest of the world?'' he asked.

"Who knows?'' Beka said. "Lots of people immigrate to Darvell, and you don't hear of anybody leaving. But it's no place for a free-trader to do business. Everything works through a government middleman—no chance to talk to the locals and strike your own bargains—and the port captains and consignment inspectors are supposed to be above reproach.''

"What does that mean?'' asked Ari.

Beka looked grim. "Nobody has *ever* bribed one.''

Ari thought about that for a while. "You're right,'' he said finally. "That does sound frightening.''

Dinner that night turned out to be a silent and edgy affair. Ari didn't find lack of appetite a problem—not after hours of hard work punctuated only by short breaks for cha'a and sandwiches—but he still excused himself from the table as soon as he could.

Nobody else was showing any tendency to linger over dessert either, which helped. He didn't get any arguments when he made his good-nights to the rest of the *Hammer*'s crew and went back to his room. It wasn't until he'd pulled the sheet up over him and kneaded the pillow into an acceptable state of yieldingness that he realized he'd started reverting to the hunting lessons of his adolescence on Maraghai.

Sleep well, youngling, Ferrdacorr had told him again and again. *Once you're on the blood trail, you can't stop because you're tired.*

Yawning, Ari wondered what his father's old friend would have said about this particular hunt. He decided that the Selvaur would probably have approved. The Master of Darvell—powerful, cunning, and a predator in his own right—made a quarry worthy of anyone's hunting. And the Lords of the Forest didn't think much of the thin-skins' habit of handing over the dirty work to paid help like Security and the Space Force.

At least this time, thought Ari, *I get to carry a blaster.*

On the Long Hunt, the solitary expedition that by Selvaur tradition had made him into a full adult member of the clan, things had been different. One by one, on Midsummer Night, he and his agemates had set out from the river-valley settlement, heading into the mountains to stalk the carnivores of the high slopes. Great predators like the cliffdragon, the darkstalker, and the muscular, lean-bodied *sigrikka* were the only beasts on Maraghai that could match the strength and ferocity of a full-grown Selvaur. Taking such a prey by strength and skill alone would prove that the blood of the Forest Lords had not run thin.

Therefore, as custom decreed, the youths had gone into the mountains unarmed. Some of the Old Ones had proposed that Ari be allowed a hunting knife, to make up for the lack of serviceable teeth and claws, but Ferrdacorr had turned down the concession. If his friend Jos Metadi's thin-skinned cub wanted to come into the clan, let him do it according to the rules.

By their own rights, though, neither Ferrda nor the Old Ones had been unreasonable. Since it wasn't Ari's fault that he'd been born without a thick scaly hide, they hadn't forbidden warm clothing and good stout boots. By the third fruitless week of his hunt, he was feeling grateful for even that small indulgence. Selvaur youths had gotten trapped in the high ranges by the coming of winter before, and while most of them lived through the experience to make their hunt again, even a Selvaur could freeze if the weather got cold enough.

If I do have to winter over in the mountains, Ari thought, sitting on a pile of sun-warmed rocks that gave a good view of the deep, tree-filled valley below him, *at least I'll have a jacket between me and the cold until something better doesn't run fast enough.*

He took a bite of his breakfast—a cliffmouse that had failed to dodge a thrown rock—and pondered future courses of action while he chewed. *Suppose you do have to winter over? You haven't had any trouble keeping yourself fed so far—it's only the big ones that seem to have taken themselves someplace else. Find yourself a snug little cave somewhere, get a steady fire going . . . you could probably make it through until spring.*

He tore off another mouthful of the uncooked meat. *Only one problem. If you don't come back before the snow falls, Ferrda's going to feel honor-bound to let Mother and Father know about it . . . and Father might be willing to let things ride until the thaw, but Mother never would. There'd be rescue teams all over the place before you could sneeze, and Ferrda would never live it down.*

He couldn't cut his hunt short and go back empty-handed, for the same reason. But in three weeks on this side of the mountains he hadn't turned up track or sign of anything larger than a rock hog, and it was beginning to look like he might have to change his hunting grounds. If another cub had been hunting the same range, the two of them together might well have driven off all the other predators.

So if I do go over the mountains, I'd better head out today so I'll have a fighting chance of finding something and getting back home before—

A distant cry, borne up to him on the wind from the valley below, stopped him in midthought. He knew that sound, high-pitched and angry like a ripsaw chewing through green wood. Somewhere down among those trees, a *sigrikka* had finished a successful stalk.

Maybe I could— he began to think, but then more noises came up from below: a Selvaur's fighting roar, cut off short, and once again that ripsaw yowl.

Ari dropped the bloody remains of his breakfast and started downhill into the valley. One of the Forest Lords was in deep trouble, and not even the Long Hunt took precedence over that.

He found the injured Selvaur more by luck than anything else, luck and the sharp hearing that let him make a good guess at the direction from which the sounds had come. Once he reached the valley floor, though, smell and not sound guided him the rest of the way. Compared to a Forest Lord he had no sense of smell at all, but even a thin-skin's nose was keen enough to pick up the sweet, heavy scent of hot blood on the clean mountain air.

Moving as fast as he could without making a racket that would arouse the whole forest, Ari followed the smell upwind, his ears straining for any sound that might help him in the search. When he heard one, he didn't like it.

I've never heard a grown Selvaur whimpering like that, he thought moving faster. *Only sick little ones . . . the babies and the younglings. And when they cry that way, you don't waste time sending for a medic, you put them in the settlement aircar and go looking for one.*

He started running, and the hell with the noise. The smell of blood filled his nostrils, and he knew he was nearly there. Another two strides, and he almost tripped over Issgrillikk—his agemate, friend, and foster-cousin— twisted around himself in pain at the base of one of the Great Trees, his claws gouging up the rough, grey-brown bark and tearing long white streaks into the inner wood.

"Issgrillikk!" Ari dropped down to his knees at the foot of the tree, and called to his cousin again. "Issgrillikk!"

He choked on the name as he saw how the *sigrikka* had laid his agemate open from crotch to breastbone with a single slashing blow, leaving the contents of the body cavity to spill out onto the moss-covered ground and taint the air all around with the smell of death. *It didn't even finish the kill,* thought Ari. *It had all the time in the world to do it, and it didn't even bother.*

''Issgrillikk!'' he called again. This time, the pain-clouded eyes showed recognition, and his cousin said *Ari Rosselin-Metadi* in a feeble growl.

It was like a Selvaur, to bring out his full formal name at a time like this; Ari swallowed a laugh that was mostly a sob and said, *What happened, Issgrillikk?*

I was tracking . . . . sigrikka. Didn't know . . . it was tracking me. I never even . . . smelled it com—nnnghrrr! The sentence ended in a wordless cry of pain, as Issgrillikk's claws dug deep furrows into the wood of the tree. When the spasm ended, Issgrillikk looked at him again. *Ari . . . I need . . . ***

The Selvaur's voice failed him then, but his eyes still held Ari's, and Ferrdacorr's thin-skinned fosterling knew what his cousin and agemate required of him.

Even if I could carry him as far as the settlements, Ari thought helplessly, *he'd die before we got there. He's dying now—but it's too slow. The rock hogs don't care whether or not their food is still breathing, as long as it doesn't fight.*

He looked down at his hands—big, heavy hands, clenched so hard that under the dirt of three weeks' hunting the knuckles showed white. Strong hands, for a thin-skin.

At his knees, Issgrillikk whimpered in pain, as he had done before his agemate showed up and pride had made him stop. Even pride wasn't helping now. Ari heard the sound and swallowed hard.

Forgive me, cousin, he said, and struck with all his strength.

Ferrdacorr had taught his foster-child thoroughly and

well. One blow was all it took, and then Ari pressed his forehead against the rough bark of the Great Tree, and cried like an unblooded child. But even while he wept, some part of his mind he hadn't known existed kept asking why a hunting beast would have left a wounded prey alive when there was ample time to finish off the kill.

When a darkstalker goes rogue and begins attacking the settlements, the Forest Lords stake out a fanghorn to draw it in . . . the way Issgrillikk drew you in . . . live bait to trap a predator hunting in another's range. . . .

His brother Owen would have said that he took his warning from the currents of power that held the universe together. But Owen didn't need to hear the padding of heavy paws on soft loam, or to smell the meat-eater scent as the wind shifted—and Ari knew better than to claim a sensitivity he didn't possess. Only Ferrdacorr's training and his own sharp ears kept him from following down the road Issgrillikk had already taken. He spun around and set his back to the tree, just as the *sigrikka* roared and began its charge.

Ari knew better than to run; the *sigrikka* had hunted running animals all is life. His only chance lay in letting the predator close in, and then keeping out of the way of those sharp, gut-slashing claws long enough to make his own kill. A fighting cry tore its way out of his throat, and he pushed himself away from the Great Tree to meet the *sigrikka*'s charge.

The *sigrikka* slammed into him like a pressor beam coming on at full power, and the weight and momentum of the charging animal pushed him backward. He let himself topple over, wrapping his legs around the *sigrikka*'s body and locking his ankles tight as he fell, so that his belly was pressed against the beast's when they hit the ground.

Over and over they rolled on the bloodstained earth, gripped together by the pressure of Ari's legs. The *sigrikka*'s claws raked at his back and ribs, shredded his clothing and lacerated the flesh beneath. Hot amber eyes glared into his face, and long teeth flashed as the *sigrikka* made a try for his throat.

He snarled like an animal himself. *Try to rip me up, will you? We'll see about that!*

He jammed his left forearm sideways into the predator's gaping mouth, and pressed back. Powerful jaws closed, and the *sigrikka*'s teeth pierced his leather jacket and sank into the muscle beneath like so many white-hot knives.

Enraged by the pain, he snarled again. *Bite me, will you? Stalk my cousin and use him for bait, will you? No more!*

He braced his right arm against the back of the *sigrikka*'s neck and pushed hard into it with his left, forcing the animal's head up and backward. The *sigrikka* tried to jerk free, but found itself trapped by its own teeth, set deep in the muscle of Ari's forearm. Ari gritted his teeth on renewed pain as the *sigrikka* fought to tear itself loose, and failed.

Now—you pay—for Issgrillikk! he choked out, and put all the strength of his broad shoulders into a relentless pressure that levered the *sigrikka*'s head further and further back, until a snapping sound came from inside the beast's neck, and its muscular body twitched and then lay still.

VII. Asteroid Base

NYLES JESSAN made another restless circuit of his sleeping quarters, pausing to watch the sunset outside the wide picture window. The window had been producing vistas of Khesat for him ever since he had taken up residence, and the sun tonight had been setting for a couple of Standard hours over the fountains and flowers of a Khesatan water garden.

As always, he spared a moment to admire the Professor's artistry. The garden view didn't have the almost painful reality of the room from the Summer Palace, but as a courtesy done for a guest it was impressive: the *leriola* blossoms floating on the long rectangular moon pool opened as he watched, while the upper edge of the sun slid below the faraway horizon.

He turned away from the window and began roaming again. He wasn't in the mood for a moon viewing tonight, even if the moons and their reflections had been real.

The little holoprojector he'd carried as Crown Prince Jamil lay on the bedside table next to a porcelain vase holding a set of Khesatan reed flutes. Stretching himself out full length on the bedspread, he picked up the projector and turned on the last act of *By Honor Betray'd*. This time, though, the grandeur and majesty of the classic drama failed to move him. When he realized that he hadn't followed two consecutive lines of the Farewell Soliloquy, he punched the Off button and killed the projection.

He sat up on the rumpled bedspread and—for lack of any other occupation—began pulling reed flutes out of the vase. They'd been produced by the Professor's robots out of synthetic reeds, and only one of the lot appeared playable. He tried a note or two, found the tone adequate, and went on into the first bars of a half-remembered practice piece.

But even the fifth Mixolydian Etude failed to have the same soporific effect it had possessed in his boyhood. He shoved the flute back into the vase with the others, stood up, and began prowling the room once more.

His eye fell on the sable form of one of the Professor's robots, standing in its niche by the door. Like a skilled organic servant, the robot wouldn't speak until spoken to, or act unless it saw a need.

"Tell me," he said, and saw a flash of crimson light behind the robot's blank mask as the mechanism blinked into life. "What would you do if you couldn't sleep?"

"I really couldn't say, sir," said the robot. "But if I may make an observation—"

"By all means."

"I would say then, sir, that you are experiencing an excess of energy. Were you a robot like myself, I would recommend that you discharge it in some manner."

"Well," said Jessan, "I'm not a robot, but the suggestion has merit. You know the facilities here better than I do—is there anything special that you'd recommend to an organic sentient looking for something in the energy-discharging line?"

"As a matter of fact, sir, there's a section of the base I

believe you would find extremely interesting in that regard.''

"Is there?" asked Jessan. "Then lead on.''

In the darkness of his room, Ari lay awake in the huge bed. All his earlier sleepiness had vanished, as he should have known it would. Thinking about the Long Hunt might bring the comfort of knowing that short of death, few things in a thin-skinned galaxy could stop one of the Lords of the Forest—but the comfort, like the knowledge, always had a price tag attached.

The *sigrikka* he'd killed had turned out to be the biggest one ever brought down by a cub on the Long Hunt. Ferrda still had the polished jawbone, fangs intact, hanging on the wall in a place of honor. Ari carried his own memorabilia with him everywhere. The white scars on his left arm and along his ribs had shocked his mother into silence the first time she saw them—but Ari took pride in his hard-earned right to call himself a member of Ferrda's clan, and he'd never thought of having the marks erased.

The hunt itself, though, he avoided thinking about as much as he could. He'd never been able to put his memories into compartments, the way some people seemed to. Always, the feeling of Issgrillikk going from life to death under his blow spread out to color the whole episode with the darkness of grief and regret.

Ari flopped over onto his back and stared at the ceiling. *Why can't I ever remember just the good parts?* Even now, thinking of what he'd had to do for Issgrillikk made him feel the same slow-burning, helpless rage that had broken the *sigrikka*'s neck and then torn free the carnivore's jawbone for proof of the kill.

At least that time he'd known the target and the reason for his anger—and if the *sigrikka*'s death hadn't changed anything, nevertheless some kind of balance had been reached by it that would let him sleep at night. The only other time he'd felt as bad as that had been after his mother died, and the anger then had been a dark and frightening thing.

It hadn't gone away, either. It only waited, quiescent, for a few days or weeks or months at a stretch, until something happened to stir it to life again, and he felt himself tensing to strike out blindly at the first person who gave him a reason. Not the least of his motives for joining Beka in her campaign had been the chance to drown that anger in blood and be done with it.

And I'm supposed to be the quiet, respectable one, he thought, with a humorless smile. *If people only knew.*

The carpet in Llannat's room was dark green, and soft as woodmoss. In the center of the room the Adept sat cross-legged, her eyes unfocused, her breathing slow and even. Deep in meditation, she sensed the currents of power moving through the asteroid base, and traced their luminous patterns with a clarity she had seldom before attained outside the halls of the Retreat. At length she perceived another presence that mirrored hers—and knew that somewhere on the asteroid base, a mind prepared itself for tomorrow in meditations like her own.

I'm not alone here after all, she thought, coming out of the trance. She rose to her feet, picked up her staff, and set out through the shadowed corridors toward the Entiboran room.

A pale, cold light was flooding the long chamber when she arrived, giving a bluish cast to the wainscoted walls. Outside the row of tall windows, a full moon was rising over the Entiboran hills. At the table, the Professor sat gazing out at the landscape he had created, bleak moonlight shadowing the folds of his white shirt and touching his grey hair with silver. A crystal decanter filled with dark liquid stood among matching glasses on a tray at his elbow. One full glass, untouched, rested on the table in front of him, and his fingers curled lightly around the fragile stem.

As she stepped into the room, he turned his face toward her. "You're awake late, Mistress Hyfid."

"I was meditating," she said. "It seemed necessary."

"So it is, Mistress." He gestured toward the decanter. "Will you join me?"

"I'd be delighted," she said, taking a chair at his right hand. "You're awake late yourself. It's going to be a long day tomorrow, and a long trip after that."

"And it's been many years since I was young?" he asked gently, pouring liquid from the crystal decanter into one of the glasses. Despite the shadows, she could see him smiling a little as he spoke. "True enough, Mistress. But I'll last out the trip to Darvell, never fear."

She took the glass he handed to her and sipped at the contents, a fiery distillate that made the Uplands Reserve she'd tasted on Nammerin seem crude by comparison. "And then?"

He shrugged. "As you said yourself, Mistress, reading the future is an uncertain thing. Does the brandy appeal to you?"

"Like satin and knives," she said. "Entiboran?"

"Yes. I picked up a dozen bottles of it in the year I swore fealty to House Rosselin, and this is the last."

She swallowed a mouthful of the fragrant, burning drink and watched a cloud glide past the face of the moon. The room dimmed, and then filled again with faint grey light. They sat in silence for a few minutes, until finally she looked away from the window and voiced the thought that had been in her mind since she began her evening's meditations.

"Darvell gives me a very bad feeling, Professor."

"You'd be a fool if it didn't, Mistress. The Master of Darvell is a man to be reckoned with." The Professor's grey eyes, pale in the moonlight, met hers. "My lady wants him dead because of what he's done—but you, I think, see what he may yet do."

She nodded, slowly. "I get the Mage-smell in my nose whenever I think about him."

"There's treason at work in the galaxy," said the Professor. "Schemes within schemes. It wasn't chance, you know, that brought an Adept into my lady's crew."

"I'm afraid you haven't got anybody heroic here," she said with a rueful smile. "I'm barely fair-to-middling with a staff on my good days, and the only Mage I ever met in the flesh was nearly the death of me."

"The galaxy has always had all the heroes it needed," said the Professor. "If it's produced a Mistress Hyfid along the way, I'd say that it probably needs her as well."

He looked out the window for a moment, and Llannat waited in silence until he turned back toward her and spoke again.

"All fighting is a matter of training and practice," he said, "and I've used enough weapons in my time to know that robots and holograms make poor substitutes for a living opponent." He pushed back his chair and stood up. "If a match between friends would amuse you, I could oblige."

He gestured, and the shadows appeared to solidify and take shape within his hand. Llannat stared as the moonlight glimmered off the silver fittings of an ebony staff that hadn't been there a moment before.

I should have known, she thought, and rose to her feet. "Master," she said, and bowed.

He shook his head. "No. I forswore sorcery long ago, when I gave my oath to House Rosselin. 'Professor' will do as well as any other name."

Her voice came out in a harsh whisper. "Adepts don't practice sorcery."

"No," agreed the Professor. "Adepts don't."

"Then that Magebuilt scoutship in the docking bay—"

"Was always mine. Yes."

She stood looking at him for a long time, while the night clouds chased each other across the Entiboran sky. "Why?" she said at last.

His face, what she could see of it in the dim light, was sad. "What does it matter? The Magelords would flay me for a traitor, if they knew I still lived after all this time— but I found a world and a way of life deserving of loyalty, and gave my oath gladly to them both.''

"The word of a Mage?'' she asked.

"*My* word,'' he said. "Which is a somewhat different matter. House Rosselin has had no cause to regret accepting that oath from me—nor will it, while I live. Does that satisfy you, Mistress?''

She looked at him, a slight, grey-haired figure standing alone in a room full of memories, and inclined her head. "Amply, Professor . . . and I would be honored by a match between friends.''

Jessan turned and fired, then turned again and flung himself onto the ground. The aircar passed low overhead, firing as it came. He rolled, and fired up at its belly.

A long trail of smoke streamed out behind the aircar, but the vehicle kept on going and started up into a loop. At the top of the loop, it rolled upright to head back the way it had come, and went into a thirty-degree dive— straight in at Jessan's hiding place, with all its bow guns firing.

A blaster against an armored aircar, thought Jessan. *I must be crazy.* Weapon at the ready, he crouched on the cracked and tilted pavement behind a broken wall while the bulk of the aircar grew steadily larger against the dull red of the sky.

The armored craft loomed huge above him. He saw a single burst of light, brighter than any he had ever seen, and the aircar vanished. The sounds of battle grew dim, then stopped altogether, and the red sky faded to black.

The lights came back up again. Jessan blinked at the bare white room and lowered the mock blaster still ready in his hand. From somewhere overhead, a disembodied voice said, "Final score, four hundred sixty-seven of six hundred possible in two thousand, nine hundred and sixty moves. This gives you the overall rating of Walking Wounded. Would you like to play again?''

Jessan shook his head. "No," he replied. "I think I'll try to find a pot of hot *sulg* instead." He put the weapon back onto the rack, toggled open the door, and went out.

Outside the game room, the dim lighting of the base's night prevailed. He walked down the hall and took the turning that led to a small after-hours galley. The galley was no more than a wide spot in the passageway, but it was brightly lighted, with a dining booth, a snack dispenser, and a drink machine sporting a row of ten identical, unlabeled buttons.

"Somehow," he murmured to himself, "I don't think much of my chances of getting hot *sulg* out of this box."

"I make them a thousand twenty-four to one against," said a familiar voice behind him.

He half-turned, and saw Beka sliding into the other side of the booth. *Looks like I wasn't the only one awake after all,* he thought. "Are you telling me that every combination produces a different drink?"

"I don't know," she said. "I haven't tried the whole thousand-odd to make sure. But so far, they've all been different—and some of them are damned weird, let me tell you. But I do know the combo that nets cha'a. Want some?"

"Sure," he said. "And thanks."

He cradled the resultant mug of steaming cha'a between his hands. During local night, a distinct chill tended to settle over the mostly empty base. "It's late," he said. "And you'll be piloting tomorrow. What are you still doing up?"

"I couldn't sleep," she said. "So I decided to take a walk and do some thinking." She sipped at her own mug of cha'a, and half-smiled at him through the steam. "What's your excuse?"

"I was just over in the game room having a go at Deathworld," he said. "The Professor's got a better version here than any commercial one I've ever played, but I still get nailed in the same place every time. I know the solution's got something to do with the pair of opera tickets, but I can't figure out how to get past the door with the combination lock.''

''Violence isn't an answer?''

''When I try violence, I get caught even quicker. But I have an idea for the next time I play. . . .''

He lapsed into silence. Beka sipped her cha'a for a while, then slid back the chair and stood. ''Are you planning to open Deathworld back up?''

''Not right now.''

''Like to walk around a bit?''

He looked up from his cha'a. ''Why not?'' he said, after a moment. He put his mug down onto the table and stood up. ''Lead on, Captain.''

Ari gave the pillow a disgusted punch and sat up in bed. ''The hell with it.''

A red light blinked in the darkness, marking where the valet robot stood at rest by the door. ''Yes, sir?''

''Is anybody else still awake?''

More lights blinked, and Ari caught the faint sound of electronic beepings as the robot and its series-mates conferred. ''Yes, sir.''

''Good,'' said Ari, swinging his legs over the side of the bed onto the carpet. ''There wouldn't be a night-robe of some sort around, would there?''

''One moment, sir,'' the robot said, and trundled over into the closet. It came out again with a pair of soft shoes and a dark robe in the same thick-piled fabric as the enormous bath towels. ''Will this do?''

''Admirably, and thank you.'' Ari stood up, belted the robe around him, and slid his feet into the shoes. ''Can you tell me where I can find whoever's up?''

''I'm not sure, sir,'' the robot said. ''Lieutenant-Commander Jessan left his chambers some time ago for the game room. But according to the gaming log, the commander played only one round of Deathworld and then closed the room down.''

"So he's still up," said Ari. "Maybe I'll run into him. What about the others?"

More blinking and beeping. "They appear to be wakeful as well, sir. Captain Rosselin-Metadi, for example, has been sighted in several locations by the maintenance units."

"And the Professor?"

"I can't say, sir," the valet said. "He left instructions that he was not to be disturbed under any circumstances short of a threat to the physical security of the base."

Ari shrugged. The Entiboran wouldn't have made a very good late-night companion anyhow. "And what do your series-mates tell you about Mistress Hyfid?"

"I'm afraid, sir, that she is no longer in her room, and therefore she must have left it—though her valet did not see her leave."

"Tell him not to overload his circuits worrying about it," Ari said. "She's an Adept. That means if she didn't want anyone to notice her, they wouldn't. Someday let me tell you about my younger brother who walks through force fields."

After a pause, the robot said, "I thank you for the advice, sir. In addition, Mistress Hyfid, wherever she may in fact be, has taken her staff with her."

"She's an Adept," said Ari. "She probably sleeps with the damned thing."

He started for the door. "If you could show me the way as far as that game room you mentioned, I can probably handle the rest. From what you tell me, I'm bound to find somebody awake somewhere."

His wanderings with Beka, Jessan realized, had brought him into a portion of the base that he didn't recognize. Beka seemed familiar with it, though, and the Khesatan was content to follow her lead. She strode along the dim passages without speaking, her hands shoved into the pockets of her quilted jacket, its collar turned up against the chill. Finally, she gave him a sideways glance he couldn't interpret.

"What are you doing here, anyway?" she asked. "I know why the Professor is with me, and I know what brings Ari into it—and Mistress Hyfid is an Adept, which means she has her own reasons for everything. But this isn't even your quarrel, and you've turned down the chance to get out of it twice already."

"Well," he said, "for one thing, they burned down my clinic."

She looked away from him, toward the floor. "That was my fault," she said. "And I'm sorry—not that 'sorry' is going to do you much good."

"What else could you have done?" he asked. "Besides, rendering aid to distressed spacers is in the Medical Service charter. Read the fine print if you don't believe me."

"I believe you," she said. "I'm still sorry. You were proud of that place, weren't you?"

"I never thought about it much," he said. "But I suppose I was."

She gave a soft laugh. "Nyls Jessan holding down a paying job. What would they say on Khesat if they knew?"

"The Professor's been telling tales, I see."

"Come on," she said. "I grew up with galactic politics. Maybe there's more than one family with a name like yours—but there's only one family that counts."

"Damn," he said. "My secret's discovered. How did I manage to give the game away?"

She smiled at him. "Tell me every Space Force medic has the royal bloodlines for the civilized galaxy on the tip of his tongue, and I'll call you a liar to your face. And Crown Prince Jamil was too good to be anything but real. Which of your relatives was he, anyway?"

"Now that," he said, "would be telling."

"So why aren't you doing something like that yourself right now—losing a few hundred credits at cards between teatime and dinner, instead of getting ready to go get slaughtered?"

He shrugged. "Because I got so good at cards that nobody would play with me, and the rest bores me out of my mind. Why didn't you stay on Galcen and play Domina of Lost Entibor for the rest of your life?"

The humor went out of her face as he watched. "Because I spent seventeen years watching my mother die by inches every time she had to put on her damned tiara and be a prop for idiots to play sick little nostalgic games around. And I wasn't going to let them do that to me. So I left."

"On the first freighter out of Galcen?"

"Something like that," she said.

She had stopped walking, and stood with one hand reaching out toward the lockplate of a door indistinguishable from any of the others along that stretch of corridor. "I had my pilot's license—I got it the day I came of age, and the examiner knew better than to ask how I'd already managed to practice without being legally old enough— and I was good. Once people stopped asking questions about my name and let me show what I could do, I never had any trouble finding a job."

Beka still hadn't palmed the lockplate. She seemed uncertain about something, which wasn't like her at all. Jessan raised an eyebrow. "What's on the other side—more holoprojections? Or pit traps and deadfalls?"

She shook her head. "I'll show you, if you're curious."

"Always," he said. "My fatal flaw—next to talking to much, of course."

She gave him a quick glance, and palmed the lock. The door slid open.

They entered a dim, unfurnished room. A few large cushions lay scattered about, and the floor itself felt springy under Jessan's feet. In the far corner he spotted a pile of blankets, neatly folded.

"Your room?" he guessed.

She nodded.

"It's not much like the others."

"I don't like fake scenery," she said. "But watch."

She pressed a wall plate near her hand, and all the lights went out, leaving the room in total, cavernous blackness. He heard a low humming noise—and then the ceiling split from side to side, like massive jaws opening to let in the stars.

The gap opened wider and wider as the walls rolled down, until the floor floated on the starry void like a tiny square of light. Jessan heard a distant keening like a high wind, and a cold breeze stirred his hair. *Ventilation systems*, he told himself, but he shivered anyway.

"This used to be the observation deck, I think," said Beka. "But I sleep here when the *'Hammer*'s docked."

"I can see why," Jessan said. "It's beautiful."

"It's all I ever wanted," she said. "My own ship, and the freedom of the stars, with nothing to hold me back . . . damn it, Nyls, why does everything always have to cost so much?"

Something in her voice drew his eyes away from the glory blazing above them both. He saw the silvery tracks of tears on her pale cheeks, and shook his head. "I don't know," he said. "It just does."

He reached out a hand to touch her shoulder, and found that she was trembling. "I'm sorry," he said. "I wish I could help."

She put her hand up to grasp his wrist. "Then don't go. Please."

He bent his head and kissed her, and stood back a little, waiting.

She looked at him for a moment, her lean, angular features as unreadable as ever. Then he felt the warmth of her hands on either side of his face as she drew his lips back again to hers.

VIII. Asteroid Base

IN THE Entiboran room, Llannat stepped away from the table and leaned her staff against her chair. "Just a moment. Formal blacks weren't really designed to practice in."

She took off the jacket and hung it over the back of her chair, so that she stood dressed like her opponent in shirt and trousers alone. Then she retrieved her staff and came to guard, holding the weapon two-handed at the horizontal before her.

Green fire flickered to life in the air about her, but she was careful not to draw more power into herself than befitted a match between friends. Working with all the energy at one's disposal had a lethal beauty that could dazzle onlookers—she'd seen Master Ransome and Ari's brother, Owen, spar that way once or twice, for the edification of students at the Retreat—but a match like that demanded control far beyond her own.

A few feet away from her, the Professor also picked up his staff. The silver and ebony rod was much shorter than hers, and plainly meant for one-handed use. He held it loosely, almost casually, but the power of his aura flowed about him in streamers of deep violet against in the moonlight.

"Shall we begin?" he asked.

Llannat nodded, and waited for the Professor to come to the guard position in his turn. The shift to guard never came. Instead, the former Magelord moved without warning, striking for the left side of her head with his ebony staff.

Llannat blocked high and to the left.

The Professor must have anticipated the classic reply. He dropped the tip of his ebony rod to pass below her block, and his attack came back in toward her right cheek.

She shifted her block to the right. The Professor, still holding the rod in that loose-looking one-hand grip, let it return to vertical. His next attack threatened her unprotected abdomen. In response, she pushed her staff straight forward and down against his, but the Professor neither stepped backward nor extended his attack. Instead, he spun his weapon outward with a quick twist of his wrist.

The violet aura around him flared high, and Llannat felt her weapon snatched from her hands. The flickering green light of her own summoning vanished as her staff clattered against the opposite wall.

The Professor crossed over to the fallen staff, picked it up, and handed it back to Llannat. "Shall we try again?"

She drew a deep breath, and took position. "I'm ready."

Once more, the Professor stood with the ebony rod held loosely at his side. The other hand rested lightly on his hip. "Begin," he said.

For a long time, neither of them moved. Power flickered around them in a glowing nimbus of green and violet. At last the Professor attacked, the end of his short staff flashing toward Llannat's left side in a whistling blur.

She blocked. The staves touched; then, somehow, the Professor's ebony rod was coming in toward her other flank. She blocked again, the two weapons kissed in a flare of green and violet light—and the Professor's staff flashed over to strike at the left side of her face.

Llannat blocked left.

This time, though, there was no moment of contact with the other weapon. Instead, she felt the ebony staff tap lightly first against her left leg, and then against her right. Too late, she dropped her guard downward to counter the blows—and felt the light contact a third time on the side of her neck.

"You win," she said, lowering her staff. "I'm dead."

The Professor stepped back, and bowed to her in salute. "Mistress, attack me. I shall do no more than defend myself."

"Right," said Llannat, and swung her staff down toward the Professor's head.

He blocked it with ease. She followed with a quick series of blows from either end of her staff. They filled the air with the whistling of their passage, but the Professor met them all without shifting his stance. Only his right hand and his extended arm moved at all, catching and deflecting each stroke as it came.

At length, Llannat took a step back and regarded the Professor. He appeared calm and unruffled. Her own forehead and neck ran with sweat, even in the chill of the base's night, and her breath came in shallow gasps.

"Mistress," inquired the soft voice, with its incongruous Entiboran accent, "where is your guard?"

Llannat took in her stance. She was out of line, and badly extended. She shook her head, and came back into position.

"Choose a line and guard it," said the Professor. "I can't attack you through a closed line." He emphasized his point with a series of slashing attacks to Llannat's right side—all of them falling, without any movement of her own, onto the staff she carried. "But try to guard all, and you guard none. Now—what line do you guard?"

"My right flank."

"Wrong!"

The Professor swung harder than before, and this time the strength of his blow pushed Llannat's staff away before it, so that she felt the sting of his blow against her ribs. "What line do you guard?"

Llannat shifted her grip, so that she held her staff tightly in front of her. "My head."

"Again wrong!" The Professor's weapon circled low, and the end tapped her leg just above the knee. "Your head is not in danger. What line do you guard?"

Llannat felt a hot rush of blood to her face—anger? humiliation?—and struck out with one end of her staff at the Professor's neck. "*You* tell *me*."

The Professor caught the blow and allowed her staff to slide down his as he stepped forward. Now, with the staves caught between them, the young Adept and the grey-haired Magelord stood heart to heart in the long, moonlit hall.

"Guard against anger, Mistress," he said, low-voiced. "It's a waste of energy, and it insults the power you bear."

This time she knew that the heat under her skin was embarrassment, because she'd managed to forget the first thing anybody had ever told her about the Adept's art.

"Don't ever lose your temper when you're working with power," she remembered Master Ransome saying to a group of new apprentices that had included a confused young ensign from the Medical Service. "Somebody always gets hurt."

Now the Professor nodded over their crossed staves. "I see you remember."

Without warning, he stepped back, and resumed his one-handed guard position.

I've seen that guard before, thought Llannat. Not at the Retreat, she was sure—she'd have remembered something like that, if it had ever shown up during those long hours of drill in the practice yard.

Not at the Retreat, no, but twice since, once in a clearing on Nammerin and a second time here on this asteroid, when she had been deep in her visionary trance. Whoever she had been that time, she herself had used that same short weapon, the same stance and grip.

This one's power is weak, she could remember her adversary/self thinking. *She doesn't really believe.*

But the frightened and unbelieving young Adept sent by Master Ransome to guard Ari Rosselin-Metadi had stayed at her post just the same—and Ari's blaster bolt had cut down the Mage as he raised his arm for the killing blow.

Now, standing in the moonlight of an Entibor that never was, she smiled with sudden understanding. *There's no such thing as luck or chance . . . and there's power in everyone, even a seven-foot Galcenian who claims to be about as sensitive as a brick, or a Space Force medic from a border planet where there hasn't been an Adept born for as far back as the Forest Lords can remember. . . .*

The insight flooded through her like a rush of light, and for a brief, dizzying second she could feel the universe itself, surrounding her and within her at the same time.

"I think you begin to understand," the Professor said. "Now shall we spar in earnest?"

Once more, Llannat took a guard position, this time with her staff held vertical by her right side, and waited. Still buoyed up by her moment of realization, she sensed the Professor's blow coming at her a second or more before his staff began to move. Her own staff turned with his as he tried to come under her guard.

Their auras flared high around them, surges of green and violet mingling in patterns of fire against the dark. Rather than step back, she lunged with the end of her staff, forcing the Professor to give ground. When he tried to beat her weapon aside, she dropped the tip so that he contacted only air.

"You see," he said. "You've learned one important lesson. Now let me teach you another."

The Professor whirled to the right, ducking under her blow and stabbing upward. She gave ground rather than take a hit to the arm, and felt her sense of oneness with the universe slipping away under the pressure of the immediate.

The Professor seemed to feel it slipping, too. He redoubled his attack. Once more, the unfamiliar rhythms of his fighting style began to dance around her Adept-trained blocks.

Llannat stepped back, and opened herself to power. The sensation of including and being included in the bright oneness that was the universe flowed out of its cramped little corner of memory and filled her as it had before.

It doesn't go away after all, she thought. *It's always there if you look for it.*

She turned her awareness outward again, and was surprised to see that she was attacking, moving in hard with fast, arcing swings that started back behind the shoulder. The Professor was slipping each blow, his staff redirecting the force of each smashing stroke outward and away from him, but he was giving ground just the same.

Llannat pressed her attack, forcing the Professor backward step by step until his shoulders touched the far wall. She closed her eyes for a moment. When she opened them again, the Professor stood pressed against the wainscoting, pinned by the light but unwavering pressure of the center of her staff against the flesh of his throat.

The Entiboran Magelord smiled. "Now, Mistress, I yield."

If everybody's awake, thought Ari, sliding into the booth in the after-hours galley, *you sure couldn't prove it by me.*

So far the breakfast nook, the main dining area, and the game room had all turned up empty. If there hadn't been two half-empty mugs of cha'a still warm on the table in front of him, Ari might have begun to suspect that the valet robot and its cohorts had been mistaken.

He stabbed a few buttons at random on the drink machine. A mug slid into position under the spout to receive a stream of blue liquid. Hot *sulg*, he guessed, from the look of it, and an experimental sip proved him right. He tried to remember what buttons he'd pushed—Jessan might be interested, since his friend was always claiming he hadn't been able to find good *sulg* since he'd left Khesat.

Ari gave up experimentation after his first try at a repeat garnered him a bowl of something black and sludgy that smelled like it ought to be repairing potholes in a landing pad. Instead, he sat watching steam rise off the azure surface of the *sulg*. His self-inflicted insomnia still hadn't left him, and he toyed with the idea of going back to the game room and having a go at one of the simulations himself. *It's not real, but it passes the time.*

Another of the Professor's robots came up to the table and began clearing away the two half-empty mugs.

"Wait a minute—can you tell me how long those have been here?" asked Ari.

"I really can't say, sir," said the robot. "I was last by about a Standard hour ago."

"And they weren't here then?"

"That's correct, sir."

Ari looked again at the two mugs. Both of them held straight black cha'a.

One of them's likely to be Jessan's, he thought. *This is the first place anybody would hit after the game room, and he drinks his cha'a black. The Professor's incommunicado somewhere, and Llannat drinks her cha'a with sugar and milk when she can get them . . . which leaves Bee.*

"You can go on with your cleanup," he told the robot. "And take the *sulg* and that black stuff with you."

"Yes, sir," said the robot, and trundled off.

Air watched it disappear into the darkness beyond the bright lights of the little galley. So his sister and Jessan were off nightwalking somewhere . . . he tried to decide just how he felt about that, and realized he wasn't certain.

Their problem, not mine, he told himself, standing up again. *Seems like Llannat's the only one not accounted for. I'll take one more look around; if she doesn't turn up she's probably gone back to bed, and I can spend the rest of the night in the game room practicing up to get killed.*

He left the little galley behind, and headed for the only part of the base known to him that he still hadn't checked: the sickbay and the docking area. Llannat was a medic, after all, besides being an Adept. She could have decided to double-check for anything useful the on-load might have left behind.

He was still a corner or so away from the Entiboran room and the entrance to the sickbay when he heard the noise: a faint, high hum at the topmost end of his hearing, mixed with the whistle of parting air and the crack and tap of wood on wood. He halted, frozen, in the darkness, and felt the hair rise on the back of his neck.

He'd heard sounds like that before, in a clearing on Nammerin, and he knew what they meant. He still dreamed about that night sometimes: the heavy wet-mulch smell of the rain forest, the poisoned blood pounding in his ears, and outside the downed aircar power surging and flaring in auroras against the dark as two staves met and parted and met again. Llannat Hyfid had fought for his life that night, and the Adept was—he had thought—the only person now on the asteroid base who carried a staff and knew how to fight with one.

D'Caer? Ari wondered. *Escaped?*

He began a slow stalk down the passageway toward the sound of the fight.

As soon as he rounded the corner he saw them, a changing pattern of light framed by one of the tall archways that led into the Entiboran room. The reverse side of the room's elaborate holoprojection gave him a view partially obscured by greenery and the spaces between the tall windows, but the illusory moonlight flooding the long chamber showed the two moving figures clearly enough. The light that played about them—vivid green and deep, almost indigo violet—was all he needed to see the rest.

For a moment he tensed, weighing how best to move in weaponless on a duel where both fighters were armed with more than just the staves they bore. Then he saw that the duelists were Llannat and the Professor, and that they both wore the dark trousers and loose white shirt that made up a part of an Adept's formal blacks. In the clear emerald light of her power, Llannat's face wore an expression that Ari knew all too well; he'd seen it before on his brother's face back on Galcen, when Owen sparred with Master Errec Ransome for pleasure's sake.

The two Adepts fought down the length of the room, the Professor wielding an unfamiliar, shorter staff in an odd one-handed style, and Llannat using the traditional two-handed grip. The auras around her and the Professor grew brighter, until the whole room shone with dancing streamers of colored light.

Llannat swung her weapon in sweeping figure-eight loops. By the intense, unnatural light, Ari could see how the sweat that dampened her shirt had plastered the white fabric to her torso, and how the muscles of her back and shoulders worked to put power behind the blows. The Professor deflected each stroke with easy grace, wasting no motion as he parried, and the violet light around him rivaled in brightness the medic's corona of vivid green . . . but he still gave ground.

The younger Adept pushed her opponent farther and farther across the room. Then, without warning, all movement stopped. The Professor had his shoulders pressed to the wall. Llannat stood facing him, her staff laid across the Entiboran's throat and her whole body poised to press the last blow home.

The Professor said something—he actually appeared to be laughing, for the first time since Ari had met him—and lowered his weapon. Llannat's aura faded a second later, and the candles in the chandelier overhead flamed into sudden fantasmagorical life as the two Adepts embraced.

Ari turned away. He was not, he told himself, such an inexperienced fool that he would mistake honest comradeship for a highly unlikely passion. He and Issgrillikk had clasped each other by the shoulders in much the same fashion often enough, after a hard-fought bout at hand-to-hand under Ferrdacorr's watchful eye.

But still, he found himself unwilling to watch any longer. *"Power knows its own,"* he remembered his brother saying once, and like most of the things his brother said, it had turned out to be true. As long as there were Adepts in the galaxy, Llannat Hyfid wasn't going to need anything else. Certainly not the friendship of a powerless Galcenian medic, even one who'd been fostered on Maraghai.

The game room had lost what little appeal it had held for Ari in the first place, and he made his way back through the darkened hallways to his bedchamber. His valet robot was still there when he got back. Its lights blinked as the door snicked shut, but like a good servant it asked no questions. Ari threw himself onto the bed without bothering to remove his night-robe, and pushed the button that brought the room lights up to "dim."

After a while he said, "Do you think you could find me a drink to help me get to sleep?"

"Of course, sir. What would you prefer?"

"I don't care," Ari said. "Whatever's handy, as long as it's strong."

"Understood, sir," said the robot. It trundled out the door, and returned shortly with a heavy cut-glass tumbler on a silver tray. A deep amber liquid filled the tumbler to within an inch of the rim.

"Thanks," Ari said, picking up the tumbler. He took a careful swallow, and then set to work finishing the rest.

"That was good," he said a few minutes later, contemplating the thick bottom of the empty tumbler. "But I'm not sleepy just yet. I think I'll try another round."

Harsh light streamed in through the glassweave curtains and beat against Ari's protesting eyes. Somewhere outside his skull, a maniac was playing reveille on the door buzzer while the robot announced, in dulcet tones, "Your clothing is ready, sir. My series-mates report that the others are already awake."

"All right, all *right*." He sat on the edge of the bed for a minute and then stood up, swaying a little. "Death and damnation . . . open the door and let whoever the hell that is come on in so they'll shut up.''

Ari stumbled off in what he hoped was the direction of the bathroom, the rumpled night-robe flapping around him. He emerged several minutes later, dressed in the garments that a blessedly silent robot had handed him one piece at a time, and found Nyls Jessan sitting in the chair by the window.

The Khesatan, dressed for the upcoming journey in a free-spacer's loose shirt and trousers, was smiling a little as he looked out at the holoprojected garden. He half-turned at the sound of footsteps, and his eyes widened. ''My word, Ari—what hit you?''

''About a liter of something or other that one of the Professor's robots found for me,'' Ari told his friend. ''And for space's sake, Nyls, have some respect for the dead.''

''You got drunk?''

Ari nodded, and wished he hadn't. ''It took some work, but I managed.''

''Why would you want to do that?''

''It seemed like a good idea at the time.'' Ari turned to the valet robot. ''Where's the blaster I brought with me?''

''Right here, sir.''

Ari blinked at the weapon and holster the valet robot held out in one mechanical hand. ''Ah, yes . . . I see it. Thank you.'' He belted on the blaster and turned to Jessan. ''You said the others were waiting?''

The Khesatan smiled. ''No, I didn't. And you forgot your boots.''

Ari sat back down on the edge of the bed with a curse. ''Where is everybody?'' he asked, as he pulled on first one boot and then the other. ''Still having breakfast?''

''Llannat was drinking cha'a the last I saw her,'' said Jessan, ''and the Professor was making a final check on something or other. Beka went back to get into her Tarnekep gear, and I drew the short straw.''

Ari glowered at him. ''There's nothing like friends—

thank the universe for small favors.'' He stood up again. ''Now, shall we go?''

Jessan rose lithely from his chair. ''Of course.''

In the docking bay, *Warhammer* and *Defiant* waited side by side on the deckplates. Even through his headache, Ari could hear the low hum of the active engines, and sense a readiness in the air that hadn't been there before.

''Still the same matchup?'' he asked Jessan.

''That's right. You and Llannat with Beka in the *'Hammer*, and me in *Defiant* to help watch the autopilot and bring the Professor cups of hot cha'a during the tough parts.''

Ari grunted. ''Sounds like a hard assignment—think you can handle it?''

''I'll push myself,'' the Khesatan assured him. ''Good morning, Professor.''

''Good morning, Commander.''

The grey-haired Entiboran stood next to the lowered ramp of the Magebuilt scoutship. He still wore the black trousers and white shirt he'd worn when Ari had last seen him. The short, black and silver staff he now carried tucked under his belt. Ari saw Jessan's eyebrows rise at the sight of it, but the Khesatan didn't say anything beyond ''Are the captain and Mistress Hyfid here yet?''

''Mistress Hyfid is already aboard the *'Hammer*,'' said the Entiboran. ''And Captain Portree is arriving now.''

Ari looked back the way they had come, and saw the sickbay doors closing behind a figure he hadn't seen since that first meeting off Nammerin.

Long brown hair queued back and tied off with black velvet ribbons; white spidersilk shirt frothing into pure lace at the neckcloth and the ruffled cuffs; heavy government-surplus blaster holstered low and strapped down onto one thigh—from up close, Tarnekep Portree looked like nothing so much as a foppish piece of very rough trade. Ari searched the features of that androgynous but extremely menacing young gentleman for some trace of his sister Beka, and found none there.

"Good morning, Professor," said Tarnekep. The Mandeynan's gaze flicked over to the other two men in the docking bay. "Ari . . . Jessan."

"Morning," said Ari.

Jessan only nodded.

A corner of Tarnekep's mouth turned up for a second in what might have been a smile. "Is everything ready?"

"Since yesterday evening, Captain," said the Professor.

"Then let's go. If everything works, I'll see you on Darvell."

"And what if something doesn't work?" Jessan's voice had a note in it Ari couldn't quite place.

"If something doesn't?" Tarnekep shrugged. "Then this is it, I suppose."

"Like hell it is," said Jessan harshly.

Ari stared—the words and tone were a sharp contrast to Jessan's usual flow of light chatter—and was still staring when his friend took a sudden step forward and grabbed Portree by the shoulders.

"Get yourself killed on the way in," the Khesatan said, "and I swear I'll never forgive you."

He pulled Tarnekep toward him into a hard embrace and a prolonged, almost desperate kiss. After what seemed to Ari an unconscionably long time, the two figures broke apart. Jessan turned and strode up *Defiant*'s ramp without looking back.

Tarnekep watched him go. Then—still wearing that maddening half-smile—the Mandeynan nodded to the Professor.

"Well, we're off," he said, and started for *Warhammer* at a brisk pace that was almost a run.

Ari caught up with him in a couple of long steps. "Was that last bit really necessary?" he growled.

The single bright blue eye and that unnerving eye patch looked at him for a few seconds from a thin-featured and deadly face, and then Beka chuckled.

"No, it wasn't necessary . . . but it sure was fun. Come on, big brother. Let's go set Darvell on fire."

PART FOUR

I. DARVELL: NORTHERN HEMISPHERE

HIGH OVER the Darvelline system, so high that the central star and all its planets were only brighter spots against the backdrop of the galaxy, the substance of realspace altered for a second as *Warhammer* popped out of hyper.

"There it is," Beka said, regarding the starfield before her with satisfaction. "Are we getting anything on the sensors?"

"*Defiant* entered realspace about a second behind us," replied Ari from the copilot's seat.

"We should be getting her on visual soon . . . ah, there she comes." Beka smiled as one of the specks of light outside the cockpit window grew into the distant shape of the Magebuilt scout. "Are we hearing anything?"

"The Professor sent us a quick-burst message on a tight beam as soon as he came through."

"Play it back."

Ari toggled the audio-replay switch. "Replaying now."

"Emission Control Alpha," said the console speaker.

"Activating cloaking Follow me close. See you on the ground."

The transmission broke off short on the last syllable.

"Are we going to reply?" asked Ari.

"No," Beka said. "He won't be expecting it. Besides, somebody might hear us."

"This far out?"

"You never can tell," she said. "Darvell has its own fleet. Who knows how far out they make a habit of listening?"

Beyond the cockpit window, *Defiant* wavered and faded from view. Only a blurred and distorted patch of starfield remained to mark the scoutship's position.

"There she goes," Ari said. "All our sensor screens read clear."

Beka nodded without taking her eyes away from the cockpit window. "Good. Then so should everybody else's."

Out against the starfield, the faint blurry patch began to move toward the planetary system. Beka pushed the *'Hammer* to the left and down, adding forward vector as she did so in order to bring the freighter closer to *Defiant*'s position. When the distortion covered ninety degrees of her field of view forward, she slowed the *'Hammer* again to match speeds with the scoutship.

"And that's all there is to it," she said. "As long as we keep the same distance, we can share *Defiant*'s cloak and sneak right in behind her."

"It's going to be a long slow sneak at this rate," said Ari. "And hard to do on visual alone."

She smiled. "Don't worry, big brother. Between us we can handle it."

Ari muttered something under his breath in the Selvaur speech he'd learned from Ferrdacorr. The comment—what Beka could catch of it—sounded unflattering; she ignored him and flipped on the *'Hammer*'s internal comm.

"Let's see how the rest of the ship is doing. Mistress Hyfid, is everything all right back aft?"

"Everything's just fine, Captain Rosselin-Metadi," came the reply from the common room. "Smooth as spidersilk."

"Good," said Beka. "Let's hope it all stays that way . . . gotten any anonymous notes lately?"

She heard a faint laugh. "Not even a picture postcube, Captain. Sorry."

"Don't be," said Beka. "I just love surprises. For now, Mistress, if you want to see what we're going to be up against, you can flip down the bulkhead viewer."

She nodded toward Ari as she spoke. Out of the corner of her eye she saw him begin punching in the codes that would translate the sensor data to a visual signal and feed it to the common-room screen.

Even this far up, the Darvell system made a spectacular sight: planets and moons and a yellow dwarf sun, flung out against interstellar night like jewels on black velvet. But as the 'Hammer and Defiant drew closer, the picture changed. Dim, half-seen shapes of cargo carriers appeared, shuttling among the system's uninhabited planets to pick up raw materials for Darvell's ring of massive orbiting factories. Along a narrow corridor guarded by heavy warships, freighters moved to and from their jump points in regular array. More fighting craft orbited the planet itself. A thick layer of satellites circled beneath the patrolling warships—weather and power and communications satellites in familiar domestic configurations, but also the darker shapes of spy-eyes and weapons platforms.

The Master of Darvell took no chances.

On board the 'Hammer, Beka took the conn for the final approach. As her brother had predicted, the run-in to Darvell had been a long one—three Standard days at low speed, with close maneuvering the whole way. She and Ari had stood alternating watches, four hours on and four hours off, during the realspace passage.

Defiant, normally a one-man craft, had also carried a double crew for this run. Nyls Jessan had never mentioned before that he knew his way around a spaceship's controls, but Beka hadn't been surprised to learn that he did.

"I'm qualified," he'd protested, during that last dinner back at the asteroid base. "That's all."

"Like you're only 'qualified' with a blaster?" she had asked him, remembering his cool accuracy back in the firefights on Pleyver.

He had the grace to look apologetic. "In this case, Captain, all 'qualified' means is that I've got a license.'

"A license is more than Mistress Hyfid's got," she told him. "You're crewing on *Defiant*."

Beka hadn't expected, at the time, to miss having the Khesatan around for the hyperspace transit. *Better get used to missing him*, she told herself. *Remember, you have to give him back to the Space Force when this is over.*

Stifling a sigh that threatened to turn into a yawn, she shook her head impatiently and squinted at the control panel readouts. This low-velocity, follow-the-leader approach was hard enough as it was. She didn't need thoughts like that to distract her.

Defiant led them in slow and easy, making planetfall just before dawn in the mountains of Darvell's northern hemisphere. Beka put the *'Hammer* down on the other side of the small clearing a few minutes later. The *Defiant*'s electronic cloak made a wavery dome of visual distortion over the two ships—somewhat attenuated, by comparison with the invisibility the field generated in deep space, but good enough to disguise their presence from orbital spies.

The bit of sky visible overhead had gone from dull grey to pink by the time she finished shutting down the *'Hammer*. The Professor's ship, a one-man craft not meant to carry cargo, had taken less time. When she came down the *'Hammer*'s ramp with Ari and Llannat close behind, the Entiboran and Jessan were waiting.

Jessan's glance went to the others for a second, and then came back to her. "You look like you haven't slept in a week."

Beka found herself a place to stand that would allow her to lean back against the *'Hammer*'s comforting bulk, then crossed her arms and grinned at him. "Flattery gets you nowhere, my friend. I got my beauty sleep four hours ago—can't you tell?"

"Not really."

"I can," growled Ari. "She woke me up to get it."

Beka ignored him and turned toward the Professor. "What happens next?"

"We wait," said the Entiboran. "If the locals mount a systematic air search at full daylight, we'll know for certain that somebody spotted us coming in."

"And if they don't start searching?"

"The lack of any obvious activity will not, unfortunately, prove that the contrary is true."

"Now that," said Jessan, "is what I call really helpful."

Beka snickered, and swallowed another yawn. "Seriously, people," she said, "one of us needs to head into town and pick up some information."

She heard Llannat sigh. "I'm the only person here who doesn't need a whole day of sleep to be functional. I'll go."

"Sign me up, too," Jessan said. "All I did on the way in was stand by while the Professor handled the tricky stuff."

Beka looked from the Khesatan to Mistress Hyfid and back, blinking her eyes against her own fatigue. One or the other of them, or maybe both, was lying about being rested. *Just the same, without local knowledge we'll all be stuck, and the Professor and I are about to drop.* She looked at her brother for a second, and gave an inward shake of her head. Ari probably had another solid week of work left in him—but unless everybody on Darvell was a giant, her brother was guaranteed to stand out in a crowd.

"All right," she said to the volunteers. "You two have it."

After his trip aboard *Defiant*, Jessan found himself enjoying the hike downslope to the nearest road. The air had a clean, resinous tang to it, another welcome change from life aboard ship, and he had to suppress an urge to whistle as he strolled along. *This is no time to be feeling cheerful,* he reminded himself. *Spying is serious work.*

All the same, he couldn't help smiling. After a few minutes, he became aware of Llannat's eyes on him, and turned the smile in her direction.

The Adept gave him a curious look. "You're on top of the galaxy this morning."

"Sorry," he said. "It comes from being out in the open."

"You—the outdoor type? Tell me another, Jessan."

He laughed. "Making a hyperspace transit as the second body in a one-man scout will do that to you."

They walked on. About local noon, they emerged from the trees and picked up a steep-shouldered road that followed the curve of a valley between two peaks. Up on the wooded mountainside, the air had begun to feel almost warm, but here a brisk wind blew through Jessan's hair and made him grateful for the jacket he'd pulled out of his locker.

Llannat, for her part, had ended up wearing a black sweater from Beka's old collection of dirtside gear. "I don't care whether it fits or not," the Adept had told the captain, "so long as it's warm." And warm it certainly was, not to mention somewhat snug around the chest. Llannat was considerably shorter than Beka Rosselin-Metadi, but the Adept couldn't have passed for male even in a dim light.

"The town should be downhill from here," Llannat said after a moment's consideration.

"Downhill it is, then," agreed Jessan. "Let's go."

The road maintained its general downward trend, broken only by occasional steep upgrades as it wound through the foothills of the mountain range. As they neared the crest of one such hill, Jessan became aware of a low, subterranean growling from somewhere behind them—a sound not so much heard as felt through the soles of the feet.

"Heavy ground transport," said Llannat, at the same moment. "Heading this way."

"Time to blend back into the trees for a bit, I think," said Jessan, stepping off the road.

He found himself a patch of ground in the shadow of a tall conifer. Moments later, the transport crawled into view, engines roaring as they fought the upward slope. The vehicle's nullgravs whined under the weight of bulging brown sacks piled high in the open-topped cargo compartment.

Jessan felt an idea forming in his mind, and looked over at Llannat. From the expression on the Adept's face, she'd already been thinking the same thing.

"As soon as it goes past," she murmured. "One, two, three—"

They sprinted around behind the laboring transport. Jessan jumped, and found a handhold on the first try—just as well, since as far as he could tell Llannat wasn't using a handhold at all. He scrambled over the top of the cargo compartment, and landed with a lung-emptying thud on a dirt-covered fabric bag that turned out to feel even knobbier than it looked.

"Oof," he muttered. "What are we sharing a ride with, anyhow?"

Llannat poked an experimental finger at the bag she sat on. "Edible roots of some kind, I'd say."

"Thanks for reminding me we didn't wait around for breakfast."

"Cultivate a philosophical outlook," she recommended.

"I'd sooner cultivate a hot meal. Oh, well—it'll give me something else to look for when we hit town."

They made themselves as comfortable as they could. Llannat curled up in a compact bundle, and within moments her chest began to rise and fall in the slow, even rhythm of sleep.

Jessan wondered, yawning, if dropping off that fast on a mattress this lumpy constituted some kind of galactic record, but couldn't keep his own eyes open long enough to decide. The warm sun shone down on the cargo compartment; the transport's engines grumbled in a deep, comforting monotone; and the edible tubers in the sacks piled around and under him breathed out a not unpleasant vegetable odor. He pillowed his head on his arm and slept.

He woke to the touch of a hand on his forehead, and a

familiar voice speaking—almost shouting—somewhere inside his skull.

We're coming up on a checkpoint. Hide.

He drew breath to ask a question, but the hand moved to cover his mouth.

Don't worry about me, said the voice again. *Just get out of sight!*

The transport was indeed slowing to a halt. He abandoned Llannat to her own devices and started burrowing. As soon as he'd gotten himself well-hidden under what felt like a hundred pounds or so of nourishing fibrous vegetables, he risked peering out through between two of the sacks. Llannat wasn't anywhere in sight.

"May I see your transportation request and vehicle log, please?" said an unfamiliar voice in a bored monotone.

Standard Galcenian, thought Jessan. *That takes care of the language problem, anyhow.*

"Sure," said another voice from the transport's cab. "Just a second . . . here they are."

"Hmmm . . . stamps from checkpoints BX-BY and BY-zero-two-seven dash zero-two-eight . . . you're carrying *garrutchy* from District BX-one-four-three to Central Storage?"

"That's right."

"Well, everything looks in order. I'll just do a quick visual, and then you can go on."

Boot heels rang on asphalt, and Jessan shrank even deeper into the hiding place he'd excavated. Down among the sacks of *garrutchy*, loose dirt tickled his nostrils, and he felt a sudden overwhelming desire to sneeze. He quit breathing instead.

The booted footsteps came around to the rear of the transport. Jessan heard the tailgate lower partway, and felt the bags about him begin to shift. The guard must have noticed the movement, too—there was an oath, and the tailgate slammed back up again. Under cover of the noise, Jessan exhaled and gulped another lungful of air.

"Looks all right," said the guard's voice. Jessan heard the dull, irregular thudding of an official stamp being pounded down in all the required locations on a set of forms in triplicate. Then the guard's voice said, "Here you go now. Move along," and the transport's engines growled back into life.

Jessan waited until the noise was back up to its earlier level before squirming out from under the bags of *garrutchy*. Sometime in there, Llannat had reappeared as well. The Adept was leaning back against the side of the cargo compartment with her eyes closed.

"Welcome back," he said. "Where'd you go?"

She shook her head. "Nowhere. You just didn't happen to look where I was. Time to start tidying up, I think—that checkpoint probably means we're getting close to town."

Jessan began brushing the dirt off his clothing. "Right. You drop off first, then."

A few minutes later, the transport slowed to go through an intersection. Llannat got a secure grip on the side of the cargo compartment, then swung over and out of sight.

Now it's your turn, Jessan told himself. *Think of it as another round of amateur theatricals—and you've got the part of a* garrutchy *grower in town for the weekend.*

The flight of fancy made him laugh a little under his breath. He scrambled over the tailgate before he could get stage fright, and lowered himself down to the pavement.

Beka woke up with a start. *What was that?*

She levered herself up on her elbows and listened, trying to catch again the anomaly that had awakened her, but she heard nothing—no engine irregularities, no noises of impact on the hull, only a deep and unnatural silence.

Right. We're grounded. And the power's off.

She looked over at the glowing face of the chronometer bolted to the bulkhead next to the bunk, where a turn of her head on the pillow could give her the time. *Thirteen-thirty-point-five-one Standard. Not a real useful piece of information.*

She got up, stretching to work the kinks out of her back and shoulders, and dressed by the dim blue light of the self-powered emergency glows. The question of persona had her chewing her lower lip for a moment in front of the clothes locker; then she nodded to herself and pulled open the section that held Tarnekep Portree's dirtside outfits.

Better safe than sorry, she reflected, tying the high cravat with an ease gained over months of practice. *Beka Rosselin-Metadi is dead, and Darvell is no place for her to be spotted among the living.*

She fitted the red eye patch into place and walked out through the silent ship.

Outside, the long golden light of late afternoon slanted down through the tops of the tall trees. Near the middle of the clearing, her brother sat next to a small fire. A cookpot dangled from a stick above the flames, and Ari looked around from stirring it as she came down the *'Hammer*'s ramp.

"So you're up."

She yawned. "More or less. Did I sleep all day?"

"That's right. The sun's starting to go down."

"Where's everyone else?"

"The Professor is still asleep," her brother said. "Llannat and Jessan haven't come back yet, but I think it's too early to worry. I wrestled our hoverbikes out of the cargo hold and then went hunting—mostly to see if anything Ferrda taught me stuck. Something must have, because we've got dinner."

"Why the outdoorsman routine?" she asked, as the savory smell of game stew reached her nostrils.

"The Professor cut the power levels on both ships to minimize energy leakage around the masking field. That left the power too low to run the galleys. He says we won't be staying here long anyway."

Ari tasted the stew, nodded to himself, and turned away from the fire. Beka followed the motion, and saw a heavy blaster lying with its belt and holster near his right hand.

"Is that what you went hunting with?" she asked.

Ari shook his head. "No. If I shot something with that,

there wouldn't be enough left for the stewpot. Besides, I never was any good with one of these things."

He picked up the holstered weapon by its belt and held it out toward her. "Speaking of which—I think that you're the one who should have this."

Beka took the belt, then pulled the blaster out of its holster and hefted it—not as weighty as the government-surplus models she'd been using lately, but heavier than the new Space Force standard issue. "Gyfferan," she said, after a moment. "Dadda's?"

"That's right. He gave it to me when I left the Academy. Said I might need it someday."

"Everybody needs something," Beka said. "Was he right?"

"What do you think?" asked her brother. "Sometimes I wonder about those hunches of his, let me tell you."

Beka grinned. "Trust an old starpilot. You know what they say—Adepts have power, and pilots have luck."

"And what does that leave the rest of us?"

She looked at him for a moment—damn near seven feet tall with his boots off, and all of it muscle. Not her style, but Jilly Oldigaard had daydreamed for weeks after the time he'd come home for a visit in his Academy uniform. "The rest of us? Well, big brother—you may not have power, but you certainly do have plenty of mass times acceleration."

"Very funny," he growled. "Do you want the blaster or not?"

"I'll take it, I'll take it."

She unbuckled the heavy leather belt that held her own sidearm and laid it aside, then strapped on the Gyfferan weapon. Not surprisingly, the belt was far too large for her. It settled low on her hips, sagging even lower on the weapon side.

"Needs work," she said. She caught a glimpse of Ari's face. "One laugh and I'll kill you."

II. Darvell: Northern Hemisphere

HANDS IN his pockets, Jessan strolled down the quiet, well-kept streets. Most of the people he saw had on what looked like uniforms of some kind, but others wore the sort of casual civilian clothing favored by free-spacers and others whose business took them from world to world; so far, he didn't feel too conspicuous. He spotted an announcement kiosk on one corner, and sauntered over to check out the monitors.

PLAN OF THE DAY said the heading on the largest screen. Jessan stepped closer and started to read.

"Excuse me, sir. May I please see your identification?" said a soft voice behind him.

Jessan turned. A young man stood looking at him. The friendly expression on the watcher's clean-cut features didn't offset the nightstick, the blaster, and the "Duty Guard" brassard around one uniformed arm.

The Khesatan did his best to look innocent. "Is there a problem, sir?"

"All personnel are required to read and be familiar with

the Plan of the Day prior to noon," the young man explained. "And it's way past fourteen hundred. May I see your ID?"

"Sure," said Jessan, reaching into the right inside pocket of his jacket. He brought his hand out again empty, and shook his head. "Must be in the other one . . . I'll have it for you in a minute."

He tried the left inside pocket and both the big zippered outer pockets, coming up empty each time.

"You're supposed to carry your ID in your left top front shirt pocket when you're not in uniform," the duty guard informed him helpfully. "Why don't you look there?"

"Shirt pocket," Jessan said. "Of course." Then, a moment later, "Oh, dear. I think I forgot to transfer my card when I changed shirts."

The duty guard looked dubious, and Jessan held his breath. *Let it slide, damn you.*

But today wasn't going to be his lucky day, it seemed. The duty guard shook his head and brought out a small notebook. "I'm afraid that I'll have to put you on report for failure to carry required documents. What's your unit and section?"

"My unit and section?" echoed Jessan, stalling for time while he tried to think. He saw a flicker of movement out of the corner of his eye, and then Llannat's black-clad figure seemed to materialize next to the duty guard.

"Excuse me, sir," she said, in a soft, hesitant voice. "But can you help me?"

The duty guard looked down at her. "Of course, miss. What's the problem?"

Llannat looked at the pavement. "I'm new here, and I think I'm lost. They told me to turn right and I'd see the Mini-Mart, but I got all mixed up and now I don't know where I am." She lifted her head again, and gave the duty guard a smile. "So, please, could you tell me how to find the Mini-Mart?"

"Of course, miss," the young man began.

"You're *so* nice to help me like this!" exclaimed Llannat, with a deep sigh of relief—rather too deep for realism, Jessan thought critically, but the guard appeared too fascinated by Llannat's snug black sweater to notice any minor flaws in the Adept's performance.

"Actually, miss," the guard said, managing to look serious and hopeful at the same time, "I'm afraid the directions from here might be kind of confusing. It's almost the end of my shift—why don't I just walk you there instead?"

"Oh, *thank* you!" Llannat exclaimed, treating the duty guard to another radiant smile.

Time to leave our friend to Mistress Hyfid's tender mercies, thought Jessan. *This is where I say good-bye.*

He faded out of sight around the corner and resumed his stroll down the street in the westering light, taking care not to be seen reading any more signs. As he walked, he kept hearing Beka's voice, back in the sickbay of the asteroid base: *"So calm and law-abiding it's unnatural."*

The captain had spoken truer than she knew. After rough, muddy Nammerin and gaudy, wide-open Pleyver, Jessan found this Darvelline town almost eerie in its polished perfection. Everywhere he looked along the wide, straight streets he saw nothing but order: carefully tended lawns and identical three-story buildings, painted sparkling white under their red tile roofs and set well back from the spotless sidewalks. There wasn't a scrap of litter or garbage anywhere.

A building came up on his right. The large sign on the wall by the door proclaimed the structure's occupants to be the Housing and Transportation Section, Second Level. *Local intelligence*, he reminded himself. *Time to get some.*

Jessan went in. The decor in the entrance foyer featured colorful posters (LIFT WITH YOUR LEGS, NOT WITH YOUR BACK!, in orange holographic lettering), a bulletin board announcing a dance and assorted sporting events, and a wall rack holding a selection of health and safety pamphlets. A placard over the rack suggested TAKE ONE, which meant that browsing was probably safe and possibly even required.

Jessan flipped through the available offerings. After a moment's consideration, he pulled out several, including a copy of "Welcome to Darvell—Know Your Rights and Duties."

He tucked the pamphlets into his inside jacket pocket, and looked about the foyer again. Off to his right, he spotted a door labeled SHIPPING/DISTRIBUTION—AUTHORIZED PERSONNEL ONLY in black stencil on translucent plastic. Jessan ran a hand over his breeze-ruffled hair and straightened his jacket. Then, after a moment's pause, he palmed the lockplate.

If the door asks for a clearance, I'm stuck. But if they just want to keep out sightseers . . .

The door panel slid aside. Jessan walked in, and up to the young man seated at the nearest desk.

"Comm-code listing," he said, in his best "don't ask questions, just do it" tone of voice.

The young man at the desk didn't look up from the comp screen and the stack of invoices in front of him. "Official or commercial?"

"Official."

Still without taking his eyes from the comp screen, the young man reached over to the shelf at his right hand, pulled out a directory, and handed it across. "Don't take it out of the office."

"Right," Jessan said, and stood beside the desk while he thumbed through the fat volume. "It's not in here," he said pettishly, after a few minutes. "Can I see the commercial listings?"

"We don't keep those here," the young man said. "Try Statistics and Tariffs."

"Thanks anyway," Jessan said. "You've been very helpful."

"You're welcome," said the young man, eyes still glued to the screen. He pulled another invoice from the stack. "Have a nice day."

Once back out on the street, Jessan began to feel a bit more sanguine about the whole idea of intelligence gathering. The next building along bore the label QUALITY ASSURANCE BRANCH, CHIEF. FURNITURE INSPECTION. Jessan looked at the sign for a moment, shrugged, and entered.

He walked past another AUTHORIZED PERSONNEL ONLY sign into another office, where a small group of young men and women in uniform stood around a drink dispenser. One of the men looked up when Jessan came in. "May we help you?"

"I'm hunting for a commercial comm-code listing."

The young man frowned a moment, and then turned toward the woman whom Jessan had already pegged as the senior in the crowd—a statuesque blonde about the Khesatan's own age, with more elaborate rank insignia than the others, a wider variety of colored patches and tabs on her uniform tunic, and a general air of having been around the system for a while.

"We got any of those, ma'am?" the young man asked.

She nodded. "Sure do, Starky. Printing and Distribution dropped off a whole box just last week. Go fetch Mister . . . ?"

"Jamil," said the Khesatan hastily.

"Mister Jamil one."

Starky hurried off, and the woman—Specialist One Griff, according to the nametag on her uniform—asked, "Care for a cup of *uffa* while you wait?"

"Sure."

Griff pulled a cup from a rack on the wall and worked it under the spout of the dispenser. Red liquid poured into the container. When the machine cut off, she handed Jessan the cup and asked, "Where do you work?"

He took a swallow of the *uffa*. The hot drink had a sharp, sweetish flavor, plus the familiar jolt of a mild stimulant. "Down at Housing and Transportation."

"When do you people knock off for the day? We still have ten minutes to go."

"We knock off at the same time you do. I got sent to get one of the new code lists."

The commercial comm list showed up then, in time to save him from any further awkward inquiries. He took the printout and began to thumb through it. A quick glance revealed that the twenty or so pages of small print covered much more than a single township.

"Thanks," he said aloud, folding the printout in half twice and slipping it into one of the outer pockets of his jacket.

"No problem," said Griff. "You're new here, aren't you?"

Nobody in the group seemed upset by the possibility, so Jessan ordered his heart down out of his larynx and back into the position his old Anatomy of the Vertebrate Sentients text said it ought to occupy. "That's right. How'd you guess?"

"I know most of the people down at H and T, and I'd remember seeing you," Griff said. "I'll bet you're staying over in the forty-block quarters, too."

"Right again," said Jessan, trying not to sound nervous. The Specialist One had a speculative look in her eye that he didn't like. *Maybe "forty-block" is a trick question. Fine time to think of that. And me without even a blaster.*

But it seemed that Griff had something other than Operational Security in mind. "Don't worry," she told him. "Darvell's a real friendly place. You'll get to know people fast. In fact—" She smiled at him, and the speculative look got even more speculative. "—after knock-off we're all going over to the get-acquainted mixer Civic Affairs is putting on. Want to come along?"

Jessan smiled back, almost dizzy with relief. *There's all kinds of ways to intelligence-gather. And once we're at the mixer, I can vanish on my way to the punch bowl.*

"Sure," he said.

Beka whirled around, bringing the Gyfferan blaster up from her side to the firing position as she turned. She pressed the stud, and a thin beam of light—the weapon's "tracer" setting—flashed across the clearing toward a new-cut blaze on a conifer opposite.

"Still a bit low, my lady," said the Professor's voice behind her.

She dropped her arm and turned back toward *Defiant*, the blaster in her right hand pointing once more at the ground. "I'm used to something with a bit more weight. But it'll do when the time comes."

"Nevertheless," the Professor said, "practice. The time may come sooner than you think."

The grey-haired Entiboran came on down *Defiant*'s ramp. For the first time, Beka got a good look at the short ebony staff tucked under his belt. He'd had it back in the docking bay on the asteroid, she remembered, but other things had claimed her attention at the time, and she'd filed away the black and silver rod as something to think about later.

Well, now it's later. She looked for a minute at the staff, and shook her head. "Are things going to be that bad?"

Ari had been tasting a spoonful of the game stew. He lifted his head as she spoke, and she saw him look from her to the Professor and back again. He nodded in the general direction of the staff. "You knew?"

"No," she told him. "But I can't say it surprises me." She turned back to the Professor. "Well?" she asked.

The Entiboran smiled. "There comes a time, my lady, when one ceases to worry about attracting unwanted attention."

Something ran down her spine on little icy feet, and she shivered. But try as she might, she couldn't read anything in the Professor's grey eyes except what might have been affection, assuming that her copilot was capable of the emotion.

Ari's deep voice broke the uncomfortable silence. "If nobody besides me claims any of this stew . . ."

She forced herself to relax. "Big brother, if you take

the whole dinner for yourself and leave the rest of us to break our teeth on unheated space rations, I'll use you for target practice instead of that tree over there. And I won't leave the beam on 'tracer,' either.''

"Then go get some bowls and spoons from the galley," he said. "Because this stuff's done."

The rest of the awkwardness died in the bustle of fetching utensils, dishing out the savory chunks of meat, and settling down for the meal.

"Good food," said Beka, a plate or so of stew later. "Who taught you to cook—Ferrda?"

"Mostly," said her brother.

"How'd you like a permanent job in the *'Hammer'*s galley?"

Ari shook his head. "Sorry, I just signed on for one cruise. And speaking of things like that—now that we've made it this far, what's the plan?" He gave her a dubious look. "You do have a plan, don't you?"

She couldn't resist. "No, I don't have a plan." She let the pause drag out long enough for Ari to start turning red, then nodded toward the Professor. "He does, though."

Ari turned with elaborate patience to her copilot. "Speaking as my sister's tactician," he said, "can you tell me how we're going to handle this?"

The Professor sat with both hands around a cup of cha'a from the self-heating pot he'd brought out of *Defiant*'s galley. "Much depends," he said, "upon the intelligence Mistress Hyfid and Lieutenant Commander Jessan bring with them when they return. Roughly, the plan is this: Nivome the Rolny maintains a vast hunting preserve in the heart of Darvell's capital city. So much is general knowledge across the civilized galaxy. In fact, invitations to join the Rolny for a weekend of shooting *wuxen* are highly prized in certain circles of the Republic."

"I'm sure everybody has a wonderful time," Ari said. "But what does that have to do with us? The 'House of Sapne' act's gone stale by now."

Beka shook her head. "You shouldn't have slept through breakfast before we left base. This time we're doing a straightforward smash-and-grab."

"In the middle of the capital city?"

"That's the importance of the hunting preserve," said the Professor. "Security is tight at Rolny Lodge—but Nivome's other residence is not called the Citadel for compliment's sake alone."

After dinner, silence fell over the clearing. Ari shied small pebbles one at a time across the open ground at a patch of light-colored moss. Beka worked over the leather belt of the Gyfferan blaster, first measuring it off against her old belt, then punching a series of new holes with the point of her knife. The Professor, meanwhile, had settled back against a convenient boulder and, as far as Beka could tell from looking at him, had gone to sleep.

Let him rest, she told herself as she worked the knife point through the thick leather. *That approach laid you out flat for a solid day afterward, even with a copilot to share everything but the worst parts—and you're still young.*

Ari had caught her quick glance over at the elderly Entiboran. "Fond of him, are you?"

She put a bit more pressure behind the knife and felt the leather give under the point. Another push, and the tip of the knife popped through on the other side of the belt like a tiny metal fang. She twisted the knife to enlarge the hole a little.

"I suppose so," she said, after a while. "Somewhat."

Ari looked disapproving. "Hard as nails, aren't you, Bee?"

"That's right," she said. She measured the new belt against the old one again, and began work on a second hole.

"So where does Jessan fit into your scheme of things? Light amusement?"

She laid the leather belt down on the ground and looked

across at him, balancing the knife in her right hand. "I'd say it's none of your damned business."

Ari shied another pebble at the patch of moss. It hit dead-on, like all the others had. "He's my friend, and you're my sister. I'd say that makes it my business."

She drew her lips back from her teeth. "Think again. Or shall I start asking questions about your Adept girl-friend?"

"Mistress Hyfid is *not* my 'Adept girlfriend'!"

"Then what the hell was she doing out in civvies with you on an emergency call?"

Ari reddened. "She came along as a courtesy to a medical colleague."

"Right," said Beka. "And I'm the Princess of Sapne."

"Gently, my lady," said the Professor's quiet voice. "Gently, Lieutenant. Squabbling will not bring your friends home any sooner."

Morning came. Somewhere beyond the combination of fog and low-lying clouds hanging over the mountainside, the sun had presumably risen as usual. In the clearing, Beka hunched her shoulders inside Tarnekep Portree's Mandeynan long-coat and poked at a bowl of congealing water-grain porridge with her spoon. The hole stayed behind when she withdrew the utensil, like an impression in wet concrete. She scowled at the brownish glop, and looked over at her brother.

Ari sat next to the tiny campfire, his only concession to the dawn chill a light jacket over his loose shirt, working his way stolidly through a second helping of porridge. Beka watched him for a few moments, but when he tilted the bowl to scrape out the last few thickening spoonfuls she felt her patience snap.

"Damn it, Ari, doesn't *anything* ever affect your appetite?"

He looked up. "If you can show me how skipping breakfast is going to help, I'll skip breakfast and lunch both. Otherwise, there's no point in starving."

"Oh, the hell with it," she said in disgust, shoving away her bowl and standing up. "Finish mine, too, if you're going to be so damned practical."

She stalked over to the tree she'd used for target practice the night before, and stood leaning against it with one hand and jabbing her dagger into the soft wood with the other.

"You'll just have to clean the sap off the blade later," Ari said.

She didn't turn around. "I'm not worried about it," she said, working the blade loose and slamming it back into the tree trunk. "I've cleaned off worse stuff than this by now."

Ari didn't answer. After a few seconds she yielded to curiosity and turned back around to see what was wrong. "Ari?"

Her brother sat without moving, his head tilted a little to one side. "Shh." After a few breaths, he added, in an almost inaudible murmur, "Someone's coming."

She switched the knife to her left hand, and let her right hand fall to touch the comforting presence of the Gyfferan blaster. Over by the fire, Ari rose to his feet in one smooth, soundless motion.

Now she could hear footsteps, too—and, incongruously, the delicate opening bars of Klif's Fifth Mixolydian Etude, its whistled notes pitched clear and true.

Only Jessan, she thought, biting down hard on a shaky laugh. She felt herself starting to tremble all over; it took all the self-control she had to pull Portree's lace-trimmed handkerchief out of her right sleeve and concentrate on wiping the resin off the blade of her dagger.

"Anybody home?" called Mistress Hyfid's soft alto voice.

"Just us," Ari replied, in a curt monotone. "You made enough noise coming up here to scare off all the game in the district."

"That was more or less the idea," said a second voice.

"We didn't want to get blasted out of the bushes before we could identify ourselves."

With careful, precise motions, Beka tucked the sticky handkerchief into her coat pocket, slid the dagger into its forearm sheath, and allowed herself to look over at the new arrivals. Nyls Jessan stood watching her through the morning fog, his jacket collar turned up and droplets of moisture beading his hair. Their eyes met; he came forward, smiling, from the mist-shrouded underbrush, and held out his hands.

She crossed the ground between them in a half-dozen strides. "You nearly got blasted anyway, you Khesatan idiot," she told him. "My big brother over there can hear the grass growing. If we hadn't been watching for you ever since last night—"

She stopped hard on the last word while her voice was still under control, and clutched his hands instead. Jessan's long fingers closed around hers, and she felt her trembling ease off and stop.

"We couldn't get away until past midnight," Llannat Hyfid was explaining to Ari. "And after that we had to walk most of the way back."

"Most?" Beka asked, without letting go of Jessan's hands.

The Khesatan didn't show any inclination to let go either. "We stole rides on ground transports for part of the way," he said, still smiling at her. "Easier."

"And faster," said Llannat. "We've got some interesting stuff for the Professor. In the meantime—what's for breakfast?"

Jessan and the Adept had put away a couple of bowls of cold porridge each by the time the Professor emerged from *Defiant* and joined the group at the campfire. He carried the self-heating cha'a pot in one hand and a bunch of mugs in the other. From her place across the fire from Beka, Llannat Hyfid gave the Entiboran a smile that lit up her entire face.

"You're a lifesaver, Professor—we'll even forgive you for sleeping in and missing our return."

"I was meditating," said the Professor, setting the cha'a pot down on a flat rock and laying out the mugs around it with as much care as if they had been translucent porcelain instead of cheap plastic. "To quote an Adept of my acquaintance, 'It seemed necessary.' "

"Now that we're all here," Beka said as the mugs of cha'a went round, "just what did you manage to bring back?"

"I'm afraid it doesn't look like much," Jessan said. He began unzipping his jacket pockets and pulling out pamphlets, leaflets, and sheets of folded paper. Beka reached out and picked up one of the gaudier ones.

" 'Seven Tested Tips For Hoverbike Safety'?" she asked.

"You never know what might come in handy," said Jessan. "Try the one under it, though."

" 'Welcome to Darvell,' " she read off the cover. "With a blown-in flatpic of Our Beloved Leader, suitable for framing . . . that's more like it."

"He still looks like he did the last time I met him," Jessan said. "A bit greyer and jowlier, but the same old Nivome and no mistake."

"Now that," said the Professor, as he riffled through the collection, "is gratifying intelligence. What else have you brought back?"

"A commercial comm-code listing," Jessan said, "a *Child's First History of Darvell*—with maps—and a lot of firsthand observation that someone may well find interesting once we get back. Quite a place, this planet."

"What do you mean?" Ari asked. Beka jumped a little; it was the first thing her brother had said since the Professor showed up with the cha'a.

"The whole place is regulation-happy," Llannat said. "ID cards to get into the stores, ID cards to make your purchase, ID cards to get out again . . . you get the general idea."

"If you think the Space Force likes red tape," Jessan added, "then you should see this place. Or maybe not—I nearly got hauled off just for reading the Plan of the Day at the wrong time. A guard spotted me acting suspicious and wanted to write me up for failure to carry my ID card in the proper pocket. I thought I'd had it until Llannat came along and managed to change his mind."

Curious, Beka looked over the rim of her mug at the Adept. "I thought you had ethical convictions about—what was it, Mistress Hyfid, 'invasion and compulsion'?"

The Adept lowered her eyes with a faint smile. "Take my word for it, Captain—the method I used wasn't the kind they teach up at the Retreat."

Over beyond Jessan, Beka could hear Ari choking on a mouthful of cha'a. She stared for a moment at the small woman and then began to grin.

"I think, Mistress Hyfid—"

"That's 'Llannat,' " said the Adept. "Please."

"Llannat, then," said Beka, still grinning, while Ari glowered dark-browed at them both. "I think we're going to be friends after all."

III. Darvell: Darplex; Rolny Lodge

*I*T'S AMAZING, Ari thought a week later, as he made his way through the tidy streets near Darplex Spaceport, *what you can do with maps and a comm-code listing.*

The child's history book Llannat had picked up—purchased for her, she said, by the overly impressionable guard in the course of a courtesy tour—had located them on the planet's surface. Working from the maps in the back, Beka and the Professor had been able to plot a hoverbike course to Darplex that skirted the settlements and the main roads. Once they'd slipped into Darplex proper, setting up shop in a deserted warehouse had been simplicity itself. The neatly stenciled AUTHORIZED PERSONNEL ONLY sign Jessan had added to the front door was enough to keep out law-abiding Darvellines.

But the real find of that first day's expedition had been Jessan's commercial comm-code listing. The little directory hadn't covered the entire planet, but it did cover Darplex and the surrounding administrative district, of which the small foothill town had been an outlying part.

Ari had been flipping through the directory's pages that morning by the campfire, while the rising sun burned the fog off the mountainside and his sister and Llannat Hyfid grinned at each other like a couple of idiots. A bit unnerved by their sudden accord, he had given the columns of fine print in the comm-code listing more attention than he might have otherwise.

"Licensed Establishments," he had muttered under his breath.

"Bars," explained Jessan. "A bit of well-deserved comfort for the hardworking members of the upper paygrades. At least, that's what it says in the guidebook."

"I see," Ari said. That explained some of the names— the Upper Eight Inn, the Six-Up *Uffa* Shop, and innumerable Top Three Pubs, Restaurants, and Lounges. And . . . "Hey, wait a minute."

Beka looked over at him, her face taking on the sharp-edged hunter's expression he'd come to associate with her Tarnekep persona. "Find something interesting, big brother?"

"Maybe," he said. "There's only one Five *anything* in this whole listing."

"Five," said Llannat. "What was Munngralla's shop in Namport called, Ari? 'Five Points Imports'?"

Jessan raised a skeptical eyebrow. "The Quincunx, here on Darvell?"

The Professor looked thoughtful. "That does raise an interesting possibility. But even if the establishment truly is a Quincunx front, that organization always charges whatever the traffic will bear. For anything we might require from them, the price would be very high indeed."

Ari couldn't help looking smug. "Not for a member."

Beka stared. *"You?"*

"That's right," he said. "Courtesy of Munngralla," he explained to Jessan and Llannat; and then, to Beka, "A long story. I'll tell you sometime."

"You'd better," she said. "But you know the recognition codes and everything?"

"Right again."

"In that case," the Professor said, looking as close to delighted as Ari had ever seen him get, "we are in a position to eliminate several intermediate steps and quite a bit of cargo handling from the basic plan—assuming, of course, that you are willing to contact the Quincunx on our behalf."

"Sure," he had said. "Why not?"

Right now, though, as he strode along under the white glare of the nearby portside dock lights, he could think of any number of reasons why not. Even in his most nondescript set of civilian clothes, he felt about as inconspicuous as a landing beacon. The ride across Darplex on the public shuttle had been even worse. He'd sat on a hard plastic seat between a pair of fresh-faced, wholesome-looking Darvellines, and forced himself to read the uplifting sayings on the placards above the shuttle windows as a means of self-sedation.

"Training—Your Key to Advancement," he quoted glumly to himself as he walked along. *Beka was right about this place. It's right out of a holovid horror show.*

The Top Five Lounge shared a three-story building with the Paperwork Reduction Office (Port Branch) on the top floor, and something at street level that called itself a Class Four Privilege Shop and appeared to specialize in light household accessories. The main entrance slid open as Ari came up, revealing a wide stairway leading to hinged glass doors off a second-floor landing.

If this place isn't a front, thought Ari, *I've had it.*

He climbed up the stairs, pushed open the door, and went in. No ID checker materialized. In fact, the place looked deserted. Ahead of him, a long corridor paneled in dark wood ended in an archway leading to the left. The arch opened onto a larger room with a long bar set against the far wall. Beyond that room, through another archway, Ari could glimpse white-draped dining tables. But aside from the man behind the front bar, the Top Five Lounge appeared empty.

It's early yet, thought Ari. *Father always did say portside never got really interesting until after midnight.*

He went up to the bar and took a seat. The bartender came over and asked, "What'll it be?"

Here goes, thought Ari. "I've traveled a long way for the sake of a proper word."

"Coming right up," the bartender said without blinking, and began to mix a drink from the bottles behind the bar.

Ari controlled a grimace as a splash of pink liquid from an unlabeled bottle was followed by a sprinkling of green powder out of a jar with a label he'd never seen before. *I don't believe it. I've hit on one of the local cocktails.*

Still, Ari wasn't too surprised when a man slid onto the stool beside him. He did feel a small twinge of suppressed astonishment at the sight of the man himself. Most humans who could match Ari for height tended to be scrawny ectomorphic sorts, but the big Darvelline gentleman in the well-cut evening suit carried enough muscle on him to be Ari's twin.

"Good evening," said the new arrival, whose discreet nametag read *H. Estisk, Manager.* "How'd you like to bring your drink back to the private office?" The manager turned to the bartender. "No charge. It's on me."

Without waiting for another word, the manager turned and walked off. Ari scooped up his just-delivered glass and followed him into an office that held a desk, two chairs, and a shelf full of order books and supply catalogs. A half-finished tumbler full of something reddish brown, over ice, stood on one corner of the desk.

Estisk sat, and indicated the other chair to Ari. "Well, now," the manager began. "What can we do for you?"

Let's try another check. "There are five things I need to start with, and more later."

"We deal in fives of all sorts," the manager replied. "But you're the first one of us to come through in a long time. Sorry about all the mystery, but the barman's only a local. I told him a 'Proper Word' was a kind of drink, and said if anyone ever asked for one to signal me.''

Ari sipped the concoction. It wasn't bad, if you didn't look at the color for too long. "The first thing I'll need is five ID cards, spaceport passes, and all the papers to allow me and four others free travel in the city. I didn't run into any spot checks on the way over here, but I think I got a few grey hairs worrying about it."

"No problem on the ID and travel papers—but I have to tell you there are no spaceport passes. Port access is by personal recognition only."

"That's all right," Ari said. "When can I get the papers and ID?"

"Come by my daytime shop," Estisk said. "That's the tool-issue point in Building One-two-five three-four, Outer Ring. If you can get there by nine tomorrow with flatpix of everybody you want a card for, I can have them for you by ten."

"What'll it cost?"

The manager looked thoughtful. "For a brother . . . just enough to cover my own expenses. Do you have any local cash, or would you like to try barter? The right off-world stuff can get you high prices around here."

I'll bet, thought Ari, remembering some of his father's free-trading stories, but he shook his head. "I have cash."

Estisk smiled. "I won't ask how you got it. In that case, the price is twenty marks for each ID and privilege card, and ten marks for travel permits and quarters cards."

"Right," Ari said. "I'll see you tomorrow, then, and bring the rest of my shopping list with me."

"Excellent," said Estisk. The manager lifted his glass. "Well, brother, here's to a profitable association for us both."

A few days later, metal grated on metal as the doors of Warehouse 307 slid open and then shut again with a clang. Ari crawled far enough out of the aircar's engine pod to get a view of the newcomers—his sister and the Professor, as he'd expected. Anybody else would have drawn some sort of reaction from Nyls Jessan and Llannat Hyfid, busy studying a holoplan of Rolny Lodge over at the watch desk.

"Where's Ari?" Beka asked.

"Right here," he said, leaving the aircar completely and joining the others around the desk. "I wanted to make certain our getaway vehicle was ready for a suborbital burn. Did you two find the stuff you were looking for?"

"Of course," said the Professor. "Did you get the information from your contact?"

"I did," Ari said. "But you aren't going to like it."

"Just tell me," said his sister, "and let me decide if I like it or not."

"All right," he said. "The entire estate is surrounded by an immobilizer force field, and the controls are in the gatehouse—behind the field, of course. Nobody gets in who isn't on that day's access list."

Beka bit her lip and frowned at the holoplan. "Stocking the woods with hunter/killer robots wasn't enough, was it? Llannat, could you manage . . . ?"

The Adept shook her head. "Not an immobilizer. Sorry."

"Damn," said Beka. "I know it's not your fault—but it'd take Gilveet Rhos himself to bring down an immobilizer any other way. We may have to settle for an ambush after all."

The Professor gave them a small half-smile. "I think not. I taught Gilveet everything he knows . . . but not everything I know. The force field won't give us any problems." He pulled a small grey box from his shirt pocket and handed it out to Ari. "Here are your decoy transponders."

"Thanks," Ari said. "Any trouble finding them?"

"No trouble at all," Beka said. "Transponders, ID, the aircar—that connection of yours does good work. All right, Professor, let's go over the plan once more before we leave."

"Very well, my lady," said the Entiboran. "If you will all observe the holoplan—at first light, I will take down a section of the force field here, to the northwest. Lieutenant Rosselin-Metadi and Mistress Hyfid will go over the wall of the hunting preserve and make their way to the house, neutralizing the robots as they go. They will remain by the main house as lookouts and guards, signaling us that the way is clear."

Everybody nodded and looked solemn. The Professor continued. "At dusk, Lieutenant Commander Jessan will bring the aircar down the cleared corridor and up to the house. The captain and I will accompany you on hover-bikes."

The Professor pointed to one side of the main lodge. "You will land the aircar here, next to the dining area, where Nivome will be at his evening meal. The rest of us will ground our hoverbikes next to the wall. The captain will place a collapsor grenade against the side of the house and activate it. Lieutenant Commander Jessan—"

"Right here," said the Khesatan. "I follow you so far."

"Excellent. You will have your blaster set to stun. When the wall goes, your only task will be to take our target and immobilize him. Your blaster, and yours alone, will be set to 'stun.' Lieutenant Rosselin-Metadi will enter the building, and pick up the Rolny while the captain and I provide covering fire. As soon as we have the Rolny in hand, we will retreat to the aircar, launch back to the ships, lift off under cloaking, and enter hyperspace from the nearest jump point."

"And then," Beka said, with a twitch to her knife hand that brought the blade flashing out of its forearm sheath and plunged it into the center of the holoplan, "we can think about planning something . . . nice . . . for Gentle-sir Nivome the Rolny."

Ari watched the air above the high stone wall. A pebble hung there, caught in the immobilizer field and barely visible in the grey light before dawn. *Any minute now,* he thought.

The pebble dropped.

Go.

Ari caught the top of the wall with both hands and swung himself up to lie along it. He looked back down at the deserted street, and saw Llannat draw herself together and jump.

She landed in a compact crouch a few feet away from him. Together, they surveyed the interior of the hunting preserve. The ground inside was considerably lower than the street beyond the wall—too far down, thought Ari, even for him to jump. About the Adept, he wasn't sure.

None of the hunting preserve's tall Darvelline conifers grew within reach of the wall. The Rolny's groundskeepers had seen to that. One tree, though, grew closer than the rest. Ari smiled to himself and drew his feet up under him. Gauging the distance, he leaped for the tree trunk.

He caught it, and slid down until his boots hit a branch that felt solid enough to take him. Turning back toward Llannat, he held out an arm in her direction. She nodded, and sprang forward and down from her crouched position to catch his extended hand. For a brief and disquieting moment, he felt no awareness of supporting her weight before she settled onto the branch beside him.

Without a word, he climbed down the conifer, and she followed. They lay still in the underbrush while the sun came over the horizon and the forest grew brighter around them. As soon as they had enough light to work with, Ari nodded to Llannat and stood up, unslinging his heavy energy lance and shrugging his backpack into position.

Using the skills that Ferrda had taught him, he faded from tree to tree until at least fifty yards separated him from Llannat. He pulled a set of earphones out of the backpack and settled them onto his head, placed the sun ahead and to his left and the wall to his back, and began to drift toward the house.

Morning wore on, and the air grew warmer. He kept up

his gradual stalk through the woods of the Rolny's hunting preserve, alternating long periods of immobility in the cover of shadow or underbrush with quick, silent crossings of open ground. Somewhere off to his right, he knew that Llannat Hyfid was doing much the same.

By the time the sun was nearing its zenith, he'd started to sweat. *Good thing robots don't have noses,* he thought. *Unless they've come up with a model that can run tests on the fly for particle concentration in parts per million . . . let's not think about that, shall we?*

He heard a crackling in the underbrush. Not Llannat—the Adept hadn't made a sound since the hunt began. An animal?

His ears caught the faint squeak of metal on metal, and he tensed. Not an animal. First contact.

A black-painted security robot floated on its nullgravs across the sun-dappled ground between the trees. The robot's sensor pod rotated as it moved. The Quincunx man had been right: this wasn't one of your call-the-guards robots, or even an immobilize-and-capture model. This was a true hunter/killer, with blunt boxes of armor-piercing and anti-air modules showing under its sensor pod.

He heard a clicking sound from the far side of the glade.

That'll be Llannat, he thought, as the robot began floating toward the sound. His headset came to life, interpreting the signal the robot was sending.

"This is FY eight-six. Grid Posit seven three eight eight five five. Suspicious noise. Investigating."

Ari raised the energy lance in his hand, took aim at the base of the sensor/command pod, and fired. A shower of sparks fell from the base of the sensor pod; the robot continued forward until a tree checked its progress.

Llannat stepped around from behind the tree and stood next to the robot. Ari took one of the Professor's little boxes out of his backpack, and punched FY86 and 738855 into the command transmitter he wore on one wrist. He caught Llannat's eye; she nodded, and switched the robot off as he switched the box on.

The robot sank to the ground. Over his headset, Ari heard the decoy's transmission: "This is FY eight six. Grid Posit seven three eight eight five five. Investigation complete. Situation normal. Resuming patrol."

One down, six to go.

Ari resumed his quiet walk toward the house.

Seven down, thought Llannat some time later, as the last of the hunter/killer robots sank to the forest floor. *And that's all of them.*

She looked back toward Ari, but he'd vanished once more among the trees. It was amazing, she thought, how close the big Galcenian came to not being there at all. If she stretched out her awareness to catch the patterns of power at work in the hunting preserve, she could sense him—but only as a quiet, slow-moving presence, like a Selvaur on the hunt.

She continued her own progress, effacing herself as Master Ransome's apprentice Owen Rosselin-Metadi had taught her to do. She was good at it—not in Owen's class, but good—and unless the Rolny had an Adept-level sensitive working Security for him, nobody was going to notice a small, almost negligible figure in a black coverall making her way from one patch of shadow to the next.

The hair rose on the back of her neck—*threat,* her Adept-trained senses whispered, *menace*—and seconds later a human in camouflage clothing walked into her field of vision. Like Ari, he carried an energy lance and a comm link, but he was noisy. His movements were those of a city dweller, untrained for work in the deep woods; his footsteps and breathing echoed in the quiet of the hunting preserve.

Nobody mentioned live guards, she thought. *Now what?*

She cast about once again for Ari's presence. For a moment she couldn't sense him anywhere, and came close to panic. Then she felt a faint reflection of the familiar, rock-steady aura, and traced it to a stand of berry bushes off to her left.

Once she had him located, she could see him. His aura intensified suddenly—he'd spotted her in turn. She raised her eyebrows and projected strong inquiry.

He wasn't as receptive as Jessan, who could pick up subvocals, but something seemed to get through. He made a "go on forward" gesture with one hand. She nodded and let herself become even more inobtrusive than before, then slipped past the guard like an unheeded thought. When she looked back at the berry bushes, Ari was gone.

Still self-effaced, she moved on toward their goal. The trees began to thin out; she could glimpse bits of mani-cured lawn ahead, and then something grey and rectan-gular that turned out to be a concrete blockhouse.

Her neck prickled again. *That wasn't on the plans.*

The grass was clipped short around the blockhouse for a greater distance than a man could cover in a rush. She let her mind become still, until she had no more presence than a patch of shadow on the landscape, then crossed the open area to flatten herself against the concrete wall. Ari joined her a few seconds later.

She looked up at him. "I don't like this," she mur-mured, backing the thread of sound with subvocal projec-tion. As long as he could hear anything at all, he should be keeping open enough for meanings to get through—and his hearing, she knew, was acute. "I think I'll go in and see what's there."

Without waiting for a reply, she glanced around the cor-ner of the blockhouse. A uniformed man was approaching the squat concrete building from the direction of the Lodge. *Good,* she thought, and drifted out shadow-fashion in a curving path that finished behind the newcomer. She closed in to follow a pace behind him, matching him step for step and motion for motion—becoming, as her masters had taught her, a shadow indeed.

The man reached the blockhouse door, and tapped out a sequence of keypresses on the cipher lock. The door slid open. He stepped in, turning to look back the way he had come. Still a shadow, she pivoted around and back with him.

Satisfied that all was clear, the man toggled the door shut after him and continued on down a short corridor to a second, open door. This time, one of his shadows stayed behind.

From her position near the main entrance, Llannat watched the man enter what looked like some sort of control room. She could glimpse security monitors and read-out panels, plus another uniformed Darvelline already on watch. She moved up to the inner door and listened.

"How's it going?" she heard the newcomer say.

"No change. We know they're inside—the robots have been switched slicker than anything—but they haven't reached the live guards yet. I just got done talking to post six, and he says nothing's gotten past."

Llannat peeked around the corner. The two men lounged at ease in front of a bank of monitors showing views of the house and grounds.

"What do you think's going on?" asked the first one.

The second shrugged. "I don't know. Maybe a drill of some sort."

"I've never seen a drill like this," the first guard said dubiously. "Especially not with shoot-to-kill orders."

"I don't make the rules," the second man said. "I just follow them. What's going on up at the Lodge?"

"They're about ready to head out. He's going to make for the Citadel."

This sounds bad, thought Llannat, and risked looking further into the control room. From the new angle, she could see what had been hidden before: ID flatpix, five of them, blown up to life size and tacked to the wall above the monitors.

The Professor. Beka Rosselin-Metadi. Nyls Jessan. Ari. And herself.

IV. Darvell: Rolny Lodge; Darplex

L LANNAT STARED at the row of pictured faces. *We've been sold out.*

The breath caught in her throat, almost choking her. *Don't panic,* she told herself. *Just get out of sight before one of those guards turns around.*

She faded back around the corner of the open door. Away from the evidence of betrayal, her breathing eased a little. *That's better. Now get out of here and warn Ari.*

She made her way down the short hall to the blockhouse entrance. When she got there, her heart sank: the exit door was locked, with a cipher-lock keypad set into the wall next to the jamb.

What's the odds, she asked herself, *that it's the same code to get out as to get in?*

Shrugging, she punched in the sequence that had opened the door from the other side. The door remained shut. *No joy,* she thought, with resignation—and then the door's numeric display started flashing off and on. "Incorrect access code, report to key operator," bleated the annunciator. "Repeat, incorrect access code, report to key operator."

Oh, no. Now I'll have to do something really *fancy.*

Llannat turned her back on the babbling cipher lock, ran forward a few steps to get momentum, and jumped for the ceiling.

Several seconds later, one of the two guards came out of the monitor room and headed toward the blockhouse door.

So this is what the world looks like to a spider, thought Llannat, as the guard walked down the hall beneath her. The Adept held herself suspended above the hallway with her back snug against the low ceiling, kept up by the pressure of her hands against the wall in front of her and the pressure of her Space Force standard issue boots against the wall behind. From that precarious vantage point, she watched the guard punch in a sequence of numbers on the keypad of the cipher lock. The annunciator's yammering voice fell silent.

The man turned and started back down the hallway. Llannat's muscles trembled with the effort of maintaining her position, but she didn't dare try floating on the currents of power while keeping herself unseen. The most she could do was to sneak in a little help every few seconds . . . just enough to keep her arms and legs from giving way, nothing anybody would notice.

The guard stopped and glanced upward.

Llannat forced her mind into the self-effacing patterns of calm and tranquility. *The ceiling,* she thought. *All you notice is the ceiling.*

The guard shook his head as if to clear it, and walked on forward until he was directly beneath her. "Nothing down here," he called toward the control room, "and the door's locked. What do you think we ought to do?"

The voice from the control room sounded resigned. "The way things are today, we don't have much choice. We'll have to call in a Class Two Contact Alert."

I don't like the sound of that, thought Llannat. She relaxed the pressure of her hands and feet, letting herself drop from the ceiling onto the shoulders of the unsuspecting guard. His knees buckled, and he hit the concrete floor with Llannat on top of him. She rolled with the fall, and drove the heel of her hand upward into his chin as soon as her arm came clear.

The guard went limp. Llannat came to her feet in a fighting crouch, gripping her staff with both hands. She took a step into the next room.

Inside the control room, the second guard let out a yell and grabbed for his blaster. Llannat struck out at him with her staff, a clumsy swashing stroke that nevertheless connected with the guard's weapon. The bolt went wild as the heavy blaster flew through the air and clunked to the floor out of reach.

Disarmed, the man stared at her. She fixed his eyes with her own and projected *Don't move!* with all the power at her command. He stared for a few seconds longer, then spun around and reached for a switch on the main control panel.

Enough! she thought, and swung the staff against his skull.

Ari lay on the close-mown ground next to the blockhouse wall. He still held the energy lance in one hand, but he'd removed the bulky, now-useless earphones and stowed them in the backpack. From time to time he inched forward to peer around the corner at the door through which Llannat had entered.

She's been gone too long, he thought. *Something's up.*

Without warning, a burst of green light flashed around the edges of the doorway, and the panels grated halfway apart. Llannat's head and shoulders appeared in the opening.

"Ari—get in here! We have big trouble!"

He scrambled to his feet and sprinted for the door, scraping sideways through the narrow aperture. In the close atmosphere of the blockhouse he recognized the sharp smell of air ionized by a blaster. A man lay flat on his back in the short passage, stirring like a sleeper trying to wake. Ari strode past him to the control room, and took in the banks of monitors, the row of flatpix posted on the wall, and the body sprawled across the control panel.

"Death and damnation—what happened in here?"

"Your precious contact sold us out," she said. "We've been walking into a trap the whole time."

"I can see that," said Ari. "Right now, we need some answers, quick."

Llannat's eyes went to the guard lying out in the hallway. "I don't know if I—"

Ari shook his head. "We haven't got time for the subtle stuff." He shrugged off the backpack and slung the energy lance out of the way across his shoulders. "Be ready to back me up."

The Adept raised the blaster she'd taken from the unconscious guard and moved away a few steps to provide cover. Ari pulled his own blaster—one of Beka's old government-surplus models, but good enough for a man who wasn't planning on making a career out of jobs like this—and stepped out into the hall.

He went down on one knee beside the guard. Taking the man's earlobe between forefinger and thumbnail, he gave the flesh a savage twist. The guard's eyes opened and focused on Ari's face. Ari grabbed a fistful of the man's shirtfront and surged to his feet, pulling the smaller man along with him and slamming him up against the wall.

The Darvelline's boots dangled a good foot and a half above the floor. Ari shoved the muzzle of his blaster into the man's belly just above the gleaming belt buckle.

"All right, you," Ari said. "Talk. Where's Nivome?"

"Up at the Lodge," gasped the Darvelline. His eyes went from Ari to Llannat and back again. "Who *are* you guys?"

"Fool!" roared Ari. "Don't you recognize Black Brok, Terror of the Spaceways, and his Sinister Sidekick Serina?" Behind him, he could hear Llannat stifling a half-hysterical giggle. He ignored her. "Nivome's in the Lodge—where?"

"Garage," said the guard. "Getting ready to go."

Ari gave the man a one-handed shake. The Darvelline's head swung forward and then hit the wall with a thud. "Go where?"

"Citadel."

"He's telling the truth, Brok," Llannat said. "Take a look at the monitors."

Still holding the Darvelline at arm's length against the wall, Ari glanced into the control room. In the farthest monitor to the left, he could make out the image of a long, armored hovercar pulling out through a wide garage door. A pack of armed outriders in blast-resistant vests and helmets formed up their hoverbikes on the vehicle as the car moved forward.

"You're sure they're heading for the Citadel?" he asked.

She nodded. "I heard these two talking about it earlier."

"Then we've got to alert the others before he gets there," said Ari. He shook the guard one more time and let him drop. The Darvelline slid to the floor and didn't try to stand up again. "Let's go."

"Wait," said Llannat. Lifting the captured blaster, she put a long burst of scarlet energy into the guts of the control panel. She took out the monitor screens and the comm unit the same way. Last of all, she blasted the rogues' gallery of betraying flatpix into smoking tatters.

"Good idea," Ari said.

The Adept gave him a brief smile as she joined him in the hall. "Thanks," she said. "I thought you'd approve." She held out the captured blaster. "You'd better take this for now—you're better than I am at that sort of thing."

"Right," said Ari. "Let's get out of here."

Holding a blaster in each hand, he turned to where the guard lay huddled against the wall. "If you value your life," he told the Darvelline, "stay where you are. Come on, Serina—'Spaceways and Away'!"

Without looking to see if Llannat followed, he headed out the door of the blockhouse and made for the main Lodge. The Adept came up abreast of him after a few steps.

" 'Brok and Serina,' " she said. In spite of everything, she sounded amused.

"It's all I could think of," Ari said without breaking stride. He set a good fast pace as the two of them headed for the nearest wing of the low, sprawling complex that was Rolny Lodge. So far, nobody in the main house had reacted to their presence, but he didn't know how long that bit of luck was going to last.

All we've got going for us now is surprise, he thought, as they rounded the corner of the house, *and not much of that.*

The plans had been right about one thing, at least—the garage was right where it should be. The long door through which the hovercar had made its exit earlier was sliding down as Ari and Llannat approached. Ari hit the ground and rolled through the narrowing gap.

He came out of the roll on his knees, firing both blasters. Most of the coverall-clad workers inside the garage headed for shelter among the Lodge's collection of aircars and hovercars. A few hesitated—until Llannat charged straight at them, staff upraised and the air about her blazing up into a corona of bright green flame.

The unarmed mechanics and controllers scattered as the door at Ari's back finished its closing cycle with a clang. He fired a few more bolts into the recesses of the garage before he realized that with the exception of himself and Llannat, the parking bay was empty.

Next to him, the Adept stopped. The green aura that had surrounded her flickered and died. "Looks like they all ran out the back."

"Looks like," he agreed. "How about giving Beka and Jessan the bad news while we've got the chance?"

Llannat pulled the comm link out of the breast pocket of her jacket and switched it on. A high, ear-piercing ul-

ulation filled the empty bay. She winced and turned off the link.

"What was that?" she asked.

"Nivome's got a jammer going someplace on the estate," said Ari. "Set for our frequency. Just one more thing our friend forgot to tell us. Come on, let's grab ourselves some transport and get out of here."

Llannat opened her mouth to say something—what, he never knew. The shrill whooping of a security alarm filled the garage, and a disembodied voice near the ceiling began to recite, "Intruder Alert. Intruder Alert. All hands man your intruder stations."

The lights in the parking bay went out.

"Damn it," Ari said. "They've cut the power."

"Don't move," said Llannat's voice a few feet away. Seconds later, a ball of green light appeared above her outstretched hand.

"Not bad," Ari said. "Can you do something about the main door controls?"

She shook her head. "Not in the time we've got. I don't even know where they are."

"All right, then. We do it the hard way."

Ari made his way to a small aircar close to the rolling doors and opened the side hatch. Reaching inside, he felt around on the control panel until he located the landing-light switch. He flipped it on, and powerful beams of white light shot out from the leading edges of the aircar's stubby wings.

He tossed the spare blaster ahead of him into the cockpit and followed it up with the energy lance. Then he climbed in himself and started checking over the controls by the landing lights' reflected glow.

He found the starter switch. "Jump aboard," he told Llannat. "We're leaving."

He put the brakes full on, set the fuel mix for full rich, and fired up the jets. The turbines whined as he increased throttle. The aircar began to slide forward despite the brakes.

"Ready to launch," he said. "Stand by!"

"Wait! I'm not strapped in!"

"Then hold on!"

Ari released the brakes.

The aircar jumped forward. With a shuddering jar, it hit the hangar doors and burst through. The doors wrapped like a tent across the nose of the craft, obscuring the windscreen. Blinded, Ari pushed the aircar's nose down to maintain ground contact, and felt the craft lurch to starboard as the wreckage of the doors tore free.

His eyes burned as bright outdoor light flooded the small cockpit. Directly ahead, he saw the outline of an armored gun position, its turret swinging toward them as the gunner inside brought his weapon to bear.

"Ari—"

"I see him."

Ari pulled back a fraction to gain altitude and then cut hard right, following the curve of the drive. For a second or two, he thought the starboard wing was going to drag the ground—but the aircar came around and leveled out just above the gravel.

Not far ahead, manicured lawn gave way to the dense woods of the hunting park, and the drive made a sharp left turn into the trees. Ari didn't attempt to make the turn. He cut the jets instead, and pulled the nose of the car straight up.

The aircar went into a steep climb, crashing through small branches on its way skyward. Velocity fell off rapidly; soon the aircar stalled and its nose began to fall.

Ari twisted to the left in a half spiral, so that by the time the craft was pointing at the ground he was lined up with the next leg of the drive. He increased thrust back to maximum and pulled the nose up. The aircar leveled out again heading down the drive, mere feet above the gravel.

"Very nice," murmured Llannat. She sounded rather breathless. "But what do we do for an encore?"

He didn't answer. The next corner, a half-right, was drawing nearer, and going straight up wouldn't work this time. The tracery of branches overhead had grown heavier; he felt like he was flying down a tunnel.

So let's try sideways, he thought, and swung the tail around to put the aircar into a skid. At the last moment, he made a sharp right roll, so that the aircar was flying down the drive with its belly foremost.

He felt himself pressed down into the seat. Then lift took over and the aircar slowed. He rolled the craft back to the horizontal, and they came out headed down the new direction. Judging by the way the shrubbery flashed past, their speed had hardly diminished.

But shrubbery wasn't the only thing flashing past. Heavy blaster bolts lit up the undergrowth around them.

"Find the weapon controls!" he called over to Llannat above the roar of the engines and the whine of energy fire. "Make them keep their heads down!"

"I think we're unarmed."

He reached down with his right hand and picked up the energy lance. "Use this."

He felt the weapon taken from his grip, and seconds later heard the sound of shattering glass as Llannat drove the lance butt-first through the window.

Good, he thought, as careful, unhurried energy-fire started up from the other side of the aircar. *But just once I'd like to do this in something that could shoot back.*

Ahead of them on the long drive, he saw a small group of figures: the trailing elements of the caravan guarding Nivome. At the same time, the high outer wall of the estate came into view. Ari pushed the throttle forward again, but this time got no answering roar. The aircar's engines had already reached maximum thrust.

All the same, the aircar gained rapidly on the large black hovercar and its group of outriders. The last two hoverbike riders in the column skidded to a stop and laid their bikes down in the dirt perpendicular to the road. They stretched out prone behind their bikes and began firing their blasters toward the oncoming aircar.

Few of the shots hit, and even fewer managed to inflict

damage. *Either they're bad shots,* Ari thought, *or we've got them really scared.*

He could hear Llannat returning the fire with the energy lance. She wasn't connecting either that he could see, but the lance's powerful bolts of energy tore up clods of earth all around the pair of outriders, and filled the air with smoke and dirt. Already shaken, and with their aim obscured, the two riders ducked involuntarily as Ari brought the aircar thundering over their heads.

The leading bikes in the flying wedge had cleared the gate, and the hovercar was approaching it. Ari chuckled to himself.

"What's so funny?"

"You can own a whole planet, but you can't bribe the laws of physics," he said. "We're going to close with him before he makes it through."

The long black hovercar flashed through the gate and out onto the city streets of Darplex, with the aircar only feet behind it and scarcely higher above the ground. Behind them, the gatekeeper brought the force field up again: too late by a split second to catch the aircar, but in plenty of time to shut off the rest of the cavalcade.

Ari cut the aircar left, then right, out into the open, and brought the copilot's side of the aircar parallel to the hovercar. From the corner of his eye he could see Llannat on her knees in the other seat, leaning out the broken window to take aim.

"Go ahead!" he shouted. "Shoot!"

The Adept fired a burst from the energy lance.

She hit the car, but the armored vehicle showed no damage. Around it, the remaining outriders were firing as they rode. One beam drilled a hole through the aircar's port cargo door, and the rush of air across the opening set up an eerie keening sound inside the cockpit.

Llannat leaned even further out the window and fired another burst. She seemed to be getting the hang of the unfamiliar weapon—this time, one of the hoverbikes exploded into flames and tumbled over and over, sending the rider flying through the air.

Ari cut right again, putting them directly above the hovercar. He dropped. The bottom of the aircraft hit the roof of the hovercar with a thump.

He lifted, then dropped again. Once more he smashed into the top of the car. Then a hollow boom shook the air in front of them, and a brilliant light filled the cockpit.

Ari looked up. There was a shadow against the sun. It grew larger and became an atmospheric fighter craft. He saw a twinkling along the wings of the fighter, and a series of explosions rocked the atmosphere around the unarmed aircar.

He pulled back and left on the control yoke, climbing out of the line of fire so that the fighter's next burst exploded around the hovercar itself. The strange pilot realized his error and turned to dive toward Ari.

A second fighter flashed into view, firing as it came. Llannat leaned out the window with the energy lance and fired a burst in that direction.

"Hold on!" yelled Ari. "We're going up!"

He pulled back sharply on the yoke, pulling the aircar into a loop. When the car was inverted at the top of the loop, he flipped upright again and nosed down into a shallow dive to gain speed. Now the two fighters were below him, but already snarling upward.

He glanced over at Llannat. The Adept was still there, firing out the broken window at the cockpit of the nearest fighter. He had no idea what she'd used for a handhold during the turn. As far as he could tell, she'd never put on the safety webbing.

"What do we do now?" she asked, still firing.

Never underestimate an Adept, he thought. Llannat's ability to stay aboard during the aerobatics of the past few minutes had finally given him something that passed for an idea.

"You'll have to go find the others and tell them what's happening," he said aloud.

"How?"

"You'll see," he said. "Get back into the cargo bay, and slide the door open. Leave the lance and the comm link up here with me."

"Anything you say."

She headed back toward the cargo bay. Ari pushed the aircar into a steep dive and began to spiral toward the ground.

He pulled out near street level. Tall buildings made blurry grey streaks to either side, and the air was bright with mingled energy fire and projectile explosives as the two fighters came astern of him and started firing.

He began to jink the little aircar about at full throttle, just above the rooftops—pulling up a bit, rolling to a new altitude, and then pushing down again. The two fighter pilots didn't much like following his smaller craft through the urban maze, but although he drew ahead, he couldn't shake them.

Never mind, he thought, and held his course away from central Darplex toward the crowded, utilitarian structures of the warehouse district. *Soon.*

A few seconds later, he found what he was looking for. In the sections of Darplex bordering on the spaceport compound, moving the Rolny's freight to market took precedence over landscaping. Here, the narrow streets went beneath, not over, the more important cargo lines. The mouth of one such underpass opened up ahead, and he shot into it without hesitation.

The energy fire from behind him stopped abruptly.

"Llannat!" he shouted, in sudden dimness. "Jump!"

V. Darvell: Downtown Darplex; The Citadel

"I WONDER how the others are making out," said Jessan.

Beka picked up the red optical-plastic eye patch from the table and fitted it into place. "Ari learned how to hunt from the Selvaurs on Maraghai," she said. "And Llannat's an Adept. They'll do okay."

Jessan brought his blaster up and took aim at the playing card taped to the far wall of the abandoned warehouse. A red tracer beam flashed across the intervening space. "Three out of five . . . I hope you're right." He aimed and fired again.

"Four out of six," Beka said, taking her knife from the table and slipping it into its forearm sheath. "You're getting the feel of it, I think. Of course I'm right."

The Khesatan took another shot at the card. "Five out of seven. I'll quit while I'm ahead." He lowered the blaster, frowned at it a moment, and then slipped it into its holster. "The real question, of course, is how much the stun-bolt attenuates with distance."

Beka's own blaster belt hung on the back of the warehouse's only chair, next to the black velvet Mandeynan long-coat Tarnekep Portree would be wearing against the late-afternoon chill. She picked up the blaster rig and strapped it on.

"Those models will give you a full stun out to the limit of their effective range," she said, bending over to tie the leather thong that kept the holster snug against her thigh. "They don't have the accuracy of an Ogre Mark Six, or even a Space Force Standard, but when it comes to pouring energy out the muzzle, you can't beat them with a stick."

"So why did you switch?"

"I learned on a Mark Six," she said, straightening up again. "This one, in fact."

Tarnekep Portree's Mandeynan cravat—a long strip of white spidersilk and delicate lace—lay on the table along with a comm link, a gold and topaz stickpin, and the hand-sized disk of grey plastic that was the collapsor grenade. She picked up the piece of cloth and started to wrap it around her neck.

Jessan came closer. "Here. Let me help you with that."

She shook her head. "I don't need . . ."

"I know you don't," he said. His hands were already busy arranging the strip of material. "Let me help anyway."

She stopped arguing. Jessan gave the cravat a final tuck, fastened the folds in place with the topaz stickpin, and then stepped back a pace to survey his handiwork. He tilted his head a little to one side like an art critic appraising the latest item in a fashionable gallery.

"Well?" Beka said.

"I'd call the general effect epicene but nasty." The corners of his mouth turned up in a wry smile. "Actually, I rather like it."

The tips of his fingers, their touch warm in the chill of the empty warehouse, still rested on the side of her throat. She smiled back at him in spite of herself.

"And what does that say about you?"

He gave a soft laugh. "Didn't anybody ever tell you that on Khesat decadence is considered one of the higher art forms?"

She thought about it a moment, while his hand moved from her neck to trace the line of her cheekbone just below the red plastic eye patch. "No," she said finally. "Nobody ever did."

"Well, it's true," he said, and kissed her.

His lips were warm against her own, like the touch of his hand on her face. She leaned against him, opening her mouth to his—and pulled away, swearing under her breath, at the sound of a first hammering on the warehouse door.

The hammering steadied into a pattern: three quick, two slow, three quick. The recognition code.

"Damn," she muttered again, moving away from Jessan and slapping the door switch. "If that's Ari I'll kill him myself for his lousy timing."

But it wasn't Ari. When the doors parted, Llannat Hyfid stood in the gap—her staff in her hand, her breath coming in ragged gasps, and her black coverall dirt-stained and disarrayed.

"Nivome's on to us," she said, before Beka could speak. "He's heading for the Citadel. And Ari's up there dodging fighters in an unarmed aircar."

Beka grabbed the black long-coat and pulled it on. With quick, automatic gestures she shrugged the heavy velvet into place across her shoulders and shook out the lace cuffs of her loose white shirt.

"You two take the aircar and look for Ari," she said, snatching up the comm link and the collapsor grenade and shoving them into the long-coat's capacious pockets. "I have to go after the Professor. Vector us in on the Rolny as soon as you've got him in view."

She mounted one of the waiting hoverbikes as she spoke, cut in the nullgravs with a backkick of one booted heel, and switched on the engines.

"Get out of the way!" she shouted at the Adept over the bike's high-pitched humming, and released the brakes.

Llannat was gone, and the end of the tunnel was coming.

Out with the sky above him, Ari pulled up, then cut left between two blocky grey buildings. The heavier, more powerful fighters might have the advantage in the open air, but down in the canyons of the city the prize would go to the better pilot.

Ari half-smiled. *If I can't outfly this pair of dirtsiders,* he thought, *I'll leave the family, change my name, and take up farming.*

A near-miss rocked the aircar, and Ari veered left to duck behind a tall building. Workers looked up from desks and tables to stare out the windows at him as he flashed past.

High above the streets, the two fighters circled like frustrated birds of prey, waiting for him to break clear. Ari wondered for a moment at the promptness with which the atmospheric craft had shown up. That promptness argued a high degree of training on the part of Darvell's planetary defenses—training, and possibly a timely warning passed on by the manager of the Top Five Lounge.

That last thought had a rightness about it that appealed to Ari. He smiled again.

He was certain, now, of what he should do: first, lure the air cover away from Nivome and the Citadel, and then get to the Quincunx man. He knew what sort of sentence the Brotherhood would pass on someone who used their name and their password to bait a trap, but it was likely to be a long time indeed before the Quincunx could get a working agent onto Darvell to take care of the problem.

But that didn't matter. As Ferrdacorr had taught him long ago, some things you had to take care of yourself.

The warehouse echoed to the sound of Beka's departure, and Jessan watched unmoving as the hoverbike roared out of sight. The last he saw of its rider was a fluttering of black velvet on the wind—the open long-coat and the black-ribboned queue of light brown hair, streaming out together behind the captain as she rode.

Good luck, Beka, thought Jessan, and then shook his head. By the time Llannat had finished gasping out her bad news, Beka Rosselin-Metadi had all but vanished. Only Tarnekep Portree remained—Tarnekep, who had walked into the fire of a dozen blasters for the sake of a clear shot at his enemies.

Jessan shook his head again, and shivered. He felt a hand touch his arm, and looked around.

"We can't stand here waiting," Llannat said. "Ari's in trouble too, remember?"

He drew a deep breath. "I remember. Go on and get in the aircar. I'll pilot."

The blaster made an unfamiliar weight on his hip as he climbed up and slid behind the controls. Like his friend Ari, he wasn't accustomed to going about armed. *Everything changes,* he reflected as he fired up the aircar's engines. *Even that.*

On the other side of the cockpit, Llannat was already strapped into the copilot's seat. Jessan brought the aircar forward through the warehouse doors in a scream of turbines, and lifted free as soon as they were clear. The ground fell away and the warehouse district spread out beneath them, an aerial vista of chunky grey buildings in a close-set network of narrow streets, with the rails and pylons of the cargo transit system stretching out over everything.

"Get on the comm," he said to Llannat. "See if you can raise Ari."

He heard the sound of Llannat disengaging the comm link from the copilot's side of the console, and then her steady alto voice saying, "Ari, Ari—where are you? Come in, Ari."

The speaker returned only silence. Jessan took his attention away from the aircar's control console long enough to glance over at Llannat. The Adept looked unhappy.

She's got more on her mind than just the comm link, Jessan thought. Aloud, he asked, "What happened back there?"

"We walked into a trap."

"And out again?"

She gave a humorless laugh. "Guess again. We flew."

"Ah," said Jessan. "Whose aircar did you steal?"

"One of the Rolny's."

"Any casualties?"

"Two dead."

Jessan whistled. "Already? Ari isn't messing around."

"Ari didn't kill them," Llannat said. "I did."

"Would you mind repeating that?" asked Jessan. "I thought I heard you say that you killed them."

"That's right."

The Adepts were fighters, back in the Magewar, Jessan reminded himself. *It looks like they still are.*

Silence filled the cockpit for a few moments. Llannat seemed to have given up on the comm link as a bad job. Then Jessan heard her draw a sharp breath.

"Look," she said. "Over there."

He glanced away from the controls and followed her pointing finger toward the horizon, where a snarl of fighter craft circled like carrion birds above a column of black smoke.

"Somebody's crashed," he said. "Can you tell if—"

"No," she said. "He—goes away—when he's hunting."

"Right," Jessan said. If Ari's Quincunx contact had played them false, the big Galcenian would certainly be hunting now. If he was still alive.

Beka leaned the hoverbike into another turn. How long, she wondered—how long had it been for the Professor, waiting for Ari to signal from Rolny Lodge, before Nivome's Security troops decided to end the charade and move in? She bit her lip in frustration, and fed more power to the hoverbike's engines.

From up ahead came the zing of a blaster, and a few seconds later an ambulance rushed past her in the opposite direction, its siren keening. Relief surged through her, and she laughed aloud into the wind. *Small-arms fire and casualties—the Prof's still in there fighting!*

The sound of energy weapons grew louder. She rounded another corner and saw a clot of emergency vehicles in the street ahead, parked behind a temporary barrier marked SECURITY ZONE—DO NOT ENTER. Beyond the barrier, Security enforcers crouched for cover around corners and behind walls, firing down the street ahead of them. The enforcers had their heads well down, and with good reason—red fire flashed back at the Security men as she bore down on the barrier.

She marked the source of the fire with a tight smile, and took her right hand off the bike's controls to free her own Mark VI from its holster. The Security barrier rose up front of her. She pulled back one-handed on the hoverbike's control bars and jumped the barricade, firing her blaster into the nearest group of enforcers as she came up and over.

One of the bolts took a man in the back before he could turn. He fell facedown onto the pavement. Some of the others slewed around, warned by his fall or by the noise of the onrushing hoverbike. One or two fired—but they'd crowded themselves when they took cover from the blaster-fire up ahead, and the shots went wide.

Too bad, thought Beka, without sympathy. She dodged her bike through the security lines, skidding from side to side and firing as she came.

Then she was past them, and saw the muzzle of a blaster poking around a door jamb over on the right-hand wall. A bolt zipped down the street toward a second Security barricade set up at the far corner.

Beka let out a yell. That was the Professor in the doorway, and no mistake. He turned toward her and brought

his blaster up to bear. She yelled again and he changed
his aim to fire down the street behind her. She pulled to
the right and bore down on the slight, grey-haired figure.

The Entiboran held out a bent arm—his left—and fired
again down toward the security barrier with the blaster in
his right. Beka veered as close to the wall as she dared,
and extended her own right arm, also bent at the elbow.

"Grab on!" she shouted.

Don't drop your blaster, now, she reminded herself, and
then their arms interlocked.

She came close to losing the weapon just the same. At
the speed she was going, even the Professor's light weight
was almost enough to pull her sideways off the bike. Then
the Professor swung himself up onto the pillion seat, and
she was firing her blaster at the Security enforcers ahead
as the bike swept them both away toward the far barrier.

The sound of her blaster became a two-note chord as
the Professor added his fire to hers. With most of her own
attention given to steering the bike, she knew that she
wasn't accomplishing much herself beyond putting out an
impressive amount of sound and light. A sudden falling-
off in the fire from up ahead told her that the Professor
was making an impression of an entirely different kind.

The barricade loomed ahead of them. *No way I can
jump this one,* thought Beka. *Not carrying double.*

"Hold tight!" she shouted to the Professor, and crashed
through it instead. Then, with the barrier a pile of broken
wood and plastic behind her, she gave the hoverbike's engine full power and concentrated on getting as far away
from the scene as possible.

Several minutes later, she and the Professor were cruising down a wide parkway at little more than the speed of
the surrounding traffic. Even carrying double, the bike
moved nimbly among the hovercars and nullgrav transports. Far behind them, sirens wailed as the Security enforcers who'd been at the barricades gave chase—but the
same traffic that masked the hoverbike's progress impeded
the ones who followed.

We must have hit the noon rush hour, thought Beka.

She felt the Professor tap her on the shoulder. "Captain!" he shouted over the wind and the engines. "Where to?"

"The Citadel!" she yelled back. "We have a job to finish."

The sounds of the chase behind them had faded almost to nothing, and her quick glance over her shoulder had shown the pursuit far away, almost out of sight. But now, from close behind and to their right, the sound of a lone Security siren cut through the rumble of traffic.

Damn it, thought Beka, *I didn't come all the way to Darvell to get arrested for speeding!*

But the Professor was tapping her on the shoulder again. "He's alone—get his bike!"

Beka nodded. A few moments later, another quick glance to the rear showed the approach of a single rider on a hoverbike with Security markings. She held her own course for a moment longer, and then pretended to see the other vehicle's flashing amber noselight for the first time.

The Security rider came up on her left and drew even with her. He gestured for her to pull over. She hit the thrust reversers and cut hard right instead. The rear of her bike skidded left and slammed into the side of the Security vehicle.

Jarred by the impact, the rider lost his grip. Beka threw herself sideways and seized the control bars of his bike. She swung her body across the gap between the two vehicles, kicking out with her legs and knocking the Security rider from his seat. The first hoverbike, controlled now by the Professor, pulled away out of danger. Beka landed in the saddle of the Security bike in time to watch the enforcer hit the pavement and roll out of sight under an oncoming hovercar.

She looked back over her shoulder one more time. The Security enforcers from the barricades were still far behind, but starting to make headway through the downtown traffic. It wouldn't be long before somebody thought to call a general alert and get all nonessential vehicles off the streets of Darplex.

If we're still out here by then, Beka thought, *we're sunk.*

Letting go the right control bar, she reached into her pocket, pulled out the comm link, and keyed it on. "Jessan," she said into the pickup. "Come in, Jessan."

She heard a whine and a crackle, and then a voice. "Jessan here. Who's calling?"

"Portree. Do you have the target in sight?"

"Better than that—I have you and the target both. Turn right at the next corner."

"Thanks. Any word from Ari?"

A pause. Then: "Nothing."

Her eyes stung for a moment, and she blinked hard. *It's this damned wind. Blast it, Ari, why did I ever want to take you with me to Darvell?*

She swallowed. "The big guy can take care of himself," she said into the pickup. Her voice sounded tight and hard—Tarnekep's voice, not her own. "See you do the same, do you hear me? Portree out."

She clicked off the comm link and shoved it back into her pocket in time to grab both control bars for the approaching corner. She rounded it without slacking speed, heeling over so far into the turn that her bike lay out almost flat on its side. Over on the other bike, the Professor did the same without a word.

"Take care, Tarnekep," murmured Jessan—but he was speaking to a dead link, and he knew it.

He handed Llannat the pickup and put the aircar into a steep left bank. The move gave him a good view of the ground below, and of the four broad boulevards that divided Darplex into quadrants. Where the boulevards met at point zero-zero, a featureless black ziggurat rose up from the earth like a mountain.

"The Citadel?" asked Llannat.

"Just like the flatpix in the guidebook," Jessan said. "Only bigger and in worse taste."

Down below, a pack of outriders and a long black hovercar headed at speed up one of the broad streets leading to the black ziggurat. Up another—a wide parkway lined with heroic statuary—two hoverbikes dodged in and out through downtown traffic. About six blocks behind them followed a moving knot of bikes and hovercars, all with flashing amber lights.

"Security," said Llannat, from the copilot's seat. "And gaining fast."

"Not for long," Jessan said. As he spoke, he reached out a hand to the console and switched on the targeting computer.

"You're planning to use the guns?" Llannat asked. She didn't sound disapproving, Jessan noted. Just thoughtful.

"That's right," he said. He pushed the aircar into a dive. "I'm not in Ari's class, but—"

"But you have a license," finished Llannat.

"That's right," said Jessan, his eyes on the targeting computer as the aircar screamed downward. "And I might even be able to pull us out of this before we hit the pavement."

Losing the pursuit hadn't taken long. The game of follow-the-leader had ended in a corridor so narrow Ari took the little aircar through it standing on one wing. The fighters had tried the same trick, and a column of black smoke on the distant horizon marked how well they had succeeded. Ari grounded the stolen aircar near the workshop that had been his Quincunx contact's daytime address, and looked around.

A sign met his eyes: LANDING ZONE RESERVED FOR LEVEL NINE AND ABOVE. That brought a smile. Whatever Nivome's private aircar might or might not be, it undoubtedly had all the right tags and stickers to roost undisturbed in this particular spot.

He picked up the comm link Llannat had left behind, then laid it down on the copilot's seat with a shake of his head. What he had to do next would go better without interruptions.

He climbed out of the aircar, stretched his shoulders, and made his way without conspicuous haste to the tool-issue point in Building 125-34, Outer Ring. As on his earlier visits, the front room was empty when he entered. A buzz-plate on the wall over the big workbench had a sign underneath reading, TOUCH ONCE FOR SERVICE.

Ari palmed the buzzer. After a few seconds, H. Estisk emerged from the storeroom in the back, wearing his daytime uniform and a smile.

"Welcome again, brother. What else can I do for you?"

"Two things today," said Ari, smiling back. A Selvaur would have taken note of the canine teeth the smile revealed, and walked warily—but Estisk wasn't one of the Forest Lords, though he was big enough for one. "Let's start with a weapons suite for a Gosy One-twenty-eight aircar."

Estisk looked thoughtful. "Tough to do on short notice."

"How about some bolt-on air-to-air weapons?" asked Ari. "I'm in a bit of a hurry."

"Nothing here," Estisk said. "But I can get some by tonight. Now, about the second thing—"

"New plans for the Rolny Lodge grounds," Ari said, stepping closer. "The real ones, this time."

Estisk didn't blink or change expression, but a blaster appeared as if from nowhere in the big Darvelline's right hand.

Ari cuffed it away. "Fight."

Estisk didn't even seem to notice that the blaster was gone. With one fluid motion, he aimed a fist at Ari's jaw.

The swing connected, but Ferrdacorr had never pulled his punches in training. Ari rode with the blow and twisted under it. He grabbed Estisk's arm and helped the Darvelline into a classic shoulder throw.

Estisk, too, must have had good teachers. Hitting the floor should have stunned the big man, but he went with the throw rather than resisting it as an amateur might, and rolled to his feet in a balanced guard position.

Ari smiled again. He drew his blaster slowly, watching the other man all the while, and threw the weapon aside.

Howl at the moon and die, traitor, he said in the Forest Speech, and lunged forward to grip the other man by the wrist.

Estisk slipped the hold, following his escape with a leg sweep to the back of Ari's knee. Ari went down, rolling under a table to avoid the smashing downward kick that skinned past his ribs, and came back to his feet.

Estisk vaulted the table to face him. The two men stood unmoving for a few seconds, taking each other's measure. Ari guessed that he might have an inch or two on the Darvelline in height and reach, but Estisk had a broader chest and carried more muscle in his shoulders and upper arms. Now the Darvelline used that muscle to good advantage in a series of closed-fisted blows, right and left, to Ari's chest.

Ari blocked and slipped the blows with his arms. *Remember what Ferrda taught you,* he thought. *Let the other guy tire himself out before you strike.*

The out-of-rhythm blow that smashed into the side of his skull came as a complete surprise, rocking his head back and flashing a bright white light in front of his eyes. But Ferrda's training held. Ari counterpunched and landed a heavy blow to the other man's ribs under his extended arm, so hard that his opponent gasped for breath.

Ari shook his head to clear the fog away. As it lifted, something dark and formless stirred inside him and came to life, and he recognized the anger that had never really left him since his mother died. This time, he welcomed it, and let it grow.

"Come on and fight me—brother," he said, smiling again at his opponent across the little space of ground that separated them. "This is going to be good."

VI. Darvell: Darplex; the Citadel

"WHAT DO you mean, demanded Llannat, "you think you can pull out before we hit the pavement?"

"Relax," Jessan said, his eyes on the altimeter. "It worked fine in the simulator." The ground was very close now. *Only three more seconds,* he promised himself. *Two. One. Now.*

He leveled out a hundred feet above the surface of the avenue. The street lay empty beneath him. All the everyday traffic had pulled over by now, or turned off onto side streets. But the gang of Security bikes and hovercars was coming in his direction and putting on speed.

He nosed the aircar into another, shallower dive. This time, he kept his attention on the targeting computer. When the cross hairs met the cluster of small blips and started flashing red, he felt with his thumb for the firing button set into the control yoke, and pressed it all the way down.

Streams of colored fire shot out from beneath the aircar's wings—*Energy guns,* he thought, *very nice*—and carved long smoking pits into the road ahead of the Security enforcers. He kept on firing as the aircar passed over the oncoming vehicles, and then pulled up into a steep climb. A quick glance over his shoulder showed him a flaming tangle of men and metal in the road below.

"Not bad for a first try," he said aloud. He felt irrationally cheerful. "Let's go see if we can slow down the Rolny."

"I don't think so," Llannat said. "Look."

He glanced in her direction for the first time since he'd said good-bye to Beka over the dead comm link. The telltales on the Adept's side of the instrument panel were blinking red.

"Just when I was starting to have fun," he complained. "Find me a good spot to set down, will you?"

"Off to port," Llannat said at once. "Behind those trees."

He looked out the cockpit window. "Near the building?"

"Left of that. In the alley."

"Got you."

Jessan pulled left and began to nose down. Landing proved to be trickier than he'd thought, mostly because the aircar's control panel locked up during the last few feet of the approach. Still, he managed to set the craft down with several yards to spare before the alley ended in a stone wall.

"A bit bumpy," said Llannat, unstrapping.

"Everybody's a critic," he said. "You don't like it, you try it next time."

"Thank you very much," the Adept said, "but no. Let's get out and start troubleshooting."

Beka Rosselin-Metadi laughed under her breath as the aircar swooped down and past her. *That has to be Jessan,* she thought, listening to the energy guns ripping up the pavement. *Showing up in style.*

She put the Khesatan out of her mind. They'd have time for that later, if later came at all. For now, the Citadel loomed ahead of her, so big and close she'd have needed to tilt her head backward to see the top, and Nivome's cavalcade was coming into view on the intersecting boulevard.

"My lady!" shouted the Professor over the noise of the bikes. "Your siren!"

Siren? she wondered, and remembered that she was riding a stolen Security vehicle. She found the switches, and brought both the siren and the amber noselight on-line.

The siren's mechanical wailing crescendoed in her ears. She gave the throttle another twist forward. The avenue down which she rode still had half a dozen blocks to run before ending in a traffic circle around the base of the Citadel, but the huge structure rose up in front of her like a wall of black marble, blocking more and more of her vision as she drew closer.

Getting out of here's going to be worse than getting in, she thought. *I hope Jessan stays handy with the air support.*

She was at the traffic circle now, with the Professor still keeping position on her right. Together they leaned into the turn, swooping along toward the point where Nivome and his escort would enter the circle from the intersecting road.

The Rolny and his men were closing fast. She slacked off a little on the power to the hoverbike, not wanting to beat the Rolny and his guards to the meetpoint and have them behind her on the circle.

We're going to catch Nivome after all, she thought. *Just barely, but we're going to catch him.*

So far, the Professor's notion of using siren and lights had paid off. The outriders hadn't taken alarm at what they must be tagging as downtown Security enforcers showing up to join the cavalcade. A few seconds later, Nivome's hovercar and its flying wedge of guards shot onto the traffic circle only a few lengths ahead of Beka and the Professor.

"Now, my lady!"

Beka pulled her Mark VI from its holster with a yell, and gunned the hoverbike's engine. The vehicle surged forward beneath her, and then she and her partner hit the rear of the Rolny's cavalcade at full speed.

She fired three times and connected twice before the guards realized that their reinforcements were shooting at them, and began shooting back. All around her, hoverbikes veered and skidded out of control under their killed or wounded riders. She counted more than two guards down—many more—and yelled again. The Professor, as usual, hadn't missed.

She kept on firing, pressing her hoverbike forward through the milling pack, ducking close to the control bars as energy bolts began to zip over her head. Not all of Nivome's outriders were trying to miss their buddies; one bolt singed the hair on her neck, and hit a man beyond.

Nivome, she told herself, still firing—picking targets now, not like the half-random shooting she'd done to keep heads down back at the barricade. *The important thing is getting a clear shot at Nivome.*

Blasters whined and spat above the roar of engines. She and the Professor were in the middle of the pack now, riding with it, coming nearer and nearer to the long black hovercar.

You aren't getting away from me, Nivome. You killed my mother, but you didn't quite kill me. That was your big mistake, Nivome, because now I'm coming after you.

The hovercar veered left. She followed, drawing closer to the target—and realized, too late, that the entire cavalcade had turned off the traffic circle and was speeding down the Citadel's entry ramp.

Heavy doors at the foot of the Citadel yawned open. The hovercar and its attendant swarm entered, bearing Beka and the Professor with them, and the blast doors closed behind them all.

* * *

"Well, well, well," said Jessan, and wriggled out from under the grounded aircar.

He brought out his find, a small cylinder with hose fittings on either end, and showed it to the Adept. "Tell me—what do you make of this?"

Llannat poked at it with one finger. "It says 'Filter' on it. What's the trouble?"

"It's the source of the leak in our control lines, that's what's the trouble. And look at this—"

Jessan worked a grimy fingernail under one end plate, and levered off the bit of plastic. Llannat picked it up and turned it over in her hand a couple of times, her frown deepening.

"I'm no mechanic," she said at last. "But this looks wrong."

"Give the Adept five points," Jessan said. "That's not a filter at all."

"So what is it?"

He shrugged. "Looks more like an inertial switch than anything else. I think it was put there to sense a high-gee maneuver and break the vacuum line."

"Sabotage," the Adept said. "Can you fix it?"

He shrugged again. "I think so. Given time." He turned back toward the aircar. "And I don't know how much of that we've got. I'll get busy. You stay out here and keep watch."

"Sure thi—"

The Adept's voice cut off in midword. He spun back around in time to catch her as her knees folded. She sagged in his grip for a few seconds; then the faintness seemed to pass, and she shrugged his hands away.

"What's wrong?" he asked.

"Sorcery," she said. "Magework and dark sorcery. And I can't find Beka and the Professor at all."

The blast doors crashed shut.
There's no way I'm going to get out of this one, thought

Beka, as the Rolny's hovercar came to a stop. *But Nivome buys it first.*

She cut engine power to the bike, and raised her blaster for a shot at the windows of the hovercar. A beam of red light burned a hole through the cuff of her long-coat, and another beam passed by her head so close she could smell the charged air. She stood up in the bike's stirrups for a better aim, and fired.

The bolt from the Mark VI hit the passenger-seat window of the hovercar and dissipated in a splash of crimson light.

"Force screen! You bastard!"

"My lady! Down!"

The Professor jerked on the hem of her long-coat, pulling her off the hoverbike and onto the floor. She hit the concrete in time to see two red bolts and a green one flashing through the space where she had stood.

She scrambled up to her knees under cover of her still-hovering bike. Next to her, the Professor crouched, firing around his own vehicle as more energy bolts whined and zipped overhead.

Suddenly, the noise of the blasters began to fall off and die, giving way to a low hissing sound. She looked up and saw thick white vapor issuing from unseen openings all about the entry bay. One curling tendril of mist touched a group of the Security men. They choked and fell forward.

Intruder gas, thought Beka. *Only one chance left.*

The fog rolled closer. She dropped her blaster and groped in her coat pocket for the collapsor grenade. *If I can just set the detonator before that stuff gets us . . . and if a collapsor's any good in an open space . . .*

Her fingers closed on the disk of the collapsor. She pulled it out and began to enter the arming sequence. Nivome's hovercar was out of sight, hidden in the fog. *Don't breathe,* she told herself. *Just get the code set, and everything will be all right.*

The Professor's hand closed on her wrist before she could complete the sequence. "No, my lady."

She stared, unbelieving, as the device in her hand cycled back to zero.

Beside her, the Entiboran rose to his feet. The white fog touched him and writhed about him. Her own chest burned with the effort not to draw breath, and she waited, despairing, for her partner to stagger and fall. Instead, he raised an empty hand and called out, "Enough!"

The fog halted, then billowed and dispersed as if torn by a high wind. The lights in the entry bay flickered and went out. In the silent dark, the long black car hovered on its nullgravs inside a nimbus of light, a corona discharge of pale orange fire that crackled outward to the floor and walls.

The heavy vehicle lifted toward the ceiling, pitching and yawing as it rose. *What am I seeing?* Beka thought, remembering at last to breathe. At her elbow, the Professor stood with one hand upraised, the play of unworldly light on his features changing her Entiboran copilot into something disturbing and unfamiliar.

What is he doing?

Out in the center of the bay, the hovercar was still rising. Slowly, it began to rotate around its vertical axis. The metal side panels curled away from the frame, and the doors peeled open a fraction at a time. With a silent explosion, all the glass in the windows flew outward in a sparkling cloud.

Nothing remained now of the still-rotating hovercar but its frame and engine. Three men clung to the seats inside the twisting frame—one in the driver's position, and two in what had once been the passenger compartment. One of those two she did not know; but the other—

Nivome, she thought, and raised her blaster to fire.

The Rolny's companion lifted a black-gloved hand, and the two men in the back of the hovercar vanished.

The hovercar hung suspended in midair a moment longer. Then the Professor closed his fist and brought his arm back down to his side. The hovercar crashed to the floor and started burning. Silence filled the entry bay.

Beka shoved the collapsor grenade back into her pocket, retrieved her abandoned Mark VI, and pushed herself up onto her feet. She cast an uneasy glance over at the burning wreckage before turning to the Professor.

"What now?" she asked.

He pulled the ebony staff from under his belt. "We take them in their hiding place," he said. "Are you with me, girl?"

Beka stared at her copilot. *He's never spoken to me that way before—it's always been 'Captain,' or 'my lady,' with him. Whatever he just did . . . changed him.*

And saved my life. Again.

"I'm with you," she said to her partner. "Let's go."

Ari and Estisk circled each other amid the wreckage of the tool-issue point in 125-34 Outer Ring. Ari's muscles burned, and his left eye didn't want to focus. Across from him, Estisk was bleeding freely from the nose, and seemed to be favoring his right foot when he moved.

Ari brought the edge of his hand down against the other man's collarbone. Estisk grunted in pain, but the bone didn't break, and the Darvelline retaliated with an elbow strike to Ari's belly.

Panting, Ari fell back, but not quite far enough. Estisk wrapped one arm around Ari's neck and began slamming the other fist into his ribs like a hammer.

Ari grabbed for the hand on his shoulder, caught it, and twisted under. Estisk turned with him—it was turn, or go down with a dislocated shoulder. As the Darvelline came round, Ari let go and lashed out with a kick that took the other man in the right kidney.

Estisk stumbled forward into the half-demolished workbench and caught himself on the table edge. Ari stood his ground, waiting. Slowly, Estisk pushed himself back around to stand with his hands braced against the bench behind him.

Ari eyed the sagging Darvelline. *Isn't he ever going to*

go down? That kick would have put most guys into the healing pod for a week.

Without warning, Estisk launched himself forward, swinging a twelve-inch length of pipe snatched up from the workbench. Instinctively, Ari blocked up and out. The impact made his left hand and wrist go numb, but the pipe crashed onto his forearm instead of his skull.

Before Estisk could pull the pipe back for another swing, Ari reached over with his right hand, grabbed the other man's wrist, and bent arm and pipe backward together toward Estisk's right ear. At the same time, his nerveless left hand lay in the crook of Estisk's right elbow, pulling down. Between the two, either the arm would break, or Estisk would yield to the pressure and fall onto his back.

And then—what was it Ferrda used to say? *Jump on his head until he stops moving*? Ari laughed a little between his clenched teeth. *Sounds like a good idea to me.*

But Estisk still had a lot of power in his barrel-like chest. The hand holding the pipe reached his ear, went a little farther back, and then stayed there.

Ari pushed harder.

A crashing pain exploded in Ari's right side—Estisk had dropped the pipe from his right hand to his left, then smashed it upward into Ari's floating ribs.

Ari let go his hold on Estisk's arm and fell back. A kick came from out of nowhere toward his chest. He caught the ankle and heaved upward.

The Darvelline hit the ground hard, and rolled upright.

Ari stared, feeling a sharp pain in his side with every indrawn breath. *What the hell does it take to keep this bastard down?*

Estisk smiled through bloody lips, and gestured to Ari to come closer. "Come on, then—brother. I thought you wanted to fight."

Llannat pushed herself away from the side of the aircar. Jessan was busy under the belly of the craft; she couldn't see him, but she could hear him talking himself through the repairs in High Khesatan. From the few words she could catch, the repair job looked like taking a while.

But time was running out. She didn't worry about the fighter craft still circling overhead, or the sirens howling in the streets. She could hide two people and one small aircar from a search like that. But the Mage-smell hung in the air like the reek of a slaughterhouse, heavy and growing closer.

Time. She had to buy time for Jessan and the others.

You're as ready now as you ever will be, she thought. *Quit stalling and show Master Ransome he didn't make a mistake when he gave you a staff and called you an Adept.*

She left the aircar behind and walked down to the point where the long alley branched out into two wider streets. Stepping into the center of the junction, she lifted her staff overhead in both hands, holding it high against the deep blue of Darvell's midafternoon sky.

Magelords! she shouted with wordless intensity. *Magelords—here is an Adept! Come to me!*

She heard a rustling in the alley ahead of her. A masked figure stepped out from among the stacks of shipping crates. The newcomer held a short, dark staff in one black-gloved hand.

"So it's true," he said. "We have an Adept in our midst."

"A very young and foolish Adept," added a voice to Llannat's right. She resisted the urge to turn her head for a glimpse of the speaker.

"How long has it been," the new voice went on, "since an Adept was rash enough to walk openly on the streets of Darvell?"

"Longer than either of you would know," a third voice said, and another tall, black-robed figure came forward out of the shadows in the alley to her left. "Not since the wars, at least. But I remember."

Like the first speaker, the newcomer wore black robes and mask, and held a short black staff in the Magestyle one-handed grip. Holding her own staff two-handed before her, Llannat turned half-right, bringing the second, hitherto unseen speaker into view. This one, too, was robed and masked in black.

Three of them, she thought. *I never expected to face this many.* But many or few, she still knew better than to let them choose their own time and manner of attack. She threw a sudden blow toward the rightmost of the three, taking his staff against hers while the green fire of her power flared up to illuminate the air around her.

The man she had targeted spun to divert her blow. She turned with him, putting all three of the blackrobes in front of her as she had intended, with their backs to the grounded aircar. Beyond them, in the cul-de-sac, Jessan was for the moment inaudible as well as invisible.

Good, she thought. She'd pulled the hunters away from him for a little while at least. *Let him finish the repair work. Then I can break away from whoever's left and we can both get out of here.*

Then the time for thinking was past. The blackrobe to her right, the nearest of her three opponents, attacked with a backhanded blow to her leg, trying to pull her out of line and give his fellows an opening. Llannat dropped the tip of her staff and allowed his blow to slide off it. When he withdrew, she followed with an attack of her own, aiming the butt of her staff at his solar plexus.

He turned to avoid the thrust, and the enemy on Llannat's left attacked in the moment when she stood extended. She stepped backward, turning to meet and block the stroke.

So far, her staff had served her well. But staffwork alone couldn't help her now. Just as she had done back on the Professor's asteroid, she drew a deep breath and opened herself to the universe.

Strength came to her—not the rush of well-being she had known before, but a calm, steady certainty. Using both ends of her staff, she threw three blows in quick succession at the man on her right, aiming for the head, the leg, and the head again. Her opponent stumbled back a pace; she feinted toward the man in the center, then came back to press down the right-hand blackrobe's weapon with the center of her staff.

If she pushed the blackrobe's ebony rod down far enough, she could shove the center of her staff up into his throat and take him out of the fight. But before she could complete her move, she felt the patterns of power shifting around her. The opponent on her far left was making ready his own assault.

She whipped her staff under the right-hand blackrobe's defense, bringing it up and leftward in time to block the new attack, and then countered with a blow of her own that diverted at the last moment to smash against the biceps of her central opponent. He cried out in pain, and his staff dropped to the ground with the loss of strength in his hand.

"First touch to you, Adept," said the tall Magelord, the latecomer to the crossroads, as the wounded man fell back a pace and went down on his knees in pain, grasping his injured arm with his good hand. "Shall we go on?"

Llannat said nothing.

The two unwounded men circled her slowly to left and right. The tall one swept his staff upward; she turned, dropping to one knee as his blow came smashing down, and swung her own staff in a flat arc into his diaphragm. He crumpled forward.

The patterns of power changed again as he fell. She pulled her staff back toward her and brought the center up over her head into a horizontal block. Wood struck against wood as she caught and stopped a blow from behind.

She somersaulted backward, forcing the only Magelord still standing to leap over her or be knocked down. He jumped; she rolled to her feet, pivoting into a guard position as he hit the ground and spun to face her. He lunged. She turned a little to let the ebony rod go past her, and whipped the butt of her own staff forward and up into his masked face.

The wood caught him below the jaw, shattering the

plastic mask and the bone and flesh beneath. He went down, clutching his face, and the blood ran out between his black-gloved fingers.

Of the three who had come out to answer her challenge, now only the one she had first wounded remained—oddly fitting, she supposed, since he had also been the first to appear. He had regained his feet, and held his staff in his good hand.

Llannat came to guard position with her staff before her. Her opponent let his arm fall to his side. Llannat stayed in guard, having learned from an expert how fast that one-hand grip could move the short rod up and into action. The Mage gave a faint laugh.

"You've done well so far, Adept," he said. "Can you do as well with this?"

He gestured, and she felt a hand close on her throat.

"Adepts understand the structure of the universe," said the other's mocking voice. "But we Magelords control it."

The grip on her throat tightened. *Illusion!* she insisted, and threw herself open to the flow of power. The unseen hand loosened its stranglehold and fell away.

"Very good—for an Adept," said the Mage. "But we've only just begun."

VII. Darvell: Darplex; the Citadel
The Void

LLANNAT SCREAMED as the currents of power around her warped and twisted. Dark sorcery pulled at her, dragging her someplace she couldn't see, couldn't understand. She fought back in the only way she could, struggling to ride the flow of the currents even as the sorcerer kinked and knotted them.

The wrenching and pulling came to a peak and stopped. Llannat opened her eyes and looked around.

The alley, and everything in it, had vanished. She and the Mage stood in a place of grey mist; no zenith, no horizon, no ground underfoot. The creature that ranged itself alongside her adversary seemed to be made out of mist as well—darker and more solid than the rest of this place, but just as featureless and shifting.

The thing lashed out at her with a whiplike extension of its body. Llannat blocked. The shadowy flail dissipated as her staff hit it, but already another pseudopod was coiling out to strike her on the side of the head.

The scalding, unexpected pain almost blinded her. She

counterattacked by reflex, her staff passing through the arm as if through mist. The agony receded, leaving her light-headed and slow. She took a long step backward and away from the hovering creature.

The Mage swung his short ebony staff up into a whirling strike against her ribs. She knocked the weapon aside, but her counterattack dissolved in searing pain when another of the shadow-creature's misty arms looped out and curled around her torso. She cried out and twisted away.

"The creature follows you," said the Mage. "I willed it so—and here in the Void, what I will becomes what is real."

Llannat took one more step backward, and came to guard. She had to fight now; she had no choice. Already she could feel the emptiness of the Void sapping her energy, as the place would ultimately drain the energy from any living thing that traveled through it, but the Mage's creature made matters even worse. Her body ached wherever the pseudopods had touched, and energy flowed out from those touches like blood from a wound.

She gripped her staff tighter, and ran in toward the Mage. He met her with his own staff upraised. She beat on it with all the strength of both arms, and his guard came down.

She started the blow that would smash his skull, and aborted it as the Mage's creature flung out another pseudopod. She ducked under the whip of grey-black fog, but even the near-miss left her stinging all over.

I can't afford to take hits from that thing, Llannat thought. She blocked against another flailing extrusion and dissolved it into grey rags, blocked a blow from the other staff, and dodged the stroke of a third pseudopod almost as an afterthought. *But I can't touch its master unless I do.*

She steeled herself to make another assault. But something new touched her awareness, and she held back.

More Magelords? she wondered, dodging and parrying by reflex. But the auras she'd caught didn't feel like Mages at all, and she felt a surge of renewed hope. *If I can just get to them . . . in a place like this, even neutrals count as friendly.*

Llannat broke away and ran.

Ahead of her, emerging from the mist, she could make out three figures: a man and a woman, guiding a third person between them. The man paused, with the distinctive stillness of one who reads the patterns and currents of power, and halted his two companions with a gesture.

A glance over her shoulder showed Llannat that the Mage had started running also, narrowing the gap between them. His creature drifted with him, a pace or so ahead.

Llannat ran faster, expending energy at a reckless rate. She could feel the Void drawing more life-force out of her with every breath, but if she didn't reach the strangers and find help, none of that would matter anyhow.

Something grey and snaky curled down over her shoulder in a lazy looping motion. She dropped and rolled away from the pseudopod's caress, but two more ropes of living mist whipped out and caught her by waist and ankle as she came up.

Pain-blinded, she struck out at the shadow-creature's body. The misty substance thinned a little, but not enough. Before she could strike again, a third pseudopod lashed out and caught her right arm by the wrist.

Her staff fell from her hands. Then, suddenly, two of the strangers stood over her.

One, the woman, carried a Magelord's short ebony staff, but wore an Adept's formal black. The man with her was dressed like a mechanic or a spacehand in a worn grey coverall—but he bore the staff of an Adept, and his aura shone with the blinding white of a captured star.

They're Adepts! she thought, exultant, even as the man called to her, "Get back!"

She staggered away, and felt herself falling. Somebody caught and supported her—the third stranger, unarmed and holding away from the melee. Llannat got a fleeting impression of someone unknown but somehow not unknown, muffled to the eyes in a hooded cloak of heavy white wool.

A friend, at least, she thought. *But I know the others. I know them both.*

The male Adept faced the Mage, their fight swirling before her as if they were partners in a deadly dance. Owen Rosselin-Metadi had still been an apprentice the last time she'd seen him, but there was no mistaking that aura, or the fluid economy of his technique. And the woman—shorter than Owen, and darker—whose staff kept the shadow-creature and its pseudopods at bay . . . Llannat had seen her before, too.

Every time I pass a mirror, she thought. *But she's older than I am . . . and Owen's different too, somehow. . . .*

"Don't worry, child," the stranger said. "Leave the Mage and his pet to them. It's time you went back. Ari needs you."

The stranger's voice was comforting, and oddly familiar. Llannat relaxed against the rough fabric of the woolen cloak, and her eyes closed. She thought that she felt a hand stroking her hair . . . and then there was sunlight beating down on her face and hard ground under her back.

"Llannat," a voice was calling in her ear. "Llannat, we have to go now. Wake up, Llannat. Please wake up."

Ari drew his breath in through his teeth. He felt another jab of pain from his cracked rib, and ignored it. He'd taken worse from the *sigrikka* he'd killed on his Long Hunt, and the *sigrikka* hadn't smiled and called him "brother," either.

He growled in his throat, a wordless sound of disgust. He'd been fighting like a thin-skin all along, when this smooth-voiced betrayer didn't deserve that much consideration.

That does it, Ari said in the Forest Speech, and took a step forward. *I'm through with play-fighting. Now I'm going to kill you.*

He took another step, and Estisk drove in a punch at

him. This time, Ari didn't waste time blocking it. He let it smash into him, ignoring the pain, and kept on moving forward.

Estisk punched him a second time, and a third. Then Ari was inside the Darvelline's reach and grabbing the false Quincunx man by the collar with his left hand. The Darvelline struggled, fighting to slip the hold. Ari twisted the handful of fabric tighter and slammed his right fist into the other man's stomach with all the strength of his back and shoulders.

Then, like a *sigrikka* in a killing fury, he shook Estisk twice with neck-snapping force and flung the Darvelline away from him into the front door of the tool-issue point. The wooden panel burst outward under the impact.

Ari went out between the hanging splinters. Estisk lay on his back in the street, dazed and blinking.

Ari reached down and pulled the Darvelline upright. "On your feet, you bastard."

Estisk swayed, but stayed up. Ari's cracked lips curved into a grin.

"Good," he said, knotting his hands together like a club. "I'm not done with you yet."

On the last word, he brought his locked fists up from his hips, smashing them against the side of the other man's head with an impact that split the skin over his knuckles and lifted the Darvelline clear off the ground. Estisk staggered, going down on one knee for a second, and hauled himself back upright.

Ari swung his clenched fists up from the other side. This time he heard bone crack as they connected. Again the Darvelline stumbled backward, but still he refused to go down.

Again and again, Ari pounded the other man, driving him step by step across the street. Not until Estisk reached the far side of the road, and his heels met the curb, did the big Darvelline fall at last and lie staring upward with eyes that did not blink.

* * *

I don't think I like this, thought Beka.

The Professor held the short ebony staff in front of him. A glowing red aura surrounded him and reflected off the polished walls of the echoing reception chamber. Beka followed, blaster in hand, feeling superfluous—as she had felt ever since those last moments in the entry bay, when the Professor had run past the wreckage of the hovercar to a door she'd never even spotted, and opened it with one touch of his staff.

He'd taken the stairway beyond at a run, and she had followed him through a maze of corridors—all of them empty and lightless through what Beka uncomfortably thought might be the Professor's sorcery.

This is the man who saved your neck back on Mandeyn, she reminded herself. *The one who broke his arm for you in Flatlands Portcity. He's on your side.*

They kept on, always moving upward: up stairs, up ladders, up ramps, through rooms and along corridors. Nothing and nobody came out to stop them, but she still felt watched and followed by eyes she couldn't see. From time to time the Professor would pause, point without explanation to a particular tile in the floor, then leap over it. Or he would throw an object through a door before entering it himself. She followed his lead—jumping where he jumped, pausing where he paused—and still her feeling of wrongness grew.

They made it as far as a large reception chamber somewhere in the Citadel's upper reaches. There they stopped. Now the Professor stood in the center of the hall, turning first one way and then another. The scarlet glow that surrounded him made shadows move in the corners like living things.

He's looking for something, Beka thought. *And I think he's found it.*

The grey-haired Entiboran—or whatever he really was—raised his left hand. A circle of greenish flame sprang up from the floor in front of him. He said something, too low for Beka to catch the words, and a black shape appeared inside the fiery circle, shifting and elongating to become a black-robed figure. A mask hid its features, but it carried a short, silver-bound staff like the Professor's own.

More sorcery, she thought. *Now I know I don't like this.*

The Professor lowered his upraised hand. The circle of witchfire died, but the figure in black remained. Beka's copilot walked forward into the shadowy form. It solidified, taking on outline and detail as the Professor's white shirt and black trousers lost resolution, until the two were one.

''So you've come back at last.''

Beka whirled toward the unfamiliar voice, her blaster coming up in her hand, but the black-robed man standing at the far end of the hall never even gave her a look. She recognized the second man from the Rolny's hovercar as he continued, ''I told them that if I waited long enough, you would return.''

''Half a thousand years,'' the Professor said, ''is a long time to wait.''

''Not to avenge treason.''

''I suppose not,'' the Professor said. Beka couldn't see his face behind the immobile features of the molded plastic mask, but the familiar voice sounded weary, and a little sad. ''Well, now I am here.''

''True,'' said the stranger. He lifted his staff. A pale red-orange glow surrounded him, in contrast with the Professor's deeper scarlet aura. ''Guard yourself, traitor.''

The Professor brought his staff up into what Beka supposed was a guard of some sort. ''And you do the same, my friend.''

''No friend of yours,'' the stranger said. ''Keep that word for the ones you serve.''

''As you will,'' the Professor said. His staff whipped out at the stranger in a fiery blur.

The other's staff caught and stopped it only inches from his neck. Then Beka, watching, saw a passage-at-arms such as she had never seen before—a fast-moving fight of advances and retreats, stamping feet and swirling black robes. The glowing auras wove a colored tapestry in the air about the two men as they fought, and arcing streamers of colored fire crackled like small lightning bolts, making the high-ceilinged reception room resound with their echoes. But the Professor was smaller than his adversary, and more slightly built; little by little the stranger seemed to gain the upper hand.

Beka gripped the Mark VI blaster so hard her fingers ached, watching her copilot's blows come slower and slower while his blocks and counters made it with less and less time to spare.

I wish Owen could see this. Or Llannat. Maybe they'd be able to make sense of what's going on. I certainly can't.

She bit her lip, and concentrated on keeping the Mark VI trained on the stranger.

An opening came that she couldn't see, and the stranger lunged. His staff struck the Professor full in the torso. The crimson aura died, and her copilot slumped to the floor in a puddle of black robes.

Beka raised her blaster and took aim.

A hand fell on her wrist, pressing the weapon downward. "Gently, Tarnekep," murmured a familiar voice beside her. "Watch."

Out in the center of the floor, the stranger bent over the fallen form. He removed the mask that covered the dead man's face, and recoiled upward with a cry.

Beka felt the weight leave her arm. The Professor stepped forward and away from her, still dressed in the shirt and trousers he'd been wearing when all this started, his staff ready in his hand. The stranger saw the movement and turned.

"Surprised?" asked the Professor. "You shouldn't be. You spent all your strength and passion in fighting yourself."

The stranger gave a harsh laugh. "You always were good at illusions; that much hasn't changed. But don't worry. I still have enough strength left for you."

The Professor raised his staff. His aura flared up in a blaze of red, far deeper and brighter than the stranger's.

"We worked in the same Circle once," her copilot said to the stranger. "You can still yield."

"You betrayed our Circle!" shouted the other. "With you as First, we could have had the galaxy . . . and now look at us. Bodyguards for the likes of Nivome the Rolny!"

"An honorable profession," said the Professor, "if you choose to make it so. Once more—do you yield?"

"No!" cried the stranger, and struck out.

The Professor beat the other's staff aside, and lunged for his head. The other blocked, and the two men sprang apart.

If the fighting Beka had seen before had been deadly and beautiful, what she watched now had a vicious elegance that made the previous exchange look like a back-street brawl. She let her blaster fall to her side—the combat was moving too fast for her to keep the weapon trained.

Attack built upon attack, counterattack followed parry at a pace that never slackened. Both men were moving easily, and neither had been hurt; it seemed to Beka that the two of them might well keep up their duel forever, while the Citadel waited in some kind of suspended animation for them to finish.

Suddenly the fighting stopped. The two men froze, facing each other in guard. At last, the stranger lowered his staff. "You have won," he said. "I admit defeat."

The Professor lowered his own weapon as well. "Stay, then, and fight beside me again for old times' sake."

He tucked the staff back under his belt while he spoke. And as he did, the stranger raised his weapon and swung on the older man.

Beka cried out. Her blaster was down at her side, and the Professor, damn him, was right in the line of fire. But her copilot ducked under the staff as in came in, and caught the stranger by the shoulder with his left hand. With the other, he embraced his foe.

She finished her sidestep and took aim, then lowered the blaster without firing. The Professor pulled away his right hand to reveal a bloody knife.

The black-robed body sagged forward. The Professor caught the stranger as he fell, and the two men sank together to their knees. Tongues of pale green witchfire flickered about them both as the Professor cradled the other in his arms.

At length Beka walked forward. "Professor, we have to go. We have things to do."

The Professor looked up. "What? Oh, yes."

"We have to go," she said. "Now. We have to find Nivome."

"Nivome."

"You remember," she said urgently. "He killed my mother."

"I remember," said the Professor. His face was older than she had ever seen it—old, and tired. "Nivome has little enough time left, child; give him a moment more. This man was my friend, once."

"I heard," she said. "Do whatever you have to."

She stood by, watching, as the Professor laid out the other man on the floor, folding the black-gloved hands around the ebony staff. The dying witchfire clung to the body, outlining it in eerie light, even after the Professor rose to his feet.

"That way," he said. He pulled his own staff free of his belt, and pointed to an archway at the other end of the hall. "It's not much farther."

The aura surrounding her copilot was deep purple now; it gave only the faintest of illumination, and the air all about them was chill. Beka shivered inside her black velvet long-coat as she and her copilot walked together through the archway into yet another corridor.

Once outside the reception hall, the Professor shook off whatever emotion had been holding him in its grip. He strode along at a rapid pace, looking to right and left as if searching for something. He began to speak aloud as he walked, a thing he hadn't done earlier.

"Along this way. Third turning, then up. Down the hall. Door on the left. Two rooms . . ."

He stopped.

Beka looked at her copilot. His foot was touching a floor tile that had somehow sunk a quarter-inch below the level of the rest. Above that tile, a mechanical spear had thrust out of the wall on his right, and the bloodied metal tip protruded from his side. He looked back at her over one shoulder.

"My lady, I am sorry. I had hoped to be with you until the finish." He glanced down at the spear, and a look of confusion passed across his features. "Oh, dear. I seem to have ruined my shirt."

The staff dropped from his hand. The violet aura died, and the hallway was left in total darkness.

She couldn't see anything. "Professor?"

Nobody answered.

"Professor!"

She grabbed blindly for his arm. It was limp and unresponding—no life there. She was alone in the heart of the Citadel, and the pitch-black darkness pressed around her.

Then the black ziggurat came to life like a giant waking. She heard the hum of electronics, loud after the long silence, as the light panels returned; then a whirring started, and the automatic cameras mounted at intervals along the ceiling switched on and began to track.

But she didn't care; she didn't care about any of it. She grabbed up the Professor's fallen staff even though Tarnekep Portree had no use for such things, then raised her blaster and shot out the nearest spy-eye before it could come to bear.

"Third turning, then left," she muttered.

Gently, Tarnekep, the voice of memory whispered in her mind.

"Gently, hell!" she snarled, and blasted another spy-eye as she ran forward. "If I see them, they die."

VIII. Darvell: Darplex; the Citadel

J ESSAN SLID shut the access plate and crawled out from under the aircar. "Well, Llannat, I think that just about does it . . . Llannat?"

No answer. The alley was quiet. Jessan looked around. A black-clad body lay facedown in the alley ahead.

"Oh, no."

He ran forward to the junction, skidding down onto his knees by the body. It wasn't Llannat. The unknown wore black robes instead of the Adept's plain black coverall, and someone had smashed in his face. A molded mask of black plastic hid what was left of his features. A short ebony staff lay on the pavement next to the unknown's body.

Jessan checked for a pulse: none. *Not surprising—the poor bastard probably choked on his own blood.*

He sat back on his heels and looked around. Another blackrobe lay nearby, as dead as the first.

Slowly, Jessan stood up. "Llannat!" he called out. "Llannat!"

Nobody answered. He looked down the main alley

toward the street—nothing. No bodies, no tracks, no blood. He drew his blaster. Holding it at the ready, he ran down the other alley to the next fork and checked to right and to left.

The right-hand alley dead-ended in a ground-transport loading dock, its doors down and locked. In the other direction, he could see a hint of green somewhere beyond the alley's mouth. He turned left.

He stopped where the alley opened out into the main road. The greenery turned out to belong to a little park across the street. Inside the park, two black-clad figures sprawled on the close-trimmed grass, surrounded by a small knot of people. One of the bodies wore black robes like the first two—but the other—

Jessan reholstered his blaster and strolled across the street to the edge of the crowd.

"Let me through," he said. "Let me through. I'm a medic."

He kept on walking forward as he spoke, and the circle parted. The smaller of the two bodies was Llannat Hyfid, all right. He knelt and put a hand to her neck. Her pulse was thin and weak, but it was there.

She's alive. I don't see her staff anywhere, though. He checked the second body: no pulse, no anything. *Dead. Time to get out of here, I think.*

"Anybody see what happened?" he asked the crowd in general.

"There wasn't anybody there at all," said a voice from the back somewhere. "Then all of a sudden, there they were."

"Yeah," said another voice. "Like they fell out of the sky or something."

Interesting . . . but not what I'd call useful. We still have to make it to the aircar before Security gets here.

He bent over and put his mouth next to the Adept's ear.

"Llannat," he called softly. "Llannat, we have to go now. Wake up, Llannat. Please wake up."

Her eyelids flickered a little, and her lips moved. Jessan bent closer.

"Ari?" she asked.

"It's Jessan," he said. "Wake up. We'll go find Ari. Wake up. Ari needs you."

Her pulse grew stronger, and her breathing deepened. She began to stir.

"Get back, everyone," Jessan ordered. "Give her air."

The crowd moved back a little. He slid his arms under Llannat's knees and shoulders, and stood up.

"Hey, wait a minute," someone said. "You shouldn't move her."

Jessan sighed. *There's always somebody.* "I have to get her to the hospital," he said. "My vehicle's over that way."

A shadow glided over the grass as he spoke. He glanced up, and saw an aircar with Security markings circling to make another pass.

"NOBODY MOVE," bellowed a voice from the sky. "STAY WHERE YOU ARE OR I WILL OPEN FIRE."

Jessan looked at the alley—only a street's width away, but too far to run while carrying another. He kept on walking.

"HALT OR I SHOOT."

Jessan froze in midstreet.

Maybe I can break for the alley once they've grounded, he thought, without much optimism.

"Put me down," said a faint voice. "I can walk."

"You're probably lying," he muttered, lowering the Adept to her feet. "But what choice have we got?"

He put one hand on his blaster, and the other around Llannat's shoulders. "The alley, on three."

The aircar circled over them again. "DROP YOUR WEAPONS."

"One . . . two . . . three!"

They dashed for the alley. Jessan supported Llannat as much as he could. He hated to think what reserves of energy the Adept must be drawing on to match his pace.

Overhead, the Security aircar whipped around in a tight turn and started firing down at them. Jessan drew his blaster and fired back, still running.

Energy bolts chewed up the pavement to either side of them as the aircar passed by overhead and climbed away, trailing black smoke from a hit to its underbelly. The aircar made a rollover at the top of its loop and headed back toward them for another run.

I've been here before, thought Jessan, staggering into the alley with Llannat in tow. *In the Professor's game room. And I didn't like the way it ended.*

They plastered themselves against the wall as the Security aircar made a second pass, then stumbled on down the alley to their own craft.

"Blast," said Jessan, panting. "We can't take off with our nose against the dead end like that. Feel up to helping me turn this boat in place?"

"No time," Llannat said.

"Blast," Jessan said again. The Adept was right: he could hear sirens converging on the area from all directions.

"Get in the aircar anyway," Llannat said.

"But we don't have room for takeoff!" he protested, helping the Adept into the cockpit ahead of him as he spoke.

"Don't worry. Switch on the engines when you think it's time."

"When I—right."

Llannat closed her eyes and placed both hands on the aircar's instrument panel. The console started to vibrate, and its readouts and telltales blinked from green to amber to red to green again. A moment longer, and the whole aircar began to shake. Then, slowly, it lifted straight up.

Energy fire came down the alley from behind them.

I think it's time.

Jessan hit the main engine ignition switch. At the same instant, he fed forward power. The craft began to move through the air, building speed until true lift took over.

He put the aircar into a climb and looked over at Llannat.

"Now what?" he asked.

The Adept had collapsed back into the copilot's seat. Her face was mottled and her jacket was soaked with sweat. She didn't open her eyes as she spoke. "Set course for *Warhammer*."

"What about Beka and the Professor?" he demanded. "What about Ari, if it comes to that? You were worried enough about him five minutes ago."

"We can't help them here. Please, Jessan. . . ."

Almost angrily, he punched the *Hammer's* coordinates into the aircar's little on-board navicomp. "All right. We're heading home."

He pushed the throttle all the way forward and banked the aircar into a turn. The Citadel, looming black and featureless on the horizon, slid from the cockpit's front windows around toward the side as he added, "But we don't lift from Darvell without the captain."

Llannat didn't respond. The Citadel disappeared from the side window, and reappeared in the rear monitor. In the tiny screen, the tip of the black ziggurat blazed for a second with a burst of brilliant light. Heavy smoke followed, billowing out to hang over the Citadel like a low-lying cloud.

"Now that looks interesting," Jessan said. "Check it out, Llannat—Llannat?"

He glanced over at the Adept. *I ought to have my license revoked*, he thought. *Labored breathing, shivering, cold sweat—she needs to be flat on a hospital cot, not running around Darplex levitating aircars.*

"What we want now," he said aloud, "is the autopilot. Get this bird headed for home, and I can forget about playing daredevil flier and go back to taking care of casualties."

He reached out to lock in the automatic controls, but his hand never got there. Alarms began pipping all over the console instead, and seconds later colored light boiled in the air outside the cockpit windows.

Fighters, thought Jessan. He cut right to ruin the other pilot's firing solution, then left to regain track. *I wish I were better at this.*

"Up the stairs," the Professor had said.

Beka took the metal staircase two steps at a time, the Mark VI ready in her hand. Something moved on the upper landing, and she fired.

Beka Rosselin-Metadi sometimes missed; Tarnekep Portree never did. The hunter/killer robot disintegrated in a shower of white sparks and fragments of hot metal, and Beka kept on running.

She reached the landing. The door out to the corridor began sliding open. She fired into the gap as it widened, then took the door in a low dive, firing again as she came up.

A man lay in the hallway, his torso a mess of bone and seared meat. A second Security guard crouched in the shelter of his partner's body. He fired, and the blaster bolt whined over her head into the now-closing doorway.

She held her fire. The security man half-rose to get a second shot at her; she pressed down the firing stud on the Mark VI and held it there. When she released it, the second man was as dead as the first.

Something rolled under her hand as she pushed away from the floor and stood up: the first guard's blaster. She tucked the Professor's staff out of the way under her belt, and picked up the blaster with her free hand.

More movement—hunter/killers, floating into action at either end of the hall. She fired both blasters. One robot exploded and the other went wild, caroming off the walls and firing at random.

" 'Down the hall,' " she recited, like an incantation. " 'Door on the left.' "

A half-dozen strides, and the door was in front of her. She took out the lockplate just as the Professor had taught her, with a precision burst from her right-hand blaster. The doors started to slide apart.

She brought the two blasters up waist-high, and stood in the open doorway firing at everything that moved. She didn't stop until the room was still.

Beka went inside. Dead men and burnt-out security monitors were everywhere. The room smelled of blaster fire and burning electronics. A mobile fire-extinguisher unit emerged from its cubbyhole and began scuttling about amid the corpses, spraying the smoking comp units with inert gas. She watched it work for a second, and then shot it as well.

"Let the damned place burn," she muttered, looking about at the wreckage. " 'Two rooms . . .' "

The sign on the far door read, simply, DIRECTOR. She walked up to it and shot out the lockplate. The door slid open.

A man sat behind a massive desk on the far side of the room, in front of an allegorical tapestry representing the Sundering of the Galaxy. "You didn't need to do that," he said. "The door wasn't locked."

Unless all the flatpix and Jessan's memory were lying, this was Nivome the Rolny. She took a step into the room and looked about. Nivome kept his hands flat on his desk.

"Ah," he said. "Tarnekep Portree. I've heard of you. In fact, I've developed more than a casual interest, ever since you were spotted on-planet."

Go ahead and talk, she thought, still checking out the room. Her blasters never wavered from their target. *See how much good it does you.*

"For the last year or more, Captain Portree," Nivome continued, "you've delighted in interfering with our plans. May I ask why? Who could possibly be paying you enough?"

She had the holoprojector spotted now, and shot it out by way of answer. Nivome and the desk both vanished.

The tapestry remained; she took a moment to set her right-hand blaster to low stun, then strode up to the wall hanging and yanked it aside. She wasn't surprised to see another door behind it.

Pulling aside the tapestry must have sent some kind of signal, because this door opened before she could even touch it. A blaster bolt flashed out, taking her low in the right side.

Beka fired back, right-handed, and the man who had shot her crumpled. She looked at the unconscious body.

It was Nivome for real, this time. Except for the two of them, the room was empty. She walked over and prodded the Rolny's motionless form with the toe of her boot.

"I ought to kill you right now, you son of a bitch. But I want to give you to someone for a present."

She tucked the spare blaster into the waistband of her trousers. The movement hurt; she felt blood starting to seep out of the wound in her side as the cauterizing effect of the blaster bolt wore off.

She pulled Tarnekep Portree's lace-trimmed handkerchief out of her coat sleeve and stuffed the delicate fabric in between the wound and her shirt to stop the bleeding. Her fingers came away red and sticky. She looked at them, and the reality of the situation hit her at last.

There's no way I can possibly get out of here.

Beka thumbed her blaster setting back to Full, and pointed the weapon at Nivome. Then she lowered it again.

No, not yet. There's still one move they might not be expecting. But I can't do it alone.

She switched the blaster to her other hand and reached into the pocket of her long-coat. She found the comm link, and keyed it on.

"Ari," she said. "Ari, this is Bee. I'm in trouble. Please get me out."

Ari shifted positions in the pilot's seat of his stolen aircar, trying to find some way to sit that didn't make his cracked rib hurt even worse.

Blinking hard, he checked the instruments again. He was having trouble seeing out of his left eye, and the readouts kept blurring when he tried to bring them into focus. *Level flight . . . good attitude . . . low altitude . . . no contacts on the scope . . .*

"Ari," said a voice from somewhere in the cockpit. "Ari, this is Bee. I'm in trouble. Please get me out."

"Dammit, Bee," he muttered. "You always pull these crazy stunts, and then expect me to take care of you."

His jaw hurt and his head felt thick. Something was wrong. He was alone in the aircar—that was it. He shouldn't be listening to a sister who wasn't there, and who sounded scared.

"Ari!" came the call again, through the ringing in his ears. "Ari, are you there?"

The voice seemed to be coming from right beside him. He turned his head that way, grimacing as several more sets of muscles protested the move, and squinted at the copilot's seat. *Nobody there. Maybe I* am *crazy.*

Then the afternoon light shone through the cockpit window and glinted off something small and metallic lying on the seat cushions: the comm link he'd left there when he went into Building 125-34 to settle accounts with Estisk. He picked up the comm link and keyed it on.

"Beka, this is Ari. Where are you?"

"I'm in the Citadel, at the top. Come get me?"

She was scared, he realized—scared or angry, or maybe both. "Sure thing, Bee. How do I find you?"

He heard his sister laughing over the comm link, and the sound made the hairs on his neck stand on end.

"Watch for my signal, big brother. You can't miss it."

The link clicked off. Ari turned the aircar and headed for the Citadel.

Nobody bothered him. The aircar's built-in identification devices must be signaling that it had permission to enter that airspace—one of the advantages to stealing the head man's personal runabout.

He put the aircar into a climb, bringing it up to the altitude of the black ziggurat's upper levels. Suddenly, he saw a flash. One wall on the topmost floor crumpled outward, falling down and away like an avalanche. A cloud of thick black smoke hung in the air for a few seconds before beginning to drift on the wind.

"You're right, Bee," he said aloud. "I couldn't miss it."

He toggled the side cargo door open, and turned the aircar into the smoke.

Beka clicked off the comm link and stuffed it back into her pocket. She pulled out the collapsor and peeled off the film covering the device's adhesive surface.

Do it right the first time, she told herself, pressing the flat disk hard against what she hoped was an outside wall. *One try is all you get.*

She dialed the collapsor up to maximum power, then set the timer and entered the arming sequence. The glowing red numbers on the readout started their march down to detonation. She hadn't allowed herself much leeway; reinforcements would be showing up any minute now, and none of them would be for her.

You'll die before I do, she thought, looking at the Rolny's unconscious form. *But maybe—if I'm lucky—not just yet.*

She crouched by his head and slapped him across the face with her free hand, back and forth until he grunted and started to come out of his stun.

His eyes blinked open; she made certain that the first thing he saw was the muzzle of her blaster. She kept it trained on him as she stood.

"Get up," she said. "We're going for a little walk."

Nivome staggered to his feet. "Whatever they're paying you, I'll double it."

"There's not that much money in the universe," she told him. With a sudden motion, she grabbed Nivome's wrist in her left hand, twisting his arm up between his shoulder blades. She pressed the muzzle of her blaster into the small of his back.

"Walk," she ordered.

The Rolny walked. Together, they moved out through the false office and the security room, and into the corridor.

Beka flattened herself against the wall, holding Nivome in front of her like a shield. Down the hall, someone peeked around a half-open door, and seconds later a blaster bolt sizzled against the wall by her head.

"Don't shoot, you idiot!" Nivome shouted. "It's me!"

"Very smart," said Beka, sending a return beam down the hallway. "You may just live past today after all."

But I wouldn't bet the family silver on it, if I were you, she thought, waiting for the sound of the collapsor. *Only a few seconds left to go.*

The grenade went off with a sound like a mountain blowing itself apart. She wrenched Nivome back around, and shoved him ahead of her through the doorway.

The shock of the collapsor blast had thrown the sliding doors apart all the way back to the rear office. Where the wall had been was now a cloud of dense smoke . . . but the cloud was shot through with sunlight, and from somewhere outside she could hear the sound of an aircar's engines.

Still pushing Nivome before her, Beka went forward toward the light.

IX. Darvell: The Citadel; Darvell Nearspace

BEKA PUSHED Nivome torward the gap the collapsor had made in the wall of the Citadel. The floor ended an inch beyond the toes of her boots, and she didn't like to think about how far below her the ground might be. Somewhere out in the smoke, the aircar purred closer.

She still had her prisoner in the come-along grip. He was too groggy from the stun-bolt to protest much, even if the blaster pressed against his spine had left him any choice.

"If I pushed you right now," she said, just in case, "you'd fall a long way down before you bounced."

The Rolny didn't reply. Sometime in the past couple of minutes, he'd apparently decided that Tarnekep Portree was too crazy to reason with.

Funny thing about that, thought Beka, as the approaching aircar gradually became visible through the smoke. *He's right.*

The aircar flew past the side of the building, close

enough for her to see that the cargo door gaped open. Then the craft veered off into the smoke and came circling back toward the Citadel to make another pass.

The drone of its engines changed to a ragged growl as the pilot reduced speed.

"Not so slow," she muttered. "You'll lose lift."

The aircar came in close . . . closer . . . if the wall had still been there, the aircar's right wingtip would have broken against it. The open cargo door yawned like a cavemouth, only yards away and drawing nearer every second. She could see the leap she'd have to make, several feet out and a long step down if she missed.

If I were an Adept, she thought, *I'd just grab hold of the currents of the universe, and hitch a ride on over. But I'm not an Adept, so—*

"You'd better hope I'm lucky," she said to Nivome, and pushed him ahead of her as she jumped.

Beka felt a split second of weightless panic. Then she was falling hard against the far wall of the cargo compartment as Ari banked the aircar left. Nivome landed under her; she still had his arm up in the come-along. She thumbed the blaster in her other hand back down a notch to Heavy, put the muzzle behind his ear, and shot him again. He went limp and slid down onto the aircar's decking.

Behind her, the cargo door slammed shut with a clang. She scrambled over and dogged it down, then clambered forward and collapsed into the copilot's seat.

Ari looked around from the controls. "Strap in, baby sister. Where do you want to go?"

She stared at him. A bruised and bleeding gash marked the right side of his jaw, his left eye had puffed almost shut, and his hands on the control yoke were red-knuckled and swollen.

"What the hell happened to you?" she asked.

"I got in a fight," he said. "Where's the Professor? Still taking care of things in the cargo compartment?"

"That's Nivome back there." She leaned her head back

against the seat cushions. Her right side was hurting her now; it felt like someone had shoved a burning torch into it. "The Professor won't be coming."

"Dead?" Ari asked.

She closed her eyes. "That's right."

"I'm sorry, Bee."

"The hell with sorry," she said. "Where's Jessan?"

She heard her brother sigh. "I don't know."

"Dammit, Ari, I told him and Llannat to take the aircar up and go looking for you—don't sit there saying you don't know where he is!"

"All right. I won't. Now tell me where you want to go."

"Set a course back for *Warhammer*," she said without opening her eyes. "They'd head there if anything went wrong."

The aircar droned on in silence for a few minutes. Her side throbbed in rhythm with the engines.

Ari exclaimed something under his breath. She dragged her eyes open again.

"What is it, big brother?"

"Look up ahead," he said. "I think we've found them."

She pushed herself away from the seat back and looked out the front window. Yes, there was the aircar that should have been their getaway craft. One of the Darvelline atmospheric fighters was on its tail, getting lined up for a firing pass.

Dodge him, you Khesatan idiot—dodge him! Frantic, she searched the copilot's side of the console for weapon controls. "Bloody hell, Ari—aren't there any guns on this damned ground-hugging boat of yours?"

Ari pulled the aircar up and added throttle. "Don't worry about it."

She bit down hard on her lower lip, and watched in silence as Ari began to sneak up on the Darvelline fighter from behind. Another moment, and he was in tight beside the Darvelline, flying with his left wing under the right wing of the fighter.

Ari put the aircar into a hard bank, and the left wing tilted up to strike the underside of the wing above it. The fighter flipped down into a vertical spin.

"Not bad," she said as the Darvelline spiraled earthward.

Her brother looked pleased with himself. "I told you not to worry."

Jessan's voice came over the comm link. "Is that the Terror of the Spaceways back there?"

"None other," said Ari. "Get on the deck—we have to switch to your aircar. This one's just about had it."

"No trouble. Taking it down."

A minute or so later, Beka felt the aircar settling to the ground. She unstrapped the safety webbing. The movement pulled at the wound in her side, making her head spin.

How much blood have I lost? she wondered. *Just let me get* Warhammer *into hyperspace before I go under, that's all I ask.*

She pushed open the cockpit door on her side and started climbing out. "You get Nivome," she told Ari over her shoulder. "Damned if I'll carry the bastard."

She heard Ari muttering under his breath and then his footsteps clunked back toward the cargo compartment.

She leaned her forehead against the side of the aircar. *How long have we got before somebody else shows up to shoot at us? The Professor would have known . . . the Professor . . . damn you, Nivome, I hope your Citadel burns to the ground.*

"We've got to stop meeting like this," said a familiar voice at her elbow.

"Jessan!" she exclaimed, turning.

He embraced her, hard; she hugged him back, harder, in spite of what that did to the pain in her side. He must have noticed something, though, because he let go and stepped away to look at her.

"If I ask whose blood that is on your shirt," he said, "will you pull a knife on me again?"

She shook her head. "No. It's all mine, this time."

"Bad?"

"It'll keep until we make the jump," she said, and turned back toward the cargo compartment. "Ari!" she called. "Have you got our passenger yet?"

The door clanked open behind her. "I have him, Bee," said her brother, emerging with Nivome slung over his shoulders like a rolled-up rug.

"Good." She moved away from the side of the aircar, heading for the armed craft Jessan had set down not far off. "Let's get out of here before the law shows up."

Minutes later, the getaway aircar lifted with Ari at the controls. Beka sat beside him in the copilot's seat that had held Llannat Hyfid not long before.

She didn't know what was wrong with the Adept, only that she was out even colder than Nivome. Ari and Jessan had argued diagnoses the whole time they'd been strapping Llannat into one of the fold-down cots in the back, and Beka had gotten the impression that they didn't know either.

"Massive internal bleeding?" she'd heard Jessan wondering aloud at one point. "Or is this some weird Adept thing they didn't teach us about in class? *You* tell *me* what's normal for somebody who pops out of nowhere and moves aircars around just by thinking about it hard enough. . . ."

The console readouts were blinking; she glanced at them, then at the screens for confirmation.

"We've picked up a tail," she said aloud.

"How many?" asked Ari, from the pilot's seat.

"Just one, so far. Can you lose him?"

"I can do better than that," Ari said. "Watch."

He banked hard left and put the aircar into a dive. Beka saw a Darvelline fighter below them and climbing. Their energy guns went off with a zinging whistle, and the fighter exploded.

"Got you!" crowed Ari as their own aircar rocked in the turbulence.

"Big brother, you amaze me sometimes."

"Compared to everything else I've done today," Ari said, "that was so easy it ought to be illegal. Now the real fun starts."

He banked again to a new heading, tilted the aircar's nose up, slid the throttles all the way forward, and flipped on the thrust inducers. The roar of the engines changed to a high, tooth-aching whine, and inertia pressed Beka down into the seat cushions. Her side hurt; she could feel it bleeding again.

Ari cut the engines back to minimum throttle. The pressure on her chest and her wounded side disappeared as the aircar went into free-fall.

She heard a yell from the cargo compartment. "Lords of Life, what are you two doing up there?"

"Taking the quickest way home," she yelled back. "We've just gone ballistic."

"Coming into final approach," Ari said. "So far, so good."

Beka shook her head. "Too good, big brother. It shouldn't be this easy."

Dazzling white light filled the front window as she spoke. She shut her eyes.

"Massive energy strike," said Ari's deep voice next to her. "Right about where our calculated landing place should have been. Somebody must have figured out we had a spaceship hidden somewhere, and decided to take it out before we could get his boss on board."

Decided to take it out. My ship. Just like that. She pulled the knife out of her sleeve, and started to unstrap.

"Bee, what the hell—"

"If the *'Hammer* is gone, I'm not waiting any longer. The Rolny buys it right now."

Next to her, Ari chuckled. "Relax and strap back in. I deliberately overshot when I plotted this thing. There was a whole mountain peak between that blast and the *'Hammer.*"

"Dadda would be proud of you," she said, sliding the

knife back. "Uh-oh . . . more contacts on the scope. Big ones, low and slow, matching course."

"Troop carriers," Ari said. "They'll wait until we set down, then try to run a rescue."

"Burn them."

Her brother shook his head. "No good—they'd just send more. Groundside's probably tracking us from one of those spy satellites we saw on the way in."

"Damn." She bit her lip, and watched the winking points of light on the scope. "Ari, you packed the first-aid kit for this aircar. Did you throw in anything strong enough to bring someone out of heavy stun in a big hurry?"

She saw him frown. "It's taking a chance on turning his brains to scrambled eggs."

"I don't care what he thinks with," she said. "Just so he can walk."

She turned her head and shouted back into the cargo compartment. "Jessan! Crack open the first-aid kit and bring the prisoner round! Ari, set us down a little way outside *Defiant*'s cloaking field."

"Got you, Bee. Going down."

By the time Ari got the aircar grounded, the troop carriers were closing. Beka could see one of them from the cockpit window, hovering on high-step nullgravs not a hundred yards away. She unstrapped the safety webbing and stood up, grimacing as the motion pulled at her wounded side.

"Get Llannat," she said to her brother. "Jessan!"

"Captain?"

"Status on the prisoner."

"He'll walk."

"Good." She was in the cargo bay by the time she finished speaking, and saw that the Khesatan had been as good as his word. He had Nivome on his feet and semi-conscious, hands bound behind him with tape out of the first-aid kit.

Her brother already had Llannat out of the other cot.

The Adept looked like a child cuddled next to Ari's broad chest. Beka tried to reconcile the picture with Jessan's comment about moving aircars around by force of will, and had no luck.

"She still with us?"

"In and out," Jessan said. "She keeps waking up and looking for something that isn't here."

"Her staff, you idiot," growled Ari. "You don't think she left it behind on purpose, do you?"

Beka pulled the Professor's staff out from under her belt, and gave it to her brother. "Here. Give her this if she asks again. It's not the same, but maybe it'll help. And I sure haven't got any use for it."

Ari looked unhappy. "Bee, you don't have to—"

She ignored him. "All right. We're going out the cargo door and heading for the ship. Ari, you're in the middle with Llannat. Jessan, get out your blaster and bring up the rear."

She undogged the door and slid it open. Then she pulled her knife. "The Rolny and I are going first, just to make a nice show and impress the dirtside troopies." She twisted Nivome's bound hands up behind him, and put the point of the knife at the juncture of his throat and jaw. "Walk, you."

Nivome obeyed. Outside, she could see another troop carrier hovering not far from the first. Foot soldiers in blast armor had already formed up into a skirmish line outside the vehicles. At the sight of Nivome, they held their fire.

She pitched her voice to carry. "You know who I've got here. One funny move, and I start cutting pieces off of him. I want an armed spacecraft and safe conduct into hyperspace, and I want them now!"

She crossed the few yards of open ground between the grounded aircar and the trees with her dagger's point nuzzling the Rolny's throat every step of the way. She didn't dare look back to see whether Ari and Jessan had followed her—not until she'd marched Nivome well into the woods, and passed with him through the area of visual distortion that marked the edge of the cloaking field.

Only after she'd confirmed that the 'Hammer and Defiant still waited for them unmolested did she let herself look around. Ari was there, holding Llannat and looking grim, and Jessan, reholstering his blaster. The Khesatan gave her an encouraging smile.

"You menaced them most convincingly, Captain."

"It helps if you mean it," she said. "If we're lucky, they'll waste some time trying to talk us into coming out of the woods with our hands up. Let's get on board and lift ship."

She watched as Jessan, the only member of the party with a free hand, punched the security codes into the 'Hammer's entry panel. "I hate to leave Defiant for those bastards to take apart," she said, "but it's going to take all of us just to get the 'Hammer up and into hyper."

The ramp came down. She prodded Nivome up it with the tip of her knife.

"Everybody aboard. Ari, you strap Llannat down for lift-off and then start warming up the engines. I'll be up to the cockpit as soon as Jessan and I get Dadda's birthday present secured belowdecks."

Ari headed forward, still carrying Llannat. Beka thumbed the ramp closed.

"Cover him," she said to Jessan, and stepped away from Nivome to open one of the 'Hammer's cargo holds. She gestured toward the opening with the point of her dagger. "You—Nivome—get in there."

The Rolny obeyed. She dogged the airtight hatch back into place and straightened up again. This time she couldn't help the stifled noise she made as the hole in her side opened and bled afresh. Again, Jessan reached out a hand. She moved away.

"It'll keep until we make hyper, I tell you," she said, throwing the compartment's external lock switch as she spoke. "Let's get forward."

In the cockpit, Ari was bending over the copilot's couch

and fastening the safety webbing across Llannat's unconscious form. Beka checked the control panel (*Automatics well advanced on the lift sequence*) and the view outside the cockpit (*Still no troopers in the clearing*) before turning to her brother.

"What do you think you're doing?"

"You know a better-cushioned place to strap someone in for lift-off?" He straightened, and gave her an appraising look. "You'd better take a gun and let me lift ship, Bee—you look like they forgot to bury you."

She shook her head. "Like hell you're flying my ship. You go shoot."

"Bee, you're hurt bad and you know it. If you pass out we're all in trouble."

She felt her temper rising, and held on to the back of the pilot's seat with both hands. *Gently,* she told herself. *Gently.* "Listen to me, Ari. You're hell on wings in atmospheric craft. I admit it. But I fly spaceships for a living, and you don't."

"She's right, Ari," said Jessan.

"Damn it, Nyls, *look* at her!"

"I know," said the Khesatan. "I know. Just pass me the first-aid box. Now, Captain, if you'd let me take your coat . . . good . . . you sit there and finish running down the checklist, and I'll see about doing a patch-and-go job that'll hold you together until we make hyperspace."

She took the pilot's seat and started flipping switches, only half-aware of Jessan still murmuring to himself as he cut away the blood-stiffened fabric of her shirt and probed the blaster wound with skilled fingers.

"Looks like it missed all the major organs . . . but it *is* a nasty one, no two ways about that. Straight into the healing pod as soon as we get home, and no argument . . . lend me a hand here, Ari? . . . thanks. There. That pressure bandage ought to keep the bleeding under control—let me get you some fluids before we lift."

She shook her head and pointed out the window. Darvelline troopers, several squads of them, burst into the clearing and started firing.

"No time," she said. "Get to battle stations—I'm lifting in thirty seconds whether you're in place or not."

Jessan counted under his breath as he and Ari ran aft for the guns.

". . . twenty, twenty-one, twenty-two . . ." The captain had been generous with her estimate. On "twenty-three" he felt the *'Hammer'*s forward nullgravs tilting the ship's nose upward, and on "twenty-five" the acceleration hit.

He made it the last few feet to the Number Two gun position in an uphill fight against gravity. He found the Arm switch after a moment's panicky search, pushing it left-handed while his right hand worked the straps on the safety webbing.

Something exploded, down below. The white flash filled the gun bubble, and after the light faded he could see an angry red ball mushrooming upward toward them.

"What went off dirtside?" he called over the internal comm as he settled the headset into place.

He heard Beka's unsteady laugh. "That was *Defiant* blowing herself to pieces. I guess the Professor didn't want anybody else messing around with her, either."

Outside the gun bubble, the sky was going from blue to black. A few stars came out, and a brighter disk-shaped spot appeared against them.

Satellite, Jessan thought. Over the headset, he heard Ari's voice muttering something about gratuitous violence, and then Number One gun fired.

"Keep doing that and they'll spot us as hostile for sure," Jessan said.

"If they don't already have us down as hostile," came Ari's reply, "then they never will."

What the hell, Jessan thought, and picked out a satellite of his own to shoot at. *I could use the practice.*

* * *

A beam of energy streaked forward past the bridge from the dorsal gun bubble. *Trigger-happy lunatics,* thought Beka, as the *'Hammer* emerged from atmosphere. *They're not going to hit a damned thing at that range.*

She brought the acceleration up as high as she dared—*Don't want my gunners blacking out on me*—and divided the rest of her attention between the sensor readouts and the realspace vista out the cockpit windows. Neither view looked encouraging. On the control panel, the *'Hammer*'s sensors were showing multiple transmissions on frequencies usually used by fire control and homing mechanisms. And outside, the sky was full of tracking devices, most of them pointed straight at her.

Time for the jammers, she thought, and flipped the newest addition to the array of switches on the control panel. *That's one more thing I owe you, Professor.*

Another touch, and airtight doors throughout the ship sighed closed. She rotated the *'Hammer* about her axis once to look for a clear route out, found a line that had fewer ships along it than the rest, and set the navicomps to work checking for a jump point.

"Don't get picky on me now," she muttered. "Just put me in the galaxy someplace. I can find my own way home."

The guns hammered out a quick burst, and a flash of light erupted nearby. "Where the hell did he come from?" she demanded, as shrill pippings from the control panel warned of lock-on. She switched on the *'Hammer*'s range gate pull-off transmitter in an attempt to divert any missiles homing in, and checked the sensor readouts again.

"Damn," she muttered. "Damn, damn, damn . . ." One of the satellites below was spinning, bringing its weapons to bear.

A bolt of fire streaked out, and within seconds the blackness of space around the *'Hammer* turned into a wire cage of crossing beams. She increased velocity and changed course again, gasping as the force tore at the wound in her side.

Another alarm shrilled in her ears: loss of internal pressure in the forward cargo hold. *The bulkheads can hold it.* She slapped the siren off.

A ship the size of a Space Force cruiser came into visual range behind and beneath her, dropping off one-man fighters as it came. *Look at the good side,* she told herself, increasing the velocity again. *You made it past the orbital stuff.*

The cruiser was falling behind now, dwindling out of visual—the 'Hammer's outsized engines had done the trick again. "That's a girl!" Beka crooned to her ship. "Fastest pair of legs in the galaxy . . . oh, damn!"

The 'Hammer's guns beat out their staccato rhythms, and more silent explosions lit up the blackness. Another cruiser had left its picket duty to come up ahead of her.

She checked the navicomps. "Come on, come on! Give me a jump point, will you?"

But the "working" lights kept on flashing. *All this twisting and dodging keeps changing the equations. I need to get clear of these warships and take a straight run.*

She cut hard left and spiraled again to get clear of the warship in front of her. Energy bolts traced across the 'Hammer's ventral surface as a fighter sped by. Fire from her own guns followed him as he ran.

"You're doing good," she called over the internal comm to the gun bubbles. "Just keep them off me while I head for jump."

Nyls Jessan slewed Number Two gun around to take aim at another incoming fighter.

"I hear you, Captain," he said to Beka over the headset, and to himself, *Keep cool. Pretend it's a simulation.* He fired, and the fighter blew up.

"Not bad," Ari said through the earphones.

Jessan fired again. A miss, this time. "I'll have you know that I'm a graduate of the Space Force Gunnery Familiarization Program."

He heard the sound of Number One firing, and then

Ari's voice again. "You mean the course that teaches medics how not to accidentally blow up the guys on their own side?"

"That's the one."

Something out there beyond the armor-glass exploded in a dazzle of white light. Jessan fired blind, letting the targeting computer swing the gun position around for him. *If it moves, it's hostile. Simplifies things a lot.*

He heard a noise like a thunderclap—*Lords of Life, that was close!*—and felt the *'Hammer* shudder. Over the headset, he caught Ari muttering something in the Forest Speech that the big Galcenian saved for serious cursing. *Something must have gone wrong.*

A second later, he realized just how wrong.

The sound of the engines had stopped.

Now we're really in trouble, thought Beka. A hit aft from one of the fighters screaming by had prompted the engine-room damage-control systems to take over and cut power. The *'Hammer* kept on moving forward with her speed intact, but the readouts on the cockpit control panel showed that the ship was no longer accelerating.

Using the realspace engines now would mean a chance of burning them out. On most ships, DC systems couldn't be reset until repairs were made, anyway. *But the 'Hammer isn't most ships,* thought Beka. *And we'll never make it up to jump speed like this.*

She reached up above her head and cut in the overrides.

The *'Hammer* surged to the side before picking up her forward acceleration again. Beka frowned: the engines were a bit skewed.

"Jump speed," she told the ship. "That's all I ask."

Another warship showed in the forward screen, coming up fast toward visual range. She checked its position.

Hell. It's sitting right on our jump point. She cut and spun left and downward to find another point. *Give me room to run and I won't care about the calculations—I'll jump blind if I have to, just let me get velocity!*

The maneuver flashed more alarm lights from the engine readouts: Tube One was fluttering on the edge of burnout already. Another Darvelline fighter zipped past, shooting as it went. The power-level indicators for the 'Hammer's weapons bobbled in reply.

At least we're still shooting back.

The starboard engine went out, then cut back in at half-thrust. She bit her lip in frustration, and cut power in the port engine to keep from spinning out of control with the off-center push. Once more, the acceleration readout slowed.

She bit her lip again, harder. *I have to do something. The engines aren't good for more than a few seconds longer, and I'm nowhere near up to jump speed.*

Any time now, she knew, one of the Darvelline cruisers would come alongside, match speeds, and pull *Warhammer* into a docking bay with tractor beams. Then they'd cut through the hull, there'd be a brief fight on board the 'Hammer, and everything would be over.

But they won't get me alive. Or Nivome. She shifted a little in her seat—even that small movement made her wound throb—and patted the blaster at her side. *'He has little enough time,' the Prof said. He just didn't tell me I wouldn't have any more than Nivome did.*

"We'll make it."

Beka startled. The voice had come from the copilot's seat. She glanced over at the Adept. Llannat's eyes were still closed and she sounded bone-weary, but she looked nowhere near as close to death as she had only a few minutes before.

"We'll make it," Llannat repeated. "I met myself, and I was older." The Adept exhaled on a long breath, and her features relaxed into the smoothness of sleep.

Wonderful, thought Beka. *At least I know it can be done.*

She looked out the cockpit window at the stars. The idea taking shape in her mind made her skin prickle. *I think I am crazy. But they can't block that jump point, for sure. Now all I need is the velocity.*

Beka spun the *'Hammer* around on its vertical axis, and fired the engines one more time.

The readouts flickered and went red. She pushed the throttles farther. The frame of the ship began to shake and vibrate, but the control panel showed acceleration picking up.

More throttle. The rear sensors started coming up with garbage—shards of metal, that would be, sloughing off the engines. All around her, the ship started to make a strange, almost subaudible noise, one no spacer should ever have to listen to: the sound of realspace engines destroying themselves from the inside out.

Beka felt like crying. Instead, she looked at the velocity readout. Yes, there it was, an increase that was more than the crippled engines could account for.

She looked ahead. It was going to be close. But already the central star of the Darvelline system was taking up more and more space in the cockpit window. No warship would sit on her jump point this time.

"Bee!" shouted her brother's voice over the internal comm. "Bee! What the hell do you think you're doing?"

She laughed aloud. "Just one more crazy stunt, big brother—maybe the last one ever. Put the guns on automatic and come on up front for the ride."

By the time Ari's heavy footsteps and Jessan's lighter ones sounded on the cockpit deckplates, she'd already blacked out the windows against the Darvelline sun's increasing light. "Can't do that for the bubbles," she said without turning her head away from the velocity indicator. "Gunners like their visuals too much. But anybody who's still with us now is only following along to watch us fry."

"Just what are you doing, Bee?" her brother growled from somewhere close behind her.

"I'm getting an assist from gravity," she told him. "We're doing a tight parabola around the sun. Either we make it to jump speed before we burn up, or we don't."

"Where are we jumping to?" That was Jessan, on his

knees beside her; the Khesatan was already busy changing the bandage he'd put on her just before lift.

Glad somebody besides Llannat thinks I'll be around long enough to need it, she thought, and shrugged one shoulder. "We'll know when we get there."

Jessan finished changing the bandage and stood up. "What if you've miscalculated?"

Beka turned her head just long enough to look at him. "Then I'm sorry I dragged you along to a family party," she said. "But what the hell—it was fun while it lasted."

She turned back to the velocity readouts. *Another five seconds . . . three seconds . . . one second . . . now!* She reached out her arm for the hyperdrive enable.

"And whatever happens, Nivome the Rolny is dead."

Epilogue
Innish-Kyl: Waycross

COMMANDER GIL leaned his chair back against the wall and listened to the ice melting in his tumbler of Galcenian brandy.

At least, the cantina's barkeep had claimed that the pale amber fluid was Galcenian brandy; along with his drink, Gil was nursing a dark suspicion that the liquor had never come nearer to the galaxy's capital than a holding vat in a middle-planet distillery. Gil's companion had opted for the local wine instead—but then, Jos Metadi had been drinking that vintage since well before the Magewar ended.

Gil shook his tumbler to hurry up the dilution a little, and smiled in spite of himself. *I have to admit, this tour of duty hasn't been dull. Artat, Pleyver, Ovredis, and now Innish-Kyl . . . where next, I wonder?*

This particular outing had started a few days ago, with a message Gil had brought into the General's office at Prime Base on Galcen.

"Relay from the merchantman *Blue Sun*, out of Ophel—personal to you, sir."

The General had looked curious. Ophel was a privately owned planet that fell into the Republic's sphere of influence, but the Ophelans had some interesting neighbors, and the rumors coming out of that sector had been even more confusing than usual lately.

"What do they say?"

"It's a bit of an odd one," said Gil. He quoted by memory from the printout flimsy he held in one hand. "No names, just 'You sold me something a while back. Want the final payment? Same place as before. We'll wait for you.' "

"Do they mention a date?"

"Yes, sir," Gil said. "A week from today, Standard."

"Wait for me, hell," the General said. "I'll be there first."

Gil suppressed a sigh. "Excuse me, sir—but where, exactly, is 'there'?"

Metadi didn't answer. He was already clearing his desk by the brute-force method, glancing at each item and tossing it into either the main drawer or the waste-disposal unit.

"Get a ship ready," he said, still sorting. "And tell the pilot to take some time off. This will just be me flying."

"Alone?"

The General paused, the folder in his hand suspended between the drawer and the disposal unit. He gave Gil a long look. "Take some leave if you want to, and come along as copilot. You've earned it."

He hadn't explained any further, though; and so far, Gil had found himself no more enlightened than before.

After a flight to Waycross, of all places, at the General's habitual speed of faster-than-safe, they'd docked the little unmarked craft in one of the bays, changed into civvies, and headed for the Blue Sun Cantina.

The establishment's name made Gil's eyebrows go up a bit—*Freighter out of Ophel, did they say?* At least, he reflected, he and the General were properly dressed for a spaceport rendezvous: civilian clothing and concealed weapons.

Just what armaments the General had tucked away under his dark jacket Gil wasn't sure, but he knew for certain Metadi would be packing something. The commander himself had taken to carrying a hand-blaster up one sleeve ever since Beka Rosselin-Metadi's wake. The figure waiting in the shadows that night had turned out to be a friend—next time, though, they might not be so lucky.

What's good for the General is good for the aide, Gil reflected, taking a cautious sip of the brandy. *I never did think much of going after the villains armed with nothing but an empty beer mug.*

The security panel by the cantina doorway beeped once. Along with most of the other customers, Gil let his gaze travel in that direction. *Well, now,* he thought. *What have we here?*

The new arrival paused for a moment in the dim interior light. A smallish, dark woman in a plain black coverall, she drew speculative looks from the cantina's regulars: *Not a spacer,* Gil could almost hear them thinking, *and not a hooker, so what's a respectable dirtsider doing up there at the bar?*

Then the speculative glances hit the black and silver staff tucked into the belt of her coverall, and slid away into the corners of the room.

The General chuckled. "You don't push an Adept."

"What in the world is she doing here, though?" Gil wondered aloud.

"She'll tell us if she wants to," said the General.

And in fact, the Adept was heading for their table. As she drew nearer, Gil felt another piece of the puzzle clicking into place: he'd last seen this particular Adept on Ovredis, playing duenna to royalty.

She slid into the empty seat at the table, and looked from Gil to the General and back again.

"Good evening, gentlesirs."

The General nodded. "Good evening, Mistress. Mind telling me what brings you to a place like this?"

"I have a message," the Adept said. " 'Crystal World, Bay One-three-eight.' "

"That's it?"

It was the Adept's turn to nod. "That's it. Shipboard's safer, if you know what I mean."

Metadi smiled at her. "I was playing this game before your captain was born, Mistress. Finish your beer and let's go."

The Adept's dark skin darkened a bit more. "We can go right now," she said, pushing the mug away. "I've had worse beer than this, but not lately."

The walk to the docking bays didn't take long; the narrow alleyways of portside Waycross were almost deserted in the afternoon heat. In the stark, yellow-white glare of Innish-Kyl's sun, the exquisite little blue and silver yacht in Bay 138 looked to Gil like a spacer's idea of a bad joke. The General seemed to think so, too. His brows drew together in a frown, and he followed in silence as the Adept led them up into the spaceyacht by the crew door.

Belowdecks, though, *Crystal World* was all business—compact, powerful, and discreetly armed. The General's scowl began to clear as they passed through Crew Berthing, and by the time they'd ascended the steep metal stairs from the bridge and emerged onto the observation deck, he was almost smiling.

The observation deck gave an illusion of spaciousness that the lower portion of the ship had lacked. Holoprojections on three sides of the carpeted area showed a formal garden extending into parkland in the misty distance. White-metal lawn furniture with green plush cushions completed the effect. Lieutenant Ari Rosselin-Metadi rose to his feet from a low hassock as they entered, his massive height a jarring note against the delicate formality of the surroundings.

The General regarded the young man for a moment.

"It's good to see you again in one piece," he said finally. "Mind telling me what this bit of fancywork is doing in a working spaceport?"

Lieutenant Rosselin-Metadi and the Adept looked at each other. "It's a long story," the woman said after a pause.

"In that case," said the General, strolling over to take a seat in one of the wrought-metal chairs, "the two of you had better get started on it."

"Beka . . . Captain . . . wake up."

She pressed her face into the pillow and shook her head. "Too tired."

"Our visitors are here."

She sat bolt upright. "Already?"

Her head spun. She felt Nyls Jessan slipping an arm around her shoulders, and leaned for a moment against his unobtrusive support.

"Damn," she said. "That approach left me in worse shape than running the Web out of Pleyver."

"You weren't fresh out of the healing pod when you ran the Web, either," the Khesatan said. "We should have stayed at the base another week so you could get some rest."

Beka shook her head. "No. I want to get this over with."

She straightened up again, and felt his hand tighten briefly on her bare shoulder before relaxing and letting go.

"I'll have plenty of time on my hands while the *Hammer* is in the yards," she continued, pushing herself up from the narrow bunk in the captain's quarters on *Crystal World*. She stood a few seconds with her feet braced apart on the deckplates; then, satisfied that her legs would hold her, she crossed the tiny cabin to the clothes locker.

She pulled out garments one at a time, tossing each item over onto the bunk until she'd assembled a complete set of dirtside clothing.

"You said 'visitors,' " she commented as she pulled on the trousers. "Who's the extra?"

"An aide, looks like, or maybe a bodyguard."

She snorted. "Since when did Dadda have a bodyguard?"

Jessan picked up the loose white shirt from the bunk and held it up for her like a valet. "An aide, then. Llannat says he's all right."

As he spoke, he eased first her right arm and then her left into the full sleeves of the Mandeynan shirt. Beka accepted his help without argument. For one thing, the new skin and regenerated flesh in her right side were still tender, and apt to protest at stretching or abrupt movement. For another . . .

Don't think about what you can't help. You knew from the start it was going to finish this way.

"Dadda wouldn't bring him along if he wasn't all right," she said, looking away from Jessan and concentrating hard on tucking her shirttails into the waistband of her trousers. That finished, she picked up the cravat and began tying it. "Where did you put them?"

"On the observation deck. Ari and Llannat are keeping them entertained while you get ready."

"I can imagine," she said. She sat down on the bunk and reached for Tarnekep Portree's high, polished boots.

Jessan took them away from her before she could bend over to pull them on.

"I'll do that for you," he said. "You'll overstress the new muscle if you try to do it yourself."

The Khesatan knelt down and started working the tight-fitting boots onto her feet and up over her calves. He was deft and gentle about it; she sat looking down at his bent head and bit her lip to keep from saying anything stupid.

You thought losing the Professor was bad enough—shows how much you know, doesn't it, girl?

Jessan finished with the second boot and rose to his feet. "Are you all right?" he asked.

"I'm fine," she said, wondering what she'd done that he had noticed.

Standing up, she took her blaster rig off its hook and strapped it on. The knife and its leather sheath, of course, hadn't left her arm in the first place. Jessan stood by the cabin door watching her, his grey eyes troubled.

She bit her lip again and reached out for the red plastic eye patch. Then she drew back her hand. She'd gotten into this as Beka Rosselin-Metadi, not Tarnekep Portree, and that was the way she was going to get out again—"maybe not quite the same as before," she admitted, under her breath. "But then, who is?"

"Who indeed?" inquired Jessan. The Khesatan bowed, and held out an arm in his best Crown-Prince-of-Sapne manner. "Come, my lady. Your family awaits."

". . . so Bee pointed *Warhammer* at the sun, and jumped us as soon as gravity pulled the ship up to speed."

Some people, Commander Gil reflected, could make even melodrama sound routine and prosaic. Lieutenant Rosselin-Metadi clearly worked hard to be included in that category. His tale of the *'Hammer's* adventures had enough holes in it to make a lace curtain, and the big medic hadn't even tried to disguise the gaps.

The General only smiled. "Are you sure that's all?"

Lieutenant Rosselin-Metadi shrugged. "What else is there to tell? We popped out of hyper in open space. There's more of that around than anything else, so you can't even say we were especially lucky. And the rest was easy."

"Don't believe him," said a Khesatan-accented voice from the metal stairway. "Qualification in field surgery is no help at all when it comes to repairing starship engines."

"Whatever works, Commander," said the General. "How's the patient?"

"Still in Intensive Care at Sunrise Shipyards on Gyffer." The reply came not from Lieutenant Commander Nyls Jessan, but from the remaining member of *Crystal World's* complement, the one who was coming up the stairway a step or two behind the Khesatan. "But she'll make it."

Beka Rosselin-Metadi stepped out onto the observation deck. The General's daughter appeared paler and thinner than Gil remembered her, either as Tarnekep Portree or the Princess Berran of Sapne. *But that's not surprising,* Gil told himself, *if even half of what her brother says happened is true.*

Beka sat down in the deck's remaining empty chair, and

Lieutenant Commander Jessan settled himself cross-legged on the carpet not too far away. The General smiled again.

"Sunrise, eh?" he asked. "They still do custom upgrades?"

His daughter nodded. "I'm having some done on the 'Hammer while they're fixing the engines. Computers, mostly, and some weapons-control stuff."

Lieutenant Rosselin-Metadi stared at his sister. "Computers—weapons—Bee, what in heaven's name are you planning now?"

"Don't worry about it, big brother," she said. "You don't need to know."

The medic reddened. Beka sat watching him with a challenging expression.

I wouldn't touch a line like that with a pressor beam, thought Commander Gil; but the lieutenant seemed made of stronger stuff. Gil heard him draw breath between his teeth for a reply.

The General suppressed another smile. "Down, both of you." Then he looked hard at Beka. "Mind telling your father what you've got planned?"

Beka glanced over at Llannat Hyfid. "Did you tell him about D'Caer?"

"He knows about the Mageworlds jump," the Adept said.

"Not the rest of it?"

The General turned to the big lieutenant.

"What 'rest of it,' son?"

"I was getting to that," he protested.

"If you and Bee keep on squabbling," the General told him bluntly, "we'll get to it sometime next week."

Lieutenant Rosselin-Metadi looked affronted—an impressive sight, but one his father ignored. Instead, Metadi let his gaze rest first on the Adept and then on the Khesatan officer sitting cross-legged on the deck. Finally, he made his choice and nodded at Jessan.

"Finish the story for us, Commander. The rest of you keep quiet and let him talk."

The captain of the *Crystal World* opened her mouth to say something. Her father silenced her with a quick glance.

"That means you too, Beka my girl. All right, Commander—report."

Jessan straightened. "Yes, sir. The repair work we did after coming out of hyper from Darvell only brought back enough engine function for one jump, so we picked the planet with the best shipyards. We made it to Gyffer just before all the systems went down hard, and put the *'Hammer* in the yards and the captain in the hospital. As soon as the captain came out of the healing pod, we chartered a vessel for the trip back to base."

"About that base, Commander—"

"It's disguised as an asteroid somewhere, sir," said the Khesatan, with a bland expression, "but I'm afraid I don't have the foggiest notion of the coordinates. The captain insisted on punching in the navicomp data herself."

"Understood," the General said. "I'd have done the same thing in her position. Go on."

"Yes, well—we'd left for Darvell with Gentlesir D'Caer stashed in Maximum Security. When we got back, he wasn't there. If all the robots and sensors and intruder-alert systems are telling the truth, then nobody broke in to get him, and nobody knows when he left."

"I see," the General said. "And what does your Adept have to say about that?"

"Magework," the Adept said at once. "Sir. They got a line on D'Caer somehow, and pulled him out before he could talk."

The General leaned back in his chair and gazed out at the simulated landscape beyond the observation-deck windows. "So the bastard's still kicking around the galaxy."

"It's possible," said the Adept dubiously. "But the Magelords don't take kindly to failure—and Ebenra D'Caer failed them at every turn but the first."

"Want to clarify that a little bit for us, Mistress?"

But it was the General's daughter who answered, the lace cuff on her Mandeynan shirt falling away from her wrist as she ticked off her statements one by one. "Suivi Point hasn't been thrown out of the Republic," she said.

"Dahl&Dahl are still as powerful as they ever were. And the Mageworlds involvement isn't a secret anymore."

"Space Force Intelligence isn't totally incompetent," the General said. "We've been getting reports of increased activity in that quarter for quite a while. Nothing this solid, though . . . and getting the Senate to listen to an old general's suspicions is next to impossible these days. But if Darvell's been supplying war matériel to the Mageworlds, the politicians will have to listen for a change."

"They'll want hard proof," the General's daughter pointed out. "Which means you need somebody out there where it's all happening."

Her brother surged to his feet. Standing, he towered over everybody and everything else on the observation deck, and his voice, when he spoke, was a controlled roar. "The Mageworlds? Bee, you're crazy!"

Commander Gil—already busy calculating which of Darvell's regular trading partners could be counted on to answer discreet inquiries—tended to agree, and thanked heaven that his own sisters had never shown any desire to leave Ovredis. But Jos Metadi only shook his head.

"No, son," the General said. "Your sister isn't crazy. Her mother used to get the same look in her eye whenever she decided it was up to her to save the galaxy." He turned to Beka. "Am I right, girl?"

"Tarnekep Portree's a merchant captain," she answered, a flush of bright color coming into the pale skin over her high cheekbones. "Why shouldn't he work the Mageworlds if he wants to? As for his other profession— word of these things gets out. Nobody is ever going to believe that the raid on Darvell was a private grudge match. I expect that Captain Portree is going to get some very interesting offers over the next couple of years."

"I wouldn't be a bit surprised," agreed the General dryly. "So your mind's made up?"

She nodded.

"The last time we struck a bargain," said her father, "all I asked for was a couple of names. By the time I got them, you'd left a trail of dead bodies and missing persons across five systems, blown the top off the strongest private fortress in the known galaxy, and damn near flown *War-hammer* through the middle of a sun. I'm afraid to ask you for anything else.''

Beka's chin went up a fraction higher. ''Who's asking anybody anything? I'm going to try my luck around the Mageworlds for a while, that's all.''

''Then I'll take whatever intelligence you can dig up, my girl, because I have a feeling the galaxy's going to need it one of these days.'' The General's expression hardened a little. ''While you're out there, keep an ear open for word of D'Caer. If he's alive, he still owes the family one.''

''My pleasure,'' Beka said. ''I'll see that he pays up.''

The General rose to his feet and extended a hand toward his daughter. ''Done, then?''

Beka rose also, but kept her hand at her side. ''Not quite yet. There's a bit of leftover business from our last deal that we have to take care of first.''

Now the Adept was on her feet as well, her dark features flushed with agitation. ''Captain, you can't just—''

Beka's fists clenched. ''Dammit, Mistress, don't tell me what I can and can't do!''

The Adept met Beka's angry blue gaze without flinching. Time stretched out interminably as the two women faced one another in silence. Then Gil saw the captain's clenched fists slowly relax.

In a calmer tone, Beka went on, ''We all agreed, remember? This one is for Dadda to decide.''

''I don't think I like the sound of that,'' the General said. ''What 'bit of business'?''

''It'd be easier to show you,'' Beka said. She started for the sliding doors at the rear of the observation deck. ''Just come this way.''

Lieutenant Rosselin-Metadi and the Adept remained behind—partners in disapproval, Gill suspected—but everybody else trooped along as the General's daughter led the way down a narrow, exquisitely paneled corridor. She didn't take them far before halting to palm a lockplate set into the bulkhead. A gilt and ivory panel slid aside, and she stepped through the doorway. One by one, the others followed.

Like the hallway they'd left, the stateroom was tiny, but elegant in its design and appointments. On two walls, mirrors in artful positions reflected the room's furnishings in such a way as to stretch its apparent size, and on the unmirrored walls Gil saw blank holoprojection windows. For a different passenger, the captain of *Crystal World* might have let the ship's computer run landscapes like the one up on the observation deck. *But not for this passenger,* thought Gil.

Hands caught tight in metal binders, Nivome the Rolny lay on spidersilk sheets in the middle of the bed, and stared out ahead of him at nothing. Not even the appearance of the General brought any reaction to the Rolny's grizzled, jowly features.

Metadi frowned. "I can see your Adept friend's problem. What happened?"

"I stowed him in the hold while we made our run to jump," his daughter said. "And we lost our pressure down there from a hit we took. I think the oxygen deprivation got to him."

The General glanced over at Jessan; the Khesatan shrugged. "That's a possibility. Then again, it could be stun-shock syndrome, or it could be that his mind snapped under the stress and he's blocking out reality."

"Whatever you say," the General said. "You're the medic." He turned back to Beka. "Well, girl—you've got him. What do you want to do with him?"

Beka looked at Nivome for a long time. At last, she shook her head. "If I'd seen him like this right after we came out of hyperspace, I'd have told the gang to cycle him out the airlock and get it over with. But I didn't, and they didn't, so I'm sticking to the original plan."

She pulled her blaster out of its holster, and handed it butt-first to the General. "He's all yours."

I don't believe I'm watching this, thought Gil.

Metadi took the blaster. He checked the weapon over and brought it up to point at the bound form of Nivome the Rolny.

Something—the talk, the blaster, the crowd in the little stateroom—had finally gotten through to the man on the bed. His eyes focused on the muzzle of the Mark VI, and then on the face above it. Gil saw the Rolny's eyes go wide with fear and recognition.

Metadi smiled. "That's right, Nivome, it's me. You should have stuck to hunting *wuxen* and left my family alone." He thumbed the blaster's safety over to Off.

In the tiny space, the click of the toggle-switch flipping over sounded louder than an explosion. Nivome closed his eyes and whimpered. Gil felt sick.

The General looked down at Nivome for a moment longer. "The hell with it," he said suddenly, and lowered his arm. "Shooting's too good for him. Take the binders off, and drop him in the alley out back of the Blue Sun. Then tip off local Security that they've got an incompetent vagrant cluttering up the street."

The General's daughter looked at her father for a moment. Her lips began to curve upward. "And the Master of Darvell can spend the rest of his life in a public mental-health ward. Dadda, I like your style."

"Good," said the General curtly, handing her back the blaster. "See to it, then." He turned on his heel and left the stateroom without another word.

Beka stood looking down at the blaster in her hand. For a few seconds Gil thought she was going to shoot the Rolny anyway. He wondered if he should try to stop her if she did.

But she gave Nivome one more disgusted look and shoved the Mark VI back into its holster. "You heard the man—he goes out back of the cantina."

"Right," Gil said. He turned to Jessan. "Commander, you and I are going to have to do the drunken-buddy routine through the back streets for this one."

"Let me get the binders off him first," Beka said. "The lock's keyed to my thumbprint."

She took a step to the head of the bed, and reached out to

key the binders open. Gil heard the faint snap of the metal parting, and then all hell broke loose in the crowded room.

Somehow, Nivome had the Mark VI—*Grabbed it when she undid the binders,* Gil thought—and was bringing it up to fire. But Beka Rosselin-Metadi was the General's daughter in more ways than one. Light flashed off something steely and wicked-looking that appeared in a blur out of her left sleeve, and she drove the dagger in toward the Rolny's gut.

Two weeks in a healing pod, however, make poor conditioning for a close-in fight. Nivome seized Beka's knife wrist as it came forward. She blocked out and upward with her left forearm, and the Mark VI went off like a lightning bolt and scorched the mother-of-pearl frame of the nearest mirror.

Nivome was already coming up off the bed, pushing the General's daughter over backward under his weight. Gil felt his own grip closing on something small and deadly, and realized that he'd flicked his concealed hand-blaster out of its grav-clip without even thinking.

He raised it and took aim, but the struggling bodies were too close together. Before he could move to get a clearer shot, another figure vaulted over the bed and onto the Rolny's back: Lieutenant Commander Nyls Jessan, wrapping a bent arm around Nivome's throat, pulling the heavier man backward and up.

Still too close, damn it, thought Gil, trying again to aim into the knot of bodies. Another second crawled by, and the Khesatan's attack pulled Nivome back a few more inches. The Rolny fought to bring the heavy blaster into line for another shot. Gil fired, and Nivome fell dead on top of the General's daughter, drilled neatly in the temple by the energy beam.

The whole episode had taken about five seconds from start to finish. The sound of blaster-fire had scarcely died before the General reentered the room at a run, his own weapon drawn. Lieutenant Rosselin-Metadi and Mistress Hyfid came charging in close on his heels.

The General made his blaster disappear again. "All right, what happened?"

One glance at Beka and Jessan convinced Gil that he wasn't going to get any help from that quarter. The Khesatan, oblivious of the corpse at his feet, was holding Beka in a tight embrace and murmuring disjointed phrases under his breath. She, in her turn, stood shaking against him, her face buried in his shoulder and the long knife forgotten in her hand.

Resigned, Gil caught the General's eye and nodded toward the body. "Shot while trying to escape, sir."

"Simplifies things a bit," agreed Metadi. "Looks like I owe you, Commander. If there's anything I can do—"

Gil slid his hand-blaster back into its grav-clip. "Take me off the cocktail-party circuit before I drown in weak punch?"

The General smiled. "I think I can swing that one. Your tour on Galcen's almost up anyway: how do you feel about being bumped up one rank, and getting your choice of ships?"

"I'll take it," Gil said. "What's the catch?"

"The catch," Metadi told him, "is that you'll be commodore of the Mageworlds fleet. Trouble's brewing out there, and I want a man on the spot who knows how to make the right decision in a hurry."

"That's just fine for you, Dadda," said Beka Rosselin-Metadi, pulling away from Jessan's grip and slamming her knife into its sheath. "But now that the Space Force has taken care of everything, why don't all of you go back home to Galcen Prime and let me get my ship the hell out of Waycross?"

"Because everything isn't taken care of," Jessan told her. "Not yet."

The General raised an eyebrow. "How's that, Commander?"

"I'm resigning my commission," said the Khesatan. "Effective immediately."

In the doorway, Ari Rosselin-Metadi stared, dumbfounded. "What—? Nyls, have you lost your mind?"

"Probably," Jessan said. "It doesn't matter."

Beka caught her lower lip between her teeth. "I don't understand."

"You can't run the *'Hammer* in the Mageworlds without a copilot," Jessan explained. "And the Professor is gone. So unless you've got somebody else lined up for the job . . ."

"You mean you're not going back to the Space Force?" asked Beka.

"No," he said, and kissed her again.

Some time later, the General cleared his throat. "Well, Commander—if you're convinced that my daughter is worth more than a promising career in the Medical Service, I'm certainly not going to hold it against you."

Still keeping one arm around the General's daughter, Jessan inclined his head—very much, Gil thought, in the manner of the Crown Prince of Sapne. "Thank you, sir."

"You're welcome, Commander," said the General. "But I'm not going to accept your resignation, either."

Beka stiffened. "Dadda!"

Metadi ignored her. "Consider yourself transferred to Space Force Intelligence," he told Jessan. "Your first assignment is detached duty with *Warhammer* on the Mageworlds border. I'll take care of all the paperwork."

Beka was looking at the General as if he had promised her a luxury tour on the pride of the Red Shift Line instead of a hard stint of dirty, dangerous work with little prospect of thanks at the end of it. Gil winced slightly—he knew on whose desk the paper would ultimately fall—but he couldn't really bring himself to begrudge the effort.